DAUGHTER, MISSING

JILL CHILDS

B

Boldwood

First published in Great Britain in 2025 by Boldwood Books Ltd.

Copyright © Jill Childs, 2025

Cover Design by Lisa Horton

Cover Images: Adobe Stock, Shutterstock and Mark Owen / Trevillion

Every effort has been made to obtain the necessary permissions with reference to copyright material, both illustrative and quoted. We apologise for any omissions in this respect and will be pleased to make the appropriate acknowledgements in any future edition.

A CIP catalogue record for this book is available from the British Library.

Paperback ISBN 978-1-80557-269-5

Large Print ISBN 978-1-80557-270-1

Hardback ISBN 978-1-80557-271-8

Ebook ISBN 978-1-80557-268-8

Kindle ISBN 978-1-80557-267-1

Audio CD ISBN 978-1-80557-276-3

MP3 CD ISBN 978-1-80557-275-6

Digital audio download ISBN 978-1-80557-274-9

This book is printed on certified sustainable paper. Boldwood Books is dedicated to putting sustainability at the heart of our business. For more information please visit https://www.boldwoodbooks.com/about-us/sustainability/

Boldwood Books Ltd, 23 Bowerdean Street, London, SW6 3TN

www.boldwoodbooks.com

For Ann

1

THEN

Kate

It could have been a perfect summer. If it hadn't been for him.

When Kate thought back to the early weeks of the school holidays, she could almost feel the warmth of the sun on her face. It must have rained. It was England, after all. But what she recalled was the sight of the girls, legs kicking up, hair flying, running out into the garden after breakfast, seizing the day, with Coco bounding excitedly at their heels, and Simon, in slacks and a floppy sunhat, acting the lord of the manor as he pottered around their new home, content and away, for once, from the pressures of work.

They were all thrilled by the house. The quaint nooks and windowsills, the eccentric sloping passageways, the grand staircase and steep back stairs, the attics where the girls kept their dressing-up clothes and played Mummies and Babies with their favourite dolls. The glorious views of the overgrown, rolling lawns and, hidden at the bottom, the wooded stream that trickled into a small pool where the girls could splash.

And then Jonathan had come to visit them and, suddenly, paradise was lost.

He was such a strange boy. Kate had felt it from the start. The way he'd climbed out of Simon's car and stood, stiffly, on the drive, arms by his sides, his face a blank canvas.

She'd hurried forward to greet him, determined to make an effort for Simon's sake. 'You must be Jonathan! Welcome!'

He hadn't answered, just looked her over with a slight crease in his forehead as if he already found her lacking.

She tried hard not to mind. She'd known, when Simon suggested this landmark visit from his estranged son, that playing the role of stepmum, even for a few days, wouldn't be easy.

She adored her girls. There was no love like it. It had over-whelmed her, from the start. There had been nothing in her life as special as the moment each of them was first placed in her arms, scrunchy and red-faced and glorious, and she'd whis-pered: *Hello, beautiful! Welcome to the world. I'm your mum.*

She'd do her very best to be even-handed and fair while Jonathan was here but, in her heart, she knew it wasn't totally honest. Her daughters would always come first.

She pushed back her shoulders and forced a smile. It was an awkward situation, all round. She tried to imagine what it was like for Jonathan. After all, he wasn't to blame for any of this. Apparently, he'd barely known that Simon was his father, until recently. This was the first time his mother had allowed him to come and spend time with Simon and his second family.

Kate still wasn't clear why Jonathan's mother had thawed. She suspected that Simon had made overtures, perhaps even offered more financial support. He'd always been generous.

Simon hated talking about his disastrous first marriage and Kate had learned not to ask. He was never good at talking about his feelings, especially important ones. She blamed his upbringing and all those years at boarding school. But she sensed, from the little he had said, that he felt profoundly guilty, and perhaps embarrassed too, about his first wife and what a mess it had all been. Being a father to the girls was so important to him. He must have hated feeling that he was failing in his duty to his son, even if it wasn't his fault.

'How was the train?' Her voice sounded more pinched than usual. 'Come inside. I expect you'd like to see where you'll be sleeping?'

Jonathan stayed silent, just turned his head to look out at the grounds, taking it all in.

'The girls are around somewhere.' Her smile was starting to feel strained. 'I'll call them in for lunch soon. You can meet then.'

He shrugged and said, almost under his breath: 'I don't hang out with girls.'

Kate didn't answer. He was a ten-year-old boy. He was bound to be shy, meeting them all for the first time, meeting a father he'd never known. She took a deep breath. They'd muddle through. Besides, it was only for a few days.

She ushered him indoors and glanced across at Simon. He was pulling the boy's suitcase from the back seat, shutting the car door. An old-fashioned, battered case.

* * *

At lunch, the girls stared across at Jonathan with round eyes and nudged each other.

Bella, the leader, asked the questions. 'What's your favourite colour? Mine's red. Clara's is yellow.'

He looked at her with disdain. 'Only babies like bright colours.'

Kate, listening, bit her lip. The girls were only trying to make conversation. They'd been excited about meeting this unknown half-brother. It appealed to their sense of drama. She glanced across at Simon but he didn't catch her eye. She wasn't sure if he'd heard.

Bella, undeterred, went on. 'Have you got a pet? We've got a dog. Coco. He's brown and white. He's a beagle.' She looked round for Coco, checked under the table.

'I've got a horse,' Jonathan said. 'Two horses, actually.'

'Have you? Really?' Bella looked uncertain. 'What are they called?'

He didn't hesitate. 'Thunder and Starlight.'

Clara whispered to her sister and Bella whispered back and both girls giggled.

Kate saw the boy flush. Of course, he didn't have horses. But, even so, the girls shouldn't make fun of him. 'Don't whisper, please, girls,' she said. 'It's not polite.'

Bella said: 'I'm going to be a vet when I grow up. I'll look after your horses, if you like.'

Clara gathered her six-year-old courage and spoke up: 'I'm going to be an astronaut.'

He sniffed, dismissive. 'Girls can't be astronauts.'

Clara flared at once: 'They can! Tell him, Mummy. They can, can't they?'

'Of course they can,' Kate said. 'Lots of women have gone into space.'

There was an awkward silence. The girls had finished eating and were kicking their legs, getting restless for dessert.

The boy bowed his head over his plate. His shoulders were thin and tense. Kate wondered if the girls had noticed how badly his clothes fit. Everything looked a size too small. She'd have a word with them about it, make sure they didn't tease him.

Bella, the peacemaker, tried again: 'So, what are you going to be, when you're older?'

He said in a fierce rush: 'Rich. Super-rich. I'll have a bigger house than this, much bigger, and a whole stable of horses and my own helicopter.'

Simon set down his knife and fork. 'A helicopter, eh? Well, that's something. I could use one of those.'

He smiled benignly at Jonathan. He seemed oblivious to the boy's anger.

Kate stood and started to gather the plates. She was supposed to be kind, to set a good example to the girls. It wasn't the boy's fault if he was awkward. He'd had a tough start in life.

She took the crockery over to the dishwasher and stacked it. There was something in that boy's attitude that really rankled. He seemed to assume the two males, man and boy, were destined to be the ones making money. And he seemed so contemptuous of the girls. Telling Clara that girls couldn't be astronauts! How dare he. She wondered if Jonathan's manner towards her was dismissive too because she was a stay-at-home mother at the moment.

She had a good mind to tell him what she'd done in her career, about all the times she'd reported from war zones, from riots, not to mention toughing it out in a testosterone-fuelled newsroom. She'd given up a lot when they had the girls. She didn't regret it. They'd agreed that one of them ought to be at home and Simon earned so much more than she had. But she did miss it.

She shook her head and told herself to calm down. Jonathan had probably absorbed most of his attitudes from his mother.

Kate had never met Monica Bancroft, the boy's mother and Simon's first wife, but she'd heard bits and pieces.

Simon should never have married her. He'd never said as much but it was clear from what happened. The two of them had met as students, both far too young for anything serious. Kate suspected that Monica, a New Yorker, had taken the reins from the start. Simon, fresh out of boys' boarding school, had barely even dated.

Then Monica had announced that she was pregnant and morally opposed to a termination. Simon, being old-fashioned, duly proposed, hoping to make a go of it, for the child's sake. It had lasted barely a year before Monica had thrown Simon out.

Monica had made a mess of her life ever since. A heavy drinker, according to Simon. She'd always had a string of strange partners. None of them lasted long. Simon had tried to stay in touch. He'd desperately wanted to play a part in his son's life. She'd refused to let him even see the boy, until now. She'd always accepted his money, though.

'Ice-cream?' Kate said brightly. 'Jonathan, we've got choc ices and lollies. Which would you like?'

He shrugged, as if he didn't much care.

Bella leaned forward. 'Have a choc ice. They're really good.'

Coco skidded in from the garden, nails clattering on the kitchen floor, and disappeared under the table. Bella leaned down, cupping her hand to him, and Coco nuzzled it, then moved on to Jonathan. He nosed into Jonathan's groin and snuffled. Jonathan pushed back his chair and jumped up in alarm, shoving the dog's head away with force.

'It's OK.' Simon reached for Coco's collar and held him still, gesturing to Jonathan to come and stroke him. 'He just wants to make friends.'

Jonathan glowered at the panting dog.

'That's how he gets your smell,' Clara said. 'Sniffing your bottom.'

The two girls looked at each other, then burst into giggles.

Jonathan turned on his heel and strode out of the kitchen.

Kate, following with the plates, was just in time to see him wrench open the back door and run out into the garden, head down.

She pulled two choc ices out of the freezer and took them through to the girls. While they unwrapped them and started to nibble, she said to Simon in a low voice: 'Should we go after him?'

Simon seemed unperturbed. 'He'll be fine.' He reached a hand to Kate's arm and stroked it. 'We've got to be patient, that's all.'

2

Later, when the children were settled in bed, Kate and Simon sat side by side on the patio in their new loungers, enjoying the cool of the evening and sipping a glass of white wine.

He reached for her hand and squeezed it. She knew that squeeze. He had something difficult to say.

He cleared his throat and said in a low voice: 'I had a chat with him earlier.'

Kate had seen the two of them, man and boy, walking across the lawns together when she was chivvying the girls upstairs for their baths. It had struck her how different they looked. Simon, broad-shouldered and kindly, the boy so scrawny and tight.

It crossed her mind to wonder if he really was Simon's son or if Monica had lied. Monica sounded the type to play him for a fool and persuade him to pay maintenance for another man's son. It wasn't a thought she could ever voice to Simon. He was such a decent person himself. He'd be horrified that she could even suspect such a thing.

'How did it go?'

'Well, he seems a bright boy,' Simon said. 'A little shy, perhaps. I had to draw him out. But definitely bright.'

Kate thought: *Not as bright as the girls.* She didn't say it aloud, of course. It was petty of her. She had no reason to feel defensive. She owed it to Simon to welcome this boy, if that was what Simon wanted. He was part of Simon's past.

There was just something about Jonathan. That sense of disquiet, which had dogged her from the moment he first stepped out of the car, hadn't left. Normally, she shared her feelings freely with Simon, all the more so since they'd moved out here to the country and she had fewer friends around, but this was sensitive territory. She needed to tread with care.

'What did you talk about?'

'Oh, this and that. Cricket. He plays a bit at school.' Simon smiled. 'And books. He loves reading. He was telling me about some adventure series. I'd never heard of it. About a boy spy. Sort of James Bond for kids.'

'Well, that's good.' Kate tried to sound positive. 'Sounds as if we'll have plenty of ideas for Christmas and birthday presents. There are so many good books out there.'

Simon didn't answer. After a moment, she felt the hand squeeze again.

'I know he's a bit of an oddball,' Simon said slowly. 'But it could just be that he needs a father.' He paused. 'That he needs me.'

Something in Kate tightened. She wasn't sure how she felt about the prospect of Simon getting more involved with Jonathan from now on. She took a breath. It had to be Simon's choice. She'd known when she'd first met Simon that he'd been married before and had a son. She'd just never seen Jonathan until now. He was suddenly terribly real.

She bolstered her resolve. If this was what Simon wanted, she should support him.

'We've got plenty of room. He's always welcome.'

'Let's see how it goes.' Simon gave her hand a final pat and withdrew it. 'But, yes, maybe this is my chance to step up to the plate. If his mother lets me.'

Kate stole a sideways glance at Simon. His face was calm but she sensed tension in him too. She wondered if he was more uncertain about all this than he sounded.

'You can only offer,' she said. 'You're already doing a lot.'

Financially, she meant. She knew Simon sent his ex-wife a generous allowance each month. She didn't resent it. Simon always tried hard to do the right thing. She loved that about him. Besides, they were lucky. They could afford to be generous. Simon earned a lot and managed money carefully. Their new home was testament to that.

She looked away, down the garden. A stout shadow emerged, snuffling, from the bushes and scampered across the bottom of the lawn. Coco looked as if his beagle nose had latched on to some exciting new scent.

Kate smiled. It was six years since Coco had come into their lives, not long after Clara was born. He was just a puppy then and his huge brown eyes had melted their hearts. Now, it was impossible to imagine family life without him. This place suited him so much better than the Victorian terrace they'd owned in London, however smart the postcode had been.

She sipped her wine. Maybe Simon was right. Maybe Jonathan was just a sensitive boy, grappling with a difficult situation. She should make more of an effort to engage with him.

She just wished she could understand why he unnerved her so.

3

The following morning, Bella and Clara started the day with painting at the kitchen table, side by side.

Clara was doing a portrait of her favourite doll, Mimi. She'd spotted her in a toy shop several Christmases ago. Kate had been reluctant to buy her, at the time. Mimi was made from cheap, hard plastic, with straw-coloured hair and garishly painted cheeks and lips. Kate had been sure there were much lovelier dolls. But Clara had been desperate for Mimi, from first sight, with all the heartfelt longing a three-year-old can bring to bear. Mimi had slept in Clara's bed ever since.

Now, Mimi sat on the table with her legs splayed. Her hair, pulled, plaited and mangled over the years, hung in clumps around her head.

The tip of Clara's tongue was just visible between her lips as she concentrated on doing Mimi justice.

When Kate called Jonathan down and asked if he'd like to join them, his eyes ranged contemptuously over the two girls, their painting aprons, the jam jar of brushes and the water-colours.

He nodded at Mimi. 'What's that thing?'

Clara looked up. 'That's Mimi.'

'You still play with dolls?'

'Mimi's special.' Clara stuck her chin out, defiantly. 'She's my baby.'

Jonathan glanced down at Clara's painting, sticky with fresh paint. 'Is that the best you can do?'

Clara flushed and dipped her head.

Bella squared her shoulders. 'There's no need to be mean.'

Kate took a breath. 'Would you like to join them, Jonathan? There's plenty of room.'

'I'll pass, thanks.' He plucked an apple from the bowl on the sideboard, turned on his heel and sauntered out into the garden, a book in hand.

Bella glared after him. 'He's so rude.'

Kate bent down and kissed the top of Clara's head. 'Don't let him upset you,' she said, evenly. 'He must find it strange here, that's all.'

She stood for a moment at the window, watching Jonathan make his way across the lawn towards the trees. He paused as Simon, pruning his roses, lifted his hand and called out to the boy as he passed. Jonathan shrugged in response and carried on, disappearing a moment later into the copse.

Clara, recovering, leaned forward to reassure her doll. 'It's all right, Mimi. Don't be sad.'

Kate went back to peeling carrots for lunch. *One more day*, she thought. *One more day and he'll be gone.*

* * *

The scream reverberated through the house. High-pitched and terrified.

My God. Kate found herself on her feet in seconds, her body shaking. The book she'd been reading slapped to the floor. She shouted: 'Girls?'

She headed for the stairs at a run. It had been so quiet in the house, since lunch. Simon had taken the car out, in search of petrol. Jonathan had sloped upstairs somewhere, on his own. The girls had played cards for a while in the lounge, then announced they were heading up to the attic.

Kate, panting, reached the first floor. She paused on the landing and listened. Faint but wild sobbing sounded from higher up the house. She took the next flight of stairs, two at a time.

'Bella? Clara?'

Bella's voice drifted down. 'Up here!'

Kate found them both in the attic, huddled tightly together on the floor. Bella had her arms wrapped round her little sister. Clara was sobbing hysterically into Bella's skirt. As Kate ran in, Bella turned wide eyes to her.

'What happened?' Kate couldn't breathe, her chest tight. She dropped to her knees and reached for Clara, drew her little body onto her lap and hugged her close. 'Is she hurt?'

Bella couldn't speak. She raised a hand to point. Kate, clasping Clara tightly, lifted her eyes to look.

Something was hanging from a low beam. A baby. It was strung up, a rope noose round its neck, its plastic limbs flailing. Kate's mouth sagged. She blinked. Mimi. A trickle of blood matted her dirty hair, then ran down the side of her face, pooling in the puckered red lips.

Kate twisted Clara away, putting herself between her daughter and the horrific sight of her favourite doll. She started to rock her.

'It's OK, Clara.' Kate's hand stroked Clara's hair. 'Mimi's fine, really. It's just a silly trick. A very nasty, spiteful trick.'

Clara, sobbing, screamed: 'Get her down, Mummy! Please!'

Kate fumbled to undo the knots. She wiped off Mimi's spattered face on a tissue. Red paint, after all, not blood.

She tried to comfort Clara with a steady stream of words as she unwound the cord from the doll's neck and handed her down. 'It's OK. She's fine. It's just a splash of paint. It'll wash off.'

Clara snatched Mimi from her and bent her body round, rocking her, just as, a moment earlier, she had been rocked herself. Her words were barely audible through her sobs: 'I'm sorry, I'm so sorry, I'm a bad Mummy; I should have looked after you.'

* * *

Jonathan's bedroom was empty. So were the other bedrooms and the bathrooms and the rooms downstairs. Kate stood for a moment in the middle of the kitchen, getting her breath back, thinking, quivering with rage.

He must have sneaked out into the garden. Hiding. He thinks I'm too stupid to find him.

She whistled to Coco. He jumped up obediently from his basket and clattered across the kitchen floor. 'Good boy, Coco.' She picked up the sweatshirt that Jonathan had left on the table and gave it to Coco to sniff. 'Where is he, Coco? Where is he? Come on, let's go find him!'

She led him outside. For a moment, he scurried in circles, confused. Kate imagined the boy's scent criss-crossing the patio and the garden paths like invisible snail trails. Finally, Coco's beagle nose seemed to pick up a fresher, stronger scent and he set off, bouncing across the lawn, nose down. Kate ran after him.

Together, they skirted the main part of the garden and headed into a wild area, not yet cleared, on the far side of the copse. It was dense with wild bushes and thick, ancient trees, strangled by ivy.

'Where is he, Coco? Good boy!'

Coco hesitated, running back and forth across the mossy ground. A moment later, he barked and was off again, pressing his body low to crawl under a fallen branch and heading into the undergrowth. Dry twigs cracked like gunshots as Kate pursued him.

She arrived just in time to see Jonathan emerging from a dry bush.

'Get off.' He scrambled to his feet, kicking out at Coco as the dog, excited, tried to lick him, tail wagging.

'Here, Coco!' Kate called him back and gave him a treat from her pocket. 'Good boy! Clever boy!'

Jonathan, panting, stared across at her sullenly. 'Was that you, setting that stupid dog on me?'

'Coco wouldn't hurt a fly. He was just showing me where you were.'

Jonathan gazed at the dog with undisguised hatred.

Kate thought about Clara's screams. She took a step towards him.

'Was it you? Did you do that to Clara's doll?'

Jonathan didn't answer, just smirked.

'She's six years old. You frightened the life out of her.' Looking at the insolent expression on Jonathan's face, her hand twitched at her side. 'Do you even care?'

Jonathan shrugged. 'It was just a joke.'

'A joke?' Kate could hardly speak. 'You think that was funny?'

'Don't get your knickers in a twist.' Jonathan rolled his eyes. 'It's not real, you know. It's a doll.'

Kate blew out her cheeks, turned and marched briskly away, back towards the house. Coco bounded back and forth around her. She was shaking. She didn't trust herself around that boy; she was too close to losing her temper completely. He was obnoxious. Spiteful. Malevolent.

Simon didn't seem to see it, or didn't want to admit it. What should she do? He'd be back soon. She didn't want to sound spiteful herself, telling tales on a ten-year-old boy. Simon was bound to be infuriatingly rational about it. She could just imagine what he'd say.

It was a horrid thing to do, obviously. But it was just a prank, a very ill-judged one, but still a prank. He is a child, Kate. We have to cut him some slack.

She slammed into the kitchen and headed back upstairs. One more day and he'd be gone. Until then, only one thing mattered to her and that was looking after her girls.

4

The next morning, Kate found herself counting down the hours to Jonathan's departure.

To compensate for her guilt, she made Jonathan an extravagant packed lunch for the train, adding a piece of fruit cake and two bars of chocolate.

In the middle of the morning, Simon appeared in the kitchen, carrying Jonathan's case.

'We should probably go,' he said. 'It's a bit early but he mustn't miss his train.'

Kate didn't argue.

The girls had disappeared together somewhere, off with Coco, probably. In other circumstances, she would have called them and insisted that they said goodbye. Today, she didn't.

Jonathan appeared in the doorway. She handed him his lunch, then leaned in and gave him an awkward peck on the cheek. His face was inscrutable.

'Thank you so much for coming to see us,' she said brightly. 'I hope it's been fun.'

He didn't answer, just headed outside to the car. She stood

on the gravel and watched as Simon settled into the driving seat. Beside him, Jonathan strapped himself in.

It was as Simon started to ease the car out of the drive that Kate thought she caught, through the passing blur of reflections across the passenger window, the gleam of Jonathan's odd smile.

* * *

'Where's Coco?'

Kate looked at his bowl, puzzled. It was untouched since she'd put it out that morning. That wasn't like Coco. He loved his food.

Bella, drawing a picture at the table, shrugged. Beside her, Clara was manically crayoning.

Kate tried to remember when she'd last seen Coco. Usually, he was in and out of the house all the time.

'Did you play with him this morning?'

'Nope.' Bella reached for a rubber. 'We were in the attic.'

'That's odd.' Kate felt a sudden chill. She tried to shake it off. He was probably just off chasing a squirrel. She looked again at the dog bowl. 'Maybe we should go and look for him, make sure he hasn't got himself trapped in any prickly bushes, silly dog.'

The girls, intent on what they were doing, didn't move.

Kate stood on the patio and called Coco's name. Birds, startled, took to the air from a nearby clump of bushes. She scanned the treeline at the far end of the garden for sudden movement, for the sight of a brown and white furball flashing joyfully into view and scampering up the lawn towards her. Nothing. She frowned.

She strode briskly down the garden, whistling now and then and calling Coco's name. She checked under bushes and along the boundary fence. There were no telltale signs that he'd forced his way out.

The lawn dipped towards the stream and she followed it down. The water, bubbling up from underground, glistened in the sunshine, rippling noisily round mossy stones. Kate followed it along its short course, narrow and fast-flowing until it finally pooled and deepened.

Her eyes flitted ahead. The girls had left something on the far side of the pool, half in the water. A bag perhaps, or a sweatshirt. That was careless. She moved closer, peering, trying to get a better look.

She let out a scream. Her body stiffened with shock. She stood, staring, unable to move.

Finally, she shook herself and ran towards it.

Coco was lying motionless, his hindquarters submerged, his shaggy head low in the water. His nose was only inches from the muddy edge. His eyes were open and glassy.

She reached down and touched his wet, matted fur. A cloud of flies rose into the air around her. He was already cold.

5

Simon was digging a hasty grave under the trees.

'But how?' Kate kept saying, her hands pulling at each other. 'How could he have drowned? He could swim. He loved water.'

Simon threw his grief into digging, pressing his foot on the shoulder of the spade and gouging the earth free with a sudden, violent release. Clods flew and settled.

'I don't know,' he panted. 'Maybe he was spooked by something and panicked.'

Kate shook her head. She imagined Coco, flailing desperately in the water, frightened, unable to breathe. She thought of the girls, inside, kept away, sobbing and clinging to each other. She thought about Jonathan and his cold strangeness and the hatred she'd seen in his eyes as he'd glared at Coco the previous day. The boy's parting smile, glimpsed through the glass.

'He did it. Jonathan.' She paused, feeling the weight of the accusation. 'He drowned him.'

'Jonathan?' Simon sounded astonished. He clearly understood nothing at all about the boy.

She heard herself say: 'Out of spite.'

Simon paused in his work and leaned on his spade, breathing hard.

'That's a terrible thing to say.' His face darkened. 'Honestly, Kate—' He broke off, turning back to his digging. A moment later, he added: 'I know you're upset but—'

Kate folded her arms across her chest. 'He hated Coco. I told you how he glared when he was hiding out here and Coco led me straight to him. It was chilling.'

Simon looked up. 'He's a child, Kate. Yes, he's difficult. I can see that. But that doesn't mean—'

She took a deep breath. 'I don't want him coming here again, Simon. I'm sorry.'

Simon shook his head. For a moment, there was silence between them, filled only by the soughing of the breeze in the trees and the sharp, bright song of a robin.

Finally, Simon said quietly: 'You don't mean that.'

'I do.' Her jaw was set. 'You see him on your own, if that's what you want. That's up to you. But I don't want him near the girls. He's upset them terribly in the last few days, even before this.' She gestured at Coco's inert body. 'There's something wrong with that boy, Simon. Terribly wrong.'

'Kate, please!' His voice was imploring. 'You can't really—'

Kate didn't stay to listen. She turned abruptly and strode back up the lawn towards the house to be with her grieving girls.

There was no point in arguing about it. Simon couldn't see the darkness in Jonathan that she saw. She couldn't even articulate it. It went beyond insolence and rudeness. She thought about Mimi, hanged in the attic. And about Coco. Angrily, she wiped away tears.

She'd never be able to prove that Jonathan had killed Coco. She'd never convince Simon. But in her own mind, she was certain. He'd done it out of malice because he'd taken against the dog and he knew how much she and the girls loved him. He'd sensed, at the age of ten, exactly how best to hurt them.

6

SIX YEARS LATER

Kate went alone to the solicitor's office.

This was Simon's world. This man, David Reed, was his friend, not hers, a pal from his schooldays. She was angry with David because, really, she was angry with Simon. Her husband had no business leaving her. He'd lied when he'd said they'd grow old together. Missing him was too crushing a weight to bear.

She sat in the waiting room, her eyes ranging unseeing over the dusty bookshelves and framed certificates. She was still trying to recover from the horror of the funeral. Clara's thin face, white with shock. Ankle socks had made her twelve-year-old legs look all the more gangly beneath her black dress. Bella, two years older, was taller and already womanly. They'd looked so lost.

Kate didn't know how to shield them. It was overwhelming. The musty smell of the church, steeped in centuries of incense and the smoke of snuffed candles, the murmuring voices and faces turning to see, the horror of the wooden coffin with its polished brass handles and the knowledge that, inside, lay the still, cold body of their father.

None of it seemed real. It had happened so suddenly. Simon had left for work as usual, settled in his favourite corner seat on the train and, at some point in the journey, simply slumped, as if he'd fallen asleep. No-one had even noticed until they reached Paddington and, by then, it was too late. He had no business having a heart attack. It wasn't fair. He'd played tennis days before.

Now, David Reed swept through and ushered her into his office. He was professionally soft-voiced and kind, full of apologies for keeping her waiting. He offered her coffee and discreetly set a box of tissues on the table in front of her while he fussed with the coffee machine.

She heard Simon's voice in her ear, his wry jokes about David's rapidly receding hair, his spreading paunch. She sensed Simon sitting there beside her, secretly rolling his eyes when David spilt milk on the counter and made a performance of wiping it up.

Finally, when he sat down with his file of papers, David drew a pair of gold-rimmed glasses from a spectacles case and set them on the end of his nose. He looked Dickensian, with his glasses and balding pate. All he needed was a tall stool, quill and ledger. She'd make a story out of this later for Simon, she thought, then her stomach fell away, a missed step in the dark, when she remembered he'd gone.

'Because almost everything passes to you, you're not liable for inheritance tax,' David was saying in a plodding, funereal tone. 'We do have to apply for probate but that should be straightforward. In the meantime, with regard to your joint accounts, you can access funds as normal.' He pulled a printed sheet from the file and slid it across the table to her. 'I've made a list of the institutions you need to contact to inform them of Simon's passing. Banks, investment houses and so on.'

Simon's *death*, she thought. Her husband had died, not passed or crossed over or been borne away on the wings of angels. Simon hated euphemisms and so did she.

'You'll find that most require a certified copy of the death certificate.' He removed his glasses to look her in the eye. 'If there's anything you need help with, Kate, anything at all... I can only imagine how hard this is for you.'

She reached for her coffee. Money didn't matter, nothing mattered, but she supposed she was wealthy now. Everything – the business, the house, her husband's savings and investments and private pension – was hers. The girls would be well provided for, at least.

Something snagged in her mind. She blinked. 'You said "*almost* everything" passes to me?'

They'd made the wills together, soon after the girls had been born. They'd been simple mirror wills, which just left everything to each other. Had he changed his, without telling her? No, Simon would never do that.

David cleared his throat. 'There is one additional bequest. I'm sorry, I thought you'd be aware.' He reached across the desk and set a printed copy of Simon's will in front of her, then indicated a paragraph with a stubby finger. 'Just here.'

To my son, Jonathan Bancroft, the sum of thirty thousand pounds.

She felt her heart rate quicken. They hadn't seen Jonathan again, not since that terrible visit. He'd become a forbidden subject between the two of them. Simon never mentioned his name and Kate didn't either. She was sure Simon would have carried on making payments to Monica, Jonathan's mother, but that was his business. She focused on their life together and on the girls.

Now, she took a deep breath and steadied herself. Simon had every right to leave Jonathan money, of course he had. She just wished she'd known.

David said carefully: 'His son from his first marriage, I believe?'

'Yes. They weren't close but he always provided for him.'

A watchfulness in David's face gave her a sudden stab of doubt. She wondered what Simon had told his friend, if he'd discussed his feelings towards Jonathan and her own distrust of the boy.

'I take it he's been informed?' he said. 'Only at the funeral, I don't remember—'

'He wasn't there. Neither was his mother.' She paused, remembering. 'I did notify her, of course. She said Jonathan was about to sit his GCSEs and she didn't want him to know until they were over.'

'I see.' David looked thoughtful. 'Of course, that's another issue. The question of his school fees. Assuming he wants to stay on for sixth form.'

Kate blinked. 'School fees?'

'Well, yes.' David looked startled. 'At Greyforth's.'

Greyforth's. Simon's old school. He'd often talked about his time there, all boys' own japes and cricket teas. *Jonathan, there?* She shook her head, dazed.

'I'm so sorry. I'd rather assumed—' David shuffled papers on his desk, hiding his face.

Kate watched him. 'Is he boarding?' David was as awkward

discussing emotions as Simon had been. And yet he'd known about this and she hadn't. 'Since when?'

'Well, since year seven, I believe. That's when we started. Aged eleven.'

Something slipped into place in Kate's mind. Jonathan's sudden visit, at the age of ten, the summer before the admissions process. It must have been in Simon's mind all along. Maybe that had been the lever he'd used with Jonathan's mother, the promise of sending their son away to an expensive school.

'And I assume Simon's been footing the bill?'

David gave a slight nod. He seemed suddenly rather frightened of her. 'I only know because he mentioned visiting, once or twice, you know, to take him out. He remarked on the changes, since our day. There's a new science block, apparently. And a rather marvellous swimming pool. It sounds extraordinary. Apparently, it's got a moveable floor. They can lower it hydraulically for diving competitions.' He trailed off, aware, perhaps, that she was only half listening. 'I am sorry. I really thought—'

Kate felt flushed. Simon had visited Jonathan there? She'd had no idea. She imagined the pride he must have felt at seeing Jonathan at his own school, the pleasure in reviving memories. He'd kept it all secret, all this time. Not just the fees but the fact he'd continued to have a relationship with the boy.

She rummaged in her bag for a tissue. It was partly her fault. She remembered how furious she'd been about Coco's death. She'd been the one who'd closed the door on the subject, not him.

'So we're talking about two more years there, assuming he does want to stay on?' She swallowed. 'I could offer to cover those. I'm sure it's what Simon would have wanted.'

David lifted his pen, getting back to safer ground. 'I could certainly inform his mother on your behalf to that effect, if that's what you decide to do. It would be a generous gesture.'

Kate considered. She could afford it, she knew. 'Would Jonathan have any claim to the rest of Simon's estate?'

David raised his eyebrows. For a moment, silence pressed down on them both, broken only by the distant strains of voices from a nearby room and the stolid ticking of the wall clock.

Finally, David spoke. 'Well, he could contest the will, I suppose. Or rather, while he's legally a minor, his mother could, on his behalf. Then it would be a matter for the courts to decide. The fact he's clearly acknowledged by Simon as his son would strengthen his claim.' David paused, weighing the argument. 'But on the other hand, the will is legally robust. Simon has provided generously for him in the past, as you say, and he is a beneficiary. Personally, I'd think it unlikely a court would grant in the son's favour.'

Kate sat straighter in her chair. 'I don't want him bothering us in the future.'

David fiddled with his glasses, then scratched a few figures on his notepad. 'Your offer to fund another two years at Grey-forth's is already generous. I'd need to clarify with the bursar but I'd expect it to be close to a hundred thousand pounds. Plus, Jonathan is receiving another thirty thousand in the will.' He nodded. 'I could draw something up, making it clear that if his mother chooses to accept your offer, they won't attempt any further claims.'

She paused. 'Is that legal?'

David looked thoughtful. 'It's not watertight, legally speaking. He might argue in the future that he wasn't able to give an undertaking himself because he was under age. But if he did decide to take you to court, it would certainly help your defence.'

Kate exhaled. 'Good.'

'I'll prepare something and send it across to you.'

Kate blew out her cheeks. She thought about the strange, cold little boy who'd stayed with them that summer, years ago, and the bloated body of their beloved Coco.

'Thank you,' she said. 'Let's hope that's an end to it.'

* * *

In the coming weeks, grief stalked them. It lay in wait in unexpected places.

In the smell of Simon's dressing gown, stray hairs still clinging to its collar. In the junk mail that continued to arrive for him, offering discounts on his favourite brands of shirts and sweaters. In the lawn that grew lavishly without him to cut it.

David sent a legal document to Monica, outlining the offer of school fees and the understanding that no further claim would be made on Simon's estate. Kate didn't know how much say Jonathan had in the matter but Monica duly signed it.

Kate heard nothing from Jonathan himself. She didn't expect it. He'd probably forgotten about them all, long ago.

Then, a week after the thirty thousand pounds had been transferred into a savings account in Jonathan's name, Kate received something odd in the post.

There was no letter, no note in the envelope. Just a faded, rather crumpled picture cut roughly from a colour magazine. It showed a brown and white beagle, very similar to Coco.

She turned it over with a frown. It wasn't an advertisement. She had no idea why anyone would have posted it to her.

She went to drop it in the recycling. It was only then that she noticed something strange about it.

The paper had been cut. It was a careful, surgical slice, as if by a razor. She held it up, curious. It ran horizontally across the picture, for all the world as if someone had deliberately severed the dog's head from its body.

She shivered, crumpled it into a ball and threw it away.

7

DAMIAN

London, Four Years Later

Bella had dyed her hair.

Damian kept his face neutral but inside he frowned. He could tell even at this distance. She shouldn't have done that. The blonde streaks were tacky. They made her look cheap.

She owed him more than that. He'd come to London for her, given up his new life in Amsterdam, as an up-and-coming wheeler-dealer, and headed here to find her. For two years now, since he'd left school himself and started making his way in the world, he'd bided his time, tracking her and her sister on social media. She had no idea how well he knew her.

He'd noted every photograph they'd posted. The exotic holidays they'd taken with their mother, the girls' faces smiling and bronzed. The family gatherings at that picturesque house in the country. Summer get-togethers on the patio. He remembered it well. Christmas drinks in front of a burning log fire. Bella had blossomed into a beauty. She'd looked so pleased with herself as she and her friends celebrated their end-of-school exam results.

King's College, London, here I come! Look out world!

It had been the cue he'd been waiting for.

Now, for the last hour or so, he'd been following her in Oxford Street. Yes, he definitely preferred her hair before when it had been completely brown, her natural colour. It had suited her much better.

She drifted in and out of boutiques and emerged with purchases in firm, square bags with rope handles. Plumes of red tissue paper rose like flames from inside. She treated herself in a smoothie bar, then spent an hour in a tech store, browsing the latest models of smartphone and chatting with a sales assistant before finally emerging with a new phone in a glistening box.

He watched. Afterwards, he followed her all the way back to her student halls. He saw her stop and pull out her new clothes, tear off the labels and stuff them roughly into her rucksack, then discard the shiny packaging in a nearby skip. He'd smiled to himself. They were two of a kind, after all, he thought. Chameleons.

She was a rich girl, pretending to be poor. He was a poor boy, pretending to be rich. The difference was that, one day soon, he really would be.

* * *

He spent the afternoon in the flat, shut in his cramped bedroom, drinking pots of tea and reading. The flat was one of half a dozen in the block owned by the father of his flatmate, Rupert. It stank of stale, pungent smoke. The previous night, Rupert had staggered home in the small hours, drunk, with several colleagues from the investment bank where he worked. Damian, shaken awake by them, had dragged himself out of bed with a forced smile to provide dope and Ecstasy, a round-the-clock service that heavily subsidised his rent.

Damian had worked hard to cultivate Rupert, a moneyed idiot of the kind he recognised from his days at school. He hadn't had a home here since his mother left and headed back to New York. He knew why. With Simon's death, the financial well, into which she'd dipped ever since Damian had been born, had finally dried up. He didn't blame her. He'd have done the same.

A light tap. Damian looked up from his laptop as Rupert poked his head round the door. He looked like an anxious rabbit.

'A man's hanging about downstairs. Looking for you.'

Damian raised an eyebrow. 'For me?'

Rupert nodded, embarrassed. 'He looks, I don't know, rather unsavoury. Short hair. Stocky.'

'How odd!' Damian tried to feign astonishment. 'And you're sure he's looking for me?'

Rupert swallowed hard. 'He stopped me on the steps and asked if I knew you. I told him to clear off or I'd call the porter.'

Damian hid a smile. Rupert was lucky the guy hadn't pulled a knife.

'He sounded East European.' Rupert was still hovering, still bruised by the encounter. 'I don't know. Bulgarian or Romanian, maybe.' He gestured to his cheek. 'He had a scar here, down the side of his face.'

'He must have me mixed up with someone else. Don't worry about it. Sounds as if you sent him packing, anyway.' Damian reached across to his drawer. Rupert looked stressed out. 'You fancy a smoke?'

He fell to rolling a joint for Rupert, making small talk to soothe him while his mind dissected the importance of this unexpected visit. He knew exactly who it was. An Albanian guy, a supplier he'd first met in Amsterdam and used once or twice here, until one of his rivals had offered him a better price. Clearly, the Albanian wasn't happy and he wasn't the sort of guy it was wise to upset. But how the hell had he got this address?

Rupert, perched now on the end of Damian's bed, took a deep drag and blew out smoke.

'I got a really bad vibe from him.' Another puff, another long, slow exhalation. 'I don't know. He looked really dodgy.'

Damian smiled benignly back. 'Don't worry. Like I said, it's probably a mistake. I doubt he'll be back.'

It wasn't a mistake. Of course he'd be back. Damian shut down his laptop, thinking fast. As soon as he could, he should head back to Amsterdam. But, first, he had an old score to settle.

8

Bella turned into the Aldwych and hurried towards the entrance to Bush House.

Damian smiled to himself as he followed. He knew exactly where she was heading. The same place as the previous Friday night. She should be more street-smart and vary her routine. You never knew who was watching. He breezed through security with a smile and headed to the first-floor student bar.

It was rammed. The thumping music vibrated through his body, setting his teeth on edge. He had to brace himself to press his way in through the stink of male sweat and spilled beer. It wasn't just the fact he was several years older than the rest of this crowd. Sticky floors and blocked toilets had never been his style.

He eased his way through the press of hot bodies to her side and tapped her on the shoulder. He had to press in close to make himself heard in the din. Her perfume, mellow and expensive, reached for him.

'Excuse me, but weren't you in *Antigone*? Eurydice, weren't you?' He glanced at his feet, as if he were suddenly shy. Hand-made shoes, well polished. 'You were fabulous.'

Bella smiled. 'Blink and you'd miss me, I was barely on stage. You sure you've got the right person?'

'Definitely.' He put out his hand. 'Damian Black.'

'Bella Grosvenor.'

Her hand was soft and smooth. He heard his mother's voice in his head, sneering: *Never done an honest day's work in her life.*

'Well, Bella Grosvenor,' he said, 'tell them to give you a better part next time. If you don't, I will.'

Bella's friend twisted round to check him out. He'd seen her hanging around Bella before, a brassy-looking girl with too much make-up. He didn't care what she thought of him. He didn't want to look like the young men in their crowd, all frayed jeans and faded T-shirts. He was happy with his crisp, tailored shirt and designer chinos. He winked at her and she stared him out.

He turned back to Bella and nodded at her glass. 'You look as if you're ready for another. What're you having?'

She hesitated for a moment, unsure. He liked that. She was right to be careful. There were some strange people out there. After a while, she shrugged, drained her glass and held it out to him. 'G and T, please. No ice.'

The brassy friend, seeing him take Bella's glass, leaned in. 'I'll have a white wine, if you're buying.'

When he came back from the bar, he managed to ditch the friend and steered Bella out onto the tiny concrete balcony off the side of the bar, with a distant view of the Thames. It was cold out there, the breeze whipping in from the water. It fingered her hair, carrying a few strands across her cheek. It was quiet enough out here for them to talk.

'So what're you studying? Let me guess.' He made a show of

searching her face for clues. 'Psychology. That's how you understand character so well.'

She laughed. 'Oh, please. English. You knew that, didn't you?'

He grinned, showing her his even, white teeth. 'Maybe. Bet you can't guess what I'm studying?'

She narrowed her eyes and scrutinised him. He wondered if there was some part of her – some locked-away, far-off part – that remembered him. He doubted it. She'd been so young when they'd last met. Besides, it wasn't only his name he'd changed. That had been the easy part. If he'd learned anything at boarding school, it was the ability to shape-shift. He'd had to.

'Is that a trick question?' She was weighing him up with interest. 'You don't look like a student.'

'Only partly a trick. I'm in my final year. Business studies.' He dipped his hand in his pocket and waved his fake student ID at her. 'I might head to New York next,' he added airily. 'I've got dual nationality.' That part, at least, was true.

Her eyes brightened. 'Cool! Lucky! New York's such a great city. I just spent the summer there.'

I know, he thought. *I've seen the photos*. Picnics in Central Park, parties, gigs, always surrounded by beautiful people.

'No gap year, then?'

'Bumming around for a year?' She shrugged. 'Nah, never really appealed.'

He almost laughed at that. He already knew the real reason: that she'd had to stay on for an extra year at school to retake two of her A levels. Let her have her dirty little secret.

'I spent a year in Amsterdam, before uni.' He thought of the network of drug pushers and pimps he'd cultivated in his time there. 'Met some great people. Learned a lot, too.'

She considered him. 'You sound like my sister. She's still in sixth form but she's already got a map of Europe stuck on her wall. She's got all sorts of crazy plans for next year.'

He nodded, filing the information away.

She rattled on. 'So, what're you going to do in New York?'

He named one of the city's top investment firms and saw that it impressed her.

'I'm going places,' he said calmly. 'You watch.'

She looked intrigued. He was sure he was different from the guys who usually hung around her.

'What about you?' he asked. 'What's your story?'

She looked into her glass as if she expected to find the answer there. 'Oh, I don't know yet. I'm still figuring it out.'

He raised an eyebrow. 'Let me see... You're rich but the money embarrasses you so you're playing at slumming it with the rest of the student crowd. But not too much. You'll live on baked beans and pot noodles in term time, so long as you can make up for it in the holidays when Mummy's paying. Right?'

She looked stung. 'You don't know the first thing about me.'

'Is that right?' He smiled. 'It's my superpower, reading people. A sort of hobby. Those leather boots of yours. Hand-made, aren't they? And those diamond studs in your ears. They're not cubic zirconia, they're real. Then you offset the good stuff with that baggy, faded T-shirt that probably came from a charity shop. You'll have to hide it from Mummy when you head home.' He held up a hand in a gesture of mock self-defence. 'I'm not judging. The boots look great, by the way. And comfy. It's good to take care of your feet. But your mates would faint if they knew what you paid for them.' He paused, taking in her reaction. 'Don't worry. Your secret's safe with me.'

For a moment, she looked about to turn and leave him. Then she seemed to reconsider. She took a deep breath and said coolly: 'OK, what's going on here? I mean, are you just being a jerk for fun or is there a point to all this?'

'A jerk?' He felt himself tense. 'That's not very polite.'

He looked at the expensive jewellery, the blonde highlights, the flawless skin, all luxuries paid for with money that was rightly his. He remembered the way she'd laughed at him when they'd met as children, how she and her sister had giggled and whispered together behind their hands. The white-hot humiliation he'd endured. And Bella's conniving mother who'd turned his father against him. They must think he didn't even know, but he was smarter than them. He understood only too well.

The memory had stayed with him for all these years, a rat gnawing at his gut with sharp teeth. He thought about all that family wealth that had passed so smoothly from their father to her smug mother. She wanted it all to go to her darling girls, did she? He'd fix that. And they'd tried to pay him off with thirty grand? That was small change to them. It was an insult. Was that really all they'd thought he was worth?

Bella hesitated. Her eyes were uncertain. He sensed how confused she felt, unsure what to make of him.

He broke into a smile. 'You've got me all wrong. We're two of a kind, you and I. And you know it.'

She didn't answer but her eyes stayed on his.

'I've got some good stuff on me tonight.' He gave her a meaningful look and patted his jacket pocket. 'I'm selling the usual but, as well as that, I've got something extra special. Pure as the driven snow. Like you. And, also like you, it's not for sale. There are some things money can't buy – right? I just share it with people I really like.'

He watched her face and waited. It could go either way. In that moment, she looked perfectly balanced in her indecision.

She might take the challenge or she might turn and walk away. What happened next wasn't his responsibility, it was up to her.

'There you are!' The brassy friend had appeared at the door. She narrowed her eyes, looking them over, trying to read the situation. She glared at Damian, then focused her attention pointedly on Bella. 'I've been looking all over for you. Come on. We're leaving.'

'Coming.' Bella put her glass to her lips, drained it, then set it on the edge of the concrete balcony. She started for the door. He didn't move, just stood there, drink in hand, poised, waiting.

On the threshold, Bella hesitated and turned back to him.

'We're off to a party,' she said. 'In Peckham. Come, if you want?'

He nodded, feigning indifference. 'Sure,' he said. 'Why not?'

9

KATE

The phone call came at 1.29 a.m. The digits on Kate's phone burned into her memory.

The screen flashed Bella's name. It wasn't like her to call in the small hours. She was eighteen now, living in halls, old enough to sort herself out if she ran into problems.

Kate groped to accept the call, shaking off sleep. 'Bella? You OK?'

The voice was shrill and breathless with panic. 'Is this Bella's mum?'

'Who's this?' Kate sat up, suddenly wide awake. Anxiety roiled in her stomach. 'Has something happened?'

'I'm Iris. She's, I mean, I can't—' The young woman broke off, sobbing.

Kate strained to make out the noises in the background. A tannoy, choppy with static. An echoey indoor acoustic. A station? An airport? 'Where are you?'

'Hospital.' Iris was barely intelligible through tears.

'No!' For a moment, Kate couldn't breathe. She wanted to

put the phone down. She didn't want to hear another word. She didn't want what was coming next. She refused it.

Bella. Her girl, her baby, her firstborn. That big-hearted little girl who tried, from the age of two, to look after them all. She used to stand by Clara's cot, still in nappies herself and clinging to the bars to steady herself, singing a barely recognisable version of 'Incy Wincy Spider' as she tried to stop her little sister crying. Here, in this bedroom, after Simon died, she'd crept into Kate's bed when she'd heard her sobbing in the night, pressed her face against Kate's back and wrapped her arms around her. *My Bella. Please God, not her.*

Kate realised she was somehow out of bed and pulling clothes from a drawer. 'Please. Which hospital? What's happened?'

Kate carried on firing questions, her voice rising in volume with frustration, until a calmer, male voice came on the line and cut across her.

'Hello? Is this Mrs Grosvenor? Bella Grosvenor's mother?'

'Yes.' Kate was shaking so hard she had to grasp the phone with both hands. 'Who are you? What's going on?'

The voice at the other end sounded unnaturally calm in the chaos of noise. 'This is Doctor Tang. I'm the on-duty doctor in A and E at King's College Hospital.' He paused as if he were gathering his strength. 'I'm afraid I have some bad news. Bella was brought in by ambulance shortly after 1 a.m. We did everything we could but—'

Kate focused on the far wall and the stain there, caused by last winter's damp. She'd meant to get a decorator in to strip back and repaint. Life had just been too busy. First, getting Bella and Clara through their exams, then sending Bella off to university. Now, she never would. Now, nothing so banal would ever matter again.

'Mrs Grosvenor? Are you there?' The voice was still in her ear, trying to reach her.

Her legs gave way and she fell heavily onto the edge of the bed. She saw the unused second pillow beside her own and felt a surge of anger. Simon should be here. He had no right to die so young, to leave her to face this. She couldn't get through it without him.

She thought of Clara, still asleep in her room across the hall. Kate didn't want her ever to wake and find their lives destroyed, a second time.

'But what happened?' she said in a daze. Maybe the man on the phone had just explained it all. She had no idea. She just kept asking: 'What happened?'

10

Kate realised afterwards that she'd driven herself up to London in the darkness. She had no idea how. She must have been on automatic.

Later, she remembered only snapshots.

She saw herself lying prostrate over Bella's body in the hospital corridor, clawing at her daughter, trying somehow, through her grief, her denial, to bring her back. It was as if Kate too had left her own body and was hanging above herself, watching this distraught, desperate mother as if she were a stranger.

Someone had cut open Bella's baggy cotton T-shirt. How dare they! Bella would be furious. She loved that top. She was wearing her new jeans, the ones Kate had bought her on a shopping spree a few weeks earlier. And those beautiful hand-stitched boots. Bella had been so desperate to have them.

Her hair was matted at the side. Kate fingered it. The blonde highlights harked back to when Bella was a child and her hair was bleached on summer holidays by the sun and the chlorine of the swimming pools. She remembered all the styles, the bunches and plaits and topknots, then the French braids Bella had perfected in adolescence. It was loose now and tangled. Kate had a sudden urge to comb it for her, then to cut it off and take it home where it could be safe.

She supposed Bella's friends were there; they must have been. She never saw them in the pictures that ran on a loop inside her head.

She remembered wailing and tearing at her own face and clothes. An unearthly keening she didn't recognise. A man was there; she didn't know who he was. He lifted her off Bella's body and held her firmly, his arms round her, as she sobbed and struggled until her legs finally buckled.

Her phone kept ringing. Morning must have come. Clara had woken, found herself alone in the house, confused, her mother's clothes in disarray, and was trying to reach her.

She rang, again and again. Kate couldn't answer. How could she? How could she tell her? She couldn't make it real. All she wanted was to hold off the day. Every passing minute seemed to drag Bella further from her. Every hour.

Stop it. Please. I'll give anything. Take me. Just not Bella. Not my beautiful girl.

* * *

It took time for the truth to come out. Bella's friends told the police that she'd never taken anything before, as far as they knew. None of them had. At the party, they'd each had a tab of Ecstasy. Just one. They thought Bella had taken the same.

At first, when she slumped against the wall, they'd thought she was sleeping. They weren't thinking clearly. They were out of it themselves.

Then someone bent over her and screamed that she'd

stopped breathing. They called an ambulance and she was rushed to hospital. It was too late. They were sorry. Everyone was so sorry. There was nothing they could do.

Why wasn't I there? I'm sorry, Bella, so sorry. I should have been there. I'm your mother. I should have looked after you. I should have saved you.

11

Late at night, Kate pored over the media reports about Bella's death, trying to bite back her frustration. They were mostly poorly written pieces, full of clichés. Her daughter deserved better.

London party girl dies after fatal drug overdose

Bella Grosvenor, 18, collapsed at a student house party in Peckham late on Friday after taking a tablet of the illegal drug, Ecstasy. Paramedics, who attended the scene, found her unresponsive. Ms Grosvenor, a first-year English student at King's College, was described as a bright, fun-loving young woman with a promising future ahead of her.

But what should have been an exciting night out ended in tragedy. The coroner described her death as 'devastating' and said illegal recreational drugs such as Ecstasy were 'a plague on society'. Her mother, Kate Grosvenor, called for all those who supply drugs to young people to face tough penalties.

A representative of King's College said the student community was in shock. She described Ms Grosvenor as a 'friendly and talented young woman who would be sadly missed'.

A detective constable, who was involved in investigating the cause of Ms Grosvenor's death, confirmed that a police file had been passed to the Public Prosecution Service (PPS).

* * *

Kate clipped all the articles, long and short, even the ones that misreported Bella's age or misspelt her name. Everything she found online, she printed off and added to her old-fashioned, cardboard file. *It's all evidence*, she told herself. *It's all part of the story.*

Kate couldn't put the feeling into words but it gave her some comfort to process what had happened to Bella, as if it were another one of the news stories she'd worked on so many years ago. It was already becoming her own personal investigation and, at a time of pain and despair, it gave her a shred of purpose.

In her mind, Bella hadn't just been unlucky, as everyone else seemed to think. Her daughter was the victim of a crime and the perpetrator hadn't been caught. It was her final job, as Bella's mother, to bring the criminal to justice.

Kate had initially placed her hopes in the police. In her first interviews with the officer assigned to Bella's case, DC Whittaker, she'd come away hopeful that action would be taken.

'We're tracking down all those who attended the party,' DC Whittaker assured her in her soft, lilting voice. 'These interviews with friends and fellow students will form a key part of the evidence file on Bella's case, along with your own statement and the forensic examiner and coroner's reports.'

But days turned to weeks. The coroner's verdict – 'death caused by the consumption of the illegal drug, Ecstasy' – seemed to bleed life out of the case. Suddenly, Kate had the feeling that no-one was any longer interested in the broader questions of how and why Bella had come to take the Ecstasy. It became harder to get DC Whittaker to return her calls.

In what was to be her final police appointment, Kate sensed a new toughness in DC Whittaker's approach. The officer seemed to have run out of patience.

'Mrs Grosvenor, I do understand how distressing this is for you. Believe me, I do.'

Kate didn't respond. *Words, words, words.* She was certain that DC Whittaker didn't understand at all.

'But I'm really not sure what more I can tell you.'

Kate perched on the edge of the hard plastic chair. The lighting in the interview room was so stark, it hurt her eyes. She forced herself to stare across at DC Whittaker. 'What I need to know is when are you going to find the person who gave Bella that drug?'

DC Whittaker's jaw clenched. 'As we have already discussed, the matter is no longer in my hands. The role of the police in a case of this nature is to prepare an evidence file and submit—'

'Submit it to the PPS,' Kate interrupted. 'Yes, I know. But then what? They're a prosecution service. How can they recommend a prosecution until you've caught a suspect, the person who supplied that drug?'

DC Whittaker clenched her hands together. She spoke slowly and carefully as if to a child. 'As you are aware, we have been unable to establish who supplied the contaminated tablet that led to Bella's tragic passing.'

Tragic passing? Please. Kate struggled to tamp down irritation. *Don't patronise me.*

'According to several accounts from people at the party,' the DC continued, 'the drug Bella took was not part of the batch consumed by the other students that evening. None of them suffered ill effects. It is possible that Bella was already in possession of the tablet—'

'When she arrived at the party,' Kate finished. 'Yes.' She tried not to raise her voice. 'But that just means we need to widen the investigation. Find out where else she might have got hold of it. Track down people who saw her that day, even if they didn't go to the party. People at the university, in her student accommodation, maybe. You've hardly scratched the surface. I can't see—'

DC Whittaker withdrew her hands from the tabletop and rose to her feet. 'I do understand your frustration, Mrs Grosvenor, I really do.' She gave a tight smile. 'You've suffered a terrible loss. It's only natural to want to find answers. To want to hold someone accountable for what happened to Bella. But I'm afraid that often, in police work, frustrating though it can be—' She gathered together her papers and gave Kate a brisk nod.

'So that's it?' Kate stared at her in disbelief. 'Case closed?'

'I'm afraid that, at this time, the PPS has ruled that there are no grounds for prosecution. However, if—'

'Only because you haven't done your job properly.' Kate had scraped back her chair and was on her feet. 'Only because—'

'Mrs Grosvenor, I'm afraid I must bring this interview to an end. I wish you well, I really do.'

The detective constable swept out of the room, leaving an embarrassed constable, barely older than Bella, to see Kate out of the building. Kate knew, as she handed over her security pass and headed towards the main doors to the street, that she had just seen DC Whittaker for the last time. Unless, of course, she managed to produce fresh, compelling evidence of her own to present to her.

'No!' Kate banged her hand on the table. Hot coffee slopped out of the mug and made a muddy ring at the base. 'She was a victim. This was a crime. Why can't they get that?'

Rosa, her closest friend, lifted the mug and ran a tissue over the wet patches on the table, mopping up. As soon as she'd heard, Rosa had dropped everything and come to stay. She found practical jobs for herself, making Kate endless cups of tea and coffee and keeping the fridge filled and taking out the rubbish. Mostly, she just listened.

'I can't stand it.' Kate was brittle with grief, with anger. 'The police need to take this seriously. I've got to make them. I owe it to Bella.'

Kate felt as if her mind were fracturing. At night, the past ran behind her eyes like an old film, filled with images from Bella's eighteen years.

Bella as a toddler, laughing so hard she could hardly stay upright, her jaw hanging open helplessly, her eyes creased, her small arms clutching her waist.

Bella at the age of three, running through a meadow, bathed

in afternoon sunshine. They'd gone away to the countryside for the weekend to visit friends. Clara, strapped into a sling, could barely walk but Bella was seized by the glorious, open freedom of the fields and had raced, her short legs pumping, the long grass on either side of her a swiftly parted sea. Such joy.

Bella at eight, excitedly exploring this house, their new home with all its nooks and crannies, running everywhere with Coco and Clara at her heels.

Other memories forced their way in until she felt her head might explode with them. Of Simon, resplendent in his floppy hat, tending to the roses. Of late suppers on the patio, the two of them, enjoying the country air and the failing sunshine, knowing the girls were already asleep in bed.

How could they both be gone? Two of the people she loved most in this world. She should have protected them. By sheer force of love, she should have kept them here.

She lifted her hand, ready to bang it down again. She was tired of *sorry for your loss*. She was tired of life smashing her in the face and destroying the people she loved, the people she *needed* to stay alive, and expecting her to take it. She wouldn't.

Rosa reached in and gently took Kate's raised hand in her own.

'I'm not giving in.' Kate realised she was shaking. She took a deep breath before she carried on. 'Her death wasn't accidental. The coroner was wrong. That stuff was lethal. Someone gave it to her. They killed her.'

Rosa didn't answer for a moment. It was still early. She'd only just come downstairs. Kate – sitting, shoulders hunched, at the kitchen table – followed her friend's movements as Rosa crossed to the kitchen counter, reached for a mug and poured herself a coffee from the fresh pot, then came back to sit beside Kate.

It was dark outside. The garden was heavy with shadow. Kate sensed movement beyond the lawn, down near the copse of trees, and strained to see. For a moment, she thought she saw the low, nosing shape of Coco emerging from the gloom and her heart stirred.

It moved again. No, a fox, lifting its muzzle to stare. It turned and trotted soundlessly back into the bushes.

'I know you want to fight,' Rosa said gently. 'You're angry. I don't blame you.' She paused, feeling her way. 'But it won't bring her back.'

'I know that.' Kate sounded feistier than she felt. Beneath a thin, hard crust, she was nothing more than liquid. 'That's not the point. Whoever did this can't be allowed to get away with it.'

For a while, the only sound was the slow tick of the kitchen clock and their own breathing.

'Kate, I can't imagine what you're going through. How hard it is.' Rosa's voice was calm and quiet. 'But this isn't about finding someone to punish. No-one forced Bella to take that tablet. Her friends took them too. She was just terribly unlucky.'

Kate bit down on her lip and looked round the kitchen at the worn cabinets and wood-fronted units. She and Simon had chosen them together, when they'd first moved in. Beside them, on the narrow strip of kitchen wall, was the family's impromptu height chart. The succession of pencil marks had tracked, each summer, how tall the two girls had grown.

'I keep having this dream,' she said. 'Well, nightmare. About Bella.'

'Oh, Kate.'

'She's only little, about four, and she's got away from me, let go of my hand somehow, and she's running through a crowd, hundreds of people, and I'm trying to chase after her. But she's so nimble, dodging through people's legs, so quick, and I'm so slow and lumbering and people are angry with me; they won't get out of the way and I can't reach her. She's in danger and I can't reach her and...' She paused, out of breath. 'And then I wake up.'

Rosa gazed at her with compassion. 'I'm sorry.'

Kate pulled a wry face. 'Yeah, no prizes for guessing what that's about.'

They sat in silence for a moment, lost in their own thoughts.

Kate said suddenly: 'I'm going to sell the house.' She didn't look Rosa in the eye. 'Don't try to talk me out of it. I've decided. I'll put it on the market as soon as I can. I'll move back to London.'

Rosa hesitated. 'Why?'

'Lots of reasons.' Kate didn't want to discuss it. She didn't want to be challenged. She had to leave. She was drowning in memories. They were everywhere, waiting to ambush her at every turn. Memories of Bella, of course, and of Simon too, as if losing her daughter had somehow torn open again the wound of losing her husband.

Rosa looked worried. 'What about Clara?'

Kate hunched. 'She'll be off travelling next summer, anyway.'

Rosa said: 'Kate, it's a big step. Have you even talked to her about it?'

Kate sipped her coffee. Outside, the black of the night softened to grey as the light grew. The outlines of the patio furniture and the bird table emerged more sharply.

'Please don't rush into it,' Rosa said at last. 'You've been through such a lot here. Losing Simon. And now Bella.' She paused, glancing at Kate. 'Try to think about what's best for Clara too.'

'Of course.' Kate gazed out through the draining shadows at

the garden. She didn't know if she could bear to leave. But she didn't think she could bear to stay either.

She thought about Bella and the drugs that had killed her and found herself creasing forward, her arms across her stomach, absorbing the pain.

She'd never worried about them smoking cigarettes. She and Simon had never smoked and the girls had always hated the stink of tobacco, thought the whole idea of buying 'cancer sticks' was too stupid for words. Kate had had to shush Bella once, when she'd been about four years old. They'd walked past a young woman in the street who was brandishing a lit cigarette. Bella had turned to scold her, with all the self-righteousness of a child. *You shouldn't do that! It's bad for you!*

She and Simon had laughed about it afterwards, amused and secretly proud. *Look at us, doing such a great job!*

She'd talked with them both about alcohol. They knew it all. Never leave a glass unattended, in case it gets spiked. Drink plenty of water. Never abandon a friend who's had too much to drink.

They were sensible girls. And school taught them all this stuff too, nowadays. It was part of the curriculum.

The girls had rolled their eyes when she'd tried to lecture them. *Yes, Mum. We know! We get it!*

And drugs, she'd talked to Bella about drugs; she knew she had. Sitting here, in this kitchen, shortly before Bella had left for New York. She'd warned her to be careful. They'd talked about peer pressure and gateway drugs and the slide into addiction. She knew they had. But had they talked about faulty batches?

Was it her fault? Had she failed, in all the noise and fret of being a parent, to give the one piece of advice that might have saved Bella's life?

Oh, Bella, why did you take it? That one tiny tablet. If you'd just said no. Oh, my beautiful girl. I'm so sorry. I should have been there.

The pain in her stomach kept her doubled over. How would she live? How would she get through this, day after empty day, without her daughter?

She felt a hand, warm, on her shoulder, gently stroking.

Rosa said: 'It will get easier. It will. I know it mightn't feel like it now but I promise you.'

'It's not over,' Kate said. She pulled herself upright. Something coursed through her. Resolve. 'I'm not giving up.'

If no-one else was going to search for the truth, to find out who gave Bella the tablet that killed her, then she would. That's what she'd do in London. That would be her purpose. She'd let Bella down terribly. She'd never forgive herself. But she could at least do this. It might save other girls from the same fate.

She blew out a long, steadying breath. She would investigate. She knew what to do. It wasn't so different from covering a news story. She'd find out who was responsible and she'd expose them.

It was the least she could do for her dead daughter. Bella deserved justice. Kate wouldn't rest until she found it.

13

Kate was suffocated by belongings.

Every day, after Clara left for school, Kate emptied drawers and cupboards onto the nearest stretch of carpet and sat beside them, wearily sorting through the flotsam and jetsam of the last eleven years. It wasn't just a tide, it was a tsunami.

Each afternoon at three, she stopped, piled filled bags and boxes into the car and drove some to the charity shop in town, others to the skips at the municipal tip. She made sure she'd finished by the time Clara came home.

Clara stomped in, tight-faced, grieving for her sister, over-whelmed with exam stress and throbbing with anger about the plan to move. Kate, feeling numb, cooked for her and sat with her at the table, picking at her own food, and trying to coax Clara into conversation. Clara barely spoke.

Kate couldn't share her grief for the possessions she felt forced to let go. It was too painful to put into words. She felt hijacked by so many random things, now useless to her in any practical sense, but imbued with the past: Simon's fishing gear, his shelves of books about the Second World War, about ships and cars, and the last of his clothes, including the suit he'd worn for their wedding, mothballed for years in the back of a wardrobe.

She sat for a long time in Bella's room, just looking around, feeling her daughter's presence. Everything spoke of her. The theatre posters on the wall, dog-eared now. The corkboard, over-flowing with jumbled photographs of holidays and school-friends. The random souvenirs Bella had brought back from her summer in New York – a replica Times Square street sign, a tiny New York yellow cab and a grease-stained popcorn bucket from her first and last ball game.

She boxed up Bella's make-up and jewellery and labelled them to keep, at least for now. She went slowly through old boxes of schoolwork. There were all the bulging files of notes from the A levels Bella had resat. Kate knew how humiliating it had been for her to stay on for that extra year at school, without her friends. She'd been so proud of the way Bella had doubled down. She'd been determined to get the grades she needed to go to London.

Now, staring at the lists and pages of cramped writing, Kate wondered what it had all been for. What if Bella hadn't done all this? What if she'd just shrugged and given up and accepted somewhere less prestigious through clearing, first time round? What if she'd never gone to London... Maybe she'd still be alive today. *What if.* It was endless. It tormented her.

Kate pushed the files into a recycling sack and moved on. There was so much from primary school they'd never thrown away. First spelling books, filled with wobbly lettering. A battered family tree, showing Mummy, Daddy, Bella and Clara perched on branches, each of them illustrated by a round childish face with a huge grin. She sat for a moment, considering them. The four of them. Their family.

Kate pulled out four of Bella's oldest, favourite soft toys to keep, kissed them gently, then stuffed the rest hastily into a bin bag before she could change her mind.

In the evening, once Clara shut herself in her room to study, Kate pulled on stout shoes and a thick coat and took silent walks round the garden in the darkness. She walked the length of the stream where the girls had once played and stood for a while at the pool, mesmerised by the refracted shards of light skimming the surface in the gloom and remembering the day she'd found Coco there, lifeless. The trees, many choked by ivy, stood guard over Coco's unmarked grave.

She wondered what Simon would have made of her decision to leave, if he'd have thought her a coward. She wondered what Bella would think.

* * *

After that, each time Kate took the train up to London to look at properties, she tried to arrange another meeting on the side, linked to Bella's death.

It wasn't easy to track down the students who'd been at the party that night. Iris and another of Bella's friends started her off with the names and contact numbers of people they knew and she widened her search from there, keeping meticulous notes on her laptop.

One or two never answered their phones or replied to Kate's messages. A young Scottish girl called Vanessa with long, straight, auburn hair, met Kate in a coffee shop in Covent Garden but cried so hard in the time they had together that Kate didn't learn a thing.

One young man, an engineering student, was too defensive to say anything helpful, beyond confirming what she already knew – yes, he was a student and yes, he had attended the party.

'Do you know anything about who was supplying the drugs there, either during the party or before it?' she'd asked.

He'd looked strained. 'I am not aware of any drugs being consumed at the party,' he'd said stiffly.

She tried to put him at his ease. 'Come on, it's OK – everyone knows there were drugs there. I'm not the police. I'm just Bella's mum.' She leaned in. 'Imagine if this had happened to you and it was your mum trying to find out what happened.'

He'd fingered his collar nervously. 'I really can't help. Sorry. I've already told the police. I didn't see anything.'

'But you must have known other people were taking drugs, yeah? Even if you didn't take any yourself.'

His eyes slid past her to the door. 'I'm afraid not.'

'OK. Could you tell me who else was there, please? Just the names and contact numbers of people you knew. I know it won't be everybody – but to help me extend my interviews a bit, yeah?'

His eyes doggedly refused to meet hers. 'No-one,' he said at last. 'Sorry. I just, er, just heard about the party and turned up on spec.'

'So you're saying you didn't know anyone there? No-one at all?' Kate tried not to sound incredulous.

She asked him a few more questions but it was clearly pointless.

He wasn't the only one who seemed frightened to open up. She did understand, however frustrating it was. No-one wanted to get into trouble. No-one wanted to risk being thrown off their course. No-one wanted a criminal record.

The most helpful interview was with Iris herself.

Kate finally met her on the South Bank one afternoon and took her for a coffee and sandwich in the British Film Institute.

Iris wrapped her hands round her mug and cradled it. Kate saw the way the rim shuddered against Iris's teeth when she sipped. Her wrists were thin and bony. Her hair, a bright blonde, was crimped into waves. When she dipped her head to pick at her sandwich, darker roots showed, running down the centre of her scalp.

Kate set her phone to record and put it on the table between them. Iris eyed it warily as Kate started to ease her into questions about what happened that night.

'A few of us met up in the bar, in the student union,' Iris said. 'Bella had been in halls in the afternoon, washing her hair and getting ready. She'd joined us there around eight.' She blinked, remembering. 'It was heaving. Typical Friday night. The drinks are cheaper in the union than in the pub, you see, so everyone gets tanked up.'

'Did Bella drink much?'

Iris shrugged. 'A couple of G and Ts.'

Kate nodded, waiting. 'So what time did you head off for the party?'

Iris considered. 'Maybe nine? It was someone's birthday. It wasn't someone we really knew. A chemist, I think. There were lots of science types there. Someone had given the address to one of the boys in halls.'

Kate lowered her voice. 'Tell me about the drugs. E, right?'

Iris nodded.

'How many times had you taken it, before the party?'

Iris glanced at the recording phone. She lowered her eyes, pulled a piece of tomato from her sandwich and nibbled it.

Kate nodded at her phone. 'I can switch it off, if it bothers you.'

Iris gave a nervous nod. Once the phone was switched off and back in Kate's bag, she found fresh courage.

'I've never taken anything like that before. Honest.' She lifted frightened eyes to meet Kate's. 'Someone else brought them. They were passing them round, handfuls of these of little pills, all different colours and shapes. They just looked like sweets. The lads were making a game out of deciding what colour you got, messing about. It wasn't easy to tell, it was so dark. I think mine was light blue. It was a funny shape, like a dog's bone. I had a beer and I just swallowed it back with that. I know it was stupid. I won't do it again. Ever.' Her eyes filled with tears. 'I really didn't—'

Kate reached forward and gave her shoulder a squeeze. 'It's OK.' She wondered how honest Iris had been with the police. Bella's death had clearly shocked her to the core. Maybe she'd have the sense to stay away from drugs now. She just wished Bella had.

Kate prompted: 'Where was Bella when this was going on?'

Iris blinked hard. She pulled a ragged tissue from her sleeve and blew her nose. 'She'd been dancing with us. She seemed fine, I mean, a bit wild but only like she was getting into the party vibe. I remember when Ned, he's the guy who offered me the pills, when he opened up his hand and offered them to her, she brushed him away. He said something, teasing her, I think, and she laughed and shook her head and said something like: *no, it's not that, I'm already sorted.*'

Kate cut in: '*Already sorted?*'

'I think that's what she said. It was so loud in there and hot, and I was starting to feel pretty buzzy, to be honest. We all were. We started high-fiving each other and giggling and we were all sort of, you know, jumping about.' She paused. 'I've asked Ned and he just says he can't remember. I think he's scared, you know, because, well, he was offering.'

Kate said: 'But if she didn't get the tab from Ned, where did she get it from? Someone else at the party?'

Iris looked anxious. 'I don't know. I'm sorry. I've thought about it such a lot and I just don't know. No-one wants to talk about it. We all used to hang out together and now, since the party, they're all avoiding me. Like they blame me.' She started to cry again, pressing the tissue to her face.

Kate shook her head. 'They probably don't know what to say, that's all.' *You're just kids*, she thought, *all of you. Bella too.* 'Look, try to eat something. Please.'

Kate watched Iris wipe off her face, then obediently pick up her sandwich and bite into it. Her chewing was mechanical. Kate wondered what support they were getting from the university. They were very young to deal with all this.

As she watched Iris eat, Kate's mind was working hard. How had Bella already been sorted? Who else had been doling out drugs?

'Was Bella hanging out with anyone else at the party, I mean, anyone outside your group?'

Iris shook her head. 'The police asked me that. I told them, no, not really. We didn't know many people. We sort of stuck together.'

Kate hesitated. Something in Iris's phrasing struck her. 'What about before the party? Did she meet anyone else, before you went?'

Iris frowned as she remembered. 'Well, only the guy from the bar.'

'What guy?'

Iris set down her sandwich and reached for her coffee again. She took a long gulp. 'She met this guy. I don't know his name. He just came up to her in the bar and got chatting and he bought us both a drink. I got the sense he didn't want me around. Something in the way he looked at me. Rude and, I don't know, arrogant. Like he was looking down his nose at me.' She sniffed as if it still rankled. 'Maybe he just wanted Bella to himself. She seemed to like him. I mean, when we left, she asked him to come with us.'

Kate's senses sharpened. 'So did he?'

'He got on the bus with us. It was pretty full and he and Bella found seats together, upstairs, at the back. Then he bailed out around Camberwell, not long before we got to our stop. I asked Bella; she just said he'd changed his mind. Didn't fancy it, after all.'

Kate pulled out her notebook. This was the first she'd heard about this guy.

'Did you tell the police about him?'

Iris wrinkled her nose. 'I don't think so. Well, maybe. They didn't really ask. Only about, you know, the actual party crowd.' She hesitated. 'He didn't look suspicious. I mean, I didn't like him but he was smart, not dodgy-looking. I don't think he's the kind who'd be into drugs.'

Kate nodded. 'What else can you remember about him? Anything at all?'

'I didn't pay him much attention, to be honest. Like I said, we didn't exactly hit it off.' Iris blinked rapidly as if she were straining to remember. 'He was quite good-looking. Confident. Older than us. Dark hair, tall, quite fit. He felt posh. The way he carried himself, his clothes. Not like your average scruffy student. I got the feeling he had money to spend.' She paused, considering. 'Like Bella, I suppose. She always seemed like that too.'

Kate dipped her eyes to her notebook and took a moment. *Oh, Bella, my love.* Bella had always been so torn, as a teenager, dying to have the best clothes, the best bags, the best make-up, knowing they could afford it but worried too about fitting in with her friends. One of her greatest fears was that anyone would call her arrogant or accuse her of showing off. It had been so important to her, all those years. Now, it would never matter again.

Kate pulled her mind back to her questions.

'What about his name? Even just his first name? Did he say what he was studying?'

Iris looked pained. 'Honestly, he didn't even talk to me. He was only interested in Bella. She's the one who'd know.'

They looked at each other. Maybe this guy wasn't important. Maybe he wasn't relevant to Kate's search for the truth. But as she stared back at Iris, Kate sensed a cold cramping, deep in her stomach.

Bella would know. That was true. But whatever she could have told them about this man, whatever clues she might have given Kate about him, it was too late to ask now. That knowledge had died with her.

14

The commuter train out of Paddington was packed, the windows fogged with breathing.

Kate spent the fifty-minute journey huddled in her corner seat. She didn't know how Simon had endured it, day after day. Her head ached.

At Swindon, she picked up the car and drove the final leg out to the house. By the time she pulled into the driveway, her nerves were shattered. She switched off the engine and sat for a moment at the wheel. The house loomed in front of her, light leaking from Clara's upstairs window and from the hall.

She remembered the first time she'd seen it, *they'd* seen it, she and Simon, at the end of a second long day driving around Wiltshire villages, looking at house after house, the girls deposited with his parents for the weekend.

She always searched with her heart, turning a blind eye to problems. She became determined to shoehorn them into each property they saw, whatever the snags, convincing herself they'd make it work. Simon was more pragmatic.

'It *is* charming, I agree, but that kitchen, I mean, it would need gutting. And only one bathroom? It'd be a big building project.' Or 'Kate, it's just too isolated. Did you hear what he said about the village bus? You'd have to provide a round-the-clock taxi service for the girls.'

But this house... she'd known, really known, as soon as they'd pulled up and the house had risen in front of them, in all its splendid architectural confusion, hinting already at its quaintly crooked floors and passageways, its grand front stair-case and steep back stairs for servants. It had been silently waiting for them, all this time. Their new home. She hadn't said a word, frightened of spoiling it, just held her breath.

After a few moments, Simon had reached for her hand and given it a small squeeze and she'd known then that he felt it too, that it was true, that it would really happen.

And now she was selling it. It still didn't seem possible. Another family would make it their own. She felt the sickness of betrayal but she wasn't sure if she had betrayed the house or if it had betrayed her, with its promise of happiness.

Kate shook herself back into motion and headed inside. Ever since she'd seen Iris, a thought had been running quietly but insistently underneath the surface of her mind.

Who was he? Who was that smart student who'd befriended Bella in the bar? Was he the one who'd given her that tab of Ecstasy? How could she find him?

On the train, she'd composed a hasty email to DC Whittaker. *It feels like an important new lead,* she'd typed. *I'd be most grateful for your help in pursuing it on our behalf. In my opinion, we really need to find this man and interview him, if only to eliminate him from inquiries. Please.*

Inquiries? She remembered DC Whittaker's expression as

she'd swept out of their final interview, her parting words as she wished Kate well. Case closed, it had silently declared. Already, Kate knew in her heart, DC Whittaker had moved on.

Now, she put the kettle on and slotted bread into the toaster. Dirty dishes and two stained mugs were piled in the sink and she rinsed them and stacked them in the dishwasher.

'Clara!' she hollered up the stairs. 'You OK? I'm home.' Silence.

Back in the kitchen, the toast popped up and she buttered it, made herself a cup of tea and sat at the long, deserted table to eat. It was hard to be in this huge, empty house and, most of all, here in the kitchen. It had been the beating heart of their home once. Bella was here. Simon too.

Afterwards, she locked up and headed to bed. The house creaked around her as it settled for the night. She paused at Clara's door to knock and, when there was no reply, pushed it gently open.

'Hey.' Kate gave a friendly smile. 'How was your day?'

'Fine.' Clara was slouched in bed, reading. Her hair fell loose around her shoulders. Her legs made lumpy mounds under the duvet.

Kate paused. 'I'm sorry I'm late back. It all took longer than I expected. Did you heat up the soup?' She tried to ignore the hostility in the air. A scream threatened to rise inside her: *I can't do this, right now, Clara. Just cut me a bit of slack, OK? I'm doing my best.*

Kate took a few steps further into the room and perched on the end of Clara's bed. Clara didn't move her legs to make room. Kate reached out and put her hand on the duvet mound.

'I saw Bella's friend today. Iris. You know what she said?' Kate plunged on, regardless. 'A young man approached Bella at

King's, in the bar, before she went to the party. Iris had never seen him before. He took the bus with her.'

Clara's eyes stayed on her book, screening her out.

'Don't you see?' Kate went on. Her voice was getting louder, despite herself. *Come on, Clara, please. I need you. I need you to do this with me.* 'What if he gave her the Ecstasy? That would explain why it was from a different batch. Iris said he never actually made it to the party. He bailed out on the way.'

'Right.'

'I've emailed the police, asking them to trace him. Iris can't remember if she told them about him or not. But if she didn't, I mean, this could be it, Clara, don't you get it? This could be really important.'

Clara shifted her legs under the covers, pulling them away from Kate's outstretched hand.

'Are you OK?' Kate paused. 'What's the matter?'

Clara lifted her eyes at last. 'What's the matter? Really?'

Kate blinked hard.

Clara said coldly: 'You don't even know, do you?'

'What?'

Clara set down her book and glared at her mother. 'OK. It was the final parent–pupil sixth-form meeting this evening. Ring a bell? I spent an hour on my own, going round teachers, talking about managing exam nerves and what to do if I don't get my grades or decide I want to change my course.'

Kate felt her heart contract, tight and hard in her chest. Oh God. Tonight, that had been tonight? How could she have, how could she possibly have... 'I'm sorry, Clara. I'm so sorry. I'm an idiot. I completely forgot. I'll—'

Clara blazed on. 'I was the only one without a parent. The only one, Mum! The teachers acted like they were sorry for me. It was so embarrassing.'

Kate felt tears start in her eyes. She blinked hard. 'God, Clara, I'm—'

'Mr Hatton asked if you were OK, if something had happened. Like, what kind of emergency must have erupted to make you not be there? I didn't know what to say. *Actually, she's just obsessed with my dead sister at the moment, sorry. I don't matter.*'

Kate reeled, stung. 'Oh, Clara, that's not—'

'Isn't it?' Clara ploughed on, merciless. 'Really? I nearly phoned you to see where the hell you were but you know what? I thought: why the hell should I? Why should I be the one chasing after you all the time, trying to get your attention, when you clearly don't give a damn?' Clara's cheeks flushed with rage. 'You're obsessed, Mum. Can't you see yourself? All this paranoia about what happened? This thing you've made it into – *Project Bella* – what the hell are you even doing? What does it matter who gave her the E? It was a crap batch. She took it. End of. She's dead and she's never coming back, no matter how many hours you pour into your – your what? – your *investigation*.'

Kate struggled to breathe. 'I know it won't bring her back. I do. But I just feel, feel deeply, that—'

'You know what this is really about? You'd rather it was me, Mum, wouldn't you, who'd died? You'd rather have Bella here. It was always Bella you wanted, Bella you adored. Clever, beautiful, funny Bella. Do you even know what that's like, growing up second best? I gave up trying to compete with her. There was no point. I was just her sad little shadow. But she's *dead*, Mum. She's dead and I still can't compete. You'd rather chase after what happened to her, even though she's *dead*, than bother with me, when I'm right here in front of you. How sad is that?'

Kate tried to open her mouth, to speak, to defend herself but, for a moment, no words came.

How can you say that? How can you even think such a thing?

Kate took a stuttering breath. 'Clara, you have never been second best. *Never.* That's simply not—'

'Oh, please. Forget it, Mum.' Clara looked disgusted. She dumped her book on the bedside table with a bang. 'It's late. Go to bed.'

'But, Clara, I had no idea, you never gave me the slightest—' She leaned towards Clara, opening her arms to her. Clara pushed her roughly aside and switched off her light.

'You know what?' Clara snapped. 'I'm too tired for this. What's the point, really?'

'But it's simply not true. Of course I adored Bella. We all did, didn't we? But I loved you just as much, Clara, always, from the moment—'

'Yeah, right.' Clara hunched on her side and drew the covers up over her shoulder. 'Save your breath, Mum.'

Kate struggled to hold herself together. 'I'm sorry about tonight. I really am. Of course you're angry. You're right to be. I'll get in touch with the school first thing tomorrow and—'

'Don't bother. Please. You'd just make it worse.'

Kate made a clumsy move to hug Clara's submerged shoulder. 'And you're wrong about Bella. You really are. I've always loved you just as—'

Clara pressed her hands against her ears. 'GO AWAY!'

Kate sat for a moment, rigid. Her chest was so tight, she couldn't breathe. Clara lay, hard and unyielding, in the bed. Kate could feel the tension as her daughter waited for her to leave.

Finally, Kate got shakily to her feet, gave the bed a final pat and retreated.

Down the landing, she undressed with trembling hands and climbed into a cold bed. She hunched into a ball, feeling the cavernous emptiness of Simon's side at her back.

I'm screwing up, Simon. Why aren't you here? I can't do this without you.

She thought about Clara. Where had that come from? She'd had no idea Clara felt like that. *It was always Bella you adored.* How could she say that? Did she really mean it? Had Kate really made Clara feel second best? It must be her fault. How could it not be? Had she really failed to give her younger daughter enough attention, enough love?

And the stupid school meeting. She cursed herself for forgetting it. She'd been so sure it was next week. She wrapped her arms round her chest. *Second best?*

How could Clara possibly think that? How? She saw the two girls together, racing down the lawn towards the trees, legs pumping, hair flying. Bella in the lead, always, Clara struggling to keep up. It was normal, surely. Two years was a big gap when children were young, big enough for the older child to dominate. But why would Clara still feel in Bella's shadow? Was it because of her? The thought cut through her stomach and she curled tighter, hanging on to her own flesh and bones.

Simon, where are you? I can't do this any more, not on my own.

She felt torn into pieces. Clara needed her. Of course she did. Her daughter was grieving as much as she was, the loss of her father, of her sister, both taken from them in such a short space of time. She was hurting and Kate was failing her. *Second best? Did she really think that?*

But Bella needed her too, even now, even in death. Someone had killed her daughter. Someone was responsible. Kate was her mother. She'd promised her justice and she couldn't stop now; she couldn't give up.

As Kate started to slip, wretched, into sleep, a shadowy figure seemed to loom in her mind, just out of sight. She opened her eyes and stared with panic into the darkness. Who was he? Was this the smartly dressed man Iris had described? Was this the one who'd given Bella the tablet that killed her?

She blinked, making the blackness spangle. The police wouldn't search for him. Deep down, she knew that. They'd moved on. They didn't have the interest or the resources to reopen the file.

But how could she find him?

15

DAMIAN

New York, Six Months Later

'It was the flowers. Those flowers you sent, for her birthday. Lovely bouquet. But they were just wilting, see, on the mat. I thought it was strange she didn't take them in. We tell each other, if we're going away, so someone's keeping an eye on the place. We swapped keys too, in case something happened. Last year, my pipes burst when I was in Maine. Your mother was the first to know. It's these old buildings. They don't maintain them properly.'

Hester, his mother's stout, elderly neighbour, dabbed at her eyes with a handkerchief. Damian, tired after the flight from London, tried to be patient. He'd heard most of this before, on the phone, when Hester had called him to break the news. She'd been in such a state, she could hardly make herself understood.

He nodded gravely. 'You did exactly the right thing. I can't thank you enough.'

'Well, I hope so. To think of her. Lying there. Right next

door.' She sniffed and heaved herself to her feet. 'Anyway, shall we?'

Damian set down the cup of coffee she'd made him and followed her out onto the small landing towards his mother's front door.

It was a shabby flat. No place to die. It stank of dank, rotting vegetation. The flowers he'd sent were dying in their cellophane, abandoned in the kitchen sink.

Damian looked around. His mother had clearly rented the place furnished. This wasn't her taste: the cheap carpet, the floppy blinds at the windows instead of curtains, an all-American breakfast bar and stools instead of a kitchen table. He'd imagined coming out here at some point to visit his mother. Never like this.

Hester bustled across the small lounge, pushed a blind to one side and opened a window. The aggressive blare of traffic rose at once from the street below and pressed into the room.

Hester gave him pecking glances. 'She was through here, in the bedroom. The door was open, you see, like this.' She'd lowered her voice, as if they were in church. 'I went in, still calling to her. I thought she was asleep. But it was clear when I saw her face that, well, she was already gone.' She wiped her nose with a shaking hand. 'Such a terrible shock. I keep thinking, why would she do such a thing? And on her birthday, too? I didn't know. I had no idea she was so—' she hesitated, searching for an inoffensive word '—so *low*.'

Damian inclined his head. 'You've been very kind, Hester. Really.'

'No more than she'd have done for me, I'm sure.' She hesitated. 'We didn't know each other terribly well, your mother and I. We were just neighbourly. But I'm sorry for your loss, I really am. It's tragic.'

Damian paced across to the breakfast bar and shuffled through the unopened post there. Alongside, he found a scrappy piece of lined paper with a name and number scribbled across the centre.

'Is this the person I need to contact?'

She narrowed her eyes to peer, then nodded. 'That's the police officer. Johnson. He said to call him, soon as you arrived. He'll tell you everything. Oh, and he took a few things away. The pill bottle. And her note. I did tell you she left a note? You'll want that back, I'm sure.'

Damian didn't answer. He looked round, debating with himself whether to stay here or check into a hotel. It was a pretty grim place. No wonder his mother had been suicidal. But the rent was paid through to the end of the quarter.

Hester headed back towards the door. 'You need anything, son, anything at all, you know where I am.'

Damian put out his hand, palm upwards. She looked at it for a moment, uncertain, before she realised what he meant and handed him his mother's set of keys.

'Thank you, Hester,' he said. 'I appreciate it.'

He locked the door behind her, then picked up the stinking birthday flowers and dumped them in the trash.

16

It didn't look like his mother.

It wasn't the fact he hadn't seen her for more than two years. It wasn't even the nature of her death. At least the fact she'd overdosed had kept it clean.

She just didn't look real. Her skin was waxen. Her hair was brittle and parted in the wrong place. Her nails looked thickened and ridged.

He sensed that the police officer, at the far end of the trolley, was observing him. He wondered how he was expected to react. What did other people do? Sob? Rend their garments? Pray? He knew his mother. She wouldn't expect hysterics.

'It's definitely her.' He glanced across. 'Is there anything else I need to do?'

The police officer shrugged. 'Not on my account. If you need a little more time...?'

Damian took a final look. 'No, I'm done.' He remembered his manners. 'Thank you.'

* * *

The police officer sat across the table from him. The family liaison officer, a dumpy woman made broader by an unflattering uniform, sat between them.

The room was institutional and airless. A clock ticked on the wall. A cardboard cup of cheap coffee sat in front of him, unasked for and untouched.

The police officer was in the business of handing him things.

He dipped a meaty hand into a plastic evidence bag and pulled out a tall cylinder. He pushed it across the table.

'This was found beside your mother, on her bed. It's prescription medication.' He indicated the printed label with a fat finger. 'The details are printed here. They were prescribed for her by a psychiatrist, Doctor Madelyn Price. She was treating your mother for depression. The prescribed dosage is perfectly safe but, unfortunately, seems like she took the lot. Forensics have confirmed they were the cause of death.' His hand dipped back into the bag. 'This was also found by the... by your mother.' He drew out a sheet of paper and pushed it across to Damian.

Damian recognised his mother's untidy handwriting at once, even though she'd seldom written to him over the years. He'd harboured no illusions, once he'd been sent away to boarding school, that she'd missed him. Even so, the sight of her note gave him a jolt. It was a final link to the one person in his life who hadn't completely abandoned him.

He folded it hastily and pushed it into his pocket. He'd read it later, in private.

The police officer folded his hands together on the table. He clearly bit his nails. A fat wedding ring dug into his flesh.

'We've checked your mother's medical records. Dr Price had only recently prescribed this medication. She made a call to check on your mother that morning, the morning of her death, and described her in her notes as being in a stable, indeed positive, frame of mind. There was no reason to suppose she was at risk. I'm sorry for your loss.' He didn't look sorry. He looked bored.

The female liaison officer picked up. 'We are now in a position to release your mother's remains.' She pushed across a bundle of commercial leaflets from undertakers and funeral parlours in the city. 'I thought, seeing as how you're not from New York, you might want these. Please be advised that this does not constitute a recommendation by the police authority but merely a furnishing of information.'

A furnishing of information. Damian felt suddenly conscious of being a stranger in a strange land. 'Her death isn't being investigated, then?'

'No further investigation is deemed necessary.'

Damian walked two blocks from the police station and settled in a coffee shop with a decent brew and a chocolate chip cookie. Only then did he withdraw his mother's note from his pocket and open it on his knee. It was short and roughly scribbled.

> *I'm forty-two today and all alone here. I guess this is as far as I'm going. I can't face another year, not the way things are. I'm all used up. Pills can't help what's wrong with me. They just make everything worse. Maybe I'm a hopeless case. But they are good for something – they can at least help me out of this mess that is my life. Tell my son not to mind too much. I don't suppose he will. I was never much of a mother. He's better off without me. I guess you all are.*

Damian folded his mother's suicide note again and put it back in his pocket.

She hadn't been much of a mother; she was right about that.

He'd learned from a young age not to call for her in the night if he had bad dreams. She never came. He'd figured out early how to dress himself for school and slip out, hair uncombed, biscuits in his pocket, taking care as he closed the front door not to wake her and whichever man might be in her bed. Sometimes, especially if she'd been drinking, she terrorised him.

He thought more about the note. Did he *mind too much*? He considered. He wasn't sure what he felt. She had been his mother. Beyond that, he'd never really reflected on how she'd treated him. But, as she'd prepared to end her life, she had apparently thought of him. That was something.

He looked over the leaflets from the funeral parlours. He planned to keep proceedings as simple as possible but there was still a lot to arrange.

He sipped his coffee and took a bite out of the cookie. He didn't rate American cuisine very highly but it had its moments and a good chocolate chip cookie was one of them.

He drew the emptied bottle of pills from his other pocket and checked the details on the label. Dr Madelyn Price. She shouldn't be hard to track down. He brought out his phone and searched up the medication, sertraline, online. He spent a while reading what he could find.

The police officer's information about his mother's medical records interested him. He was intrigued in particular by Dr Price's description of her phone call with his mother on the morning of her birthday when she'd reported her to be in a positive state of mind.

Damian reached thoughtfully for his cookie and chewed. He'd tried multiple times himself to get through to his mother on the morning of her birthday. He knew how depressed birthdays always made her and, besides, he wanted to be sure she'd received the flowers. Every time he'd tried, her phone had been switched off. It was the only way of reaching her. The rental didn't have a landline.

It was only when he'd arrived from London that he'd understood. Her phone wasn't just off, it had run out of battery. Once he'd recharged it and checked the call log, he'd found that no-one had got through to her for days. Including Doctor Price.

He finished off the cookie and wiped his fingers with care on the paper napkin.

He didn't like to be lied to, especially not about something so important.

He didn't like it at all.

17

Dr Madelyn Price ran along her usual route.

Damian knew it well. He'd spent the last two weeks living in his mother's rented apartment and doing his homework. He had Dr Price's routine down pat: the early-morning run, the short commute by subway to her plush office building, the occasional lunches with friends in smart coffee shops, the range of dingy pharmacies she searched out after hours, the evening stop-off at the deli across the street for last-minute groceries before she went home.

Now, as she ran, he trailed her at a distance, taking short cuts where he could.

She entered Central Park. As usual, she picked up a path to the right and struck out towards the wooded expanse of The Ramble.

She had her headphones on, and her limbs pumped in a light, regular rhythm. Her breath made a series of neat puffs in the dry, chill air. She was wearing black, clinging bottoms with a pink flash down the leg. As she moved, he could see the lengthening and contracting of the muscles in her thighs and buttocks.

The trees formed a bridal arch over her head. The early-morning light, filtering through the branches, changed the mottled pattern of green to gold. A beautiful New York morning.

She headed down a slope, following a dip in the landscape. Rocks rose steeply on either side as she approached a bend where the path narrowed and the bushes became dense. There was no-one else in sight. She pressed on, unaware of the danger, her pace even.

Damian narrowed his eyes, scanning the undergrowth for a shadow, for a sign of movement. Mobile phone coverage faded to nothing down here. He sped up, hurrying to close the gap between them.

It happened in a moment. The man, his face obscured by a balaclava helmet, sprang from the bushes in a flash of motion as she reached the bend. He jumped her, knocking her sideways across the path.

Damian, sprinting forward now to reach her, sensed her shock. One minute, she'd been running, at peace with her surroundings, lost in the steady rhythm of her own stride. The next she was under attack, stumbling, battling to stay upright, her arms flailing as she tried to fend off her assailant.

The guy grabbed her from behind. One arm was tight round her throat, in a chokehold. In the other hand, a blade flashed. He breathed hard as he heaved her backwards, trying to drag her off the path towards the bushes.

'Hey!' Damian surged forward. He barely had the breath to shout. 'No!'

Damian reached them at last and threw himself at the lumbering, locked couple. He grabbed the guy's hair and snapped back his head with a jerk, kicking out at the backs of the man's knees as hard as he could. The guy's arm loosened enough for her to twist herself free of him. She fumbled at her pocket, reaching for her mobile phone.

'Don't!' Damian was too breathless to explain that her phone was useless down here. There was no signal in the dip. 'Just go!'

She seemed to understand but still didn't turn and flee. The masked man sank lower, pinioned by Damian's grip. She lifted a leg and lashed out, kicking her assailant hard in the groin. He gave a high-pitched shriek and doubled up.

'Run!' Damian had a firm hold on the man now. He tightened his arms round the youngster's chest. 'Quick!'

She hesitated, frowning. For a moment, she seemed about to come close again, to attempt another kick in the groin or maybe this time higher, in the face.

Damian shouted again. 'Go! Please. He's got a knife.'

The youngster, as if reminded, brought up the blade and stabbed wildly backwards, trying to sink it into Damian's side. His strokes met only air.

Damian grabbed at his wrist and twisted his arm backwards. The youngster screamed.

'Go!' he told her again, his voice commanding. 'Get away!'

Finally, she turned and ran, sprinting now as she raced off to raise the alarm.

* * *

It was a relief to lie on the moist earth. Damian's nostrils filled with the pungent scent of leaf mulch and tree bark and undergrowth soaked in dew.

It brought a memory of early childhood, of playing on his own in the woods, after his mother had sent him out of the house for the day. Overhead, the leaves shivered and stirred in the breeze and, even when he closed his eyes, he sensed the pattern of the shadows they made across his face. There was a stealthy rustling somewhere near his head. A squirrel, maybe, or a mouse. Higher, further, the sharp, insistent note of a bird broke the air.

His mind skimmed through memories. His mother's face came, from years ago, from a time when he was young. He supposed he had loved her, despite it all. There had been moments of kindness, of tenderness; there must have been, in amongst the drunken rages and the depression and the succession of violent, unstable men.

He'd tried hard, during his mother's short cremation service the previous week, to winkle out some positive memories of his early years. His mother hadn't been cut out for motherhood. He tried not to judge her. He wasn't exactly a people person himself.

His cheek ached where the knife had nicked it. His fat lip oozed blood. He tasted its dull, metallic tang.

Maddy's voice sounded, distant at first. Running footsteps grew more distinct. She was coming back along the path, coming to find him. There was a heavier tread, too. A man. Damian peered through barely open eyes. A thick-set man, middle-aged, in a sweat-soaked running vest.

'There!' She raced towards Damian and crouched down over him. Her soft breath was warm on his face. 'Are you OK? Can you hear me?'

Damian fluttered his lids as he nodded weakly. 'He got away. That guy.'

'Did he hurt you?' She looked so concerned.

He lifted a hand with dreamlike slowness and touched his bleeding cheek. 'I think I'm OK.' He fixed his gaze on her. 'But —?' His tone was befuddled. He tried to give the impression he was still in shock, struggling to regain his senses. 'How about you? Are *you* OK?'

18

Dr Madelyn Price and her husband lived in a fancy building on the Upper West Side, only a few blocks from the park. Damian had already checked out the floorplan online but, even so, seeing it in real life was different.

She led the way through the wide entrance hall into a spacious, open-plan kitchen-diner.

'Great place!' He meant it. He approved of her taste. She was an impressive woman, smart, driven and successful. He didn't begrudge her that. Quite the contrary. It would make the challenge all the more delightful.

He hadn't lost sight of his unfinished business back in the UK. He planned to make his stepmother pay for turning his father against him. Taking Bella from her was just the start. He still had the second daughter, Clara, to deal with. Mostly, it was the principle of the thing, although he was also aware that, once his two half-sisters were out of the way, his claim to the family wealth would be all the stronger.

He scrutinised the kitchen, a sunny expanse of lemon walls, broken up here and there by bold framed prints of line drawings. A woman's face dissolving into a dove. A stretching cat. Both, unmistakably, Picasso. Damian paused to admire the cat.

'Perfect, isn't it?' Dr Price's face softened. 'Such a genius.'

Damian said quietly: 'Exactly. Genius.'

She pointed him to one of the padded chairs at the dining table while she found a clean cloth and wrapped ice inside.

'Here.' She gestured to his fat lip. 'Try this.'

He touched it to his mouth and winced. She turned back to the kitchen and pulled open the door of a voluminous fridge. The seal gave a soft protesting suck.

'What can I get you? Juice?' She hesitated, fumbling inside. 'A beer? Or would you like something stronger?' She looked around a little vaguely as if she weren't certain where else to check. 'A Scotch?'

He raised an eyebrow. 'Perhaps a little early in the day.'

'You're right. Of course. I was just thinking, well, we've had such a shock, haven't we? Both of us.'

He said gently: 'Maybe a juice?'

She pulled out a carton of orange juice, then reached in the cupboard for two glasses and poured them both a generous measure. Her hand trembled when she came to join him at the table, setting down the glasses and sliding into a seat across from him.

He stole a glance at her. Her cheeks were pale and pinched. Delayed shock, he thought.

'Dr Price, are you sure you're OK?'

She lifted her glass with both hands. The rim shuddered against her teeth as she drank. She took a deep breath. 'I'll be fine in a moment. And call me Maddy, please.' She raised her eyes and he felt her appraising look. 'I love your accent. British, right? I guess you get that a lot, people commenting on the way you speak.'

Damian concentrated on sipping his juice as if he were embarrassed by the compliment.

When he'd first started at boarding school, his accent had been a bizarre mix of his mother's American vowels and whatever he'd picked up at his local state primary school. It had been another reason for the other boys to bully him, another flag that he didn't belong to their privileged set. He'd worked hard to change it. School had taught him a valuable life lesson, just not the one they advertised to parents: adapt or die.

Here, the rules were different. He'd already discovered that most Americans couldn't differentiate between one British accent and another. Here, he could be whoever he wanted to be.

She gave him a thoughtful, appraising look. 'What's your name again?'

'Damian Black.'

'Damian Black.' She nodded. 'Well, Damian, you really saved me back there.'

She shook her head, still battling disbelief about what had just happened in The Ramble. 'It's a weird thing. I run in the park pretty much every morning. Have done for years. That exact same route. Never had a problem before. Not once.'

Damian remembered how quiet and secluded the path had been as she'd descended into the dip and rounded the corner.

'I'm just so glad I happened to be there,' he said. 'That guy, I mean, he really looked like he meant business. That black thing he was wearing, that mask covering his face. That was pretty weird. And the knife, did you see how sharp it was?' He touched his cheek with care. Flecks of dried blood, blackened now, came away on his fingertips. 'I hope the blade was clean.'

She peered more closely at his wound. 'You should get that looked at. I'll cover the cost. Here, give me your number.' She reached for her phone and keyed in his UK number, then sent him a quick message so he had hers. 'Do you live in New York?'

'For now.' Damian allowed a shadow to flit across his face. 'Some family business to take care of. My mother, well, she passed away recently.'

'I'm so sorry.' She considered him. 'Look, let me take you for lunch sometime. Will you do that? It's the least I can do.' She batted away his attempts at a polite refusal. 'I'll text you a few dates.'

He put his hands flat on the surface of the table and pressed himself to his feet. 'I should get going.' He winced as he started to move. 'Do you mind if I just use your bathroom before I go?'

She pointed him to the right door.

Later, as they said goodbye, Maddy said: 'I still feel maybe I should notify the police.'

'Up to you, of course.' Damian frowned. 'But honestly, if this was London, I doubt they'd even log the case. What can we tell them? We didn't get a good look at the guy. He could be anywhere, by now.'

Maddy looked thoughtful. 'I guess that's true. Still—'

'We mustn't forget,' Damian added, 'how lucky you were today. I don't want to scare you but who knows what he might have done, if I hadn't been there?'

He adopted a slight limp as he set off along the pavement and kept it up until he was sure he was out of sight. He thought back to the way the guy had doubled up with pain after she'd kicked him in the groin, the way he'd waved that tinny knife around like an idiot.

He sighed. Bloody amateur. He should have followed his instincts and paid the extra hundred bucks for the ex-marine. He'd have done the job properly. You got what you paid for in this world.

Still, he thought, he shouldn't berate himself too much.

She hadn't suspected a thing. Deep in his pocket, his hand closed around the bottle of prescription meds he'd taken from her bathroom cabinet. It was exactly what he'd suspected.

He nodded to himself thoughtfully. Yes, all in all, it had gone pretty well.

19

Damian liked to get up early, to get ahead.

By 5.30 a.m., he was showered and dressed and heading out of the door, taking the subway north towards the Upper West Side. He ordered a cream-cheese bagel and a coffee and set up in the window of the café right across the street from Maddy's block.

He'd widened his surveillance now, to include Maddy's family. Their routines were predictable. First, Maddy headed out for her run, undeterred, it seemed, by the recent incident in the park.

At around seven, her husband, Dr Cushing, emerged, besuited and carrying a beige trench coat. His hair was flecked with grey at the temples and, although his body was trim, his chin was slackening. He wasn't exactly handsome but his money – the well-cut suit, the handmade leather shoes, the expensive briefcase – gave him a certain gravitas. He liked to walk, if the rain wasn't too hard. His clinic – a plush suite of consulting rooms, shared with a fellow cardiologist – was about fifteen minutes away.

Often, their teenage daughter came out soon after him, still eating a piece of toast as she tramped to the end of the block to pick up a bus to school. She was a sullen-looking girl with rows of studs up each ear and a hoop through one nostril. She had the same thick, blonde hair as her mother but it was unkempt, a fresh out of bed look which, Damian suspected, she'd spent time perfecting.

For days, Damian's careful monitoring yielded nothing. Until, finally, he struck gold.

It was a grey day, flecked with the threat of rain. The subway grilles along the pavements steamed. Damian had come to recognise the smell. The evocative mix of wet wool and damp, decades-old grime and constantly fermenting mould pervaded the city.

Maddy still wasn't home but, soon after six thirty, Dr Cushing stepped out of the apartment building and wrapped the flaps of his woollen overcoat around his body with a sense of purpose. Damian tailed him so closely that he could see the streetlights reflected in his fine leather shoes.

After about ten minutes, Dr Cushing disappeared down a narrow alley. Damian, curious, counted to thirty before slipping after him.

The alleyway was empty. It was gloomy and slightly threatening and Damian felt his heart quicken as he crept on, glancing dartingly to left and right. He wondered if Dr Cushing had become aware that he was being followed and was lurking in a shadowy doorway, ready to confront him.

It was a lower rental area, a forgotten pocket in the middle of so much fashionable modernisation. The backs of these buildings had the air of old warehouses or go-downs, in need of renovation. Some flashed signs for budget businesses. Here and there, low lighting spilled out from second- and third-storey windows where unseen people were still hard at work. The weak glow barely washed the stone walls on the far side of the alley.

Just when Damian was starting to doubt himself, a doorway appeared to the left, gleaming with red and gold. There was no signage but Damian assumed, from the soft emblems of dragons on the black lacquer surround at the entrance and the low red lighting inside, that it was a Chinese restaurant. The sort of place only those in the know would find.

Damian took a deep breath and headed inside.

The interior offered a kind of pastiche of Chinese culture for the well-heeled American. Bamboo birdcages hung from the ceiling, containing brightly coloured, ornamental songbirds. A glistening statue of a Chinese god, garishly painted, was positioned in the centre of the restaurant. A cumbersome, old-fashioned bicycle, in the style of the Chinese Flying Pigeon, was mounted on a stand nearby, garlanded with a silken strand of plum blossom.

The dimly lit room was divided into booths, each separated from the next by dark wooden panels. A grotesque twanging of Asian string instruments resonated through the speaker system. But the smells were more appealing: the rich scents of roasted duck and pork, garlic and sautéed pak choi and the pungent steamy aroma of fried rice.

The waiter, a thin-faced Asian man, bowed and showed Damian to a table where he ordered jasmine tea and a small selection of the cheaper dishes on the menu, brought out his laptop, as cover, and secretly observed.

Dr Cushing was seated a few tables away, too distant for Damian to hear his conversation but close enough for him to observe his body language. It wasn't hard to read. He'd been joined within five minutes of arriving by an attractive young woman of maybe twenty-six or -seven and there was no mistaking that the two of them were flirting hard.

She was smartly dressed in the New York uniform of the young educated professional, a provocative, clinging sheath dress of soft wool with a tailored blazer. Her legs were shapely, their contours set off by kitten heels. Her make-up was freshly applied. Even in this low light, her lips showed in a bright red slash across the lower part of her face and her eyes were outlined, Cleopatra-style, in kohl.

Damian watched as Dr Cushing leaned forward. He raised his wine glass and gazed into his companion's eyes. Her red lips parted as she pressed in closer.

Damian smiled to himself. He didn't know yet who the young woman was. What mattered was that Dr Cushing had just handed him a winning card. All he needed to do now was to monitor these two for a while and find out exactly when and where they liked to meet.

20

'It's rather special. But it's also quite a responsibility, actually.'

Damian ate his burger and fries doggedly with a knife and fork, acting the old-school English gentleman. He was clearly amusing Maddy who, like the rest of the diners, was using her fingers.

'It's a dilapidated old pile.' He smiled to himself as if recalling a fond memory. It might have been true. As he spoke about the rolling lawns, the wandering grouse, the neatly clipped hedges of the old maze, the walled garden with its herbs and shrubs, he almost believed it himself.

'The old hall dates back to Tudor times,' he went on. 'The story goes that Queen Elizabeth dined there once, in fifteen-something, when she was travelling through the north of England on a hunting trip.'

'Elizabeth the First?' Maddy's eyes sparkled. 'That's amazing.'

Damian tried to look modest. 'Well, it's just a story.' He dabbed at his mouth with his serviette. 'It's a lot of upkeep. I suspect what I'm really inheriting is a giant headache.' He reached for his water glass. 'Have you spent much time in England?'

'Only London, once or twice, for conferences.'

He smiled. 'Well, next time you're crossing the pond, let me know. You must come and see the old place.'

Maddy nodded. 'Do you have pictures?'

Damian looked rueful. 'I'm afraid not. I don't usually talk about the family much. People can be a little peculiar. Jealous, I suppose. Maybe that's just a terribly British obsession?'

Maddy smiled. 'Well, no, I guess it's pretty universal.'

Damian went back to sawing through his burger bun with his blunt knife. They were in a diner, just off Broadway. All booths and bright colours. Maddy had suggested it and, frankly, she might have gone a bit more upmarket. As far as she knew, he had saved her life.

'And you?' he said. 'You said you had a daughter?'

She looked surprised. 'Did I?'

'You did,' he covered smoothly. 'When we were in your apartment that morning, drinking juice.'

'I do have a daughter. Amy. She's seventeen now, in her senior year.'

'So she's off to college soon!' Damian felt something slip satisfyingly into place in his mind. Clara was seventeen. Maddy's daughter and Clara must be in the same school year. He could find a way to use that, he was sure. 'Where's she hoping to study?'

She smiled, shrugged. Damian sensed her awkwardness at his questions about her daughter's plans. He wasn't surprised. Amy looked like trouble.

'She's not sure yet.' Maddy sipped her sparkling water. 'To be honest, she's still finding her way. At the moment, she's got her mind set on taking a year out and touring the country with an up-and-coming rock band. Well, she says they're up-and-coming.'

'Does she sing? Play?'

'She writes songs.' Maddy pulled a wry face. 'I'm not sure they're terribly good but – well, let's just say she doesn't much value my opinion.' She picked up a fry, dipped it in ketchup and bit it in half. 'Anyway, I don't think it's love of music that's really motivating her. Her boyfriend's the lead singer.'

He considered that. He sensed that she didn't approve. 'What's he like?'

'Jed?'

Jed, he thought, storing the name away. 'The musical boyfriend.'

She didn't answer for a moment. 'I can't say it's my kind of music but he's got a pretty good voice, I'll give him that. Amy says his band's doing OK. They're called Cold as Ice. Not exactly Shakespeare, is it?' She rolled her eyes. 'They've got a regular gig in one of the Brooklyn clubs on Friday nights. The venue's kinda rough and ready. We're apparently the meanest parents in the world because we don't let Amy hang out there with him every Friday.'

He made a mental note. 'And what about him? A decent guy?'

'Well, I guess so.' She visibly squirmed.

He said gently: 'You don't sound too keen.'

'Well, I haven't had the chance to get to know him well enough. He just seems a little, how shall I put it, a little rough around the edges, that's all.'

'Not the prince you once dreamed your little girl might bring home for Thanksgiving someday?'

That seemed to amuse her. 'Well, she's practically a grown

woman. She's entitled to make her own choices. It's her life, right? I know it's a cliché but I just want her to be happy.'

Damian smelt an opportunity. He leaned in. 'You know what might do her the world of good? She should take that gap year but use it to live overseas. Europe, maybe.'

Maddy's eyes lit. 'I thought the exact same thing! Like a Grand Tour, you know? Venice, Rome, Paris – I mean, what's not to love, right?'

Damian pressed on. 'I spent time in Amsterdam after boarding school. Thoroughly recommend it. A great party scene. And the canals, the museums! It was the making of me, really.' He paused, reading her. 'I can start her off with a few contacts, if you like? Point her in the right direction? It's pretty easy to pick up casual work there.'

Maddy's eyes seemed to dim. She focused again on her food. 'That's very sweet, Damian. It sounds wonderful. But I don't think I could persuade her to leave Jed, even for a few months.' She pulled a face. 'Nothing as crazy as young love and all that!'

'Well, that's a shame.' Damian was thinking rapidly. 'It really is.'

She seemed uncomfortable and he steered the conversation onto safer ground, asking her advice about places to visit in New York. She was articulate, with the neat turn of phrase that came from a sharp intellect. He liked that about her.

When the dessert menu came, she waved it away, apologised to Damian about needing to dash and insisted on paying.

'It's been a pleasure, Damian. Really. I can't thank you enough for what you did the other day. If there's anything—'

'Well, there is one thing.' He smiled. 'Let me return the compliment, just once. Let me take you out for dinner. There's a place I'd love to try, not very far from your apartment, in fact, and it's such a bore, eating alone every night. Honestly, you'd be doing me a favour.'

She hesitated, her face suddenly wary.

'Oh no, please, I don't mean like that!' He blew out his cheeks and tipped back his head awkwardly. 'Oh my goodness, this culture divide. No, I'm not, you know, I'm not—' he flannelled deliberately, as if he couldn't bring himself to use a phrase as indelicate as *hitting on you*. 'I would never be inappropriate. I wouldn't dream...'

He was doing his best Hugh Grant impersonation, all charm and bluster. He took a deep breath as if he were collecting himself after all that embarrassment.

'Let me explain,' he said. 'In my circles, it's more usual for a gentleman to treat a lady to lunch or dinner, you see? It would be considered ill-mannered for me to accept a delightful invitation, like this—' he gestured to the soggy remains of his burger '—and then not to reciprocate. It's a matter of honour. But I'm sorry. I really am. And I quite understand. We hardly know each other. I really shouldn't have...' He tailed off.

She laughed. 'Well, if it's a matter of honour, how can I refuse? Sure, Damian. I'd be happy to catch up again. No problem. Just drop me a text, OK?'

And, with that, she was gone.

21

It wasn't hard to find out where in Brooklyn Cold as Ice was playing its regular gig that weekend.

Once he knew, Damian made a few calls to set things up, then changed into a dark blue T-shirt and jeans and headed off in the weekend rental he'd hired.

The club was in a dingy basement. The smell of mould mingled with spilt beer and dope as he descended the internal stairs into the darkness. He was enveloped by a dense cloud of sound.

At the bottom of the stairs, he stood for a moment, letting his eyes and ears acclimatise. His body vibrated with a thudding bass line.

'Need company, honey?'

He turned to find a woman at his side. She was pressing in too close and her breath smelled of garlic. When he pulled back, he saw her face, its glory already fading. He glanced down with distaste at the crepey skin revealed by her plunging neckline, shook his head and pressed on.

He stepped into the main part of the club and was assaulted

by the noise. The walls of the dingy, damp cavern were splashed with luminous paint that glowed eerily when stray flashes of light hit them. Searchlights ran to and fro across the stage where a group of three women, more punk than rock, were pounding guitars and screaming into microphones, making the speaker system squeal.

A bored-looking waitress in black leather hot pants and gladiator thongs led him through the darkness to a sticky table against the wall, then brought him an ice-cold bottle of Budweiser. He sat back, let the music pulse through him and felt an unexpected wash of contentment.

He thought about his mother and his final sight of her, waxy and cold on that cheap trolley. He thought about Maddy. He was making good progress. She didn't suspect a thing.

Now, in the shadowy basement, the strobing lights shifted and swung and became multi-coloured: red, white and blue. The punk girls with their pink and white hair had disappeared. The next act, all guys, ran on, waving guitars. An unseen voice announced them over the speaker system with a flourish: Cold as Ice.

He sat forward and narrowed his eyes to peer through the gloom at the lead singer. Jed had short, spiky hair and a lean, boyish frame. He leaped around the stage in his ripped T-shirt and jeans, making love to the microphone as if he imagined himself at Madison Square Gardens.

Damian nodded to himself, satisfied, finished off his beer and got to his feet. That was all he'd needed. He'd just wanted to look.

Outside, in the chilled, quiet air of the street, his ears rang. He strode briskly to his rental car, checked the tyres for damage and the back seat for muggers, then drove back to his mother's apartment. He felt a surge of elation as he crossed the

Brooklyn Bridge. The lights of Manhattan set the clouds aglow.

He waited until he'd parked up before taking out his burner phone and sending the text.

Back in the apartment block, he took care to knock on nosy-neighbour-Hester's door and made a point of asking her advice about local pizza delivery companies. When she dug out a leaflet, he asked her for the correct time too and made sure she paused to check. He didn't expect to need an alibi but it didn't hurt.

The pizza, washed down by a few more beers, wasn't bad.

Afterwards, he took a long, hot shower, climbed into bed and slept the sleep of the dead.

22

'How did you even find this place?'

Maddy was looking round the restaurant thoughtfully, taking in the Flying Pigeon bicycle, the bamboo birdcages. Damian had selected a table near the front of the restaurant. There was no chance of Maddy spotting the couple already hidden away towards the back in a high-backed booth. Not yet.

'Just word of mouth,' Damian said, with a modest shrug.

'Well, if the food lives up to the décor, we're in for a treat.' She turned her attention to the menu. 'I'd like to visit China someday.'

'Why not?' Damian raised his beer. 'To dreams and adventures.'

She clinked her beer against his. He stole glances at her as she perused the menu. Her forehead was tight with concentration. Her hair was fastened low this evening, at the nape of her neck.

Money, he thought. Everything about her screamed rich and successful. The tailored black trousers and the blue silk blouse that fell in easy folds across her breasts. The solid gold chain that glimmered at her throat.

She must have no idea what it was like to worry about making ends meet, to struggle to pay the bills. How dared she presume to treat others for depression, including his own mother, when her own life was so privileged?

And yet. He smiled to himself. Maddy had her own monkeys on her back. He knew.

The food came soon after they'd ordered, in a series of neat bamboo baskets. Damian took charge, lifting each lid, one by one, describing the morsels inside, then using the serving chopsticks to place an assortment of items on her plate: steamed dumplings, pieces of chicken and pork, tofu in ginger and steamed broccoli in garlic. He was deft with chopsticks. Back-street Chinese restaurants in Amsterdam had been some of the cheapest places to eat when he'd first arrived there.

'You should bring your daughter here.' Damian feigned ignorance: 'What did you say her name was?'

'Amy. Yes, you're right. She'd love it.'

He saw a shadow cross her face. 'I'm – sorry,' he made a show of stumbling, 'did I say the wrong thing? Your daughter, I hope I haven't—'

'That's OK.' She shook her head. 'Amy's just going through a tough time at the moment.'

Damian said: 'Still hanging out with the rock band? What are they called again?'

'Cold as Ice. Actually, no.' She sighed. 'That's all over, apparently.'

'Oh?'

There was a short pause, then Maddy seemed to reach a decision. She set down her chopsticks and focused on him as she began to speak.

'Something kinda awful's happened. I wasn't going to mention it but seeing as you've asked... Jed, her boyfriend, was coming out of the club in Brooklyn the other night and some guys jumped him. They had knives. One of them slashed him across the throat.' She looked shaken. 'He's in a pretty bad way. It was touch and go for a while.'

Damian breathed: 'My God. That's terrible.'

'I know! Weird thing is, they didn't even rob him.' She shook her head, incredulous. 'He had his wallet, his phone. They didn't take a thing.'

'And Amy? Is she OK?'

She blew out her cheeks. 'She wasn't with him, thank goodness. I tell you, I get chills thinking about that. That's one thing we've always fought about, her hanging out in Brooklyn. I'm so glad I put my foot down.'

Damian frowned, as if he were struggling to understand. 'And you said it's over, between her and Jed?'

'It's not how it sounds. I mean, she didn't dump him because he's hurt. Obviously. Quite the opposite.' She reached for her beer and took a gulp. 'She's been desperate to visit him in the hospital but he's refusing to see her. He sent her a message saying it's over. She can't understand it. She's a wreck.'

'Maybe it's the trauma,' Damian said. 'Maybe it's made him stop and think what he really wants. I mean, it sounds like he's lucky to be alive.'

'I doubt he'll sing again. That's all he ever wanted, apparently.' She picked up her chopsticks again and speared a piece of greasy pork. 'I admit, I didn't approve of the guy, I mean, as boyfriend material. But this? Well, no-one deserves what's happened to him.' She chewed thoughtfully for a while, then said: 'Maybe you're right. Maybe he just wasn't into Amy the way she thought and this has made him reassess.'

'I think that's right.' Damian didn't voice the thought: *or maybe the guys who jumped him made it damn clear that if he ever saw Amy again, they'd be back and, the second time, they'd finish off the job.* 'But you know what? Maybe now's the time to press that great idea you had, about her spending time in Europe next year. Why not? It could be just what she needs. I can send you some links, if you like. I know a great real estate agent in Amsterdam. He's got some beautiful apartments in the old city. Really. To die for.'

'Thanks. I'm not sure if she's quite ready...' She trailed off, lost in thought, then seemed to rally. 'But hey, why not send them over? Maybe in a little while...' She dabbed her mouth with her napkin. 'Look, I should probably get going soon.'

'I'm sorry but I'm not sure I can allow you to leave without trying the mango pudding.' He raised an eyebrow but she barely seemed to be listening. 'I've heard it's pretty special.'

She didn't answer that, just set her napkin to one side, slid out of her seat and, as she stood, murmured: 'Excuse me a moment.'

The restrooms were right at the back of the restaurant. She needed to pass every booth to reach them.

Damian sipped his beer and watched her head away from him into the dimly lit interior. There was a charge in the air. He'd pulled the pin from a grenade and was holding his breath, anticipating the explosion.

All he had to do was to sit back and savour the moment when Maddy, caught unawares, spotted her husband and his young lover in their clandestine booth, pressed close together, feeding each other gobbets of meat and sucking the grease obscenely from each other's fingers.

'I'm so sorry. I had no idea. Honestly, Maddy, if I'd had the faintest—'

Maddy sat with her elbows on the kitchen table. Her shoulders hunched. Her face was hidden in her hands. Earlier, as Damian had escorted her from the restaurant and helped her to walk the few blocks home, she'd been chalk white. He wondered what lies she'd told herself over the years about her husband and the state of their marriage. He wondered if she'd known, deep down, what sort of man he was.

He studied her with interest. She appeared to be in shock. He saw how different it was from the physical reaction she'd suffered after the attack in the park.

'Can I get you anything?' He peered round her ordered kitchen. 'A cup of tea?'

'I think you should go now.' There was a hard edge to her voice that caught him by surprise.

'Really?' He hesitated. 'I mean, you've had a shock. You shouldn't be left on your own.'

'Amy will be home soon.'

Damian nodded. He slipped on his coat and stood awkwardly in the kitchen doorway.

'I'm sorry—' he began.

She interrupted: 'Please. Forget it, Damian. Just forget all of it.'

On his way out, he paused to check the security at the front of the building. There was only one camera, wall-mounted and pointing down the pathway to the street. That was it. Nothing visible inside the entrance hall or around the lift.

He let the communal door click closed behind him. He already knew the entrance code. He'd watched Maddy key it into the pad when they'd arrived back together.

If she thought she'd seen the last of him, she was very much mistaken. This was just the beginning.

24

For two more weeks, Damian bided his time.

He kept his distance but, when he could, he took up his usual place in the café across the road from their apartment building and kept watch. He saw Maddy cross the street to the subway each morning with her neat, quick steps, her leather bag in one hand and a coffee in the other.

She'd taken to wearing more make-up but, still, she looked drawn. He sensed that she'd lost a little weight. He imagined her lying awake in the middle of the night. He half-heard the tearful, angry conversations with her husband.

Her husband and daughter came and went much as usual. They hid their crisis well. It made him shiver with pleasure to know that he was the only one, watching them, who knew the truth.

Finally, by the start of May, an opportunity presented itself. A routine online search for Maddy's name gave him the news he wanted, a post about a forthcoming psychiatric conference. It was a high-profile event, spread over three days. Maddy was

appearing on an evening panel on day one. It was to be followed
by a drinks reception.

That first evening, Damian took up his position in the café
across the street. The windows of the family's apartment were
darkening, blind rectangles. Maddy would be at the conference.
Amy was, as always, out. Damian watched intently. All he
needed now was for Dr Cushing to come home.

A light, cold rain was falling. Finally, when it was almost
nine, Dr Cushing appeared with his head lowered, his shoulders
hunched against the weather. The collar of his expensive coat
was turned up to shield his neck. Damian smiled.

Dr Cushing slipped into the corner deli and came out with a
brown paper bag of groceries. The brightly coloured corner of a
family-sized packet of taco chips protruded from the top, alongside the metal top of a bottle of wine.

Damian paid up and headed for an art-house cinema a few
blocks away. He bought himself a ticket for the next showing of
a film he'd seen before and made a point of arguing with the guy
in the booth about getting a student concession, even though
he'd 'lost' his student ID.

He made a mental note of the guy's name on his corporate
badge: JOEL. The guy was on the brink of calling his supervisor
when Damian finally backed down and, with a sulky pout, paid
the full price. He'd made enough of a nuisance of himself for
Joel to remember him later if questions were asked. He slipped
into the half-empty theatre and chose a seat at the back.

He waited until the film had started before slipping out. He
made first for the restrooms, scanning the lobby as he went. Joel
had been replaced by a young woman who was busy handling a
customer complaint.

He changed course and headed quickly through the double
doors into the darkness of the street.

He tried to focus his thoughts on Maddy. Another hour and she'd be on stage, in front of dozens of colleagues. It was perfect.

A young woman, in her thirties perhaps, was entering their apartment building as Damian approached. He shrank back into the shadows of a doorway and waited. She keyed in the security code and disappeared into the lobby. Upstairs, in Maddy's apartment, lights blazed.

Damian pulled on his gloves and climbed through the low hedge surrounding the front gardens. He popped up at the side of the building, hard by the entrance, avoiding the watching eye of the security camera on the path. He keyed in the code and the door clicked open.

He took the stairs to their floor, avoiding the lift. Outside the door, he pulled on a black balaclava, adjusted it around his eyes and fingered the blade of the knife in his pocket. He stood against the wall, out of sight of the spyhole, and rang the bell.

A pause. Damian handed it over to fate. If Dr Cushing decided not to answer, he would save himself, at least for tonight. Damian respected chance.

He was about to turn away when heavy footsteps sounded. Damian tensed. He wondered how much of the bottle of wine Dr Cushing had already consumed. The more the better.

Damian's breathing quickened. He sensed Dr Cushing on the other side of the door, just a piece of wood away. Probably, he was peering through the spyhole, wondering why he couldn't see a soul.

'Hello?' Dr Cushing's voice was muffled.

'Delivery for Señora Price!' Damian ventured a high-pitched Spanish accent. He hadn't planned to, it just happened. Actually, it wasn't bad. 'Hello?'

Inside, a security chain rattled. The door creaked open a few inches and Dr Cushing peered out.

'Delivery!'

Damian launched himself at Dr Cushing, planting his foot over the threshold before the door could close on him. He shoved Dr Cushing hard against the wall with one hand as he drew back his arm and plunged the knife between his ribs. The two men were rammed up against each other, faces a few inches apart, one hidden behind its balaclava mask, the other wide-eyed with terror.

Damian was overwhelmed by a rush of sensations. Dr Cushing's bulk was warm with pulsing life. His breath smelled of red wine and spices. *Taco dip*, Damian thought, *that piquant one with, what were they called, those hot green chillies Americans love...* even as he heaved his stuck knife out of the man's chest. It was harder to withdraw than he'd expected, like pulling Excalibur from the stone. As it gave and rushed out with a sudden wet suck, blood spurted between Damian's fingers, soaking his gloves.

He gave Dr Cushing a look of disgust and thrust in the blade a second time, a fraction higher. He rammed it so hard that the man's body rose against the wall, like a puppet. He felt a storm of strength, of power as he held him there, controlling the ebbing of another man's life.

Gradually, Dr Cushing's hands loosened their weak grip on Damian's arm. He exhaled noisily, then slumped forward into Damian's arms. Damian withdrew his knife a second time and stepped sideways to let Dr Cushing slide to the floor. Blood was pooling on his chest, spilling out from the body to form a sticky, spreading stain on the wooden floor. His eyes were glassy.

Damian closed the front door with care to make sure that no-one on the far side, passing by on the landing, could see in. He thought of Maddy. He remembered what she'd said about the attack on Jed.

Weird thing is, they didn't even rob him... Didn't take a thing.

That was a rookie's mistake. He shook his head in disgust. He'd do a better job.

He moved hurriedly around the apartment. In the living room, a flame-effect fire was burning and he bent down to switch it off. No point wasting gas. An old war film was on TV. He paused a moment to watch but it wasn't one he knew.

On the coffee table, the packet of tacos scattered its contents – the slob couldn't even be bothered to use a bowl – towards a plastic tub of dip. A glass of red wine, half finished, stood by the opened bottle. Damian almost tutted. For a cardiologist, Dr Cushing ate a very poor diet.

Dr Cushing had set his wallet and smartphone there too. Damian rifled quickly through the wallet, taking the cash – only a few hundred bucks – and a couple of cards. He'd destroy them later. He pocketed the phone. He'd destroy that too. He just wanted the police to be irritated by its absence.

He paused on the threshold of the master bedroom, taking in the sight of the neatly made king-sized bed. He wondered which side was Maddy's. She'd find it pretty lonely, from now on.

He pulled open a few drawers and withdrew handfuls of clothes, dropping them on the floor. He found Maddy's lingerie drawer and looked over a few pieces. Silk. Right at the back, hidden, he discovered a square jewellery box and pocketed the contents, just for form's sake.

The other bedroom was clearly Amy's. He shook his head. It would be hard to make this one look any more ransacked than it already did. The door to the fitted wardrobe stood open and a mess of clothes lay tangled on the carpet, bleeding into piles of papers and books. The rumpled duvet cascaded off one side of the bed. Fantasy goth posters of black skulls, crows and gravestones were dotted round the walls. He left it as it was and headed out again.

Dr Cushing's body was stiffening as it cooled. He wrenched the Rolex from his wrist and tried to prise off his rings. The gold signet ring twisted off his pinkie but his fancy wedding ring, white gold inset with a row of small diamonds, grated on his knuckle and refused to come free.

Before he opened the door to leave, he pulled off his bala-clava and thrust it deep into his pocket, then turned up his collar and closed the door with a satisfying click behind him.

He slipped back to the movie theatre and hurried across the empty lobby, head down. He returned to his seat in the dark-ness. His eyes fixed on the flickering images on the screen while his mind replayed the events of the past half an hour.

He was throbbing with adrenalin. He mustn't be complacent. There was still work to be done. He needed to burn the bloodied gloves, now bunched in a plastic bag in his pocket, and dispose safely of most of the items he'd taken. But not yet. For now, at least, he could relax.

The film would soon reach its climax. He considered heading back into the lobby for popcorn but he couldn't decide what type he wanted, salty or sweet.

He thought it over. Salty. And maybe a soda as well. He deserved a treat.

He heaved himself to his feet and headed out to the conces-sion stand.

25

'You!'

Maddy stared at him, confounded.

Damian softly closed the door of her consulting room behind him.

'Sorry,' he said. 'I could hardly use my own name.'

It was her first day back in the office. He'd only managed to book the appointment after a great deal of persuasion, spinning a cock-and-bull story to the receptionist about a personal recommendation from a top London psychiatrist.

For almost two weeks, the receptionist had tried to redirect him to a colleague, saying Dr Price was indisposed. Damian had almost laughed. It was her husband who was indisposed, he'd thought. Permanently.

Now, he settled himself into the soft, upholstered seat opposite Maddy's. He looked around. It was a tastefully appointed room, just as he'd expected. The chairs were a pale green. The walls were painted a bland, creamy brown and studded with innocuous framed pictures: a cactus in a pot, tulips in an earthenware vase and a bowl of fruit.

He imagined his mother sitting in this same seat, looking at these same walls. He wondered what she'd told Maddy about the depression that had dogged her as long as he could remember. The closing in of the darkness that had finally overwhelmed her.

Maddy leaned forward and said curtly: 'Why are you here?'

Damian smiled, trying to put her at ease. 'You need to know a few things.'

'About what?' She tutted. 'Is this a professional appointment, Damian? Because, if not, I'm afraid—' She shifted her weight as if she were about to rise to her feet.

He raised a hand to silence her. 'First, don't worry about the police. You're quite safe. I made sure of that.'

She frowned. 'The police?'

'They've got nothing to go on,' he continued patiently. 'The conference gave you a watertight alibi. There's nothing pointing to you, not really. Marital problems, sure, but that's half of New York, right? As far as they're concerned, it's just some botched robbery. Some wacko on drugs.'

She seemed to shrink into herself. 'What are you talking about?' She looked him right in the eye. 'You've read about it in the papers, haven't you? About what happened to my husband. Is that why you're here?' She seemed to be struggling to read him. 'Do you find the idea of murder fascinating, in some way?'

'Fascinating?' He considered the word. 'Well, yes, I suppose I do, at some level. Doesn't everyone? But that's not why I killed him. You mustn't think that.'

She didn't answer. He saw her jaw tighten. 'Is this some sort of a joke?'

He dipped his hand into his pocket and brought out a small plastic bag containing Dr Cushing's signet ring, the only item he'd taken from the apartment but not destroyed. He'd suspected she might need proof. He set the bag on the coffee table between them, alongside the box of sympathy tissues. She craned forward to see more closely. He watched the colour drain from her face as she recognised it.

'Where did you get that?' Her breathing was shallow.

It was a foolish question. She knew, of course, in her gut she already knew. It was just that her mind was struggling to catch up.

He spoke rapidly but clearly. He had a lot to say and they didn't have long.

'Maddy, you need to listen. I know all about you. I know what your husband did to you. Not just the affairs. There was more than one, wasn't there? Anyway, that's by the by. But the fentanyl, Maddy. Why? What made you start on it?' He steepled his hands. 'I bet it was simply for pain relief at the start, am I right? A running injury, perhaps? A bad back? But then you started to crave it, didn't you? You became addicted, horribly addicted. You wanted to stop but you couldn't. And your husband didn't get help for you, did he? Didn't pack you off to rehab. I'm guessing he didn't want to risk exposure for either of you. So, in the end, he took the easy way out, when you begged and pleaded. He just kept writing fresh prescriptions for you. Isn't that pretty much what happened?'

She stared at him, her lip trembling. He liked it, that shock in her eyes. He felt as if she were finally seeing him for what he really was.

'I followed you, you see,' he explained. 'All those dimly lit, out-of-hours pharmacies you visit, a different one every time. That's what made me suspicious. Then, when I asked to use your bathroom that time, I went through your medicine cabinets. You'll never guess what I found!' He shook his head sadly. She was such a hopeless amateur. She hadn't even changed the labels to hide the fact those pills were fentanyl. She hadn't bothered to erase her husband's name. 'You're nothing more than a junkie, really, are you?' He thought of the back alleys of Amsterdam and of the Albanian dealer in London and the contrast they made with Maddy's plush Manhattan suite. That amused him. 'A rich, white-collar junkie.'

'But why?' Maddy seemed lost. 'Why do all that?'

Damian nodded. Of course, she hadn't yet made the connection. Why would she? It was something else he'd need to spell out.

'Because of my mother.'

'Your mother?' Maddy blinked rapidly. 'You said she was the reason you came over to New York, right? Because she died.'

'That's right.' He paused, watching her confusion. Maddy had visibly blanched. 'She killed herself. She was a patient of yours. Monica Bancroft. Ring a bell?'

'Monica! My God. You're—?'

He nodded. 'Yes, I'm rather afraid I am. Is all starting to become clear?'

She seemed completely unable to speak.

'You didn't call her that morning, the day she died. I know you didn't. You lied about it in her medical notes, to cover your own back. You knew you'd been negligent. If you'd taken proper care of her, if you'd realised she was having a reaction to the sertraline, the antidepressants you'd prescribed for her, she'd still be alive today.' He hesitated, reaching for the term he'd found online. 'A paradoxical reaction, isn't that right? Not that uncommon with SSRIs. When, instead of the drugs making a vulnerable patient feel *less* depressed, they have the opposite effect. They make them feel suicidal.'

Maddy looked stricken. 'I didn't know. I swear to God. If my—'

'If your brain hadn't been doped up with fentanyl? Quite. Maybe you'd have done your job properly. Maybe she'd still be here.'

Silence pressed in between them.

Finally, she said softly: 'I'm so sorry. About your mother.'

For the first time since he'd been in New York, Damian had the sense he was hearing it from someone who actually was. He felt a moment of deep calm. It was an unusual sentiment for him and, he realised, not unpleasant.

Maddy's forehead was slick with sweat. 'So that's why you did it? Why you killed my husband? For revenge?' Her voice sounded squeezed.

He nodded. He wondered if she sensed how narrow her own escape had been. He might easily have killed her, instead. He had considered it. But her husband was responsible too, in his own way. And he'd liked him less.

After a moment, he said: 'You can't go to the police, Maddy. You do see that, don't you? First of all, you've no actual evidence against me. It would just be your word against mine. And second, I'd be obliged to tell them everything you've done. And I have got evidence, including a bottle of those fentanyl pills prescribed by your husband. You'd be struck off, at best. More likely, prosecuted. You'd lose everything.' He paused. 'And there's Amy to think of.'

'Amy?' Her face filled with alarm. 'She's just a child. She's done nothing, nothing at all.'

'Exactly!' He patted her arm. 'She's got her whole life ahead of her. So play your cards right and you'll make sure she lives to enjoy it. Right?'

26

KATE

London, One Month Later

Who was Harry?

His name had just flashed up. Clara's phone was there, right in front of Kate on the table, when it had suddenly rung. The screen lit to show the name of the caller: *Harry.*

Kate felt a sudden chill. Why did she? It was absurd, of course it was. He was probably just a new friend, someone Clara hadn't thought to mention. By the time Clara reappeared from the loo, it had stopped ringing and the screen had faded to black.

'Your phone rang.'

Clara snatched it up and turned away. 'Thanks.' She'd headed upstairs with her coffee to get back to revising. *One last time.*

Kate sat alone in the stillness, frightened without understanding why. She looked out into the shadows creeping across the garden. The view felt as familiar as her own face, as her daughters' faces, every shrub, every flower bed, the gentle slope of the lawn towards the stream and the watchful trees.

Simon was there, somewhere, forever pottering, and Bella, squeezing into bushes and shinning up trees, and young Clara, running to find her, Coco bounding at her heels.

She bit her lip. It wasn't hers, any more. Not for much longer. The removal vans were already booked.

Why had it bothered her, seeing that name: Harry? It was nothing to be alarmed about. She'd ask Clara, maybe later tonight, if she got the chance. Just casually.

* * *

'So, who's Harry?'

Clara's head whipped round. Kate, driving, felt the intensity of her daughter's stare without needing to look. She'd waited until the next morning and she'd tried to make it casual. It wasn't such a terrible question, was it? Judging by her reaction, Clara clearly didn't agree. Kate stiffened and kept her eyes on the road.

'Why are you even asking that?' Clara's tone was tight.

Kate had heard it a lot, recently, this dangerous, warning tone. It was like a dog, snapping. *Back off. Mind your own.*

When Kate put her head round Clara's bedroom door, took in the chaos of unwashed plates and mugs, the crumpled bedclothes, the piles of notes and dared to ask how her revision was going.

'*Fine*, Mum. Just stop asking, would you? *Jeez.*'

When Clara took a phone call and instantly jumped up from the table and, lowering her voice, headed out into the garden to talk in private and, afterwards, Kate couldn't stop herself from asking: 'Who was that, on the phone?'

'*Mum!* Just a friend. *OK? Get off my back!*'

And the eye-roll. Always the eye-roll.

But why? Why did her daughter need to be so secretive if she had nothing to hide?

Now, the morning after that mysterious phone call, Kate was driving Clara to school to sit her final exam. This was it. One last push and, in a matter of hours, it would all be over. The work of Clara's schooldays would be finished. A promised land of freedom awaited, gleaming and elusive. An adult land.

Now, Clara said coldly, in answer to her question about Harry: 'Did you look at my phone?'

'No!' Kate tried to sound injured. She concentrated on indicating and moving into the outside lane, ready for the round-about. 'Of course not!' She eased her way through the traffic and waited until she was safely on the far side. 'I saw his name flash up, that's all. Last night. I just wondered who he was. No big deal.'

'God, Mum.' Clara gave a dramatic flounce of her shoulders. 'Can you just stop spying on me, please? *Honestly.*'

Clara didn't speak to Kate again after that. She hunched towards the window, pulled out her phone and sent furious texts, her fingers flying over the tiny keys. Kate tried not to show that it hurt. She kept her breathing steady and her eyes on the traffic.

When they finally pulled in outside school, Kate reached across and squeezed her daughter's arm.

'Good luck, sweetheart. Last one.'

Kate didn't pull off straightaway. She sat in the car and watched Clara head down the drive. She cut a solitary figure as she threaded her way through the tumult of bouncier, younger girls. Kate could still pick her out as she approached the entrance. It was the way Clara walked. Her gait was stiffer and slower than the girls around her. There was something vulnerable in the way she tipped her body slightly forward, her arms barely swinging at her sides.

Kate drove home slowly. She planned to pack boxes today. Now the exams were over, she could speed up and not worry as much about disrupting Clara's studying. She'd hardly started on the kitchen.

Back in the house, she made up a fresh set of boxes and went back to work on her study. She'd thrown out a ton of paper already, filling bags of recycling.

She dusted off the cardboard files with Bella's obits, the news clippings reporting her death, Kate's neat pages of typed interview notes. *Project Bella*, Clara had called it. She read over a few sheets, flicked through others.

I'm sorry, Bella. I haven't abandoned you. I really haven't.

She hadn't given up. She never would. She'd just hit a dead end, that was all, trying to trace that stranger, the one Iris had mentioned. No-one else seemed to think he'd existed.

She packed the files into a box, ready for her new study. She'd have a chance to get back to it in the autumn. She'd needed to put it on hold while she focused on Clara and got her through her final year of school.

Afterwards, when the study was nearly cleared, she'd found herself wandering into the garden. The scents of early roses, geraniums, sweet peas hung heavy in the warm June air. She sat on the patio. What was the matter with her? Why did she feel so unsettled, so afraid? Was this all about the house move?

She had a sudden memory of Clara, at the age of six, riding her first proper bicycle down the path, splayed knees pumping, body swaying with effort and concentration.

It was that first summer, not long after they'd moved into the house. Kate had supported her, day after day, as Clara, wobbling terribly, had tried to find her balance. Kate remembered running endlessly up and down that path, her bent spine aching, her knuckles white from gripping the hard back of the metal seat, every muscle straining to keep Clara upright as she lurched and teetered.

Bella, already independent on two wheels, had sped past, urging her sister on.

'Yay, Clara! You can do it!'

Clara ignored her, her face a frowning mask of determination.

How long had it lasted, that dangerously unsteady phase? Maybe only a few weeks. It had felt like more.

Simon was relaxed about it. 'Keep trying! You'll get there, petal.'

She remembered how frustrated she'd been with him. He didn't seem to grasp their pain, either Clara's frustration or her anguish, as she ran, bent double, her grasping fingers numb, her lungs bursting as she struggled to keep pace, tried to save her daughter from disaster.

And then it had happened.

One day, Clara simply flew away from her and carried on, hair flying, splendidly alone.

She'd screamed: 'LOOK, everyone! Look at Clara!'

They had. They'd seen. Cheers had gone up.

'Well done, darling!' Simon had tugged off his floppy hat and waved it above his head.

'Go, Clara!' Bella, beside him, had danced up and down, arms flying.

Only Kate seemed to watch with fear chilling the pit of her stomach.

She didn't want to let go.

She saw how vulnerable Clara still was, how wobbly. She

wanted to run always beside her, hand on the seat, steadying her, ready to catch her if she fell.

She didn't want either of her daughters ever to cycle away. The world wasn't safe. It was full of traffic. They'd be menaced by the madness of crushing cars and vans and trucks. You couldn't just teach them to pedal and then let go.

The danger was far from over. It had only just begun.

27

'Clara, is there anything you want to talk about? Anything at all?'

They stood, side by side, on the station platform. Clara's bulging backpack leaned against her legs. Kate sensed the energy pulsing from her daughter in waves of nervous excitement. Clara's eyes flicked every few seconds to the screen to check if the train's arrival had clicked any nearer.

'Clara?'

'No, I'm good.'

Kate looked her over. She was still adjusting to Clara's new, spikier haircut, part of her daughter's gradual makeover in the two months since the end of exams. It still reached her shoulders, well, some of it did. Kate was grateful for that. It was just choppier and her natural blonde was suddenly highlighted with hot pink streaks.

It'll wash out, Mum! Jeez, get a grip! It's just for the weekend. No big deal.

Despite the August weather, Clara's multi-coloured woolly hat was poking out of a pocket of her backpack. Bella had laboriously crocheted it for her years ago and, although it was ragged, Clara took it everywhere.

On her feet, she was wearing her new Doc Martens. She'd been living in them for the last week, trying to stop them from looking 'too smart'. Kate knew better than to comment on how hot they'd be. At least they'd keep her feet dry if it poured.

'You will be sensible, won't you?'

Clara laughed. 'God, Mum, I hope not. It's a rock festival.'

Kate hesitated. 'You know what I mean.'

Clara's mood gave a handbrake turn, from excitement to irritation. 'Stop it, Mum. For God's sake. I'll be *fine*.'

The passengers around them surged towards the edge of the platform as the train slid into view. Clara gave Kate a quick peck on the cheek.

'See you Monday.' She manhandled her backpack onto her shoulder and clambered in.

* * *

Kate had the dream again, that night. The Bella dream. Only it was Clara, this time.

They were in the open air, nowhere she knew, and Clara was little again. Her hair was in bunches and Kate remembered thinking, in the dream, that it looked better like that, without the new choppiness and the pink highlights. And she'd slipped free from Kate's hand, just as Bella had, and she was running away, ducking and dodging through the crowd and Kate was puffing desperately after her, muscles straining, legs like lead, knowing with impossible dread that she'd never catch her but knowing she'd die trying, if that's what it took.

She woke with a start, sweaty, heart racing. She didn't know where she was. As her eyes adjusted to the gloom, the outlines of the furniture came to her. London. She was in the new house in London. It was unfamiliar, still, but it was OK.

The dream still cast a veil of dread over her, not quite dispersed. She reached for her phone. Nothing from Clara, not since Friday night when she'd sent a crazy photo of herself, pulling a silly face, her cheeks squashed by the gurning friends on either side. There were just four words:

Arrived safely. Luv ya. x

Now, disturbed by the dream, Kate tapped out a quick message:

Everything OK? Let me know. Love you, Mum x

* * *

On Saturday, Kate spent the day hacking away at the out-of-control ivy in their new, pocket-handkerchief garden. She kept her phone close to hand. There'd been no reply to her text. In the afternoon, she dialled Clara's number. It rang out, unanswered.

She left a message on voicemail: *Hi, sweetheart. It's only Mum. It's three o'clock on Saturday afternoon. Just checking you're OK. Would you give me a call when you get this? Love you.*

By the evening, when there was still no news, she called Rosa.

'I'm worried.' Kate went straight to it. 'I haven't heard from Clara.'

'When did she go? Yesterday morning?' Kate heard the hesitation in Rosa's voice. 'She's at a music festival, isn't she? Well, the music's probably so loud, she won't hear her phone. I'm sure she's fine.'

Kate paced up and down the kitchen, the phone tight against her ear. 'That's what we said about Bella, when she went off to start uni. *She'll be fine.*'

Rosa's voice was soothing. 'I know. What happened to Bella was terrible.' She paused. 'But just because something dreadful happened to Bella, that doesn't mean it's going to happen to Clara.'

'Doesn't mean it won't, either.'

A timer went off in the background. Kate heard a clatter of dishes as Rosa cooked.

'Clara's sensible, Kate. You've got to trust her. She'll be fine.'

* * *

Kate was still sorting out her new study. The mews house, narrow but arranged over four floors, was large by London standards. Everything felt scaled down though, compared with the rambling Wiltshire house they'd just left. Her Victorian desk, a present from Simon when they'd moved to the country, overwhelmed this room.

She dusted off the books as she lifted them out of packing boxes and put them onto shelves. At the bottom of the box, she found her Bella files. She sat at her desk, in a circle of light, and read through her notes, all over again. The interviews, the reports and the horror came flooding back.

She sat for a long time, afterwards, staring out into the darkness.

He was still out there. Whoever hurt Bella was still at large. How could she possibly feel Clara was safe until she knew for certain that he'd been caught?

On Sunday, Kate messaged and phoned Clara repeatedly through the day. There was no reply.

Around four o'clock, the location of Clara's phone changed. Kate had been tracking it all weekend. Until now, it had pinned Clara clearly at the giant venue, with its camping sites and refreshment tents and multiple stages. Now, she appeared to be on the move.

Kate watched the series of ragged jumps. Clara was being taken somewhere. Or her phone was. Maybe it had been stolen? She tried to slow her breathing. Maybe that was why Clara hadn't got her messages.

Soon after five o'clock, the pulse stabilised in a residential area off to the north of the venue.

Now, what, Simon? Now what do I do?

Kate sat very still, trying to force down panic. Memories ran through her mind of all the nights, after Bella's death, that she hadn't slept, lying awake at three, four in the morning, berating herself until she was physically sick. She was Bella's mother. She'd failed her when she was in danger. She hadn't been there, hadn't saved her.

Please God, don't let it happen again. Don't let me fail Clara too.

The location pulse didn't move from the residential street.

By six, she couldn't stand it any longer. She snatched up her car keys, punched the street address into the sat nav and set off.

* * *

It was after seven thirty by the time she arrived.

The area was rundown. She nosed the car slowly past a paint-peeling parade of shops at one end: a deserted laundrette, a newsagent with grilles across the windows and a kebab shop. Litter lay in clumps along the gutter. She cursed as her tyres crunched over broken glass.

She pulled in to the side of the road, halfway down. The location finder wasn't precise. It was showing her a point towards the centre of the street but didn't pinpoint a particular house. She switched off the engine and listened, wary of getting out. She checked her phone again, in case Clara had miraculously left a message, then called Clara, listening as it clicked uselessly to voicemail.

As soon as Kate opened the car door, a throbbing electronic beat set the air vibrating around her. Every now and then, human notes – shouts, high-pitched screams and raucous laughter – added to the cacophony. She looked across to one of the terraced houses in the road, the source of the sounds. Through the open windows downstairs, she could see starbursts of coloured light bouncing back and forth across the walls.

The front door stood open. Youngsters, some drawing lazily on cigarettes, stood around it, beer cans in hand. Kate hurried across. The youths hollered and waved when they saw her coming up the path. A fug of sweating bodies reached for her from the other side of the open door.

'Fancy a beer?' A skinny lad, maybe twenty, in tight blue jeans and a faded T-shirt.

His mate nudged him and they both grinned.

The mate said: 'Hey, it's not your house, is it?' and laughed at his own wit.

Kate hesitated. She imagined the party house in Peckham all that time ago and Bella, inside, lifting a tablet to her mouth.

'I'm looking for Clara?' She had to move close to the young men to make herself heard. Their breath flared with stale alcohol. 'Clara Grosvenor?'

'Clara! Ooh, posh!' Skinny jeans crossed the front yard to the open sitting room window and shouted inside: 'Hey! Clara! We got a Clara in the establishment? Mummy's here!'

A girl with straggly hair leaned out. 'Who?' She had the sweaty, bleary-eyed look of someone who'd been drinking all day.

Frustrated, Kate pushed her way into the house. Heat rose from the drinkers lining the walls of the hall. Their shirts and blouses were stuck fast to their chests. She forced her way from room to room, peering at the faces that turned to her in the gloom, screaming Clara's name in the ear of anyone who'd listen. The only responses were glassy-eyed stares and shrugs.

Upstairs, the crash of the music dulled although her ears still rang. Her heart pounded with fear, with adrenalin, as she pulled open the door of the first bedroom. A couple writhed on the bed, all limbs and emerging flesh. She made to leave but, as she turned, her eye snagged on a pair of new Doc Martens, protruding from a corner of the bed.

She rushed forward. She took in, at a glance, a mess of spiky, pink-streaked hair against the floor. Her daughter, on her back, was pinned down by a young man, his face in hers.

Kate seized his shoulder and hauled him roughly off, reached to rescue her daughter.

'Clara,' she panted. 'You OK?'

Clara's eyes widened in shock. 'Mum?' As Kate watched, her daughter's expression moved rapidly from confusion to white fury. 'What the – Mum, what the actual—'

A figure behind Kate collapsed into the hysterical giggle of the stoned.

'Clara! Darling! You *found* her!' Skinny jeans from the doorstep had followed Kate through the house. He started to clap his hands and shout: 'Mummy's here, Clara! Mummy's come to take you home!'

The lads crowded on the stairs took up the chant, clapping and shouting as if they were at a football match. They drummed Kate and Clara down the stairs and out into the street.

Kate tried to thread her arm round Clara, to lead her towards the safety of the car. Clara shook her off.

'Are you—?' Kate stared at her daughter's flushed face, struggling to understand. 'Did he—?'

'Did he what, Mum? Tell me, please.' Clara was shaking.

'Are you OK?'

'I was OK until you pitched up. What the hell do you think you're doing?' Clara twisted back to look at the gang of young, sniggering men. 'This had better be good. Really good. Please tell me the house burned down. Or you've murdered someone and you're on the run. Because anything less and I swear to God—'

Kate opened and closed her mouth. She couldn't speak.

Clara shook her head. 'How could you? Why would you want to humiliate me? I mean, really, Mum, how?' Tears started into her eyes. 'How are you even *here*?'

Kate tried to reach out a hand. The pavement seemed to curve under her feet.

Oh God, Simon. I screwed up, didn't I? She actually hates me. I embarrass her. What have I done?

'I'm sorry,' she stuttered. 'It's just that I didn't hear from you and I panicked and—'

Clara's shoulders slumped. She looked exhausted, older than her years. 'You thought I'd take something, didn't you? Like Bella.'

Kate nodded, dumbly. *She understands. She gets it. She'll forgive me. Won't she?*

Clara turned away. 'Oh, Mum. I'm sorry. It's shit, what happened to Bella. I know. There isn't a day I don't think about her. A day it doesn't hurt. But I'm still me. I've got my own life to lead. And I can't do it like this. I really can't.'

Kate felt suddenly bone-tired. The surge of adrenalin had given way to exhaustion. *It's over*, she thought. *Let's go home.* 'Where's your stuff?' She nodded towards the house. 'Let's get it in the car.'

'In the car?' Clara gave a hollow laugh. 'I'm not going in the car, Mum. I'm staying here with my mates. With my new *boyfriend*, if he's still speaking to me. And don't expect me home tomorrow, either, not after this drama. I'll sleep on someone's floor. We're off travelling soon, anyway.'

Clara turned back to the house, as if she'd finished, then hesitated and came back. Her eyes glistened in the fading light.

'Listen.' Her words came in a rush. 'I didn't want to do this right now but you haven't left me much choice. I'm eighteen. I'm an adult. This is hard to hear, I know, but I need to do my own thing for a while. I need a clean break when I'm away, from England, obviously, and from you too. You're suffocating me.' Clara's eyes flicked to Kate's, gauging her hurt. 'I know that's not an easy thing to ask. But I need you to let go. I really do. But I'm clearly, politely, telling you this: while I'm off travelling, *leave me alone*. You get what I'm saying? I mean it. Don't phone me, don't text, don't email, don't anything. Like the olden days, right? Before the internet. When people went away and you didn't hear from them until they came home – yeah? Like that. You have to trust me. I'll be fine.' She paused, her face creased into a frown. 'It won't be forever. So can you do that for me? Please?'

Kate stared. Clara's eyes weren't angry, only sad. Her tone was measured.

Kate blinked. Something in their relationship had reversed.

When had that happened? Her daughter, gazing at her now, had somehow become the sensible adult, steeling herself to handle a difficult conversation. Which meant Kate was what? The child? The problem, certainly.

'OK,' she said simply.

Clara looked relieved. 'I'll see you next week, anyway. I'll be in and out. I need to pack.'

She gave Kate a cursory hug and turned back towards the crowded house.

Kate pulled herself away. She sat for some time in the car, before she was ready to drive.

Her daughter wanted her freedom. Kate should be cheering. Simon would. He'd be waving his floppy hat right now and shouting: *Well done, darling!*

But she couldn't. Her last precious child was cycling away from her and all she could see was how menacing the traffic was and how dangerously her daughter was wobbling.

28

KATE

London, Three Months Later

The room was solid with blackness.

A noise cut through it. Kate fought her way to the surface, disorientated, suffocated by sleep. The sharp metallic ring of her phone.

She reached out an arm and groped, then cursed softly as she knocked it off the bedside table. She pulled herself up, sleep pouring like water from her head and shoulders. Her mouth was sour and dry. Her heart pounded. A memory burst over her. An echo of that other time a phone had woken her in the night. The call about Bella. Good news never came in the small hours.

She needed to hurry. She blinked hard, agitated now, and managed to focus on the dim screen, to slide the button to take the call, making her own silent bargain with God as she did so.

I'll give anything, anything you want. Just not bad news about Clara.

'Hello?'

'Am I speaking with Kate Grosvenor?' A woman. A clipped

East Coast American accent, professional in tone. The voice was distant, reaching from halfway across the world.

'Yes, I'm Kate. Who is this?' She kept her own voice level, hiding her sense of panic.

'This is Madelyn Price. I'm calling from Ann Arbor, Michigan.'

Kate's mind scrambled. Michigan? Who? The woman had given her name as if she expected Kate to know her. Price? She didn't know anyone in Michigan.

Her hand shook with adrenalin. She took a deep breath and tried to relax her chest, exhaling slowly and deliberately. Not Clara, then? The wave of nausea, which had washed over her since she was roused from sleep, eased a fraction.

She took a breath. 'I'm sorry. What's this about?'

She wondered how this woman, this stranger, had got hold of her number.

'I need to contact your daughter.' The woman sounded impatient. 'I understand she's in Amsterdam.'

Amsterdam? Was she? Kate had no idea. She narrowed her eyes to peer at the time. It was just after two o'clock in the morning. She found herself counting backwards from London time. The time difference with Michigan must be five or six hours. So, eight or nine in the evening there.

The woman said again, more insistently: 'Your daughter? Clara?' The way she raised her voice at the end of each statement made it sound uncertain but they weren't questions, not really. She seemed to know more than Kate did about where Clara was. Tightness gripped Kate's chest again.

Kate managed to say: 'Has something happened?'

'Well, yes.' A pause, dense with silence. 'I'm trying to reach my own daughter. Amy. I understand your daughter's renting a room in her apartment.' She paused, as if she thought Kate an idiot. 'They're room-mates.'

Kate felt a knife twist in her gut. She struggled to imagine this life of Clara's, sharing an apartment in Amsterdam with an American. She felt so shut out of it. It hurt that a stranger in Michigan, of all places, knew more about it than she did. Kate focused on the weak lines of light tracing the edges of the bedroom curtain, the only puncturing of the dense blackness in the room.

Kate breathed hard. 'I'm afraid I still don't—'

The woman pressed on. There was something commanding about her manner.

'I'm concerned,' the woman said. 'Amy isn't answering her phone. Or messages. She hasn't posted on social media for ten days. It's not like her.'

Kate's throat tightened. She didn't know how to explain that she rarely heard from Clara and how hard she found that. A shiny postcard of the Eiffel Tower. A joke postcard of a baguette and cheeses. The postmark was too blurry to read. The chirpy messages said nothing about how Clara really was, about her plans. They were just, as they used to say in the newsroom, proof of life. Just enough to let Kate sleep at night, to keep her racing to the mat each day when the post arrived.

'I haven't heard from Clara for a while,' Kate said. 'She's travelling.'

'Well, I need to contact her, just to confirm Amy's OK?'

Kate flung back the covers, swung her legs round and got to her feet. Cold air flooded her back, her shoulders through the thin fabric of the nightdress, icy fingers running across her skin. She had a need to be upright. Her bare feet touched the rasp of the wool mat by the side of her bed, then the floor. The worn wood felt cool but alive.

Her breathing was quick as she started to pace around the perimeter of the bedroom, touching the dark, solid shapes of each piece of furniture she passed. The bedside table, the dressing table, the back of the wooden chair. Items that were anchored in the real world. Objects that had places, that belonged, that she could trust.

'If you could give me her mobile number?' The woman on the far side of the world sounded impatient. 'Or an email address? Or – look, give me your email and I'll send you my details, OK? You can pass them on yourself. I just want to know Amy's OK. It's not like her.'

Kate stopped at the window and lifted the edge of the curtain. The street outside was a pattern of falling light from street lamps and shadow – still, silent and empty.

'I can give you my email.' A piece seemed to fall into place at last in her mind. There was no reason to think that Clara wasn't safe. She wasn't the girl who was missing. It was this other mother, so far away, who was in crisis, not Kate, after all.

Kate's mouth twitched with nervous relief. She was awake now, properly awake, and becoming brisk, regaining confidence as she dictated her email address. She saw the letters slide into view one by one as she pronounced them, superimposed in her mind on the pavement below.

'Send me your details and I'll forward them to Clara. What did you say your name was? Price?'

'Madelyn Price.' The woman paused, then added: 'Doctor.'

The American ended the call, apparently in a hurry to send her email and get the answers she needed. Kate climbed back into bed and hunched on her side, drew up her knees. The curl of her body held its own memories. If she believed hard enough, she could almost feel him there, Simon, warm against her back, firm-fleshed, a lazy arm tucked round her waist, his breath in the nape of her neck. A long time ago now. Each passing year since his death had carried him further away from her, drifting down an endless stream, his face blurring a little more in her mind.

She opened her eyes to dispel that memory, then closed them again and let another one take its place. Clara, three or four, all bones and sharp angles, restless between her parents, jabbing her with an elbow or a knee as she turned. A nightmare would have woken her. When she appeared in the middle of the night, a thin, forlorn figure with tousled hair, shivering lightly, tugging at Kate's arm and whispering urgently: 'Mummy!' she'd throw back the covers and lift her into the safe, fuggy space between them, gladly accepting the ice-cold feet against her own warm skin.

Kate thought about Madelyn Price. She might be a doctor but she was still a mother. Kate had heard the tremor underpinning the other woman's words. She sensed that Doctor Price wasn't someone who was used to making herself vulnerable or asking favours, especially not from a stranger. She feared that something might have happened to Amy, to her daughter. She was gripped by her terror of it, of this unknown. Kate understood.

Something stirred inside her as her heart picked up its pace. This wasn't just about Doctor Price and Amy. It was about Clara too. It was an opportunity to reach out to her, maybe even to speak to her.

She opened her eyes wide in the darkness, thinking rapidly. In the morning, as soon as she woke, she'd pick up Doctor Price's email and forward it to Clara. Then she'd message Clara, to let her know it was there. Maybe she'd even try phoning, despite Clara's ban on calls. Clara couldn't object, surely. Kate had just been handed a perfectly sound excuse.

She felt her body start the heavy descent into sleep. Her mind let go filament by filament. Her thoughts became slippery as they split and dissolved.

Minutes later, her eyes flew open. A cold, dead sense of foreboding gripped her, deep inside. The sudden shock of it made her shiver and she groped for the light, blinking as the room flooded and she scrambled to sit upright, to find reassurance in the familiar, solid outlines of the furniture, the door, the shrouded windows.

The nightmare had been waiting for her. Clara, small and vulnerable, running away into danger and Kate, straining, panting, unable to catch her, to keep her safe.

Her hands, clutching the sheet, trembled.

Kate read back over her email to Clara, scrutinising every word.

> Sweetheart,
>
> Don't be angry. I know I promised not to contact you but this is on behalf of Amy Price's mother who's frantic. She hasn't heard from Amy and is desperate to know she's OK. She got in touch with me – she's in the US – because Amy had mentioned your name, saying you're sharing an apartment in Amsterdam? Anyway, if you could just let us know Amy is OK, we'd both be grateful. Her email address is below.
>
> Love you, Mum x

It had been two days since she'd sent it. Two days of restlessly checking her phone, searching every few minutes for a reply. Nothing.

She turned away from her keyboard. The light was poor, the day overcast and grey. Now and then, rain spattered the large picture window. It had cost a small fortune to install it when

she'd turned this attic room into her study. She'd needed somewhere quiet to work on Project Bella, as Clara called it with a
sarcastic roll of her eyes.

The files about Bella's death were still stacked at the side of
her desk. Now and then, she reached for one, dusted it off and
began to read, hoping at last to see something new, to find some
telling detail she'd earlier missed. Despite all the time she'd
spent conducting interviews and searching for information that
would reveal exactly who gave or sold Bella that pure, lethal
drug, she'd proved nothing. Her search for the well-dressed
older man, mentioned by Iris, had gone nowhere. After all this
time.

Rosa kept nudging her to find a job. Voluntary work, maybe.
She needed a purpose, Rosa said. A routine. Everyone did.

Kate just couldn't find the motivation. She felt as if she'd
been out of journalism for too long to go back now. What else
would she do? Nothing inspired her. She was lucky; she knew
that. She didn't need to work. The sale of Simon's business, his
life insurance and savings and the sale of the big house had left
her embarrassingly wealthy, even after buying this London
home.

Out of the corner of her eye, Kate saw a new email pop into
her inbox and hurried to look. It wasn't from Clara. It was from
Madelyn Price.

Kate clicked to open it. It was still early in Michigan. She
imagined her fellow mother in a robe, fresh from a power
shower, nursing a black coffee.

It was a short message.

Hi Kate (if I may), I'm sorry to report that I've received no
reply yet from your daughter, Clara. Have you been able to
reach her, please? I'm still unable to contact Amy. Please

let me know at once if you have news. Yours gratefully, Maddy

Her mobile and office numbers were listed below.

Kate tasted the other woman's panic. Maddy? That was a sudden lurch from Doctor Madelyn Price. The gear shift told her they weren't strangers any more. They were fellow mothers.

Kate's stomach ached. Why hadn't Clara answered? Kate had tried so hard to respect her *boundaries*, to give her *space*, but this was different. This was a cry for help from someone who was frightened for her daughter's safety. Clara wouldn't ignore that. Whatever else she might be, she had never been unkind, never lacked compassion. Far from it.

Kate picked up her phone and, before she had time to reflect whether it was wise, she called Clara's mobile. After a few moments, the ringtone sounded. Her breath stuck in her throat as she waited, heart thudding. She could almost hear Clara's voice. Her body shook with anticipation, with longing. It was visceral, this need she had for her sole surviving daughter. It was overwhelming.

She saw again Clara's pale, drawn face, the intensity in her eyes: *I need a clean break, Mum. You're suffocating me.*

A click sounded on the line and she jumped to attention, hurriedly started to speak: 'Clara? It's Mum. Don't hang up—'

She was met with nothing more than a dull echo on the line. The ringtone had simply expired, unanswered. Kate stood very still, looking at the phone. She knew, in the tissues and organs of her body, even before her mind could realise, that something was wrong. She thought of Maddy in her Michigan kitchen, tamping down a similar panic.

She pulled up Maddy's email and dialled her number. Maddy picked up at once.

'Maddy? It's Kate,' she said simply. 'I can't get hold of Clara either.'

Kate heard the sharp intake of breath across several thousand miles. Her eyes fixed on the light falling into her study in weak shafts, dappled with dust motes, and pooling on the floor.

I will remember this, she thought. *This is another before.* She was afraid to imagine what might become *after*.

Maddy, far away, seemed to recover herself first.

'That's it.' Her voice was determined. 'I'm getting a flight out there.'

'Good.' Kate didn't hesitate. 'I'm coming too.'

30

Kate sipped her coffee.

A headache had gathered behind her eyes but she refused to give in, to crawl into the hotel bed and sleep it off. It had been three long months since she'd seen Clara and her body tingled with nervous excitement. Each time a distant figure crossed the lobby, she sat up straighter, strained to see if it might be Clara, felt her heart rate quicken.

She was braced. She knew Clara might be angry with her for coming out here. She hadn't forgotten what she'd said: *I need a clean break. Leave me alone.*

All the way, on the Eurostar, she'd been seized by the idea that she'd somehow sense Clara as soon as she arrived. That they'd find each other straightaway. Her need to see her daughter, to hold her, was so intense, it made her body ache. And yet here she was, sitting in a five-star hotel on the edge of the old city, trying to feel that Clara was near and failing.

It was three in the afternoon and the hotel restaurant was deserted. She'd chosen a seat facing the entrance from the lobby, next to a vast floor-to-ceiling window. The breakfast

buffet had been cleared long ago and the counters were deco-
rated instead with bowls of plastic fruit, display jars of pasta and
signs advertising Dutch beer. There was something moribund
about it all that added to her sense of anxiety.

Outside, the street glistened as watery sunshine reflected in
puddles from the recent rain. She imagined Clara walking along
this very stretch of pavement past the hotel restaurant, then
pausing at the pedestrian crossing to hurry over that bridge
towards the old centre of the city.

Kate stared at every young woman who approached, stiffening with hope, trying to see in each one's walk Clara's rather
stiff, slow gait. One by one, they came nearer and she saw by
their faces, as well as their movements, that they were strangers.

Alongside the pavement, a jangle of bikes of all shapes and
sizes jostled down the broad, dedicated bike lane. Beyond, the
multi-lane roads were efficiently busy. She watched cars and
trucks pass, flicking spray. A tram glided through. None of the
faces at the windows was Clara's.

She lifted her eyes and scanned further, searching, always,
for a sign of her daughter. In the distance, the far pavement
gently rose towards a bridge that arched over the nearest canal.
The approach was cluttered with street stalls. One dangled
plastic tourist souvenirs and fridge magnets; another was a
mobile café, offering pretzels, pancakes and coffee; a third stood
behind a row of boards advertising canal trips and dinner
dances and, finally, on the turn to the bridge, a rounded stand of
pictures showing landmarks of Amsterdam. For Kate, it was
joyless.

Eventually, she turned back to her phone and opened again
the University of Michigan website. The headshot of Doctor
Madelyn Price was glossy and carefully posed. Her blonde,
shoulder-length hair looked perfected by lacquer. Her half-

smile was enigmatic, professional yet just warm enough not to be off-putting.

The biographical detail published beside it set out her credentials. Before joining the University of Michigan's Counselling and Psychological Services as its clinical director, she'd been a psychiatrist in private practice in New York. There were references to published papers, conference appearances and media work.

The description of her role now gushed about her vision for an inclusive and diverse campus, for the mental health and well-being of the student community, about academic excellence with, at its heart, a people-centred approach.

Kate flicked back to her photo library and scrolled through pictures of Clara. Something softened inside her as she gazed at her daughter's features. Kate saw Bella there, in the heart-shaped face, framed by blonde, wavy hair. It had been the anniversary of Bella's death just over a week ago. A difficult day to survive alone. The pain had made her long all the more for Clara, made her wonder if her younger daughter too had remembered the date and was also reliving it.

She looked again at Clara's smiling face. Those were Simon's intelligent grey-green eyes looking back at her and his neat mouth. Clara's exuberance, her determination, the toughness that had crept into her personality of late, those were all her own, forged by the losses and traumas of recent years.

A sense of movement, of someone entering the restaurant, made her look up sharply.

She rose to her feet and lifted a hand in greeting. 'Maddy?'

Of course it was. The woman striding towards her, an expensive brown leather bag in one hand, seemed an older, more care-worn version of the woman pictured on the U of M website but she was still unmistakable. The thick blonde hair was tucked behind her ears. She exuded efficiency, smartly dressed in black, tailored trousers, a light blue cotton shirt and a denim jacket. She did not look, Kate thought, like someone who'd just got off a seven-and-a-half-hour flight and skipped half a dozen time zones.

Maddy extended a hand and the two women shook across the table. Maddy's fingers were soft-skinned, her nails shaped and polished. No wedding ring. Kate's own plain gold band felt so familiar now it seemed part of her flesh. Kate was conscious of the contrast between Maddy's manicure and her own stubby nails. She'd fallen back into a childhood habit of chewing them since Bella died.

The waiter appeared the moment Maddy settled into her seat. Her presence seemed to stir the dead air in the restaurant back into life. She ordered a cappuccino and a bottle of sparkling water with precise, detailed instructions, then, as the waiter scurried away, she turned her attention to Kate.

'Thank you for coming. I appreciate it. No news, I take it?'

Kate shook her head. 'Not yet. I've only just arrived.'

'Have you visited Clara since she's been here?' As Maddy spoke, her hands were busy in her bag, extracting a file of papers and spreading them out on the surface of the coffee table between them.

'No.' Kate felt herself shrink inside. She was embarrassed to admit the truth. That she hadn't even known Clara was here until Maddy told her. That Clara didn't want her to know which country she was in, let alone allow her to visit. She just said: 'I haven't seen her for months.'

Maddy pushed across a sheet of paper. 'I've typed up what I know about Amy's life here. It isn't a lot to go on. But it's a start.'

Kate scanned it at once. There were two addresses at the top, one for an apartment and one for a Bar/Restaurant Galileo.

Maddy pointed a manicured nail. 'Amy started renting the apartment in the summer. There, on the canal. She had another room-mate for a while, before Clara moved in.'

Maddy opened her phone and showed a photo. Her lip-sticked mouth was pursed. 'That was taken last month, just after Clara moved in. Maybe you've got something more recent?'

Kate couldn't answer. She stared at the two young women. Their cheeks were pressed together, their blonde hair choppy across their faces. Their mouths formed exaggerated pouts as they clamped down on separate straws that protruded from a single, bulbous cocktail. They looked fresh, at the start of a night out. Their faces were artfully made up, eyes popping with colour, cheeks contoured, lips glossy and red. Their gazes were confident, almost challenging.

Kate took a deep breath. 'Clara and I haven't been in touch for a while. She needed some space, you know. We've had a tough few years.'

Maddy's eyes were sharp and knowing. She didn't ask, just turned her attention back to the printed paper.

'I suggest we try the apartment first. I've checked Google Maps. It doesn't look far. Down this canal, here, ten minutes' walk or so. This—' she pointed at the second address, for the bar/restaurant '—is where they're both working. Maybe we'll find them there or, if not, hopefully we can find someone who can confirm they're still in Amsterdam.'

The waiter appeared and set out Maddy's order on the table with a flourish. The cappuccino with its tiny, complimentary biscuit tucked into the saucer, the glass part-filled with ice. He unscrewed the top of the bottle of sparkling water and poured it with care, one hand tucked in the small of his back, as if it were a fine wine. The ice cracked and sputtered.

Maddy nudged out another paper. Printed emails, speckled with yellow highlighter.

'There's a couple of people Amy mentioned.' She pointed to one name. 'Honey comes up a few times. American girl, also works at Galileo's. I've got a photo of her, too.' She glanced up, looking for a response in Kate's face and finding only blankness. 'And a guy called Adrian.' She pointed to more short bursts of highlighter. 'British. No photo but she's mentioned him once or twice.'

Kate considered Maddy as she set aside the papers and sipped her coffee. Maddy's hand trembled slightly as she set down her cup again, reached for the water and drank. Maddy turned her face to the window and seemed to concentrate on taking in the scene outside. Kate wondered if she too was imagining her daughter out there, trying to seek her out in those unfamiliar streets. For a moment, neither of them spoke.

Maddy seemed to make an effort to breathe evenly, collecting herself. She set down the empty glass and turned back to the restaurant, reaching again for the coffee cup.

Kate dropped her gaze to the table. Clara, she thought. She just needed to see Clara. That was all. She just needed to know she was safe.

Maddy drained her cup and pushed it aside, then dabbed at her lips with the napkin, leaving a smudge of foam and lipstick. 'OK, let's go find them.' Her voice was determined but, as she gathered together her papers and made to get up, Kate saw the tension in her face.

She's afraid, she thought. *She's just as frightened as I am about what's happened to our daughters.*

31

Maddy, following the map on her phone, strode ahead with confidence. She led Kate first along the side of the busy, broad canal that ran close to their hotel, skirting the old city, then waited on a corner, pointing the way down a narrow, sleepy tributary.

As soon as they took the turn, Kate noted the change in atmosphere. The sounds of the city – blaring traffic, music spilling from bars and cafés, the tinny commentaries from passing tourist barges – retreated and became muffled. Instead of restaurants and shops, they found themselves passing a line of thin but imposing residential buildings, pressed close together in a row that reached to the grey, threatening sky. Dates above some doors proclaimed their heritage, suggesting they dated back to the eighteenth, even seventeenth, century, the city's commercial golden age.

Kate paused in front of one of the grander ones, distracted for a moment by the thought of Clara standing here, seeing all this for the first time. She imagined Clara's bright-eyed excitement as she gazed up at such beautiful architecture with fresh eyes. She'd always dreamed of bringing the girls to Amsterdam. It had just never quite happened.

The building had an impressive façade. A ladder of floor-to-ceiling windows rose up the centre. Each set was flanked by a sturdy pair of wooden, painted shutters, flung open and secured against the wall like pinned ears. A black, chest-high railing across each window gave the appearance of a balcony. Kate peered more closely. No, not balconies, they were flush against the frame, presumably for safety. Perhaps for show.

She had the disconcerting sense that the building was falling towards her and stepped to one side to change her perspective. She was right. The whole front of the six-storey building was angled, the upper storeys leaning forwards towards the canal as if it were in danger of toppling, an old woman with weighted feet teetering to admire her face in the water. She peered more closely.

'Hoists.' Maddy, a few steps ahead, had turned to follow Kate's gaze. 'See, right up there?' She pointed to a boxed finger-like structure right at the top of the façade, sticking out from the brickwork. A large metal hook, as sturdy as an anchor, protruded from beneath it. 'They have to winch everything up the front. Settees, tables, pianos, whatever. The staircases inside are too narrow for anything bulky. That's why the fronts are angled like that.'

Kate managed a smile. Clara would love the quirkiness of that.

'Amy sent me a picture from when she moved in,' Maddy went on. 'I've got it somewhere on my phone. Her bed dangling in mid-air, then a desk. Quite a sight.'

The sharp ding of a bell brought their attention back to the street. A young woman with flowing hair swerved past them, perched upright on an old-fashioned bicycle, a panier of shopping strapped to the back.

'Here.' Maddy looked back at her phone, frowning. She lifted her gaze and pointed. 'That one, right there. Number 43.'

Kate turned. Number 43 looked as if it dated from much the same period as those around it but it was far more modest, squashed between two more impressive ones. The brickwork was blackened with centuries of dirt. The downstairs floor-to-ceiling windows were lofty, suggesting grandeur and opulent space, but as the storeys climbed, the heights seemed to shrink dramatically. The windows at the very top, five storeys up, seemed barely half size. The woodwork around the front door and the windows was flat and plain, with none of the architectural flourishes of its neighbours.

'Is this their place?'

Maddy nodded. 'Their apartment's right at the top. It's a walk-up. The front looks grand but apparently, round the back, it's pretty shabby. And the rooms are poky, Amy said. That's how they afford it.' She looked round, taking in the view of the canal, the sweep of water, dotted with tethered houseboats. 'Great spot, though.'

Kate hurried after Maddy as she took the flight of stone steps from street level to the raised front door.

At the top, Maddy twisted back, her face triumphant. 'See?'

Kate caught up and leaned in to look. Maddy had brought up a photo on her phone of Amy, standing in front of a crimson door with a brass knocker in the shape of a dragon. A door exactly like this one.

Maddy pressed the buzzer. Kate's hands slickened with sweat as they waited, straining to hear sounds of movement from the interior.

Kate imagined Clara, dashing up these steps with groceries,

standing where Kate now stood, fumbling for her keys and hurrying into the hallway on the far side. Maybe she was upstairs in the apartment right now. Maybe, in a matter of moments—

Kate hurried down the steps again and crossed the street to stand back from the building. She shielded her eyes and peered up at the truncated windows in the top storey. They were blank. The only movement was a ghostly pattern of light playing across the glass, reflections rising from the stirred currents of the canal.

Kate raised her hand in a cautious, embarrassed wave. She imagined Clara there, concealing herself, looking down at her.

She could almost sense her daughter's feet pounding down the invisible stairs inside, her hand fumbling with the latch to throw open the door. Kate faltered, bit down on her lip. And then what? A look of delight or of scorn? Kate bowed her shoulders. She knew the answer to that.

Clara would be furious with her for turning up. Maybe Amy felt the same, refusing to respond to her mother's messages because she wanted to get her off her back. Maddy and her daughter might not be as close as Maddy had implied.

Maddy turned away and came slowly down the steps, back to the street. She looked deflated. Kate could almost hear her thought: *I've travelled all this way and for what?*

The door opened. A young man of around twenty slipped out, hurried to unlock one of the dozen battered bicycles chained to the posts along the edge of the canal. His blond hair stuck out in clumps. He was wearing an oversized coat, flapping round his jeans, his neck encircled with a long, woollen scarf.

'Excuse me!' Maddy was at his side almost before he realised. 'Do you live here?'

The young man, glancing warily at Maddy, nodded. 'Is there a problem?'

He spoke clearly but with a sing-song Scandinavian accent. Swedish, perhaps, Kate thought. His eyes were ice-blue and piercing. She wondered if he and Clara knew each other. She watched as Maddy pulled up a picture of Amy on her phone.

'I'm looking for my daughter. Amy. I think she lives here. Have you seen her?'

He blinked, checked out the picture. 'Sure. She was living at the top. With an English girl.' He turned back to his bicycle, as if their business were finished.

'This one?' Maddy scrolled through her pictures. She must be pulling up the picture of the two of them together, Amy and Clara.

He nodded. 'That's right.' He paused, as if he were reconsidering. 'Why?' He gave Maddy an appraising glance, then looked across at Kate. 'Who are you?'

'I'm her mother. I just want to check she's OK.'

He frowned at that. It didn't add up, Kate could see. Amsterdam was notorious for being a backpackers' playground, a place of freedom, of hash and alcohol, of sex and craziness. No young person in their right mind wanted their mother to show up and spoil the fun.

He removed the lock, straightened up and wheeled the bike away from the post.

Maddy stuck to his side, persistent. 'Can you tell me when you last saw her? I've come a long way. I just want to know she's safe.'

He threw one leg over the bike frame, less friendly now. 'Maybe last week. Maybe the week before. I don't know.'

'Please, think hard.' Maddy stayed close to him. 'It's important.'

'Lady, I'm sorry, I hardly know them, really. I just saw them in the stairs now and then, that's all. Just to say hi.' He narrowed his eyes. 'Maybe, if you're her mother, you should call her, message her.'

'I have. I can't get hold of her.' She reached for his bike to detain him but he was too quick, pushing off at once.

He pedalled away hastily, rapidly gaining speed, calling back over his shoulder: 'Sorry.'

You're not sorry, Kate thought. *You're shaken. But why? What do you know?*

Maddy stared after him as he cycled off. Her mouth tightened. Whatever she was feeling, anger or frustration, Maddy blinked hard and shook her head, making an effort to recover herself. She twisted back to Kate, brisk again.

'Well, we know we found the right place. I guess they're just not home. We can come back.' She looked down at her phone, flicked through the screens. 'Let's try their workplace next. It doesn't look far.'

Maddy gave the closed front door a final glance, then pulled her coat more tightly round her body and began to stride away.

Kate tipped back her head and looked up again at the poky blank windows of the upper storeys. As she stared, something flickered. The slightest movement, there, to one side of the glass.

'Wait!'

Maddy, already out of earshot, didn't turn.

Something stirred and rose in Kate. It chilled her stomach, made her legs buckle. She groped backwards for support and her hand found the painted railings along the edge of the canal. The paint, flaking, cut into her pressing palms, peppered her flesh with black.

Horror washed through her. She knew this darkness. She'd been engulfed by it before.

When the phone had sounded in the middle of the night and the panicked voice of a stranger had told her about Bella, her beautiful, clever firstborn. She'd known, even as she'd tried to stay calm, to say: *maybe they're wrong, maybe she'll be OK, whatever state she's in, I'll make her better*, she'd known, deep in her gut, what lay ahead.

And all those years earlier, when Simon, just hours after leaving for work, had slumped in his seat on the train. Somehow, even as the phone had rung with the terrible news, she'd known what was to come.

Just as she knew now.

Maddy was right to be worried, to have jumped on a plane and flown halfway round the world. She wasn't being a fussy, anxious mother. She'd felt it too. Deep down. Something terrible.

Kate leaned heavily on the railing and concentrated on breathing, steady, deliberate breaths. Slowly, through the dread, her body found its rhythm again.

When she could, she narrowed her eyes and looked up again at the windows, straining to see more clearly. She was too far away to be sure if the glimmer of light on the glass was the sign of a figure inside, stirring in the shadows, or just a meaningless reflection from the shifting water.

32

'When you find them, do me a favour, will you? Tell them to come see me: Gino.'

The thick-set Italian jabbed a meaty finger at his chest. 'Tell them there's money here for them, pay from their last shift. Then they'll come running.'

Gino folded his arms, biceps bulging beneath his pale blue, cotton shirt. He sat back in his chair, making the wood creak, and regarded them. He was still muscular but on the brink of becoming corpulent, solidifying into middle age. His armpits were stained with fresh sweat. When he moved, the smell reached for them.

In the background, behind the restaurant's long, wooden bar, a younger man was taking glasses from a dishwasher, polishing them and hanging them upside down by their stems above the bar, one by one, ready for use.

It was late afternoon. Sleepy and quiet. A family of four sat at the front of the restaurant, in the bay window looking onto the street, eating garlic bread and pizza. Otherwise, the place was quiet. Even at this hour, it had the secluded atmosphere of a dimly lit cave. It would come into its own after dark, Kate thought, when the candles waiting on each table would be lit, the air becoming steamy and pungent with Italian cooking, the wine flowing.

Kate looked around, taking it all in. Clara had spent evenings here, standing by these tables as she took orders for drinks, for food, rushing to and from the kitchen with piled plates. She wondered what sort of boss Gino was, if he were old-school, too free with his hands, or if he wouldn't dare, if he knew the young women were feistier nowadays. Clara wouldn't stand for any nonsense, surely.

The walls were panelled in dark wood, the tables and chairs heavy. The only décor came from framed black-and-white photographs of Italian scenes. They exuded a sense of languorous heat, of blinding sunshine and dense shadow. A fashionable young woman walking down a cobbled street, past fruit stalls and pavement cafés. A gnarled old man sitting on a bench, forever smoking his pipe. A rural landscape, thick with pine trees, and a path showing the way through to a distant country church. Kate didn't recognise the city. Naples, perhaps. Or Syracuse.

'It's no picnic, running this place,' Gino was saying in his thick Italian accent. 'I tell the girls when I give them work. I know they won't stay forever, they're *ragazzi*, of course, young, but I tell them, please, when you want to leave, give me a little time. I won't be angry. Disappointed, yes, but not angry. I say: don't just disappear into the night. And what do they do?'

He sighed theatrically and made a fountaining gesture with his large hands: 'Whoosh!' It was the wordless story of two girls disappearing in a plume of smoke.

Maddy, leaning forward, interrupted, trying to bring him back to the point. 'But you haven't answered my question, Gino. When did you last see Amy?'

Gino pulled a face. 'Ten days, maybe two weeks back.' He shrugged his shoulders. 'Long enough to know they're not coming back. Same story for both of them. One missed shift, even two, I can forgive. But so many? No. I'm sorry. That is not OK.'

Maddy shook her head, barely containing her frustration. Kate sensed the cultural gulf between the two: Gino, with his fleshy body, his ruddy features, his emotional Italian temperament and Maddy, lean and trim, immaculate and outwardly collected but with a need for precision, for information that she was, so far, failing to secure.

Kate put her hands together in a gesture of supplication. 'Please, Signore, could you possibly check the date of their last shift for us? We're so worried. You must have daughters. You can imagine. We'd be so grateful.'

He turned to regard her, thoughtful. Slowly, he nodded his head. 'For you, Signora, let me see.' He heaved himself to his feet and disappeared into the back.

Maddy waited until Gino was out of earshot before whispering tartly: 'How can we believe a word he says? I wouldn't trust him as far as I could throw him. Which isn't far.'

Kate glanced past her to the youngster, still laboriously polishing glasses, concerned he might be able to hear. 'Let's see what Gino comes up with. We're not done yet.'

'He's hiding something.' Maddy glared at her. 'There's something he's not telling us, I can feel it.'

Kate nodded. She was dogged by the same unease. Trying to be fair, she just said: 'We don't know that.'

She considered what he'd told them, that both girls had been good waitresses, reliable, efficient and popular with customers. Amy had worked there for several months, Clara just since she'd arrived in Amsterdam six weeks ago. She'd started off by picking up odd shifts here and there until another girl quit and she took a regular slot.

'Clara is a good girl,' Gino had told Kate with a nod of parental approval. His accent extended Clara's name, giving it a hint of the exotic South. 'Steady girl. Not so crazy, like some.'

Then, he'd said, both girls had simply failed to show up for work one weekend. They'd left him in the lurch when he needed them. He was clearly still sore. He didn't seem like a man who'd be philosophical about being slighted.

Kate frowned. Maddy was right to feel suspicious. It didn't add up. Why would both girls, who'd always been reliable and needed their jobs, simply walk out without a word, leaving wages uncollected?

Gino came back, a computer printout in his hands, a pair of cheap, wire reading glasses on the end of his nose. 'Friday 12 October. *Ecco*, here.' He pointed a fat finger at the column of names. 'Amy Price, Clara...' he hesitated over Clara's family name, peering more closely, then mangling the pronunciation anyway '...Clara Grosvenor. Friday evening. Weekend. Busy, always busy. They'd both begged for extra shifts and I, just from kindness, had put them both on Saturday evening too. But see here?' He traced down the type with his nail. Both girls' names were listed but had a large cross printed beside them. 'No-show.'

Maddy shook her head. 'That makes no sense.' She raised her eyes to Gino's face. 'Surely you must have been concerned. I mean, for both of them not to show up like that. Did you inform anyone?'

Gino bristled at her tone. 'Inform who, exactly, Signora?'

Maddy faced him down. 'You tell me. The police, maybe?'

He gave a cold smile. 'The police? You think they want to hear from Gino every time some kid from another country doesn't show up for work? You have any idea how often that happens?' He shrugged his shoulders, made an expansive gesture with his large hands. 'Who knows where they are?'

Gino raised his voice as he became animated. Kate saw the young man behind the bar stiffen, as if he sensed trouble.

'At some party, maybe? Drinking, taking drugs?' Gino gesticulated as he spoke, emphasising the drama. 'This is Amsterdam. Young people come here to go crazy. You are the mothers. You think your daughters are still little girls, dressed in pink, playing with dolls. You have no idea, the things they do.' A vein pulsed at his neck, his jowly face flushed.

Kate bristled. She didn't need a lecture. Any illusion that her daughters were still *little girls, playing with dolls* had been crushed to death a year ago when Bella died. As for Amsterdam, she could imagine perfectly well what dangers and temptations lay in wait here, for Clara and for Amy too.

She saw a similar tightness in Maddy's face and put a restraining hand on her arm. There was no point antagonising this man. They might need him.

'We don't mean any offence, Signore,' Kate said. 'We're most grateful to you, really. Can I ask you one more question before we go?'

He was breathing heavily, a snorting bull, his eyes still fixed angrily on Maddy.

Kate pressed on. 'Amy mentioned a couple of people she knew here. A friend of hers, another American girl. Honey. Does she work here too?'

He pulled a face. 'That girl? Useless. I gave her a shift only because Amy begged me. She's a dopehead. Too much into parties. I told her to leave and not come back.'

Kate felt despair grip her. All their leads were evaporating, one by one. 'Any idea where we'd find her?'

He blew out his cheeks. 'No. I told you, she's not welcome here.' He folded the printout deliberately into half, then quarters and put it in his shirt pocket, then put his hands squarely on the edge of the table and, with some effort, pressed himself upright. 'Now, Signore, if you will excuse me...'

Kate got to her feet too, still talking. 'And there's an English guy she mentioned. Adrian. You ever met him?'

His features softened at once. 'Ah, Adrian! This is a good guy. He comes often here to eat, sometimes with his friends, sometimes alone. Loves my food. Always smiling. Clever boy. He knows Amsterdam and he speaks languages – English, French, a little Italian, also.'

'So he doesn't work here?'

'Here? No.' Gino started to turn away from her. 'Try the tourist shop down there on the bridge, Gift World. I've seen him working there, not so often but still... Always reading.' He tapped his forehead meaningfully. 'Big brains.'

Kate, feeling they were being dismissed, hastily scribbled her name and number on a scrap of paper and pushed it at him. 'Please, Gino, if you hear anything, anything at all about Amy or Clara, could you let me know?'

He took it with a shrug and pushed it into his pocket. His eyes fell again on Maddy who was still sitting, shoulders hunched, at the table. 'Now, please, Signore, you should go.' His arm waved them without question towards the door, past the family of four. They were tucking now into gelati and pancakes, their spoons flashing.

Outside, Maddy and Kate stood for a moment under Galileo's awning, gathering their thoughts. The light had started to fade and dusk was rolling in across the square. Here and there, in shafts of brightness from shops and cafés, drizzle fell in lit columns. At their feet, the neat rows of angled paving stones glistened with rain.

A group of tourists trudged by with tired steps, subsumed in voluminous, thin plastic cloaks. A tram slid past, then came to a halt across the road at a crowded tram stop. Off to the left, at the edge of the pedestrianised zone, traffic lights changed and a surge of bicycles pressed forward, bells jangling.

'I don't trust him.' Maddy's face was tight.

Kate sighed to herself. 'Well, OK. If that's how you feel. But it doesn't help to rile him.'

Maddy's lips pressed into a hard line. She turned her head away to face the square. Waiters in the pavement cafés were hurriedly unrolling tarpaulins and winding out awnings to give cover to early evening diners.

Kate felt suddenly exhausted, worn by the emotion of the day. She was gripped again by an intense physical longing for her daughter. She wanted to see her face, to wrap her arms around her and hold her tightly. The thought of it was so immediate, it overwhelmed her.

'So, we need to find this tourist shop, Gift World, and get hold of Adrian.'

'Why don't you do that?' Maddy pointed vaguely in the direction of the street on the far side of the square, a broad touristy avenue of shops and pancake houses, leading to a narrow bridge over a canal. 'He said that way.'

Kate hesitated. She was trying to be patient with Maddy. She understood how worried she was. She was carrying her own

166 JILL CHILDS

anxiety, about Clara. The other woman's brusque tone didn't help.

'Sure,' Kate said, evenly. 'You're not coming too?'

Maddy turned. 'Me? No, not right now. I've got an appointment at five thirty.'

Kate frowned. 'An appointment? Where?'

Maddy shot her a cool look. 'With the police.'

33

Kate set off down one of the broad, pedestrianised tourist streets.

As the darkness intensified, the neon signs from pancake houses, gelaterias and cafés flickered and dazzled, leading her down a coloured runway towards the canal. It was that dead, in-between time, when the day shoppers had left for home but the evening club and restaurant trade hadn't yet ignited.

Kate tried to fight her sense of disquiet. Why hadn't Maddy told her earlier about this appointment with the police? She'd thought they were a team, planning everything together. Now, she felt shut out. Should she be there too, reporting Clara as missing? She glanced sharply from side to side as she walked, searching always for a glimpse of Clara. The rain had driven most visitors into cafés and restaurants.

Tomorrow, she decided. If there was no sign of Clara by then, she'd go to the police too. Better another row with Clara in the future, however painful, than this endless fear that she wasn't doing enough.

It wasn't hard to find Gift World. It had a prime position at the far end of the street, facing a picturesque bridge over the canal, which was framed by black railings hung with brightly coloured flower baskets and studded with chained bicycles. It was a remnant of picture-postcard Amsterdam, even in the fading light and rain.

Kate paused outside the store, bracing herself. Gift World looked every bit as clichéd as its name. Its window was cluttered with tacky souvenirs. Cheap versions of Delft blue china, painted with windmills and figures in old-fashioned clothing, complete with Dutch winged bonnets and clogs. Souvenir T-shirts, baseball caps and sweatshirts trumpeting slogans. A pillar of fridge magnets with mass-produced scenes of Amsterdam's flower market and canals. Bowls of painted wooden tulips. Hessian and canvas bags emblazoned with Van Gogh's *Sunflowers* or *The Starry Night*.

Kate's eyes slid over it, uninterested. They fell finally on the items which, tucked off to one side and slightly hidden from first view, hinted at the other side of Amsterdam. The mugs shaped like enlarged breasts, the vulgar statuettes and bottle openers with engorged genitals. The lurid sex toys. They told a story of the city's openly flaunted sex trade and legal drugs, the freedoms that tipped at times into licentiousness. She thought of Clara and Amy and shivered. Amsterdam's dark side.

As she entered the crowded cave, hung on every side with lurid merchandise, a sign over the door proclaimed: 'We Sell Magic Truffles'.

The shop seemed empty at first, apart from a Japanese couple, huddled together in a corner, examining a set of place mats. Kate headed down the main aisle, skirted a rainbow display of scarves and found herself at the back of the store. It was a den of sorts, hemmed in by stacks of stock. To one side, a young man was perched on a stool by a wooden counter, his head tipped forward over a hefty book.

When he sensed her approaching and looked up, he gave an easy smile. He was handsome, even under the hard artificial lighting. In his early to mid-twenties, he had a mess of wavy, black hair and a pattern of dark stubble across his upper lip and chin. His eyes, when they focused on her, were a piercing grey.

'Hi, can I help?'

A native English speaker, by the sound of it, with slightly clipped, professional-class vowels. She wondered if he always addressed customers in English, a default tourist language, or if her nationality was obvious at first glance.

His look was direct and thoughtful. She felt herself appraised without knowing why.

'Bit of a strange one,' she said, feeling her way. 'I'm trying to find a contact number for someone who works here.'

'Anyone in particular?' His eyes were amused, teasing.

'It's for a friend of mine.' She hesitated, unsure if it might be him or not. 'Adrian?'

'Yep, you've found him.' He closed his book and set it on the counter. She glanced at the front. It was in Italian and it didn't look a light read. She remembered what Gino had said about Adrian and his big brain.

He extended his hand. A firm, warm handshake.

'I wasn't sure what days you work.'

He shrugged. 'That's OK. I'm not always sure myself.'

She looked round at the almost empty shop. 'Is it OK, now? I mean, for a quick chat?'

'Sure.' He reached behind the counter and drew out a second long-legged stool, then set it near her. 'Take a seat. So, who's this friend? Male or female?'

'Female. Madelyn Price. She doesn't live here. She's based in Michigan, in the US.'

He looked confused. 'And she says she knows me?'

'She thinks you might know her daughter: Amy Price. Apparently, Amy mentioned you a few times in emails.'

He smiled, relaxed again. 'American Amy? The waitress? Crazy blonde hair? Yeah, I know her. Not well but, you know, it's quite a small expat scene here. Once you meet someone, you keep bumping into them.'

Kate found herself smiling back.

He hesitated, then added: 'She's not in trouble, is she? She seems a bit wild but I think she's just, you know, young. Still finding her feet in life. Amsterdam's good for that.'

'Her mum's trying to check she's OK, that's all. She hasn't heard from her for a while. It's not like Amy, apparently, not to be in touch. She's worried.'

He looked concerned. 'I'm sorry.' He paused, looking into the middle distance as if he were straining to collect his thoughts. 'Have you tried her flat? She had a place on one of the smaller canals. I don't know the address but I could probably take you there. Top floor. Kind of poky, to be honest. I went to a party there, one time. It wasn't a huge crowd but we were packed in so tightly, we could hardly move.' He laughs at the memory. 'Come to think of it, she might not be there any more. I know her flatmate left. Maybe she couldn't find anyone else.'

Kate's pulse quickened. 'Her flatmate? You mean Clara?'

He blinked, clearly surprised. 'You know her?'

'I'm her mother.' She faltered. Unexpected tears came to her eyes and she blinked them back. 'We haven't been in touch much, recently.' She took a deep breath. 'That's the connection. I mean, that's why Amy's mum asked me to come, because the girls were sharing a place together. You say she's left?'

He dropped his eyes to his hands, folded now in his lap. 'This is kind of awkward. Sorry.'

Kate's heart pumped. Something had happened and he seemed loath to tell her. She felt her cheeks flush. She wondered what Clara might have said to him about her, about her need to get away, not only from England but from her. She heard herself say: 'When you say "left", do you mean left Amsterdam? Or the Netherlands? Tell me that much, at least. Please.'

He didn't answer for a few moments. In the silence, Kate became aware of approaching footsteps. A middle-aged woman appeared from round the rainbow scarves. A young girl, eleven or twelve, trailed after her.

The woman gave them a curious glance, her eyes resting more on Adrian than on Kate, then placed a set of postcards and a souvenir fridge magnet on the counter. She seemed to straighten a little and played with the ends of her shoulder-length hair as she waited for Adrian to jump to his feet and serve her. Her daughter pressed against her side, scuffing her shoes against the floor, bored.

Kate watched as Adrian took the woman's money and rang up the sale. His easy charm seemed natural to him but she sensed too that he was distracted. She wondered if he'd been thrown off course by their conversation. Whatever he knew about Clara, he seemed uncertain whether to tell her.

Kate felt a flurry of thoughts close in on her. Maybe Clara had simply moved on. She'd always given the impression, as she'd pored over the battered map of Europe on her bedroom wall, that she wanted to pack in as many countries as she possibly could, in her long-awaited gap year. She must surely have earned enough money here, in six or seven weeks, to tide her over somewhere new. She shook her head. But why disappear from the restaurant without a word? That wasn't like Clara. And Amy, there was Amy's disappearance too. She bit her lip.

As soon as the customer had collected her purchases and left, Kate started again.

'Look, I don't want you to break a confidence. But could you at least put my mind at rest? Is Clara OK? Please, can you tell me where she's gone?'

34

Adrian blew out his cheeks. He shook his head a little, head bowed, the mop of dark hair shifting on his forehead. He seemed to come to a decision and raised his eyes to meet Kate's.

'It is sort of tricky. But, you know, I can see you're worried.' He frowned. 'You won't tell anyone, will you? I mean, the last thing I want to do is cause trouble. I didn't know Clara well – just from Galileo's and we'd say hi at parties now and then. Brits tend to look out for each other here. She needed a bit of help, that's all. I was happy to give it.'

Blood thumped in Kate's ears. 'What sort of help?'

He nodded a little as if to persuade himself to go ahead. 'There's a lot of drugs here, right? Amsterdam's famous for it. Well, Clara got involved with this guy – I don't know his name. He's a charmer, gets along with everyone. He's always the one at the centre of the party crowd, the one who could get hold of stuff. Not just weed. That's legal here, you can get it anywhere. But harder stuff. Coke and poppers and E and whatever else. You didn't always know what they were. Sometimes he sold them; sometimes he just handed them out.'

Kate felt her jaw tighten. She thought about Bella and the student who'd handed out tabs of E at the party as if they'd been sweets, scattering them so liberally that no-one had been sober enough to notice when Bella first slumped.

Not you, Clara. You wouldn't get involved with a low-life like that, would you? Didn't Bella's death teach you anything?

Adrian went on: 'He had another side to him. A dark side. You don't get big in the drugs scene without knowing how to operate. I don't know much more. I steer clear of all that. Not my thing.'

Kate leaned heavily on the counter, anchoring herself. 'You said she got involved with this guy. Involved how?'

Adrian's eyes slid back to his hands. 'Pretty heavily, from what I heard. She really fell for him. What can I say?'

Kate battled to hold herself in check. She wanted to scream, to tell him he was wrong, that he'd mixed up her daughter with someone else. Something dark was opening up inside her. A fear.

Did she truly know Clara? Had the gap between them become such a gulf in the last year that she could fail to recognise her own daughter? She remembered how floored she'd been when Clara had suddenly accused her of loving Bella more, of wishing that Clara had been the daughter she'd lost, instead of Bella. How could she have thought such a thing? Now, hearing all this, she felt just as lost.

'She knew about the drugs? Are you sure?'

He gave a non-committal pout. 'Sure. I mean, I assume she and Amy were using too. They seemed pretty into it. You don't hang around with that crowd and stay clean. It's just not like that.'

Kate felt stiff with adrenalin, every sense heightened. Her

voice, when she spoke, was stretched string-tight. 'Well, go on. You can't leave it there. What happened?'

Adrian raised his eyebrows nervously. He seemed unable to meet her eye. 'A lot of it's hearsay, OK? Gossip at Galileo's, at parties. I don't know for sure.'

She cut through. 'What did you hear?'

'That this guy got heavy with her, knocked her about a bit. I can't be sure. I didn't know her well enough. But she came into work one night with a shiner – I did see that. She'd tried to cover it up with make-up but it was a mess. She made an excuse about it, laughed it off, but, well, I'm not stupid. I told her to watch her back.'

Kate's hands balled instinctively into fists. She could hardly bear it. She was gripped by a sudden need to punch someone, she who had never hit another person in her life. A picture came into her head of Clara, her lovely girl, battered by a man's fist. Cringing and crying, her hands to her face. *Why didn't you tell me?* She felt a surge of nausea and swallowed it back. *I would have been here in a heartbeat. I would have done anything you wanted. You know that.*

Adrian stuttered on. 'After that, I didn't see her for a while. I didn't think much of it, to be honest. I'm sorry. I didn't know her that well.' He lifted his eyes for a sudden, shame-faced look. 'Then I bumped into her in Dam Square. She was waiting for a taxi with a load of luggage, big rucksack, suitcase, bags everything. Too much to carry. I asked her where she was going and she said to Schiphol. She hadn't even bought a ticket yet; she just said she needed to get the first flight out.'

Kate felt her daughter's panic. 'Did she say why?'

Adrian sighed. 'She said something about going where he couldn't find her. I assumed, you know, it was that guy. That he'd threatened her or maybe hurt her again and she wanted out. She didn't want to talk about it.'

'How did she seem?'

'In a state, frankly.' He glanced up and seemed to read the horror on Kate's face. 'I'm sorry. I didn't mean to – I mean, maybe I shouldn't—'

Kate steeled herself. 'You're fine. Just tell me. I need to know.'

He nodded. 'She seemed frightened. Nervous. I got the feeling she just wanted to get the hell out of there as soon as possible. I offered to go out to the airport with her and she started to cry. Anyway, I did and when we got to Schiphol, it all fell into place. She got a cheap ticket to Rome. I gave her some extra cash, just what I had on me, about a hundred euros, maybe. That was the last time I saw her, heading through passport control.'

'How long ago was this?'

He pursed his lips, thinking back. 'Maybe two weeks? Yeah. About that.'

'And you're sure it was Rome she was heading for?'

'Definitely.' He nodded. 'She'd talked about heading to Italy next. Venice, maybe, or Rome. Gino and the guys at Galileo's – half of them are Gino's sons or cousins or whatever – they talk about Italy all the time. You can imagine. Praising it to the skies. The sun and wine, *la dolce vita*. Maybe she got the idea from them. I don't know.'

Kate nodded. It rang true. Clara had always loved Italy. They'd been there as a family a few times, when the girls were young. They'd rented a villa in Tuscany one year and stayed in an expensive hotel in Sardinia another. And then they'd lost Simon, and her appetite for holidays in the sun had dwindled.

So, Clara had packed up and left Amsterdam in a hurry. Kate felt suddenly very deflated. Ever since she'd arrived in Amsterdam, she'd been searching for a glimpse of Clara, on every street corner, alongside every canal, in every café she'd passed. It had all been pointless. No wonder she'd failed to sense her here. Clara was already long gone.

'And Amy?' she said. 'What about her?'

Adrian shrugged. 'I don't know. I haven't seen her around for a while. She might still be here; she might have moved on. I don't know. People kind of come and go here, you know? It's pretty fluid.' He considered. 'Have you tried Galileo's?'

Kate nodded. 'We spoke to Gino. He said neither of them had shown up to work recently.'

Adrian pulled a face. 'Well, maybe she moved on too. She'd been here a while; she was probably getting itchy feet.'

'Thanks.' Kate found it an effort to get to her feet, she felt so weary. She nodded at the book on the counter. 'You speak Italian?'

'I'm studying it, when I get the chance. And French. It's a great place to practise.'

She frowned. 'Amsterdam?'

'Sure, half of Europe's passing through.' When he flashed a smile, the sun came out. 'It's a lot more fun here than England.'

'Well, thanks.' She turned to leave. 'Good luck.'

'Wait.' He reached out to put his hand on her arm. 'Tell Amy's mum not to worry, will you? I'm sure she's fine. Like I said, people come and go all the time here. It's that sort of place.'

Kate nodded, then headed back out, past the stands of over-priced plastic kitsch, back out into the dark and rain.

She dragged her feet down the dripping pedestrianised road, past the cheap takeaway joints and tacky tourist shops. Bubbles of tinny pop music engulfed her, one by one, as she headed towards the hotel. She felt utterly alone. The headache, which had been brewing behind her eyes all afternoon, pounded. She needed to eat something, take some paracetamol, then, as early as possible, shower and sleep.

She checked her phone. Nothing from Maddy. She sent her a quick message, suggesting they meet for a quick bite in the restaurant once they were both back, to share what they'd learned.

Around her, the rain was becoming more intense, sending tourists scurrying for shelter. It streamed in a steady torrent from the sagging corners of awnings and gutters. Kate hunched her shoulders and quickened her pace.

She wondered if Maddy had made progress with the police, if she'd persuaded them to take her seriously. Gino had been derisory when Maddy had suggested that he might have alerted the authorities when the girls failed to turn up for work. She could see his point. They were adults, after all.

As for her, what did she have to add? Little of any comfort. All Adrian had said was that both girls had been taking drugs, possibly dangerous ones, that Clara had fled the country and Amy had vanished.

As Kate emerged from the paved areas and went to cross the road to the hotel, her mind was leaden with thoughts of Clara. She couldn't rid herself of the pictures in her head, of her lovely daughter battered and bruised by a thug.

She thought of the image Adrian had painted, of a frightened, defeated young woman desperately fleeing to the airport with her belongings. It tortured her. She should have been there. She should have protected her. It was the least a mother could do.

A thought struck her. Adrian said he'd given Clara money. She cursed herself for not offering to pay him back. She'd just been too caught up in the story he'd told. She hesitated, looked back up the street, slick with running water. No, she wouldn't go back now. He'd be shutting up shop, anyway. She'd find him again tomorrow and put it right.

She was stepping off the kerb to cross the road to the hotel when a fast-moving bicycle rang a shrill warning. It swerved through a puddle to avoid hitting her. A cascade of flying spray splashed up across her feet and legs as she jumped back. Her body stung with the shock of cold water.

She bit her lip, then, on impulse, reached for her phone and brought up Clara's mobile number for the twentieth time that day and pressed dial. She didn't care if it annoyed her daughter, not any more. What else was she supposed to do? She pressed the phone to her ear as the ringtone beat out its distant rhythm, then clicked, unanswered, to silence.

She looked at the gleaming lights of the hotel on the far side of the road, at the river of rainwater streaming down the camber, glistening under the passing wheels of cars and bikes.

She knew what Bella would say. She could almost hear her voice.

Let go, Mum. You've got to have faith. Clara's got to make her own mistakes.

She shook her head, her saturated hair dripping rainwater. 'No,' she said aloud to the empty street. 'Sorry, Bella. You can't say that. You lost that argument the day you died.'

Besides, she couldn't dislodge a sense of dread, a feeling that Clara wasn't safe to make her own mistakes. No safer, in fact, than Bella had been.

35

Maddy looked ghostly pale, as if the lifeblood had been drained from her face.

Kate, stealing glimpses at her, wondered when Maddy had last slept. She spiked another piece of pasta with her fork and tried to force herself to eat it.

Maddy had fixed her with hard eyes as Kate had described her meeting with Adrian and repeated what he'd said. When Kate reached the end, Maddy didn't comment. The two of them picked at their food in awkward, hostile silence.

Finally, Kate dared to ask: 'So tell me about the police. How did you get on?'

Maddy wouldn't look her in the face. 'They did some sort of risk assessment. Stupid questions. Whether Amy was classed as a vulnerable person, whether she was taking medication, whether she had a history of mental illness, her last known state of mind. I kept telling them that I hadn't heard from her, that it was out of character. At the end, they sent a more senior police officer into the interview room to break the news that they weren't actually planning to do anything. Let me down gently.'

'What did she say?'

'That Amy can't be classed as a missing person. There's no reason to suspect foul play, to fear for her safety. Apparently, the fact she hasn't messaged me for so long isn't enough. She told me to think about flying home to the US and giving it more time.' Maddy snorted as she remembered. 'Her tone. She talked to me as if I were a three-year-old.'

Kate set down her fork. 'So they haven't even registered a case?'

'No.' Maddy pushed away her own bowl of pasta, still almost full. 'I guess I just have to keep bothering the hell out of them, making a nuisance of myself until they start to take me seriously.' Maddy's voice was tense. 'They clearly think I'm the problem. Wasting their time, clinging on to my poor, oppressed daughter.'

Kate said quietly: 'I don't think that.'

Maddy looked up quickly. Her eyes were red-rimmed with exhaustion. The brittle, composed exterior she'd presented when Kate first met her now seemed flecked with cracks. 'Thank you.'

Kate shook her head. 'Something about all this doesn't add up. I just have a gut feeling—' She stopped. A flash of memory. The times she'd felt this before, about Bella, about Simon. She didn't want to be right. Please God, she'd give anything to be wrong, for Clara to be safe and well somewhere in Italy, eating fabulous food and drinking great wine.

And yet she was right; she knew it.

Maddy drained her water glass, then leaned in closer too. 'After I'd seen the police, I went back to the canal, to the house.'

'And?'

'I rang on the bell again.' She paused, making sure of Kate's attention. 'Someone answered the door. An Israeli guy. Said he and his girlfriend moved in there a week ago. Never heard of Amy. Or Clara.'

Kate bit her lip, thinking. 'Maybe that proves it,' she said. 'Maybe they have both moved on.'

Maddy shook her head stubbornly. 'She'd have told me. She would.'

They were settling the bill, getting ready to leave the restaurant, when Maddy's mobile rang. Kate watched as she answered. She gave a few terse responses, confirming who she was, then tensed as she listened.

Kate couldn't hear what the murmuring voice on the other end of the line said but she saw the impact it had.

Maddy slumped in her seat. Her cheeks turned grey. A moment later, she let the phone fall from her hand onto the table. It hit the surface with a clatter and slowly spun before coming to a halt.

'What?' Kate asked.

Maddy's eyes found Kate's. They were staring, large with shock. The bill in her hand fluttered violently as her fingers shook.

'Maddy? Tell me.'

For a moment, Maddy seemed unable to speak. Her eyes had an intense, glassy glare of horror.

Kate reached for Maddy's hand, still clasping the bill, and covered it with her own, trying to stop the trembling. 'Take a deep breath. OK? In. Out. Go on, with me. In. Out.'

She watched as Maddy struggled to regain control of herself.

Finally, Maddy said croakily: 'That was the police.'

'OK.' Kate's heart started to pound. She squeezed Maddy's hand more tightly. 'What did they say?'

Maddy gulped. Her body seemed in the grip of an erratic wave of emotion, beyond her control.

Kate reached in closer and set her other hand on Maddy's shoulder. She gripped it hard, her fingers pressing through to the bone. Kate's own breath came now in sharp, painful pants. Her body seemed to sense what was coming before her mind did.

'They've found something. In the water. A body.' Maddy's voice was strangled. 'A young woman.'

36

Sleep was impossible.

Kate tossed and turned in the crisp, cool sheets. Her head throbbed. Her eyes stared sightlessly at the blank walls, the stippled ceiling. She was physically exhausted, craving sleep, but her body was rigid with tension.

Her mind chased itself in endless circles. The body – what if it were Clara? What if it were happening all over again, the way it happened with Bella? *No.* She couldn't bear it. Not again. Please, God. Life couldn't be so cruel. Clara was all she had left.

Images rose in her head. Clara's lovely face, so animated, radiant with life, now darkened and decayed, the skin turned slack, the flesh falling away from the bones.

Kate's chest heaved with panic. She sat up abruptly in bed, shaking, and snapped on the bedside lamp. The room flooded with hard, artificial light. She stared round, panting. A dull, anonymous hotel room, that was all. Nothing.

Stop it. She raked her hands heavily down her face, trying to erase the horrors. *Keep it together. Clara's in Italy, remember?*

She remembered the way colour had drained from Maddy's

face. Amy was the one missing, not Clara. Kate didn't need to go to the police about Clara because Clara was safe and well and travelling in Italy, right? She made herself nod.

Her mind slipped again to imagining the bloated horror of a drowned girl. How long had she been in the water? Maddy hadn't said. But the police had told Maddy to go the next morning to view the body, not straightaway. That must mean something. Kate shuddered. Maybe they were preparing the corpse, trying to minimise the horror of seeing it.

She swung her feet out of bed and padded through to the bathroom. Her face, hanging moon-like in the large mirror, was haggard. She couldn't *want* it to be Amy. That was too selfish, too cruel. She knew what it would mean for Maddy, what would lie in wait for her. The shock. The pain. The agonising, gnawing misery of loss, not just now, here, but clinging to her for the rest of her life. No mother deserved that.

She stared at her reflection. She knew, if she had the power to choose, Amy or Clara, she knew what she'd decide. She'd save Clara. No shadow of a doubt. But what did that make her?

She splashed her skin with cold water and rubbed at her cheeks with the snowy towel. Eleven thirty. She couldn't just lie there any longer, tormenting herself. She needed to sleep. But she couldn't. The eyes staring back at her were red-rimmed. She couldn't face getting back into bed, stewing there in her own terror.

Downstairs, the lighting in the hotel lobby was dim and the reception desk deserted. She nodded to the security guard as she passed him on her way out. The automatic doors opened with a swish, leading her into chill night air.

The streets felt different. She felt the light breeze strike her cheeks and breathed in the quiet. She was glad to be out of that claustrophobic room. She crossed the road and headed back to the cobbled precinct of the old city.

The rain had stopped. The angled stones, freshly washed by the day's drizzle, gleamed in the low light falling from street lamps. Here and there, subdued neon traced the outlines of closed shops and cafés. The only sound spilled from late-night bars and restaurants.

She walked briskly, hands in her pockets, trying to give the impression to anyone watching her that she belonged here, that she was heading somewhere with purpose. Her body settled into movement and gave her a chance to marshal her thoughts.

The body couldn't be Clara. She knew that. Clara had left Amsterdam. She'd packed her bags and fled, flown to Rome. Adrian had seen her off. She wasn't a missing person, like Amy. She was an angry young woman who had already made it clear that she didn't want contact with her mother.

She nodded, convincing herself. She reached the tourist shop where Adrian worked, its windows dark now. Ahead, the bridge rose gently over the canal. She paused, found a place between the chained bicycles and tethered flower baskets and stood against the metal railings, looking down into the inky water flowing beneath her. The sour, dank smell of the canal rose to meet her.

Her mind, let loose for a moment, fluttered back to horrors. She could almost see it, there in the softly flowing current. A drowned body. Bloated limbs. Discoloured, peeling skin, already decomposed after days of saturation in dirty water. She grimaced, feeling nausea rise and choking it down.

Stop it.

She turned away from the canal and, shivering, started to hurry back to the hotel. She shook her head, trying to rid herself of the pictures crowding there.

Kate, halfway back along the pedestrianised street, snapped back to the present. Someone was behind her. She sensed them in the darkness. Someone was there.

She twisted and peered into the shadows. Blood beat in her ears. The darkness pulsed. What was it hiding? A figure, perhaps, crouching in that deserted doorway or, there, pressed back into the mouth of that alleyway. She blinked and her vision spangled.

She turned back to the street and quickened her pace. She couldn't shake off the sense that someone was following her, watching her. By the time she reached the hotel, she was slick with sweat, her breath coming in hard, unsettled bursts.

37

Clearly, Kate wasn't the only one who hadn't slept.

Maddy's cheeks were sallow. Her eyes were dull with dread. When she tried to lift her coffee cup, it rattled on the saucer.

'I'm coming with you.' Kate spoke softly. 'If that's OK?'

Maddy shrugged. 'If you like.'

Behind them, a French family with young children were squabbling. The mother scolded one of them for knocking over his juice glass and covering their table in sticky orange.

Kate turned to look. The mother, mopping at the mess with paper napkins, had tightly pursed lips. The two children had miserably shrunken into themselves, eyes downcast, hands toying with cereal spoons.

You have no idea, Kate thought, watching the angry parents. *You don't realise how lucky you are. What Maddy or I would give to be you, to have your problems: high spirits and spilled juice.*

'It won't be her.' Maddy's voice had an unaccustomed tremor. 'It could be anyone. Any young woman. Right?'

'Of course.' Kate nodded, raised her coffee cup and downed

it. *It can't be Clara*, she told herself. *She's in Italy*. Neither of them could face food. 'You just need to check, to rule it out.'

'Rule it out. That's right.' Maddy nodded to herself. She seemed far away.

Kate checked her watch. 'We should go.'

They waited on the pavement while the concierge flagged down a taxi. When it came, Kate took Maddy's arm, helping her into the back seat as if she were a much older woman.

As the taxi weaved through the streets, Maddy said: 'It's just because she's blonde. But lots of young women are blonde. That doesn't mean anything.'

'Is that what they said?' Kate's heart stopped for a moment. *Blonde? My God*, she thought. *It might be Clara*. She lifted her hands and brought them slowly down her face, breathing hard. Her shoulders tightened.

'Didn't I say?' Maddy seemed dazed. 'This morning. The woman who called me with the details, the address, she told me. There's clothing too, of course. And jewellery. Chunky beads. But that doesn't mean anything either, right? Lots of kids wear them.'

Kate turned her head away. *Please God, don't let it be Clara*. Then, almost at once, she felt guilty. How could she be so cruel. Amy was blonde. If it wasn't Clara, it might be her.

The weather was brighter this morning. Yesterday's rain had largely evaporated, giving the pavements a freshly washed air. The pedestrians they passed seemed jaunty, cheerful about the day. Kate wanted to wind down the windows and tell them to stop it, stop being so insensitive.

'I just want to get it over with,' Maddy said quietly. Her shoulders were hunched. 'Then they'll keep looking for her, won't they? Once they know it isn't her.'

Still, images bubbled up in Kate's mind. Engorged, bloated features, waterlogged skin. She didn't know how long this body had been in the water, how well they could have cleaned it up for viewing. She didn't know whether to warn Maddy. What could she say? What if the body was too badly decomposed for Maddy to know, one way or the other? If they had to resort to DNA tests, it could take days.

Kate glanced across at Maddy. Her hands twisted at each other in her lap.

No, Maddy was Amy's mother. Whatever state the body was in, surely she'd just know. Kate felt sure she would, if it were Clara.

At the mortuary, a female official and a police officer met them. Their voices were calm and soothing.

Kate reached across and touched Maddy's arm. 'I'll come in with you.' She nodded at the officials. 'Is that OK?'

The police officer looked uncertain. 'Who are you? A family member?'

Kate stood her ground. 'I'm a friend.'

Maddy seemed far away. 'No, she's not family.' She blinked at Kate as if she were struggling to see her. 'Thank you but I think I need to do this on my own.'

Kate hesitated. She wondered if Maddy understood how distressing this might be, if it really did prove to be Amy. 'Are you sure? I wouldn't intrude. I'd just—'

Maddy shook her head. 'No. It's not Amy. It can't be. But if it were...' Her voice faltered and she took a moment to collect herself. 'I'd want to be alone with her. Just the two of us.'

The officials, listening in, gestured to Kate to wait on the wooden benches in the entrance atrium. Kate backed off, sick with anxiety, and watched them lead Maddy, her shoulders stooped, down a corridor.

Kate paced back and forth, troubled. The walls were freshly painted in a creamy beige. The smell of disinfectant hung in the air.

She stood for a while by the only feature, a tiny glassed-in courtyard that housed a spindly tree. Its base was set about with rounded stones.

Please, God, she thought. Her eyes traced the pattern of the bark, young, broken only by knots announcing new, budding branches. *Please, God, look after her. Make it not be Amy or Clara. Make it someone else.*

Time passed. She settled on a bench and hunched forward, her hot head resting in her hands, listening for the sound of an opening door, of footsteps.

She thought of the photos of Amy that Maddy had so proudly shown her. The vivacious blonde with a cheeky pout, her head pressed close to Clara's. The young woman taking a triumphant selfie on the doorstep of her new home, grinning into the camera.

When Maddy finally reappeared, Kate couldn't move. She didn't need to ask. Maddy shuffled towards her, her face bone-white. The woman at her side had taken her arm, as if Maddy might fall.

Maddy didn't look at Kate as she passed her. She didn't seem to see her there. She kept her eyes on the floor and allowed herself to be led down the corridor to an office where formal paperwork was waiting. She seemed barely aware of where she was.

'I'm sorry,' Kate murmured as she followed at a distance. 'I'm so very sorry.'

Her mind was racing. It was true, then. It was just what Maddy had feared from the start.

She shook her head, trying to disperse the thoughts that crowded into her mind.

How could Amy, a healthy, young woman, be dead? Was that why Clara had suddenly packed her bags and fled?

Her arms crept round her body as she clutched at herself. More questions followed at once. Amy was dead. But where was Clara now? And what did she know?

38

During the following days, Kate did everything in her power to stay physically close to Maddy.

When Maddy lay on her bed, her body exhausted but shaking, unable to find stillness, Kate curled in the armchair across the room, wrapped round in a blanket, and watched over her.

When day broke, she cajoled Maddy to shower, to dress in clean clothes, to be led down to the restaurant and force herself to swallow morsels of food, to leave the room and take short, dazed walks in the watery sunshine.

It was painful to see the world continue to turn, to be reminded of the indifferent bustle of everyday life in the city. Every group of tourists posing for photographs, every cyclist bowling past, jangling a bell, every sliding tram felt like an affront to the dead.

Kate quietly bore witness to the physical breakdown – the inability to sleep, to eat, to be – that came with Maddy's deep and sudden grief. The loss of a child, of whatever age, was a loss of self. Kate recognised it in a way many others could not. She'd been gripped by the same grief in those desperate, desolate days after Bella's death.

'Who should I call?' Kate asked, now and then. 'Is there anyone who needs to be here?'

Maddy just shook her head, wearily.

'There must be people you need to tell. I can help, if you like. What about Amy's father? Do you have anyone else...' Kate paused, feeling her way '...a sister or brother?'

'A sister but we're not in touch.' Maddy's eyes stayed vacant. 'And not her father. He's dead.'

Kate hesitated. 'Perhaps a close friend then? Someone who'd be willing to come over, to give you some support?'

Maddy didn't respond. Amy's jewellery, recovered by the police, lay always within her reach. A set of wooden beads, hand-painted, which Amy had worn around her neck. A matching bracelet. The wood was swollen, cracking the surface of the paint here and there. The colours, a vibrant azure and gold, had stayed defiantly bright.

'I bought them in New York,' Maddy had explained, fingering the beads in a restless caress. 'The beads are hand-carved, hand-painted. Unique. Amy had always loved them. I finally gave them to her the night she was leaving. A little piece of me, I said, to take on her travels.'

Downstairs in reception, the staff extended their rooms on a day-by-day basis, charging them to their credit cards. Kate tried not to think about the empty house waiting for her in London, the silent files on Bella's death. It was traumatic to be here, locked in with Maddy's pain, but there was a part of her that felt alive, her senses keen. She didn't want to go home.

There was something else too. While she remained in Amsterdam, she felt closer to Clara. She looked for her every time she took to the streets where her daughter must have walked. She searched for a trace of her each time she made hurried visits back to the house by the canal where Clara had so recently lived or passed Galileo's with its dark interiors, knowing Gino and his relatives were there, tossing pizzas and serving up pasta specials.

It was as if Clara had left emotional fingerprints, some essence of herself, which was fading but not yet erased.

* * *

On the fourth day, the police liaison officer, the same woman who'd assisted at Maddy's identification of the body, visited them in the hotel. She sat on an upright chair in Maddy's room, her hands neatly paired in her lap, and spoke in immaculate English.

'The post-mortem examination has been completed,' she explained. 'I have the contents here.' She drew a brown envelope from her bag and set it tactfully on the dressing table. 'It's in the Dutch language,' she said. 'I can translate it for you, if you wish?'

Maddy didn't answer. She was standing at the window, her back to the room, looking out at the street. She seemed unable to stay in one place for long.

Kate interjected: 'Perhaps the main points?'

The officer nodded and opened up a sheet of printed paper. 'The cause of death is determined to be drowning. Relevant factors include a high blood alcohol level, estimated to be around 160 milligrams per hundred millilitres. Also, the presence of MDMA—' she raised her eyes from the paper to meet Kate's sharp glance '—the drug also known as Ecstasy.' The officer paused, then lowered her voice to something nearer an embarrassed whisper. 'The forensic team has advised that, given the advanced decomposition, after so long in water, more precise analysis is problematic.'

Maddy, statue-still at the window, didn't flinch. Kate wondered if she were even listening.

'What happens next?' Kate asked.

The officer blew out her cheeks. 'We have recommended a verdict of accidental death. The coroner's report is expected later today or tomorrow.' She closed the paper along crisp folds and slipped it back into the envelope.

'And that's it?' Kate narrowed her eyes.

The officer frowned slightly. 'What do you mean?'

Kate glanced at Maddy's indifferent back. 'There'll be no investigation, no attempt by the police to find out more about how she actually died?'

The officer stiffened a fraction. 'As I have said, the police department has recommended a verdict of—'

'Accidental death,' Kate finished. 'I know. I understood that. But if it were my daughter, I'd want to know more. I'd want to know what actually happened.'

The officer took a deep breath. 'I understand how difficult this must be but—'

Maddy said woodenly to the window: 'It doesn't matter. Really. I get it.'

There was a moment's silence in the room.

Kate raised a questioning eyebrow at the officer. 'So, we get the coroner's report. Then what?'

'After that, the remains will be released.'

'Released?'

The officer's eyes darted meaningfully to Maddy. 'To the next of kin. In this case, her mother.'

'Is there someone who can give us some practical help?' Kate was beginning to feel that the officer was dismissing them, that the police had lost interest in their dead American visitor. 'Some assistance, for example, if her mother wants to repatriate the remains?'

The officer rose to her feet. 'A list of local funeral directors is also inside the envelope. I should say that they are not officially endorsed. They're just suggestions that might be of use to someone in your situation.'

'I'm not flying her home.' Maddy turned abruptly to face them. 'She wouldn't want that. And a cremation. Definitely.' She nodded to herself, coming to a decision. She looked more determined than Kate had seen her for days. 'Here. That's what she'd want. Something simple. She wasn't a believer.'

Kate blinked. She wondered if Maddy had really had time to think this through.

'It's a long way for people to come,' Kate said gently. 'I know you haven't much family but what about friends? Amy's, as well as yours. Wouldn't it be easier—?'

Maddy interrupted at once. 'I told you, her father's dead. There's no-one else, not really.' She looked down and spoke to the beige carpet underfoot. 'I've decided. I want to do this here.'

She paused as if she were gathering her strength and thinking rapidly. 'I'd like to scatter her ashes in the canal.' She turned to the officer. 'Is that allowed?'

'I believe, yes, that is allowed,' she said. 'You have to make some official report before you do that but there are companies—'

'Good.' Maddy seemed to consider the matter settled. She turned to Kate and gave a brief, emphatic nod. 'Then that's what I'll do.'

39

The boat chugged slowly down the canal.

Kate sat quietly, surrendering to it, watching the row of tall, narrow buildings slide by. Her throat was tight. It was hard not to feel strangled, both by memories of Bella's death and the tsunami of grief that had almost consumed Kate in its aftermath and, linked to it, her growing sense of estrangement from Clara.

However hard she strained to feel her, late in the evening, in the small hours of the morning, Kate had no sense of Clara's presence here. Her daughter had moved on. Clara had clearly meant what she'd said: she didn't want contact with Kate. There'd been no reply to any of Kate's messages and attempts to call. Kate brooded too about the direction her daughter was taking. She hadn't thought Clara capable of getting involved with the kind of man who could hit her, who sold drugs, however charming he might appear. She just hoped Clara was safe from him now.

Kate felt her time in Amsterdam was approaching its natural end. She had helped Maddy through the simple, minimalist cremation service she'd wanted for Amy. Now, all that remained was for the two of them to scatter Amy's ashes in a final farewell.

The sky was grey and leaden. The only people on board the cruiser were Maddy and Kate, the driver, sitting up front in a glass-walled cabin, and the sombre-faced officiant, respectful in black jeans and a black long-sleeved top. It's his scattering of the ashes outfit, Kate thought. She wondered how often he had to dig it out. She tried to imagine the boat in summer, in high season, packed full of families in short and T-shirts, kids eating ice-creams, parents in sunglasses, shielding themselves from the glint of the sun off the water.

Maddy clasped the urn in her arms, hugging it close. It was soluble, the officiant had explained. He'd given them a careful talk the previous day, slow and steady in a voice reserved for speaking to the bereaved.

'We don't advise scooping out the ashes,' he'd said. 'The winds are too strong.'

He demonstrated the recommended form with a dummy urn as he spoke.

'The best thing to do is to lift the urn carefully over the side and immerse it,' he went on. 'Press it slowly but firmly under the surface of the water, remove the lid and then simply let go.' His hands spread in a solemn pantomime of release. 'Voila! The ashes slip free and disperse naturally as the urn sinks and gradually dissolves.'

It was all eco-friendly, he'd finished. No damage to the environment. They'd take care of filing the necessary paperwork to the authorities. It was all included in the package.

'How many mourners will be present?' he'd asked. On the website, there was a whole section on catering options and a drinks list.

'Just us,' Maddy had said, giving Kate a nod. 'Just two.'

The boat nosed its way forwards through the shadows thrown by the gathering clouds overhead. It turned into the secluded, tapering canal where the girls had lived. The engine's notes deepened as it slowed, softening enough for Kate to hear the slop of water against the sides. The building towered above them, gazing down at its own reflection.

The officiant leaned in to them. 'Here?'

Maddy nodded. She moved carefully forward to the front, open part of the cruiser and sat close to the side, pressing the urn against her body.

The officiant reached out and touched her lightly on the shoulder. 'You're sure you don't want me to,' he hesitated, 'to say a few words?'

'No, thank you.' Maddy cradled the urn for a moment, as if it were a child, then eased off the lid, leaned over and gently placed it into the water.

For a moment, it seemed to hang there, the lip not yet fully submerged, staying close to the surface. Kate held her breath. Then, even as they watched, as a thin trail of ash dispersed lazily and spread in a grey mess through the moving current, the water flooded the mouth and weighted the urn, dragged it deeper as steadily as if an unseen hand had risen from the bottom and seized it, until the surface closed over its curves. A moment later, it disappeared from sight, taken back by the water.

Kate blinked. It was over. Just like that, Amy was gone. She craned forward, trying to see Maddy's face, but her shoulders were twisted away, her head inclined towards the water. She seemed to be travelling through the darkness with the vanished urn, maintaining the connection with her daughter's remains for as long as she could.

Kate tipped back her head and gazed up at the compressed windows of the top apartment. She tried to imagine Clara and Amy there, drinking coffee together, looking out at the passing boats, talking about their plans.

Maddy straightened up. The officiant nodded to her, then gave a discreet signal to the driver. The engine whined.

As they started to pull away, Kate's eyes caught on a movement, there, in the shadows, close to the apartment building. She narrowed her eyes, straining to see as the boat gathered speed, drawing them away. A figure stood against the building, watching them. She shivered. Already, even as she strained to see, the insubstantial shape blurred and became lost, blending into the reflected pattern of light and shade dappling the canalside.

* * *

'You think I'm strange, don't you?' Maddy said.

The boat was nearing the end of its journey, nosing its way back towards the docking point in the centre of the city.

Kate said, too quickly: 'Not at all.'

The two of them had barely spoken since the dispersal of the ashes. Maddy had seemed lost in her own thoughts. Kate imagined that she was beset with memories, plagued by a kaleidoscope of images of life with her daughter, which had ended here, now. Kate understood that. Seeing Maddy's quiet desperation brought back so much of her own. It made her long too, more keenly than ever, for Clara.

'It's OK,' Maddy went on. 'I get it. You think it's weird that I've given in without a fight. That I didn't make more of a fuss.' She pursed her lips. 'You'd have demanded more from the police, wouldn't you? Insisted that they launched an investigation and found out what happened.'

Kate hesitated. Of course she would have. 'Well, I didn't—'

Maddy lifted a hand to stop her. 'I've thought about little else in the last few days, believe me. At night, especially.' She took a deep breath. 'This is what I think. Amy was a party girl. Always was. Clearly, she'd had a lot to drink. She'd taken Ecstasy too. The toxicology report confirms that.'

Maddy paused for a moment, then carried on. 'Maybe someone else was there but I doubt it. Most likely she was on her own. Either way, she was heading home at the end of a great night and she strayed too close to the edge. Slipped on a mossy stone and lost her footing.' She seemed to see the scene play out in her mind's eye. 'Once she was in the water, she couldn't save herself. The current's pretty strong in places. She never was much of a swimmer. Even when she was sober.'

Kate hesitated, watching her. 'You sound very...' she reached for the right word '...accepting.'

'Do I have a choice?' Maddy pulled a wry face. 'Falling apart isn't going to bring her back.' She faced the approaching dock. Voices drifted across towards them, punctuated by a sharp laugh. Overhead, seagulls swirled and cried.

'I was brought up religious,' Maddy went on. 'Church every Sunday. I dropped it as soon as I went to college. But, I don't know, maybe it never quite leaves you.'

Kate didn't answer. She had struggled to keep believing in a God that had taken first Simon, then Bella, from her so cruelly. Now that same God had let Maddy's daughter drown.

Maddy seemed to be thinking aloud. 'I guess it was her time. It's hard to understand but, like they said, it was an accident. That's all. A tragic accident.'

The boat's engine quietened as they eased alongside the

dock. The officiant gave Maddy a respectful bow as he handed her up the steps and onto the quay.

The two women walked slowly back through the narrow streets towards the hotel, breathing in the mossy tang of the breeze blowing off the canal. Around them, the clatter and clamour of the city closed in. A crocodile of Japanese tourists passed, doggedly following a waving flag. The bittersweet scent of dope wafted out from a café. The smell slowly mingled with, then was subsumed by, the aromas of frying batter and melted chocolate emerging from pancake houses.

Maddy pushed ahead, her head down. Her steps were so even, they seemed disembodied. Kate, watching her, wondered how resigned Maddy really was to the loss of her daughter. She remembered her own desperate need to find answers after Bella's death. It had consumed her.

A tragic accident, Maddy had said. Perhaps it was helpful for her to believe that. Kate didn't. Not fully. Not yet.

She hurried to catch up with Maddy who was waiting at the pedestrian lights, just across the busy road from their hotel. A whirl of cars, vans and bicycles teemed past.

Kate's mind churned. It wasn't clear exactly when Amy had died. Her body had been in the water too long for the police to be certain. Kate couldn't help wondering about the timing. Could it be more than a coincidence that Clara had so hastily fled the country at around the same time?

Perhaps it was true that Amy had simply slipped on mossy pavement and pitched into the canal, drunk and high, with no-one there to save her. Or perhaps there was more to it than that.

In the hotel lobby, Maddy turned to her, abruptly.

'I'm flying home tomorrow.' Her tone was professional. 'It's an early start so I'll take room service breakfast. I guess we won't see each other again.'

She held out her hand for Kate to shake. It was an oddly formal gesture, after all they'd been through together, as if they were parting in the same way they'd met: as strangers. Her fingers were smooth and cool against Kate's.

'If there's anything else I can do,' Kate said. 'Anything at all.'

Maddy's eyes swung away to focus on the leaping flames of the decorative gas fire set into the wall on the far end of the lobby. They lingered there for a moment, then swung back to Kate.

'You know, I really appreciate it. The fact you came over here. The way you've hung out with me these last days. It hasn't been easy, you know?' Maddy's voice cracked. She swallowed. Kate sensed how much effort it was costing her to keep herself together. 'So, anyway, thank you. And I hope, you know, that you and Clara are together again soon.'

Maddy turned on her heel and strode off. Kate, feeling herself dismissed, watched her cross the lobby towards the far bank of lifts.

She felt unsettled. Maddy seemed to think it was over, that they'd done what they came here to do. She was behaving as if she expected Kate to head back to London, to her own life, and forget all about Amy and what had happened to her.

Kate didn't think she could. She felt too involved. Clara and Amy had been flatmates. More than that, they'd been friends.

Kate headed slowly towards the nearest lift, thinking hard. This wasn't only about Amy. It was about Clara too. She could feel it. And Maddy was right. Kate was struggling to let go and accept that it was just an accident. She just didn't know.

And that led back to Clara. Clara might be the one person with information about what had really happened to her friend. She might be able to confirm if Amy had indeed met a solitary, accidental death or if it hadn't been accidental, if she'd been the victim of a horrific crime.

Kate leaned heavily against the wall. What if Amy *had* been murdered? What then? Her stomach dropped away.

That would change everything. Because, if someone had killed Amy, Clara might know their identity. And if that were the case, then, however far her daughter had run, she could still be in danger.

40

Late that evening, Kate went for a final walk through the old city.

The drizzle that had washed the city on and off all day had left glinting puddles on the paving stones. Kate picked her way with care.

The daytime cafés had closed, leaving empty windows, stripped of cakes and breads, ghostly with low lighting. Here and there, a souvenir shop still buzzed with neon, and tourists, spilling out of one of the many noisy restaurants, browsed half-heartedly through blue and white china, T-shirts and shelves covered with brightly coloured plastic.

Gift World, grand on the corner, was closed and silent. Kate paused in front of the window display. Her eyes flicked idly across the gaudy merchandise. She imagined Clara standing beside her and the disparaging comments she'd make about commercialism, about tourist tat. She started to smile to herself, then felt her mouth buckle and choked back tears.

She decided to take a different route back to the hotel. She walked on past Gift World along the edge of the canal. It was one of the smaller ones. Boats were moored along the near side. Light spilled from some and shimmered across the water. Kate imagined the people inside, eating, perhaps, or smoking weed, judging by the herbal scent on the breeze.

She stopped and considered the scene. The boats, hugging the side of the canal, edged the view. In the distance, there was a bridge with wrought-iron railings, barely visible in the gloom. She drew out her phone and took a picture. It matched her mood. The darkness, contrasting with the shards of light. The boats, the water, made mysterious with shadow.

She strolled on, her mind wandering. She tried to work out why she felt so unsettled. Her train was booked for the next day, her bag almost packed. This time tomorrow, she'd be back home, rattling round her London home, worrying about Clara. She felt her chest tighten at the thought.

When she reached the bridge, she turned to look back. The neon shining above bars and restaurants along the main strip gave it a different aspect and she lifted her phone again and listlessly took another picture.

Her eye was caught by a couple. They were standing in the shadows, under the awning of a closed shop. Even from this distance, she could sense the tension between them. The woman, casually but smartly dressed in well-cut jeans and a coat, was gesticulating angrily, stabbing the air with a pointing finger near the man's chest. The man, slight in stature, seemed to be standing his ground. He was closer to the building and obscured by the darkness.

Kate took another picture, adding the quarrelling couple to the side of the frame. Their row gave the scene grit.

It was only much later, when she sat on her bed in the hotel and looked back over the photographs, opening up the images with her fingers to scan the details more closely, that she realised with a jolt that the furious, gesticulating woman in the expensive clothes bore an undeniably strong resemblance to Maddy.

41

DAMIAN

Amsterdam, Four Months Earlier

Damian smiled to himself.

He hadn't expected to find himself back in Amsterdam so soon but he prided himself on being a man who recognised an opportunity when it arose and, already, he was relishing the sense of his plans falling into place.

In the weeks following Dr Cushing's murder, he'd followed the news closely. Naturally, the killing had caused quite a stir but the police, in their media briefings, stayed focused on the theory that it was the result of a botched, violent burglary. Apparently, by chance, it resembled a similar attack in Queens some weeks before. Damian had raised his eyebrows when he'd read that. He never trusted to luck but, at times, it played a part.

He was confident he'd left the police little to go on. No DNA at the scene, no incriminating CCTV images, no murder weapon. All he needed was to make sure Maddy kept her mouth shut and he felt he'd taken care of that.

He'd taken a risk in telling her what he'd done. But it was a calculated one. She was a smart woman. She'd understood his threat. She had too much at stake. If he told the police everything he knew about her addiction, about the fact she'd falsified medical records and lied to officials, about the malpractice that had contributed to his mother's death – and possibly other suicides too – she'd not only face professional disgrace but probably criminal prosecution too.

And that was the least of her concerns. There was also the small matter of her daughter's safety.

And telling her had been necessary. He needed her to know how clever he'd been. That was deeply satisfying. This time, there was none of the irritation he'd felt before, after Bella's death, that he'd won a sweet victory but had no-one to admire it.

From now on, he planned to keep Amy close. He could already see a way of using her. He had her pegged as a valuable asset in furthering his broader plan. And, besides, the more he engaged with Amy, the more Maddy would understand that she could never be rid of him, never be completely safe.

He'd bided his time. Amy was busy completing her final exams, getting ready to graduate from high school. With Jed off the scene, there was no obstacle to Maddy's plan to send her travelling in Europe during her gap year and, he was gratified to see from monitoring her social media posts, the seeds he'd so carefully planted about Amsterdam were starting to bear fruit.

Since her husband's death, Maddy had been deprived of her regular supply of prescription fentanyl, and he watched as she went cold turkey. Signs that others may have ascribed to grief, he recognised as withdrawal symptoms – her clammy, pale face, the sunken eyes that suggested how fitful her sleep had become, the prominent cheekbones that hinted at vomiting-induced weight loss. He nodded approval. He'd given her a fresh start. She should be grateful.

In July, Maddy put the apartment on the market.

When Damian called her office, pretending he wanted an appointment, he learned that she had ceased to practise there. He stepped up his surveillance, befriended the young real estate agent and chatted with the removal guys to find out what she was up to.

The week Maddy was due to start her new job at the University of Michigan, he sent her a good luck card. A classy touch, he felt. She'd know exactly what he meant: you may have fled New York but you can't escape me.

Finally, in late July, Amy posted a series of photographs that gladdened his heart. He'd been unsure, until then, which way it might go, whether Maddy, despite being so diminished, would somehow find the strength to keep her daughter with her, after all.

But the seeds he'd planted had taken root. He didn't know for sure if Maddy had tried to persuade Amy to forget her travel plans and move with her to safe, sleepy Ann Arbor. If she had, Amy, always the rebel, had clearly taken little notice.

Because the photographs showed Amy, in shorts and strappy top, posing outside Anne Frank's house.

Guess where I've landed up! she'd written.

In another, she was smoking a cheeky joint in a canal-side café.

City of Sin – Amsterdam! she'd captioned it. *Perfect for a Bad Girl like me!*

Damian had booked his flight back to Amsterdam before the day was out.

42

Damian settled back into Amsterdam at once, reigniting his old drug contacts with ease and charming his way into a new season of naïve, backpacking kids.

It wasn't hard to target Amy. She acted tough on the surface but he knew she was struggling inside. She never mentioned it but she was clearly raw from the shock of her father's murder and he sensed that Maddy's fentanyl addiction had driven a wedge between them in the last year or two. For all her bravado, Amy craved love and stability. It was a vacuum he was only too happy to fill.

All that remained for Damian was to lure Clara to Amsterdam to join them.

It hadn't been hard. He'd started, once Clara had arrived in Paris, by liking her photos. Gradually, he'd started posting complimentary comments beneath them too.

He'd observed these gap-year kids for some time. Once they arrived in a foreign country, they abandoned their common sense and were quick to trust complete strangers. They seemed to think it was cool to be open to new people, to new experiences, to help each other out by pooling travel tips and information. They had young, open hearts and wanted to see the best in people. Laudable but dangerous.

When the time felt right, he took his contact with Clara a step further.

> Hey! Hope you don't mind my asking but you gotta be Bella Grosvenor's little sister – right? I knew it! You two look so alike! I knew her at King's. She was so cool. We were all gutted by what happened. Tragic.

Once she'd replied, cautious at first, he started dropping hints about Amsterdam in chatty messages to her. What an amazing city it was, so much history, so cosmopolitan, so many parties.

> You should come on down, after Paris.

He kept it light.

Gradually, as he sensed that she was getting bored of France, he stepped up the pressure.

> Hey, you! Come and join us! My girlfriend needs a new room-mate. Take a look at the apartment!

He'd posted stunning photographs of the canal at dusk and a picture of Amy, beaming and raising a glass.

> Don't worry about work – we'll fix you up!

And, just like that, the trap was sprung.

* * *

Damian saw Clara emerge in the press of travellers, streaming out of the Eurostar terminal. She was weighed down by a bulging rucksack and bags. He took a moment to observe her before she reached him. Her wavy, full hair was still the same natural blonde he remembered from when she'd been a child.

She scanned the crowd ahead, searching for him. He raised a hand.

'Hey!' She broke into a relieved grin. 'I wasn't sure you'd be here.'

'But of course.' He gave her his most charming smile and reached in to lift the heavy bags from her hands. 'I'm a man of my word.'

She seemed subdued on the bus into the old city. She answered his questions – yes, the train was comfortable, yes, she'd had an amazing time in Paris but she had been ready to move on and, yes, she was excited to be here. Her attention seemed more focused through the window than on him, as if she were absorbing every detail of the city as it came into view.

She fell silent as he walked her the final stretch from the bus stop, right along the canal to the apartment. He set down her bags, produced the spare keys from his pocket and unlocked the communal door to the building, then handed her the set with a flourish.

'Your new home awaits!'

'But I haven't even seen it yet.' She flushed slightly, gazing uncertainly at the keys in his hand. 'What if I hate it?'

'Don't worry.' He pushed the heavy front door fully open, lifted her bags again and led the way off the street, into the cool interior. It smelt of varnished wood and fried fish. 'You won't.'

Clara hung back for a moment on the threshold. She twisted

and gazed at the canal with its gently swaying, tethered house-boats, the line of bicycles chained against the railing, separated by brightly coloured hanging baskets.

'It's really something, isn't it?' Damian smiled. 'Didn't I tell you?'

She allowed herself a cautious grin. 'It really is.'

* * *

Once Clara had settled into the apartment, he insisted on taking her out into the old city for something to eat.

'I promised Amy,' he said. 'Please! She already feels bad that she couldn't meet you herself. She'll never forgive me if I abandon you. Come on.'

He felt a flush of joy as he escorted her through the bustling streets to a small pizzeria. He chose one of the outside tables that spilled out onto a cobbled patio, overlooking a softly flowing canal, then waved across the waiter for a bottle of wine and two glasses.

'If you're hungry, I recommend the *calzone*,' he told Clara who was tilting the menu into the fading light and studying it. 'Trouser leg. Did you know that?'

She looked up, surprised. 'Trouser leg?'

He grinned. 'That's what it means, literally. *Calzone*. Because of the way the dough's folded over and stuffed.' He pointed further down. 'Or if that's not your thing, the pizza capricciosa is good here too. I'll order us some calamari to start with.'

He took control and let her sit back. As the wine came and the waiter poured them both large glasses, her shoulders finally started to relax. She looked across at the canal, at the light, thin-ning and dispersing now, giving way to the lights along the edge of the water, the shine from the houseboats moored there.

They picked companionably at the bowl of calamari.

'So how did you meet Amy?'

Damian tried to look bashful. 'Well, there're two versions of that story. Which one do you want?'

Clara raised an eyebrow. 'Both, of course.'

'OK.' He sipped his wine and leaned in towards her. 'This is Amy's version.' He took a deep breath and launched into story-telling mode. 'So, she's working in Galileo's one night and this guy comes in—' he pointed to himself '—handsome, charming guy, obviously, and, by chance, he gets seated in her station. And he doesn't really understand the menu – not a word of Italian.'

Clara snorted. 'Not a word of Italian? Not even trouser leg?'

'Exactly.' He winked, complicit. 'So, she has to explain half the dishes to him and he's pathetically grateful, obviously, and they get chatting and, turns out he's a pretty slow eater so he's still finishing his dessert and wine when the place is getting ready to close and she's about to come off shift. So what does he do? He does what any gentleman would do. He takes her to a late-night bar to say thank you for all her help and, well, turns out he's just arrived in Amsterdam and she hasn't been here long and, more weirdly, they both used to live in New York. Next thing you know, they can't live without each other.'

Clara rolled her eyes. 'And the second version?'

'What? You don't buy the first version?' He gazed at her in mock-offence, reached for the bottle and replenished their glasses. 'So, OK, the second version. But it's top secret. If I tell you, I'll have to kill you. You OK with that?'

She laughed. 'I'll risk it.'

Damian gave her a thoughtful look, as if considering, then took a sip of wine to fortify himself. 'So, the truth is, well, it wasn't exactly a chance meeting.'

Clara grinned conspiratorially. 'Did you know her in New York?'

'I had kind of seen her around.' Damian thought back to the hours he'd spent tracking Amy and her parents. It seemed a long time ago.

Clara's eyes widened. 'So, you followed her out here? That's creepy.'

'It wasn't like that,' Damian protested. 'I've lived in Amsterdam before and I'd been thinking for a while about coming back. Then, I just happened to be walking through the old city one evening and recognised Amy from New York.'

'Definitely a set-up, then?'

'Well, I did make sure I got a table in her station. And all that business about not understanding the menu? Well, I have to admit, Your Honour—' he put his hands in the air in a gesture of mock-surrender '—my Italian is actually pretty good. I know my *polenta* from my *parmigiana*. And yes, even my trouser legs. But I suspect Amy's figured that out, now.'

Clara shook her head. 'You con merchant!'

He laughed. 'What can I say? Now I'll definitely have to kill you.'

She smiled back. He hadn't told Clara anything that Amy didn't already know but he'd enjoyed playing with her. People liked the idea they'd been let into a secret, however slight. It drew them in.

The waiter interrupted with their giant pizzas and the two of them focused on eating.

The darkness was steadily intensifying, bringing a chill breeze from across the water. The quiet was split by an approaching tourist boat. It glided noisily past, blazing with music and raucous chatter. Clara's hair spilled out across her face and she lifted a hand to tuck it back behind an ear. She felt him observing her and lifted her head.

Damian said quietly: 'You look so like Bella sometimes. You know that?'

That knocked her down. She didn't reply for a few moments. 'How well did you know her?'

'Not that well. We hung out a bit together, you know?'

Clara set down her knife and fork. 'What did you two talk about?'

'Well, she clearly loved London but she talked a lot about home too. Big old house, with lots of nooks and crannies. Oh, and she mentioned an attic. And it had a large garden, with rolling lawns and wilderness and a strip of woodland and – wasn't there a stream where the two of you used to play?'

Clara bit her lip and nodded. He saw the sadness in her eyes as she travelled back through the years to the childhood she'd left behind.

'And of course she mentioned your father,' he went on. 'How clever he was and funny and warm. I'm so sorry, you know, about what happened.' He hesitated, gauging her reaction. 'It was clear how much she missed him.'

'Did she—' Clara swallowed '—did she talk much about me?'

'You? Too right she did.' He had a sudden memory of the two girls running at full pelt down the garden, hair flying, Clara's short legs pumping as she struggled to keep pace. 'That's why I wanted to say hi online. It was obvious how close you two had been.'

Clara looked at her plate. Her eyes had brightened with tears.

He watched her with interest. Technically, he was her big

brother. He could lean over right now and tell her that. He could make a show of comforting her. She'd welcome it, he was sure.

He took a deep breath. No. He wasn't the one who'd set them on this track. This was their doing. Those girls who'd made sport out of belittling a ten-year-old boy. Their selfish mother who'd grabbed everything for herself and her daughters and shut him out.

Clara pulled a tissue from her pocket and wiped off her eyes.

'Sorry.' She managed a weak smile. 'I didn't mean to, you know...' She trailed off, reached for her wine glass and drank.

He lifted the bottle, ready to tip the last of the wine into her glass. When she raised her eyes, still embarrassed by her show of emotion, he gave her a reassuring smile.

'Now, we need to talk about something really important – dessert! I hope you like chocolate?'

He reset the mood and she leaned in as he started to expound the virtues of the restaurant's Torta Caprese, best eaten, in his opinion, warm with double cream and, it went without saying, a glass of Amarone. She smiled and nodded, swept along by him. Her cheeks were becoming ruddy with alcohol.

As he gestured to the waiter, he thought: *she trusts me. She's even more gullible than her sister.* He found himself almost disappointed because already he could see the way ahead and that the path he'd chosen was going to be easy.

43

KATE

London

Kate had been back from Amsterdam for a week.

She was struggling to concentrate. When she sat at the laptop, her fingers pursued internet searches on cheap accommodation in Rome or Naples. She clicked on the travel photographs, imagining Clara everywhere.

The previous night, unable to sleep, she'd hatched crazy plans to fly to Rome and start combing the city for her daughter. *At least I'll be doing something*, she'd told the shadowy ceiling. *At least I'll know I tried.*

Now, she found herself pacing the kitchen, making herself cups of tea which, abandoned, gradually went cold. She had to do something. She had to find out if Clara was OK.

When it reached five o'clock, she shrugged on her coat and headed out. She knew how angry Clara would be if Kate interfered again. But if Kate happened to bump into one of Clara's friends, out and about, well, surely then she could casually ask them if they'd heard from Clara. All she wanted was to know Clara was safe and well.

Since Clara had left school and they'd moved back to London, Clara had started hanging out with a slightly older crowd. These were the youngsters who'd gone to the music festival and, afterwards, to that disastrous house party.

Kate didn't know this new set well enough to have their contact numbers but she did remember several faces. Before Clara had moved out altogether, she'd tended to meet up with her friends in and around the fast-food joints in Leicester Square or in Covent Garden or on the South Bank.

Kate jumped on the first train, made her way up to Leicester Square and did a brisk circuit, eyes sharp. Darkness had already closed in and a cold breeze whipped across the large, open square. Kate picked her way through the meandering tourists, the foreign school groups, the filmgoers gathered around the brightly lit cinemas and the final dregs of the queue at the West End ticket booth. The acrid smell of dope mingled with the fatty scents of pizza cheese and frying oil.

Kate waded through the debris of discarded burger and kebab wrappers and peered into the fast-food outlets, one after another, searching for a familiar face. Now and then, her heart stuttered when she thought she saw one, only to realise it was just a stranger.

Eventually, she sighed to herself, stuck her hands deep in her pockets and headed on doggedly towards Covent Garden, past the theatres with their huge hoardings and displays of running lights. The piazza was one of Clara's favourite parts of London and one of Kate's too. She passed the clothing shops, blaring music, and the cafés and restaurants, their chalk blackboards shouting pre-theatre menus, and reached the cobbled approach of Covent Garden.

She'd brought Bella and Clara here so often, when they were children, to watch the street performers and poke through the market stalls and top off the afternoon with an overpriced ice-cream.

The piazza was peppered with people. Clear-plastic awnings turned the restaurants' outdoor seating into pockets of damp, warm air. The scent of burnt sugar sweetened the wind.

Kate strode back and forth across the piazza. The tourists were slowly dispersing but there was no shortage of youngsters to take their place, hanging out on corners, sitting in gaggles along the steps, gathering in knots by the pillars, smoking and gossiping and debating plans for the evening.

Kate slowed her pace and cruised by them, group by group, listening in. Twice, she pulled out her phone and showed a young woman, of about the right age, a picture of Clara.

'I'm Clara's mother,' she said in a low voice, looking each girl squarely in the eye. 'Do you know her?'

They looked wary, shook their heads and turned away.

She was about to leave and head down towards the South Bank, when a flicker of light across a shop window made her spin. Her heart quickened. She wasn't sure what she'd seen. She'd sensed Clara.

She stood still, a solitary stone in the moving flow of people, and stared into the crowd.

There, on the far side of the pedestrianised street, a young woman, head down, had detached herself from a group and was hurrying away.

Kate's breath stuck in her throat. She was wearing Clara's multi-coloured woollen hat, the one Bella had crocheted for her. She was sure she was. There was no other like it. It was ragged and rather grubby now because, since Bella's death, Clara took it everywhere with her.

Kate blinked. It had just been a glance but... her heart pounded... the young woman's height and the way she walked. She'd had Clara's stiff, slow gait, her arms motionless at her sides, her body tilting slightly forward. And that hat.

Kate shook herself into action and pressed through the crowd. It was an unwieldy mass of obstructions. Cycle rickshaws, trailing plastic rainbow streamers, blocked the side of the road. A hawker cooked up smoking chestnuts on a cart. People gathered round him to look. Kate shoved her way through.

Ahead, she spotted again the woolly hat bobbing in the throng that gathered around the entrance to the underground station. It was a swirling surge of people, pressing onto the concourse, feeding lines through the ticket barriers. If she didn't rush, she'd lose her.

'Clara!' She screamed her daughter's name as loudly as she could. A couple in front of her paused and turned to stare. She didn't care. She broke into a run, pushing past the meandering tourists, clawing her way forward.

She reached the entrance to the station. The crowd was dense, pressing in tightly around her, refusing to give way.

'Excuse me. Please. I need to—'

No-one parted to let her through. She tried to force herself forward. A burly man in a padded jacket turned on her and swore under his breath. She didn't recognise the language but she understood the message.

By the time she reached the barrier, she'd lost sight of the young woman. She took a slow, crowded lift down to the platforms and turned randomly left. A train was in the station and passengers were jostling their way into busy carriages. She ran the length of it, scanning the interiors for a sign of Clara. The doors banged closed and the train drew noisily away, leaving the hanging smell of age-old dust.

She turned on her heel and ran in desperation against the arriving flow of fresh passengers, back down the platform and across to the opposite one. This too had recently emptied. There was no sign of her.

Kate sat heavily on a bench and stared at the glossy travel poster on the curved far wall. Her breath came in hard, painful pants. The colours of the beach, the sky, the laughing family's giant faces, were lurid.

She felt utterly depleted. Had it been Clara, that vanishing figure in the crowd? She'd felt so certain but now, on the dirty platform, surrounded by gaggles of tourists who were pointing at the flash of a rat across the sunken track, she doubted herself. And yet. That hat with its uneven stitches, its swirling colours. Surely it was Clara's. If only she'd managed to get closer, to see her face.

Kate boarded the next train and headed wearily home. Without conviction, she typed out a text to Clara:

> Was that you, in Covent Garden? Just want to know you're OK. Please reply. Love you so much xxx

As the train rattled along, she stared at her own flickering reflection in the window. Her cheeks were pale. Her hair was in disarray. Her eyes were so bright, they looked feverish.

44

That night, when Kate finally dozed, she had the nightmare.

Clara, a little girl again, was racing away from her through the crowd. However hard Kate chased after her, lungs bursting, she couldn't catch her, couldn't quite reach her. But she needed to. Clara was in danger, terrible danger; she knew it.

Kate woke abruptly at three in the morning with a dry mouth. The fading horror of the nightmare morphed into her memory of chasing the young woman through the Covent Garden crowd the evening before.

In the bathroom, her face in the mirror was clammy and pale. She checked her phone. Nothing. She tried to imagine Clara, wherever she was. She just willed her to be well and happy and sleeping soundly. She tapped out another text to her:

> Sweetheart, are you back in London? Please tell me. No need to meet, if you don't want. Just tell me you're OK. Please. Love you so much. Xxx

She pressed send with little hope of a response, then made

herself a coffee, drew back the curtains and sat, propped up in bed, sipping it and losing herself in the mottled patterns of the night sky.

Too many pictures were jostling for attention in her mind. Memories of Bella. Images of Clara.

Underneath them, her mind swam with unanswered questions. She needed to know if she had seen Clara in Covent Garden or not. She needed to ask Clara what really happened to Amy in Amsterdam.

On top of everything else, Kate still struggled to believe that Clara would get involved with a man who sold illegal drugs, let alone a violent and abusive one. Could Kate really know her own daughter so little? Kate didn't have any illusions that Clara was a saint. She just knew how much Clara despised people who peddled drugs.

Of course she did. Clara remembered only too keenly how her big sister had lost her life.

Kate pulled on a dressing gown, made herself another coffee, found a fresh A4 pad and powered up her laptop. She sat in front of the screen for some time, staring sightlessly at the stories cascading through her newsfeed.

She tried to push through her anxiety about Clara and shake her reporter's mind into action. She picked up her pen and wrote across the top of the pad what she knew.

Amy Price, found dead in Amsterdam. Accident (or possibly murder?)

Underneath, she wrote, less certainly: *Clara. Friends with Amy. Fled to Rome – abusive boyfriend? Knows something about Amy's death? Now back in London?*

She considered what she'd written, her mind buzzing. She had so little evidence but she couldn't rid herself of the idea that there was a connection between what had happened to the two girls. She took a long slow breath, thinking. She needed more information.

She typed *Amy Price* into her search engine and pressed return. At once, a host of references unfurled.

A minor celebrity with the same name had made the news some years ago with her 'brave battle' against cancer. Half a dozen sites carried articles and photos of her.

There were red-carpet photos and studio shots of a glamorous-looking actress with the same name.

Finally, as Kate continued to scroll, a headline swam into view.

Heart doctor stabbed to death in Upper West Side

Kate clicked through to the report, her heart pumping. It was poorly written but it set out the main facts.

Dr Arthur Cushing, a leading cardiologist, has been found dead, in the family's apartment on the Upper West Side, with multiple stab wounds to the chest. A police spokesman confirmed signs of a break-in. His wife, Dr Madelyn Price, a well-known psychiatrist in the city, and their teenage daughter, Amy Price, were not at home at the time of the assault.

Kate read on. A neighbour described the family as '*delightful*'. In the comments below, colleagues paid tribute to Dr Cushing, saying he was a devoted and inspirational practitioner. One called it a tragic, senseless loss. *Our thoughts are with Dr Cushing's family.*

The report was accompanied by an uninspiring external shot of the apartment building, cordoned off by police tape, and an inset thumbnail photo of Dr Cushing.

Kate lifted her eyes and stared at the wall. Her thoughts danced on the paintwork.

Her father's dead. That was all Maddy had said.

Kate hadn't pursued it. She'd been too focused on Amy's death and ushering Maddy through the funeral. If Kate had reflected on it at all, she might have imagined cancer or a heart attack, maybe a road traffic accident. She'd assumed it was a death that had taken place years ago, not this spring. And not this. Not a botched armed robbery and a frenzied knife attack.

Kate could hardly breathe. Maddy had lost her husband just months before she'd lost her daughter. It wasn't so different from what had happened to Kate. Only Maddy didn't have a second daughter to become the focus of her life. She'd gone from being at the centre of a family to being alone.

Kate wrapped her hands round her coffee cup and brought it to her lips, thinking about Maddy and everything she'd been through. A fresh understanding slid into place. No wonder Maddy had behaved strangely at times. She remembered the way Maddy had rushed ahead with Amy's cremation, without family or friends. Maddy must have been out of her mind with grief. The second loss must have rekindled the horror of the first, the brutal murder of her husband.

Kate set down her cup and turned her attention back to her laptop. She searched *Arthur Cushing death* and read everything she could find about his murder. Both Maddy and Amy seemed to have watertight alibis. Maddy had been speaking at a conference all evening. Amy was with a group of students at a friend's apartment until late.

There was no indication that anyone had been arrested. There were references to the police investigation, to a possible link with a similar attack in Brooklyn, but nothing about a particular suspect. The crime scene must have been left pretty clean. It had been a brutal murder and she sensed from the coverage how much it had shaken an affluent neighbourhood.

How hard for Maddy too, that no-one had been charged. She nodded quietly to herself. Maybe this explained why Maddy had been so determined to agree that Amy's death was an accident. The prospect of a second, unsolved murder of someone she loved must have seemed impossible to bear.

Kate clicked on Dr Cushing's photographs. He was a good-looking man, on the brink of middle age. His dark hair was starting to recede at his temples and forehead. His shoulders were broad and his intelligent brown eyes gazed directly at the camera. They must have made quite a couple, Maddy and her husband.

A memory rose. She thought of the woman she'd photographed in the darkness on her final evening in Amsterdam. A woman caught up in an intense, emotional argument with a man. A woman who looked very much like Maddy. Except Maddy had said she'd never been to Amsterdam before. She'd implied she didn't know anyone there. Why would she lie?

Kate turned the thought over in her mind. She went back to her laptop and entered a fresh search, this time, for Dr Madelyn Price. Studio portraits of Maddy popped up, clearly designed for professional use. The most recent one had first appeared nearly two years ago.

Kate was struck by how much younger Maddy looked then. Her skin looked fresher and her smile whiter than the woman Kate had met in Amsterdam. It wasn't only the physical change that was so evident. The Maddy of two years ago looked warmer. Happier. It was like reaching back to a glimpse of a woman in her prime, before life had reared up and hurt her.

Kate came across the press notice issued by the University of

Michigan, announcing Maddy's appointment there. It trumpeted her previous experience as a leading clinical psychiatrist in private practice in New York and highlighted a series of papers to which she'd contributed. It was illustrated by the same headshot that Kate had seen on the university's website when she was sitting in Amsterdam, waiting to meet Maddy.

Kate turned from her screen and looked out of the picture window at the emerging landscape of chimneys, sloping roofs and gardens. Dawn was already breaking. A pigeon landed on the nearest roof in a flurry of feathers and clattered along the tiles to the guttering that edged it. It perched there, its head darting nervously forwards, then again drawing back, as if it were contemplating the drop into nothingness.

New York to Michigan. Private practice to university employee. It was a curious move.

People did sometimes make dramatic changes after a major loss; Kate knew that. She could certainly understand why Maddy might have felt the need to sell the apartment where her husband had just been murdered. But, even so, it was a bizarre career move.

On the surface, at least, it looked as if Maddy had abandoned an established, affluent client base in New York to oversee a student counselling service in Michigan. The University of Michigan was prestigious but not Ivy League, and Ann Arbor, although a well-heeled campus, was a long way from the glitz and glamour of Manhattan.

Outside, the pigeon, disturbed, took clumsy flight.

Kate pushed back her chair and got to her feet. She started to pace up and down the study. Her mind, searching for answers, groped through empty air.

A feeling dogged her. A suspicion that there was some connection between Dr Cushing's violent murder and Amy's death, just months later, in Amsterdam. A connection too between the tragedies that had befallen this glamorous American family and her own life, her own broken family.

She suspected it. She was grasping for it. But, so far, it felt frustratingly beyond her reach.

45

'Why didn't she tell me about her husband?'

Kate gave Rosa a darting look. They were settled in their usual places in the coffee shop, across from each other. The flow of high street traffic, both people and cars, stopped and started on the other side of the plate-glass window.

Kate went on, keeping her voice low: 'He'd just been murdered, for heaven's sake. Don't you think it's odd she didn't mention it?'

Rosa stirred her coffee, mixing the sprinkled chocolate powder into the froth of milk. 'Maybe it was too difficult to talk about,' she said. 'Precisely because it's so raw.'

'I still think she'd mention it,' Kate said. 'It was clearly a high-profile case. The police must have come under a lot of pressure to catch someone.'

Rosa shook her head. 'It's awful, Kate. And dreadful for her, for Maddy, to lose her husband and then her daughter so suddenly. I can't imagine.' She paused, feeling her way. 'But that doesn't mean the two deaths are linked. Is that what you're suggesting?'

'I'm not sure what I'm suggesting.' Kate spread her hands and carried on. 'I just think it's quite a coincidence.'

Rosa blinked. 'Do you think Maddy's guilty in some way?'

Kate had wondered that, at first, but she slowly shook her head. 'I don't see how she can be. By all accounts, she had a clear alibi. It's hard to believe she's anything but a grieving wife in shock.'

Rosa lifted her cup to her lips and sipped. 'So what's your point?'

Kate sighed. 'I don't know. Something just feels off, that's all. And why this sudden move to Michigan?'

Rosa considered. 'You said yourself there was a lot of media attention. Maybe she wanted to escape. Her daughter's finishing school and setting off on her travels. Her husband's gone. Why not go somewhere quiet and safe?'

'Something's going on; I can feel it,' Kate said. 'It's more than just grief.'

Rosa didn't answer for a moment. Her eyes slid away from Kate's and studied the table.

Finally, she said: 'Kate, don't you think you need to let go of all this? I'm concerned that what happened in Amsterdam, to that girl—'

'Amy.'

'Yes, to Amy. I think it brought back a lot of intense feelings for you. Unresolved feelings. About Bella.'

A couple pushed past them with a laden tray, forcing their way through to the next table. Kate watched them take their seats and settle in. The woman lifted their cups and plates off the tray and set them out on the tabletop while her partner shed his coat.

Kate bit her lip. 'There's something else. About Clara.' She hesitated. She'd been trying to decide all morning whether or not to confide in Rosa. 'I think I saw her, yesterday afternoon, in central London.'

Rosa's eyes widened. 'What?'

Kate told her about the fleeting figure, about Clara's distinctive hat and the way she'd walked, about the chase through the crowds and the fact she'd finally lost her in the tube system.

When Kate finished, Rosa sat very still.

Kate said: 'I know what you're going to say. That I imagined it. That there could be another hat just like Clara's.' Kate's voice rose in frustration. 'Except Bella crocheted it. You must remember it? It's multi-coloured because she was using up odd balls of wool and it's a bit, well, lopsided.'

Rosa said quietly: 'But you were some distance away, right? And it was dark.'

'Yes.' Kate tried not to let her frustration show. 'But even so—'

Rosa reached for her hand and gave it a light squeeze. 'You might have been mistaken. But even if you're not, it is perfectly reasonable for Clara to come back to London for a while. She's got a lot of friends here.' She looked pained. 'If she is back and she hasn't been in touch with you, well, I know this is going to be hard to hear but I think that means she really doesn't want to see you right now.' Rosa added more gently: 'Try not to assume the worst.'

Don't assume the worst. Kate had heard all that before. Whenever she'd fussed about Simon's health. When she'd been anxious about Bella and how she'd adjust to university life. Look how well that all turned out. Her shoulders hunched. The silence between them stretched.

Rosa gave her friend a long, thoughtful look. She hesitated, choosing her words carefully. 'Clara's said very clearly that she wants a break from you while she's travelling. Wherever she is, back in London or somewhere overseas, I really think you should respect that.'

Kate couldn't answer for a moment. It was too late for that. Her mind was already made up. She wouldn't let go of this. She couldn't. She had to satisfy herself that Clara was OK.

'You're right,' she managed to say aloud. 'Of course I respect that.'

46

From then on, Kate staked out Covent Garden, in the hope of catching sight of Clara.

When it was dry, she wrapped up warmly and positioned herself on a bench in James Street, at the back of the piazza. She usually found herself between a street entertainer and a silent statue.

When it rained, she took shelter in a nearby café and grabbed a place as near the windows as possible. She nursed a cup of coffee and scanned the faces passing between the shields of unfurled umbrellas.

By the fourth day, Kate was finding it harder to quash rising doubts that this might be a futile exercise. As the hours passed, she sat in the café with determination and peered through steamy windows. The skies were leaden and a light rain had fallen on and off all day. Tourists hurried past at speed, heads down, shrouded in voluminous plastic ponchos.

At five o'clock, the weak sunlight gave way to darkness. The pavements glistened and shone with the reflections of coloured lights from the shops. The crowd thinned. The day trippers were heading wearily back to their hotels and Airbnbs for hot showers and cups of tea. The evening theatre and opera crowd had yet to venture out.

Kate sipped the cold dregs of the coffee she'd husbanded for the last two hours, then packed her bag and shrugged on her coat. She mustn't give up, she told herself. She'd give it another few days, at least.

She emerged from the café and stood for a moment under the awning. The drizzle sparkled in the spreading cones of light falling from the street lamps. She tasted the dampness in the air.

As she turned to thread her way down through the piazza, a hurrying figure caught her eye. It was some distance away, down a broad street lined with shops and restaurants. It was the hat. Bobbing, multi-coloured and ragged around the edges. It looked so like Clara's.

Kate stared. She couldn't see the woman's face. She couldn't tell if it was Clara. But she was Clara's height and build and, when she turned and passed close to a brightly lit shopfront, her hair shone. It was Clara's colour. And the way she walked, that stiff, forward-leaning gait.

Kate was too far away to have a hope of being heard. Instead, she threw her bag on her back and broke into a run, dodging and weaving through oncoming pedestrians. It wasn't easy. This was a busy, narrow stretch of pavement and tightly packed. Hurrying people, heads bowed against the wet, struck her in the face with the spokes of their umbrellas as she tried to pass.

Every now and then, intent on closing the gap, she lost sight of the young woman and had to stop and crane through the crowd to catch sight of her again, then, sure of her direction, renew her running.

At the far end of the road, the young woman seemed to become aware of her. She broke into a lumbering run, crossing the busy road ahead without proper care and darting down an alleyway.

Blood pumped in Kate's ears. Was it Clara? She was still too far away for Kate to be sure. Had she recognised Kate? Was that why she'd started to run? Kate was panting hard, struggling to ignore a stitch biting her side. She didn't have the breath to shout, even if she'd thought Clara would hear.

She swarmed down the alleyway in pursuit, jumping over strewn rubbish and trying to ignore the stench of stale urine and rotting mulch. At the far end, she hit a main road. The vista opened out. She stood there, hands on hips, looking this way and that, trying to pick up the trail. Had Clara darted into a building, a shop or café? Had she—

Further down the pavement, passengers were streaming onto a double-decker bus. Kate caught the bobbing movement of the woolly hat. As Kate watched, helpless to stop her, the young woman heaved herself heavily onto the bus step and disappeared into the brightly lit interior.

Somehow, Kate sprinted. Ahead, the bus doors hissed closed. The bus revved and moved forward, nosing into the stream of traffic. Kate was almost level with its back as it pulled away, gliding in a glut of engine fumes towards the traffic lights.

Turn red. Now. Please.

Her plea went unheeded. The lights stayed green just long enough for the bus to sail through, gathering speed as it drew away. Kate, hammering down the pavement recklessly towards the junction, had a final glimpse of the young woman as she swayed her way down the crowded aisle. Kate saw her find a seat and steady herself to sit down. As she moved, her coat flap fell open.

Kate ground to a stop. The image of what she saw seared

into her. She gasped for breath, feeling suddenly weak in the legs and very sick.

There was no mistaking that shape, the soft, hard curve of the young woman's lower belly. It told Kate everything. The woman she'd been chasing looked about four months pregnant.

There, in the middle of the rainy street, Kate's mind counted feverishly back. At the end of August or early September, where had Clara been? Paris? Who had she been with? Kate shivered. Her daughter had told her so little.

Kate, shocked to the core, couldn't move.

Was that why Clara was refusing to talk to her, why she'd bolted at the sight of her?

She stared at the disappearing outline of the bus.

She was struggling to take it in. Her legs juddered.

Was it really possible that she was on the way to becoming a grandmother?

47

'Kate, I'm so sorry.'

Rosa looked up from Kate's phone screen. Her eyes were full of compassion. Their cooling coffees sat on the table between them.

Through the huge café window, life was carrying on as if it were a normal day. A mother doggedly pushed a buggy with a red-faced, screaming toddler braced against the frame. A young man, smartly dressed, a takeaway cup in his hand, stepped off the pavement to circle them and hurry on. Kate's mind was numb.

Rosa said gently: 'When did it come?'

Kate took back her phone and looked again at the message there. 'Just after seven this morning.' Two hours ago. 'But what if it isn't her? What if someone's hacked her account?'

Kate reread the message. She already knew it almost by heart.

Stop following me. I don't want to see you. I know you won't approve but I'm having this baby. I want it. I'm not alone – the father's with me. If you really want to help, send money, just to see me through. I'll pay you back someday. But please – stop trying to contact me. I know it's hard but you need to leave me alone. At least for now. Love ya, C

Underneath, there was a second message with details of where she should send the money: to the Travelex desk at Heathrow Terminal 3, landside. There was a pick-up time of 1600 today, in seven hours' time.

US dollars, in my name, Mum.

Rosa was watching her closely. 'Do you think it might be a scam?'

'I don't know. It's from her number. And that's how she always signs off. *Love ya.*' Kate's voice faltered and she took a deep breath. 'Rosa, I can't be sure. She was too far away. But it really did feel like her. The girl in the street, getting on the bus. And that hat.'

'It's not like Clara to ask you for money.' Rosa looked concerned. 'She's always so independent.'

Kate remembered the time Clara had walked all the way home from a party miles away because she'd lost her wallet and didn't have the cash for a taxi. She'd finally reached home at two in the morning, exhausted. Kate had been incredulous when she found out. *Why didn't you let me know? I could have picked you up.*

Clara had given her a cool look. *Don't fuss, Mum. I was fine.*

She remembered the way Clara had refused to take money

when she packed her bags and moved out, refused to let Kate subsidise her plans to travel.

Independent? Yes, Rosa was right. On the other hand, Clara had never been pregnant before.

Rosa looked thoughtful. 'Is there some way you can check it out?'

Kate pulled a face. She'd been thinking the same thing since she'd first read the text. 'How?'

Rosa leaned forward: 'What about the police?'

'I doubt they'd be interested.' Kate shook her head. 'Especially when the alleged scam hasn't even happened yet. Clara's an adult. If they tried to open a case file on every young person who asked their parents for money, they'd explode.'

'So what are you going to do?'

Kate reached for her coffee. She felt sick but sipped it anyway, without thinking.

What was she going to do?

The noise of the café, the tinny music and low voices, the hiss of the steam machine, seemed to fill the silence between them. Rosa sat still, watching her.

When Kate had first read the text, early that morning, she'd found herself in Clara's bedroom. She'd curled on the floor, her back against Clara's bed, and breathed in the fading scents. The musk perfume that Clara loved. The fragranced hand and face creams lined up on her desk.

Mostly, since Clara had left, Kate kept the bedroom door closed. It hurt her too much to see inside. Clara hadn't lived in the London house for long but, even in that short time, she'd made her mark. Her room had teemed with life – with noisy rock music and stomping footsteps, raucous laughing when Clara was on a call to one of her many friends or the low tones of Clara's narrative voice, barely audible when Kate passed on the landing, a signal that her daughter was recording herself making some sort of video to post on one of her group chats.

Now it was too empty, too dead. Kate ran a cloth round the surfaces each week, lifting objects that hadn't been touched since the previous week. At night, as she went to bed, she went into the room, closed the curtains and said goodnight to the daughter who wasn't there. Each morning, she went in again to draw back the curtains and murmur to the vacant bed: *Good morning, my love, wherever you are. Love you.* She did the same in the spare room too, imagining Bella was there. She'd had to keep that ritual quiet when Clara was still at home.

Sitting there, desolate, Kate had thought about Maddy. She'd wondered what Amy's bedroom was like, whether Maddy sat inside it, alone, as she was now doing. An image came to her of Maddy, hunched forward in the boat, lowering the urn into the water. The grey streak as the ashes had dispersed, expanding as they spread through the canal.

Now, Clara was having a child of her own. Kate should be with her, supporting her, getting ready to welcome her first grandchild into the world. Instead, Clara had forced herself to ask for money – Kate knew how hard that must have been for her – and made it clear that she didn't want to see her mother, to speak to her, to hear from her, at least for now.

Kate had wrapped her arms round her knees as the tears came, hugging herself, and slowly, she'd begun to rock.

Now, Rosa reached out and touched Kate's hand, bringing Kate back to the present, to the crowded coffee shop.

'Don't feel rushed into anything,' Rosa said. 'Maybe there is a way of checking out if it's for real.'

'I can't wait. What if it's true and she's asking me for help and I let her down?' Kate's cup trembled in her hand, sending ripples across the surface of the coffee. She blinked back tears.

She ached to hold Clara, a pain so intense it was overwhelming. She'd let her daughter down before, after Bella died. She hadn't read the signals, hadn't been there for her. She mustn't let that happen again.

Kate swallowed hard and carried on: 'This might be my chance to prove myself to her. To show her I can give her what she needs, without asking questions. To show her how much I love her. If it is and I miss it, I'd never forgive myself.' She shook her head. 'I don't suppose she'd forgive me either.'

Rosa nodded slowly, then looked at her watch, calculating. 'If you do decide to do this, you should probably get on with it. They'll need a few hours' notice.' Rosa paused and lowered her voice. 'Are you OK for cash? I can transfer some to you right now, if you like. A few thousand?'

Kate managed a smile. 'Thank you but I think I'm OK. My balance is pretty healthy.' She hesitated. 'I was thinking maybe ten thousand dollars?'

Rosa looked taken aback. 'That seems a lot.'

Kate shrugged. 'If it is Clara and she does need help, even that won't go very far.'

She pulled out her phone and set about ordering the dollars, to be picked up by Clara at the Heathrow Travelex desk that afternoon.

When she'd finished, Rosa said: 'Of course, you could go to Heathrow yourself. Try to intercept her when she goes to collect it? She might not want to talk to you but at least then you'd be sure it was her.'

'You read my mind.' Kate gave a wry smile as she reached for her bag. 'That's exactly what I'm planning to do.'

48

It took Kate two hours to get out to Heathrow's Terminal 3. She hurried up to the Travelex desk near the entrance to security and tried to explain to the woman there that she'd ordered ten thousand US dollars in cash for her daughter to collect in a few hours' time.

'I just want to be sure it's all gone through OK,' Kate lied. 'I've never done this before and I'll be in such trouble with my daughter if I've messed it up.'

The woman gave a cautious smile as she took down the details and looked up the order. 'Yes, it's all been processed. It's been issued in your daughter's name so she'll need to come to the desk in person to collect it. We'll need ID. Her passport will do fine. Is she flying today?'

Kate hesitated just a fraction. 'I think so.'

'No problem.' The woman nodded, dismissing her.

Kate grinned. 'She's eighteen now but I still worry about her. I guess I always will. Do you have children?'

'Three.' The woman looked Kate in the eye as if she were seeing her for the first time. 'All girls.'

'Mine are girls too.' Kate forced herself to use the present tense. This wasn't the time to start explaining about Bella. 'Clara's my youngest. Just finished school. She's spending a year travelling, lucky thing. She's having a great time but she's giving me grey hairs, wondering what she's getting up to.'

'Don't!' The woman grimaced. 'My oldest is thirteen next month. Thirteen going on thirty, you know? And sassy with it.'

They exchanged a sympathetic glance, mother to mother, then the woman bent her head back to her work.

Kate felt herself dismissed. She nodded to the row of seats a little further along the concourse. 'I'll wait over there. I really want to catch her before she goes, to make sure everything's OK. Well, and to say goodbye.' She hesitated, trying to gauge how much the woman would be willing to do for her. 'Could you call me over, if she comes? In case I doze off or something. I don't want to miss her.'

The woman shrugged, without looking up.

A smartly dressed man appeared by Kate's side, waiting to be served, and the woman turned her attention to him.

Kate settled in one of plastic bucket seats and watched the movement of travellers back and forth across the concourse.

She was probably in for a long wait but she hadn't wanted to risk missing Clara. If Clara knew her mother at all, she must surely have predicted that Kate would show up in person and, with things as they were, she might be looking for a way to avoid that meeting.

Kate tried to distract herself by letting her thoughts wander. Her eyes drifted, half-seeing, over the striding business travellers, the young couples, the harassed parents tugging along kids astride wheeled cases. Slowly, painfully, time passed.

They'd had some wonderful holidays, over the years. Simon

had always loved travelling as a family. He used to get as excited as the girls did.

Until she'd met him, Kate had never liked flying. Her memories of airports, when she still travelled for work, were of dashing to catch economy flights, a stressful scramble that came from being sent at the last minute to cover some breaking news story on a low budget. Her time on board planes usually involved hastily scanning through printouts and notes to mug up on facts and, the moment the plane landed, her phone was back on as she picked up messages and made frantic calls to get information or arrange interviews.

It was something Simon had never been able to understand. For him, airports were luxurious havens, with business-class lounges and a chance to catch up with himself in peace.

He'd tried to instil the same ethos in the girls. They'd come to love standing at the spectators' windows while Simon, crouching between them, pointed out what was happening: cargo and luggage being loaded or unloaded, catering trolleys being winched on board, pilots in the cockpit getting ready for take-off.

Kate felt a sudden shiver. She thought of Clara and her unborn child. Kate was still struggling to adjust to the idea of her daughter, her little girl, as a mother. It seemed impossible. It seemed only moments ago that Clara was a child herself, clutching her battered bear under her arm, a mini-rucksack on her back with snacks and crayoning, pointing out aircraft at her father's side.

Kate took a deep breath and checked her watch. She sat up a little straighter, her eyes restlessly scanning the busy terminal. Soon, she thought. Her body was tight with anticipation. She could almost feel her arms around Clara. She could almost sense the relief of holding her close in a tight embrace.

I'm OK about the baby, she'd say. *I love you. I want to support you. If you want it, I want it too. As long as you're safe and happy, that's all that matters.*

Her eyes filled at the thought of seeing Clara again and she pulled out a tissue and brushed her tears away.

'Excuse me!' The woman at the Travelex counter was waving to her, calling.

Kate jumped up and ran across, heart thumping, scanning passing faces for a sign of Clara. 'I haven't missed her, have I?'

'I'm sorry.' The woman looked embarrassed. 'I just checked for you and apparently she's already picked it up.'

Kate felt the floor dip and roll in front of her. How was that possible? She'd been right there, all this time. How could she have failed to see her? 'But, I don't understand, I—'

'Airside.' The woman gave her a sympathetic look. 'Just five minutes ago. It's here, on the system.'

Airside? Kate's arms felt cold and empty. Clara had seemed within reach. Now she was again impossibly far away. She choked back tears, tried to gather her thoughts.

'But it was definitely going to be collected here,' Kate said. 'You checked the order, remember?'

The woman gave a brisk nod. 'Let me call through.' She picked up an internal phone and cupped her hand round the receiver as she murmured in a low voice. Kate caught Clara's name in the muffled conversation.

Afterwards, the woman put down the phone and leaned across the counter to Kate.

'Apparently, your daughter forgot she had to collect it land-side and went through security. My colleague said she turned up at the airside desk in quite a state, sobbing. Obviously, once you've passed through security, that's it – you can't go back.' She reached out a hand and patted Kate's arm. 'Don't worry. In the end, we sorted her out. We don't make a big thing of it but we always keep a good stock of dollars in the safe for walk-ups.' She gave a final pat and lifted her hand again for a thumbs up. 'So she's OK! She's got it!'

Kate hesitated. 'Is there any way I can be certain it was really her?' She saw the other woman's face cloud. 'I'm silly, I know, I'm just such a worrier. I'm really sorry.'

'I really can't—' The woman gave Kate a sharp look, then sighed and said more quietly: 'Let me have a look.' She set to work on her keyboard. After a few moments, she turned the screen so Kate could view it. 'Here. There's the scan of her passport – see? That's who picked it up. Is that your daughter?'

Kate looked. Her breath stopped in her throat. She and Clara had gone to the shop together to have that picture taken, about three years ago. It felt like another life. Clara had been a gawky fifteen-year-old girl, now she was an eighteen-year-old woman. Simon had been alive then and Bella too. They'd been a family. How could Kate possibly have imagined, when she'd paid for that photo, the circumstances in which she'd see it now? She bit her lip and nodded.

'Well, then.' The woman gave her a thoughtful look. 'I don't blame you for worrying. It goes with the job description, doesn't it? Being a mum.' She hesitated, as if wondering how much more to say. Something in her eyes made Kate wonder if the colleague on the airside desk had hinted that Clara was not only tearful but also pregnant.

Kate's mind was still churning. Something felt off. It could have been a genuine mistake. Of course it could. But what if it hadn't been? What if Clara – or someone with her – had spotted Kate here, waiting, and decided on a hasty change of plan? If they'd decided instead to head through security and try to bluff it out with the airside desk, to see if they could swing the cash there? Kate started to shake.

She clutched at the woman's sleeve. 'Was she travelling with anyone?'

The woman looked suddenly uncomfortable, as if Kate had gone too far and she was regretting whatever lines she'd already crossed for her. 'I'm afraid my colleague didn't say. Now, if you'll excuse me—'

She gestured to a young couple who'd appeared behind Kate and were waiting patiently to be served.

Kate leaned in closer. 'Please.' She heard the note of desperation in her voice. 'Did she scan her boarding pass too? I need to know where she's going.'

The woman looked at her with an expression of pity. 'We don't scan boarding passes, I'm afraid. Not for pre-paid collections. Only passports. And frankly, even if we did—'

She hesitated. Her eyes moved on to the young couple, then, a moment later, flicked anxiously back to Kate. She seemed to read the despair there. She said in a low voice: 'Look, my colleague did say your daughter was in a hurry. She said she couldn't wait because she was boarding in twenty minutes.' She looked at her watch. 'That was maybe ten minutes ago.'

Kate snatched up the woman's hand, kissed it, then turned and ran.

The departures board showed two flights that were due to start boarding from Terminal 3 in the next ten minutes. One was to Beijing. The other was to Detroit.

Kate nodded to herself. There was a reason Clara had asked to have the cash in US dollars and she doubted it was to fly to China.

As for Detroit, there was one link that came to mind immediately. It was a tenuous connection and the thought of it wounded Kate.

Clara clearly didn't want to be around Kate at the moment but it was possible she was turning to someone else's mother. Someone based less than an hour's drive away from Detroit, in the leafy University of Michigan town, Ann Arbor.

49

It had been years since Kate had flown into Detroit.

That had been in her journalism days, before the girls were born, when she'd been working on an investigative assignment about the collapse of vehicle manufacturing in the area and the fallout for the city. From what she'd seen so far, the city didn't look any richer than it had then.

Kate made sure the doors of her rental car were locked before she drove steadily through the suburbs, sipping a strong takeaway coffee in the effort to stay awake and taking care not to hit any trouble as she made her way through the city to pick up the highway.

She took in the closed factories, walls emblazoned with spray-can bubble tags, and the tired fronts of budget, bulk-buy supermarkets, their windows fortified by metal grilles. Knots of young teens, slouching in oversized hoodies and flapping, lace-less sneakers, shared cigarettes by the side of the road. The demise of local industries had been a knockout punch to a city that was already prouder of its past than excited about its future.

She'd known, as she'd hurried to the ticket desk and bought a seat on a Detroit flight the next morning, that there was no point imagining she could follow a scent. Clara would have landed hours ahead of her. The trail was as cold as death.

Kate stretched out her stiff neck and shoulders at the next stop light, then reached again for the coffee. It would keep her awake for now but she badly needed some sleep. She'd dozed as much as she could on the journey but flying was never exactly restful.

She checked her phone. She'd sent a query to a reporter friend in New York, a contact from her news days. No answer yet but Kate knew to be patient. There wasn't much her friend couldn't winkle out. Kate would just owe her a lot of favours by the time this was over.

The lights changed and she surged forward, eager to put Detroit behind her.

When she reached Ann Arbor, Kate checked into a small, boutique hotel on Main Street, which claimed to be a two-minute drive to the University of Michigan campus. She took a hot shower, forced herself to turn away from the tempting bed, and headed out, picking up a fresh coffee and muffin on the way.

She wasn't really in the mood for a university tour but, she had to admit, the U of M campus was impressive. She sat in the weak, early-morning sunshine on one of the stone benches, taking stock. The centre of the main campus smacked of privilege. It was a far cry from the depressed suburbs of Detroit she'd passed through an hour ago.

The students, striding along the tree-lined avenues and across the red paved square, to and from lecture halls or libraries, had an air of effortless affluence. Their sneakers, jeans and backpacks looked brand new. Blue U of M sweaters, with shiny gold trim, were draped casually around shoulders, the sleeves tied loosely in front for effect.

These young people had purpose. Some hurried, heads down, alone. Others strolled more amicably in twos or threes but even those who chatted seemed to keep their voices hushed. Their faces were earnest. None of them looked hungover or unshaven. No Goths. No punks. No weird fashions or theatrical make-up. Barely any smoking. They seemed to blend perfectly into the scenery: the grand clock tower with its light-brown stone tiers and green-tiled roof, the dark red-brick buildings with pillars and flourishes. The carefully tended, litter-free stretches of lawn that filled the spaces between the diagonal paths.

The sight made Kate suddenly very weary. She thought of her own student days. They'd all worn second-hand, threadbare clothes and shabby boots and carried their books around in old carrier bags or ink-stained tote bags, proud of the coolest logos, from theatre companies or low-budget shops. It was just a phase. They'd all taken the capitalist shilling eventually. But their student days had been edgy and heady, fuelled by idealism.

These students, on the other hand, were not even pretending to be children of the revolution.

Her phone buzzed. A message from her reporter friend in New York. *Madelyn Price: home.* Kate smiled to herself as she punched in a quick thank you in reply. She didn't know how her friend had come by Maddy's home address so quickly but it was exactly what she needed. She dumped the rest of the muffin in the bin, brushed crumbs off her skirt and went to pick up the car.

The sat nav guided her to Maddy's home, past row after row of substantial detached houses. The streets here were as affluent as Detroit's suburbs had been poor. The grand entrances of the sprawling brick mansions were framed with ornate pillars. Ivy, climbing towards bedroom windows, shone a luminous green with the onset of spring.

Other properties were colonial-style clapboard, freshly painted, with pointed roofs and wooden stoops.

She found Maddy's house number at last on a pair of ornate stone gateposts, topped by sculptured acorns. They led the way into a short, loose stone drive where an expensive silver hatchback was parked.

Kate drove past and pulled in at the kerb. She switched off the engine and eased open the car door. The only sounds she could hear were the distant cawing of a bird and the clatter of a squirrel's claws on bark as, startled by her movement, it darted up a tree.

Kate hesitated, breathing in the scent of wood pulp and freshly mown grass. She felt strangely detached, as if her mind were watching her body, observing the combination of caffeine, tiredness and adrenaline making it tremble. She felt suddenly lost.

Until this moment, all she'd focused on had been a driving need to see Clara, whatever way she could. It wasn't rational, this urge that had propelled her first to Heathrow and then onto a transatlantic flight. She needed to know that her daughter was OK.

In her heart, she clung to the image of Clara welcoming her, opening her arms and letting Kate hold her close, just for a moment. That alone would make the journey worthwhile. But even if Clara was furious, if she reminded her mother bitterly that she'd asked for space, asked to be left alone, well, Kate knew that would hurt but at least she could leave knowing that her daughter was safe and well.

She held her hands out in front of her and calmly observed the shake, then, before she could stop herself, she got out of the car, marched down the drive to the front door and rang the bell.

50

Kate rang and rang and, between times, she banged on the wood with the flat of her palm.

No-one came to the door.

Kate took a few steps back and stared up at the building, looking for signs of life. A light shone behind a narrow upstairs window. It was opaque glass, a bath or shower room presumably. Shadows crossed it as an unseen person moved inside.

Someone was in the house. Someone who didn't want to open up.

Kate's hands clenched into fists at her sides. It might be Clara. It might be her daughter taking a shower up there, freshening up after the drag of jet lag. The frustration was unbearable.

After some time, she retreated to her car and sat there, trying to decide what to do, how long to wait. She was still considering when a rental car drove up behind her and swung into the drive, crunching across the gravel. It parked neatly alongside the silver hatchback.

Kate narrowed her eyes and watched. A young man climbed

languidly out of the driving seat. She blinked, recognising him at once but hardly able to believe her eyes. It was Adrian, the young man in the Amsterdam gift shop who'd told her about accompanying Clara to the airport and helping her flee. He crossed to the front door and rang the bell.

Kate was still adjusting to the shock when the passenger door opened and a second person clambered out and followed him. Kate's heart leaped. Clara! My God, it really was her. Bella's crazy hat was pulled down low on her head. Her coat stirred round the mound of her stomach.

For a second, Kate couldn't move. She just gazed, washed through with such a heady mixture of joy and relief that her limbs simply refused to function. *My girl, my gorgeous, darling girl. You're safe.* A smile broke across her face.

The two youngsters were side by side at the door now, Adrian reaching protectively for Clara's hand. The door opened and Kate saw Maddy framed in the doorway, enveloped by a dressing gown, her hair wrapped in a towel. No wonder she hadn't answered the door. Kate almost laughed. It was all right, all OK. It had just been Maddy, in the shower. What a fool she'd been to panic.

Kate opened the car door and pulled herself out of her seat, ready to start towards them.

The young woman, as she moved to enter the house, tugged off the woolly hat and tipped back her head, shaking her hair free. Her mane of blonde hair. Kate stared. For the first time, Kate saw her face clearly. Her heart seemed to stop.

It wasn't Clara. She had the same figure, the same stiff walk but it wasn't her.

Kate felt as if someone had punched her hard. She staggered, gripping the open car door for support.

It was Amy. Amy, smiling in the photograph with Clara, their faces, so similar, pressed close. It had been Amy, all along. Of course Amy would fly home, to join her mother. Kate felt suddenly very sick.

Because, if this was Amy, whose body had Maddy identified in Amsterdam? Whose body had Kate helped her to have cremated? Whose ashes had she watched Maddy feed to the dark waters of the canal?

Kate started to sob, heaving sobs that scalded her chest and left her gasping for breath. Her nails tangled her hair, scratched at her skin.

It was impossible. It couldn't be true.

Whose body was it, if it wasn't Amy's?

My God, Clara, my beautiful girl. I was right, all this time. I knew it. I knew something terrible had happened.

Kate sank back into the car, blinded by tears. Her mind raced. How could she prove it? Who would believe her? There was no evidence. She'd arranged her own daughter's cremation without even knowing. She'd even helped Maddy to dispose of Clara's ashes.

Amy was the one who was alive and well and expecting a child. The new baby wouldn't be Kate's grandchild, but Maddy's. Amy was the one she'd seen fleetingly in Covent Garden, wearing Clara's stolen hat. Amy was the one who'd messaged her from Clara's phone, the one who'd stolen Clara's passport and used it to pick up that cash.

And Adrian and Maddy had been part of it all. They'd played her. Played her for a fool.

Kate battered her hands against the steering wheel, crushing and bruising her fingers in her grief, and, certain that her heart would break, she wept.

51

DAMIAN

Amsterdam, Two Months Earlier

'Oh, come on, Clara! Don't be such a party-pooper!'

Honey persisted, waving the joint in Clara's face. Clara forced a laugh, pushed Honey's hand away and reached for her wine glass instead.

'We will get you stoned, girl!' Honey was giggling to herself. 'Ain't that right, Amy? You don't know what you're missing. No point being in Amsterdam and not trying the good stuff.'

Honey wasn't the best advocate of any stuff, good or otherwise, Damian thought, quietly observing her from the sofa. She was sprawled on the rug. Her mess of blonde hair was bedraggled from the rain that was still splattering the windows along the front of the apartment. She'd kicked off her shoes and her big toe protruded from damp, torn tights. Its nail was dotted with the remnants of chipped pink polish.

It amused Damian to watch Clara's reactions to Honey. She clearly didn't like her. Honey was too loud, too brash for Clara's taste, plus she was constantly stoned, whatever the time of day.

Clara worked hard to look relaxed around her but Damian caught the occasional expression, a grimace or roll of the eyes, which told him how much she disapproved.

Clara had surprised him. Damian had expected her to dive into the party scene, once she'd settled in, especially as he took care to maintain a free and flowing supply of dope – and harder drugs – in the apartment. He liked to be generous with drugs and alcohol. It was good for business if he was known as the go-to guy for everything, legal or not.

After a matter of months, his earnings were already high, far better than they'd been in London. He'd taken a dull job at a gift shop, just as a regular place to hang out, somewhere the kids always knew to find him if they needed fixing up. It gave him a good cover if the cops got nosy.

He'd expected to start Clara on some hard stuff. E, maybe, like her sister. Or coke. Once she was trashed, he'd have no trouble arranging a little accident.

It would serve his stepmother right. She'd been the one to turn his father against him. If they'd opened their arms to him, given him his due and recognised him as his father's son and heir, none of this would have been necessary. She'd regret it for the rest of her life.

But how to do it? So far, Clara was proving more circumspect than her sister had. She had refused even a cigarette. Alcohol was the only weakness he'd found.

Now, Damian picked up the open bottle of wine and topped up Clara's and Honey's glasses.

Amy, stretched out on the sofa at his side, reached a lazy hand to his cheek.

'Can't I have a taste? Just a sip?'

'Nice try but absolutely not.' He clasped her hand and kissed it. 'Stay there. I'll get you some more juice.'

'Juice! I'm sick of juice.'

Honey rolled onto her back, waving her arms theatrically. 'Give me strength! You're all so BORING!'

They were all still adjusting to the news that Amy was pregnant. It had happened faster than he'd expected, pretty much the first time she'd been drunk enough not to realise he wasn't using a condom. He hadn't been counting on it but it was still an opportunity and he intended to take it.

The harder part had been after the pregnancy test – when he'd had to convince her that he loved her, that he wanted this baby, that, although it was early, he knew he needed to share the rest of his life with her. She was besotted enough with him to believe it.

Damian opened the windows wider as he passed. He didn't mind if Clara got high on second-hand smoke but not Amy. He didn't want her to hurt the baby.

He did want this child. He wanted a son, a miniature version of himself, a child who'd love and admire him, who'd long to be like him. He'd model his boy in his own image.

The child would have a practical use, too. He'd serve as Damian's insurance policy. Maddy had kept her mouth shut out of fear, until now. Fear of being exposed. Fear of anything happening to Amy. Now, Damian had made himself a permanent part of their family, united by blood. Maddy could never turn Amy against him now, however hard she tried. He would always be the father of Amy's child. Maddy would never be free of him.

He smiled to himself as he pulled open the fridge door and lifted out the orange juice, then opened a bumper-sized packet of tortilla chips and shook them out into the bowl on the coffee table. Honey twisted round at once and grabbed a fistful. She threw them at Clara, then got the giggles again as she snatched up more and tried to stuff them all into her own mouth. Fragments flew in all directions.

Something else to annoy Clara, Damian thought to himself, watching Clara pick bits of tortilla chip out of her hair, off her T-shirt and jeans and pop them in her mouth. She was trying to look amused but she wasn't.

Honey came round so often, Damian did wonder if she sometimes forgot that Amy, after a missed rent payment too far, had finally found the courage to ask Honey to move out and let her room to Clara instead.

Once or twice, when Damian had been staying over, Clara had come back late from Galileo's, where she'd already picked up regular shifts, and found Honey fast asleep in her bed, dead to the world. She'd clearly ended the evening too out of her head to make it home and simply crawled under the covers. Amy had just laughed and told Clara to chill.

Damian had caught Clara's expression. She hadn't seen the funny side. She had finally been persuaded to bed down on the sofa for the night but she'd done so with bad grace. It hadn't helped that Honey had also polished off the food Clara had bought for herself.

More importantly, he sensed the tension Honey sparked when she hung out in the apartment. Amy still felt guilty about evicting Honey and sorry for her because she seemed unable to hold down a job. She was quick to defend her old friend if Clara made it clear that she was less than pleased to have her around.

For his part, Damian took care to stoke it. He made sure there was always a generous stash of dope and plenty of booze in the apartment and that Honey knew where to find it. If that didn't keep her coming round, he didn't know what would.

Quietly, week by week, he worked this crack in Amy's friendship with Clara, turning it to his advantage.

Once, when tensions were high, he waited until he and Amy were alone together in her room, then dropped some poisoned words in her ear, in the guise of defending Clara.

'I know Clara's difficult sometimes,' he said, stroking Amy's arm. 'But maybe we should cut her a little slack.'

'Why?' Amy twisted round, eyes blazing. 'She doesn't own the place.'

'I know.' He paused. 'But she has problems, you know? She strikes me as kind of unstable.'

He made a show of hesitating before he continued. 'I didn't know whether to tell you this.' He paused. 'But I get the feeling Clara's got a dark side, you know? She's been getting into some pretty dodgy stuff.'

'Clara?' Amy frowned. 'What dodgy stuff?'

He squirmed. 'Maybe I shouldn't. I mean—'

Amy was all over it, at once. 'Go on. You can't stop there. What stuff?'

He'd looked her square in the eye. 'You promise you won't tell her you know? Not a word.'

'Promise.'

'OK.' Damian let out a sigh. 'Well, I've heard things about her, that's all. Guys, bragging. Apparently, she's been hooking up with men through a raunchy sex app. For threesomes and bondage and stuff.'

Amy's eyes widened. 'Clara?'

He shrugged. 'I'm not one to judge. It's her business. But I thought you should know. I don't want her bringing anyone rough back here.' He placed his hand protectively across her stomach. 'Especially not now.'

She'd smiled then and kissed him and he left it at that, for the time being.

52

As the days passed, Damian became aware of a couple of incidents that caused him alarm.

They were subtle. Amy and Honey might not have noticed. But he did.

Once, he had come along to Galileo's in the evening to eat and have a glass of wine while he waited for Amy to come off shift. As usual, he'd offered to buy Gino a glass of something too and made a point of practising his Italian with him, just to curry favour.

On this occasion, Gino had joined him at his table. He'd waved away the bowl of pasta Damian had ordered and insisted that they both have platters of the daily special, a spaghetti dish with clams and mussels, dripping with garlic butter. Following Gino's lead, Damian tied a napkin round his neck, peasant-style, and tore apart the shellfish with his fingers. Soon, his palms and chin were greasy with scented butter and his lips peppered with fragments of fish.

Gino was trying to tell him a joke, apparently an earthy one, in Italian. Damian could only half understand but when Gino burst into throaty laughter, lolling back in his chair, his stomach bulging, Damian laughed too, partly to humour his host.

He didn't know what made him glance across the restaurant at just that moment. He had a sixth sense at times, when he'd feel someone looking at him and turn to catch them. Sure enough, there was Clara, leaning against the edge of the bar, no doubt waiting for a drinks' order to take to one of her tables.

She was staring directly at him. Her look was disdainful but also knowing, as if she saw right through him, as if she knew exactly who he really was and what he'd done.

For a fraction of a second, he froze, knowing himself undone, then, just as quickly, he recovered his wits and gave her a cheerful grin. She immediately flushed and turned away to face the bar. The moment passed. But he didn't forget it.

A second time, the three of them – Clara, Amy and Damian – had gone to an overpriced ice-cream place in the old city. Amy was idiotic about ice-cream sundaes, taking forever to study the menu and fretting about what to choose, then ordering so many extras they could barely fit in the dish.

On this occasion, she was fussing Damian in a silly way about their future and whether they should live in the US or in England. She was such a child, at times.

'We'll live in lots of places,' he'd said curtly, growing impatient with her.

'Good!' Amy popped a blob of cream on his nose, trying to be playful. Irritated, he wiped it off with his handkerchief. 'Here in Amsterdam too?'

'For now.' Damian sipped his coffee. He planned for Amy to reconcile with Maddy as soon as she could and join her in Ann Arbor but Amy wasn't ready to hear that yet. She was still in the throes of an angry rebellion where her mother was concerned.

Amy hadn't spoken to her since she'd left the US after graduating high school.

'We could take vacations in England, couldn't we? Stay with your folks.' She turned to Clara who was quietly eating her own, more modest ice-cream. 'Damian's family have titles. Did you know? What are they again, baby? Lord and Lady? I guess that'll make us Lord and Lady someday. What a hoot!' She pulled a face at Damian. 'What? What's the big deal?'

Damian put his hand on her shoulder. 'Please, Amy. Clara doesn't want to hear this. You're embarrassing her.'

'But it's true. You shouldn't be so modest.' She turned back to Clara. 'They've got some great country house up in – where is it, again?'

'Amy, stop it.' He had an urge to pick up the stupid sundae and plant it in her face.

'What's the matter?' Amy grumbled. She turned her eyes back to her sundae spoon. 'No need to be so rude. Gee, you're so sensitive.'

Clara didn't answer. She kept her eyes on her ice-cream, keeping her own counsel. But Damian felt her emit something, something only he could sense. Again, it was a feeling that she knew him. She saw what he really was and what he'd done. He felt naked in front of her, his soul bared, with nowhere to hide.

Then, the following week, things came to a head.

What happened taught him that there could be no second chances.

53

It was her own fault. If Clara had just kept her mouth shut, if she hadn't gone behind his back that way, maybe he would have taken his time. But she couldn't mind her own business.

Damian had been to meet a new dealer that evening, up in Bijlmer. He was a young Egyptian guy who'd been recommended by a mutual contact. Damian came away at around ten o'clock, his pockets laced with small bags of pills. It seemed good stuff and the Egyptian was asking a fair price. He'd smiled to himself as he rattled back to the old city by tram. He hadn't realised how tense he'd been until now it was safely over. He'd have no trouble moving these. The American and South African kids, the French and Spanish, they'd lap them up. He made rough calculations on the profits he could expect as the night-lit bars and cafés rumbled past. Enough to splash out on two tickets to Ann Arbor, for sure.

He'd planned earlier just to head home, stash the stuff and get an early night. Now, though, his mood was buoyant. He'd established a good rapport with the Egyptian. He seemed a smart guy, rough but with good access to supplies. His problem was that his English was poor and his look wasn't right for the affluent Amsterdam party scene. He'd struggle to win the confidence of the international kids with dollars to burn. That was Damian's forte. Together, they could make a killing.

As the tram crossed Spui Square, he found himself jumping off. He headed into a bar for a bottle of decent white wine and then off down the edge of the canal towards Amy's apartment. She'd be finishing up at Galileo's in the next half hour. He'd surprise her. He liked to keep her on her toes. If she went out late after work, if she brought anyone back to the apartment, he wanted to know about it.

Amy's apartment was in darkness. He let himself in, locking the door behind him, stuck the bottle of wine in the fridge and made a quick check of Clara's bedroom, sliding open drawers and cupboards and lifting her folded belongings with care. He wasn't looking for anything in particular, it was just good practice. He never knew what he might find – a letter, a diary, a receipt – anything that might prove useful.

Finding nothing of interest, he moved into Amy's room and was just doing the same, keeping the light low, when he heard the scrape of a key in the lock.

Amy's voice was loud, Clara's lower, but it was clear they were in the middle of an argument. Damian snapped off the light and crouched low in the darkness, listening. He peered out through the thin crack of the half-open bedroom door.

'What are you saying? I mean, really, what the heck—'

'I'm just saying be careful, that's all.' Clara's tone was even. The front door closed behind them with a bang. A moment later, Damian heard the smack of the fridge door being pulled open and drinks being poured. 'I just think he's phoney.'

'Phoney?' Amy sounded as if she were spoiling for a fight.

'All this stuff about him living in a country seat, about his parents being Lord and Lady something. I don't believe it.'

'Just because he doesn't show off about it, that doesn't make him a *phoney*.' Amy spat the words with contempt.

They moved into the sitting room, into his line of sight. Amy, juice glass in hand, settled heavily into her favourite armchair. She kicked off her shoes and lifted her feet onto the coffee table.

Clara sat to one side, on the sofa. Her face was turned away from him, her expression harder to catch.

'Have you ever googled him? I couldn't find anything about him online. Or about his family,' Clara was saying. 'Don't you think that's weird? If his parents are titled, there should be articles about them or at least photos.'

'You *googled* him?'

Clara carried on, regardless. 'There's just something about him. Something off.'

'Why would you even do that?' Amy sounded increasingly angry.

Clara leaned forward, defensive. 'I don't trust him. It's hard to describe. It's like he's putting on an act all the time. Pretending to be someone he's not.'

Amy shook her head. 'Oh, please. You know what that sounds like? Some weird jealousy thing. First, it was Honey. Now, it's him. Basically, anyone close to me, anyone who hangs out here a lot, you don't like them, right?'

Clara clicked her tongue. 'You know me better than that. Come on, we're good friends.'

Amy sounded begrudging. 'Well, I thought we were.'

'We are. I didn't know whether to say anything or not. I just don't want you to make a mistake, that's all. I know how important he is to you and I—'

'Important? He's my future kid's dad.' Amy's hand moved

instinctively to the low mound of her stomach. 'And you know what? I don't care what you did or didn't find on Google; I really don't. I trust him and I love him and he loves me and that's that. OK?'

Damian shifted his weight a fraction, trying to ease the cramp in his leg. His face burned in the shadows. That cow. How dare she. She hadn't changed a bit. She was still the same stuck-up little girl, giggling at him across the table, determined to hurt him.

Amy set down her glass on a side table. 'I'm going to grab a shower.'

Damian stiffened. If she stood up, he'd crawl onto her bed and pretend he'd been asleep the whole time and hadn't heard them come in.

Clara stretched out a hand and gripped Amy's forearm. 'Listen, please. There's something else.'

Amy shook her off but didn't leave. 'I'm not sure I want to hear it.'

Clara let out a long sigh. 'I did check something out.'

Amy's eyes flashed. 'You've been checking up on him, behind my back?'

'Not just for you. For me too.' Clara's shoulders fell. 'I've never told you this but, well, I had a big sister. Bella. She died when she was at uni. Some drugs she took at a party. That's why I never touch the stuff.'

Amy's demeanour softened. 'Shit, Clara. I'm sorry.' She nodded her head, as if something was falling into place. She sagged back into her chair.

Clara carried on, more quietly now. 'Yeah, anyway. And you're right, it was shit.' She drew a hand down her face. 'He knew her at college. Did he say?'

Amy screwed up her face, trying to remember. 'Maybe. I

mean, he definitely said something, that you'd had people in common.' She paused. 'Awful about your sister. Poor you.'

'He was a student at the same time. The way he talked about her – well, it sounded like he'd known her pretty well. She didn't usually open up about herself, about home and family, unless she was really comfortable with someone.'

Amy looked confused. 'That's a good thing, right?'

'Sure.' Clara hesitated, choosing her words with care. 'But do you remember the other day when we were talking about that comedian who'd headlined the Edinburgh Fringe Festival and we were explaining to you what a big deal that was? And he said he'd starred in a play at the festival, *As You Like It*, when he was a student. Remember? He said they'd put it on at King's first, in London, and it did so well, they took it to Edinburgh and it sold out.'

Amy blinked. 'So?'

Clara leaned in closer. Damian had to strain to hear.

'So, I emailed Bella's old English tutor. He was really kind to us after she died and kept in touch for a bit. He takes a big hand in all the student productions. Drama's his big thing. Guess what? He emailed back to say he'd never heard of Adrian and neither had anyone else he'd asked. Pretty odd, huh? And get this... King's hasn't ever staged *As You Like It*, in London or anywhere else. He's been there twenty years.'

Amy looked thrown. 'But why? Why would he lie about something like that?'

Clara splayed her hands. 'Like I said, he's a liar, through and through. Why's he working in a two-bit gift shop? What's that all about? And all the cash he splashes about – the wine, the fancy dinners, the drugs? Where does it all come from? Come on, Amy. Think about it. I don't know what he's up to but the guy's dodgy.'

'Stop it!' Amy put her hands to her ears. 'That's enough!'

Damian couldn't stand it any longer either. He raked his hands through his hair to make it look tousled, pulled the bottom of his shirt free from his trousers and rubbed his eyes, then lurched out of Amy's bedroom, blinking hard in the light of the sitting room.

'What time is it?' He yawned, peered round through half-closed eyes. 'God, I'm sorry. I must've dropped off.'

Amy jumped as if she'd been scalded. Guilty, he thought. *Good. She's afraid of what I might have heard, what I might do.* He opened his arms to her and she pressed into them.

'I didn't know you were here.' She was shaking against him.

He tightened his grasp and, with his free hand, stroked her wild mane of hair. 'I wanted to surprise you. I missed you so much. You smell good.' He shifted her hair to one side and lowered his lips to the soft skin of her neck, felt her shiver. 'What are you doing out here, anyhow?' he murmured. 'It's late. You should be in bed, with me.'

He took her hand and led her back into her bedroom. She needed reassuring and he knew exactly how to do that.

As he turned to close the door behind them, he glanced back to Clara. She was sitting rigidly on the sofa, staring after them, her eyes wide with shock. She didn't buy for one minute that he'd been asleep – it was written all over her face. She knew he'd heard every word. And she was clearly terrified.

He gave her a thin smile. Clara looked just as if she'd had a sudden, dreadful premonition of exactly how he was going to exact punishment.

54

Damian didn't sleep much that night. He lay calmly in bed, feeling the soft weight of Amy's head on his shoulder, thinking. Planning.

At eight o'clock, he emerged from Amy's bedroom in his shirt and boxer shorts. He knocked softly on Clara's bedroom door, then opened it without waiting for a reply.

She was already washed and dressed and sitting on the end of her bed, her head bent over her phone. When she looked up and caught sight of him, she jumped.

He smiled. 'Sorry, just wondered if you wanted a coffee?'

She stared. 'No, that's OK.'

'You're up early.' He nodded at her phone. 'What are you up to?'

'Nothing.' She made a clumsy move to hide the screen.

He considered her, reading her discomfort. 'I hope it's not fallout from, well, from anything that's happened between you and Amy.'

She didn't answer.

He took a few steps further into her room, uninvited, pushing the door to behind him.

'Look, Amy didn't want to talk about it last night but I could tell she was upset. You two had a row, didn't you? It's OK – you don't need to say anything! I'm just sorry. You're such good friends.'

She sat with a rigid back, unyielding, waiting for him to finish.

He sat heavily beside her on the edge of the bed. The old mattress sagged, drawing her closer to him as she tilted, then struggled to regain her balance. For a moment, her thigh pressed warmly against his before it withdrew.

'I know it's silly,' he went on, 'but I feel close to you because of Bella. I know! I only knew her a little and you were sisters. I shouldn't presume – but then, she wasn't an ordinary person, was she? We both know that. She made a real impression. She was special.'

He paused, enjoying her confusion. He could play her like an instrument.

'Anyway, you and Amy... I think I know what the argument's about.'

He waited for a few moments as she tensed. He sensed her fear of him, of what he might do to her. It was intoxicating. He remembered the surge of power through his body when he'd plunged the butcher's knife into Maddy's husband's chest and felt the blade slice through sinews and flesh, then pulled it out with a soft, wet suck, only to push it in again, deeper.

He tried to seem grave. 'It's about Honey, isn't it? The fact she's round here all the time, acting like she still lives here, helping herself to everything. And the fact she's such a dope-head. I'm right, aren't I?'

She nodded at once. She was a terrible liar.

'And you're fed up with it,' he went on. 'You've had enough. You're even—' he nodded at her phone '—you're even thinking of looking for some place else and moving out. Or maybe moving on from Amsterdam altogether. Didn't you say you might head for Italy next and find some sunshine?'

She flushed. He was smarter than her. He'd hit home.

He reached out a hand and laid it on her knee. 'Please don't. Not yet. Just give Amy a chance to make it up to you, would you? I'll have a chat with her.' He squeezed the bone. 'She's very fond of you, you know. We both are.' He lifted his hand and, gesturing towards the window, lightened his tone. 'And you've got to admit, it's quite an apartment.'

He rose to his feet, decisive, as if a deal had been struck.

At the door, he turned back to give her his warmest smile. 'Now, how about I put the coffee on and then head out to the French bakery on the corner while it brews. I could murder a croissant and I'll get a pain au chocolat for Amy. What can I get you?' He raised an admonishing finger. 'And believe me, I won't take no for an answer.'

* * *

He reckoned that he'd probably bought himself a day or two with his touching performance. No more than that.

As the three of them sat over breakfast together, showering the tabletop in flakes of pastry, he kept up a stream of amusing chat and sensed the tension between the two women ease.

Damian felt almost sentimental as he discreetly observed the two of them. In the night, Amy had clung to him, as if she feared losing him and wanted to hold him close. The pregnancy was already changing her. It wasn't only that her ankles were thickening and her waist becoming slacker. There was an intense neediness about her which, mostly, he found cloying. There was no question in his mind, though, that the baby was his and that was all he cared about. He couldn't have planned it more brilliantly. He'd gain an adoring son and his punishment of Maddy would be never-ending. Maddy would be reminded of his poor mother's suicide every time she looked in her grandchild's eyes and saw traces of his mother's face there.

Clara seemed subdued as they ate. He wondered if she felt any remorse about having been so nosy. His blood warmed when he thought about the email she'd sent to Bella's tutor, the way she'd spied on him. He wouldn't have thought her capable. She'd had no right to poke her nose into issues that were no concern of hers.

The tip of her tongue snaked out and touched the corner of her mouth, snaring a crumb. He realised, watching her, how much he wanted her to know, when the moment of her death arrived, that it wasn't some random act, as it would appear later to the police, but that he was the person responsible. He'd like her to understand how selfish she and her mother had been in disowning him. He'd like her to look into his eyes, one last time, and finally recognise her own brother there. He'd like her to be sorry for everything she'd done to hurt him.

He reached for the coffee pot and, with a smile, refilled her cup. It was fantasy, of course. This was one job he'd have to leave to professionals. Anything else was too risky.

At the end of breakfast, she self-consciously pecked him on the cheek and thanked him for treating her. He wasn't fooled. All this rapprochement was nothing more than a sticking plaster. Clara clearly didn't trust him. She was determined to move on, he could see. He needed to act quickly.

During the morning, he sat on his stool at the back of Gift World with one eye on the security mirrors, watching a ragged assortment of tourists finger the cheap plastic souvenirs, and the other eye on the burner phone that he held low, under the counter. It was the same phone he used for dealers.

The Egyptian replied to his message within a few hours. *Yes, I have friends*, he wrote. *Good friends. They are free to do the work this evening.*

Damian agreed a price and a drop-off point.

Soon after three, when business was dead, Damian flipped the sign on the shop door to: *Closed.* He headed down the cobbled streets to his own apartment, an anonymous studio on the far side of Vondelpark.

First, he headed to the kitchen, fixed himself a strong coffee, then got to work. He stuck several roofies into a mortar with a tab of Ecstasy, grabbed the pestle and ground them to powder. Then, he made a narrow slit in the giant chocolate chip cookie he'd just bought at the corner deli and funnelled in the drugs.

He nodded to himself as he cleaned up with care. Clara loved those cookies. That one, he was sure, would put her out of action for a long time. The Egyptian's friends would do the rest.

Next, he opened up his wardrobe, cleared away the pile of shoes and bags at the back and unlocked the steel safe he'd bolted to the floor. It was stuffed with drug cash, a mix of euros and US dollars.

He counted out six thousand dollars, stuffed the wad into a large envelope and added, in block letters, the address for Amy and Clara's apartment.

It was after four by the time he reached their block. It looked quiet. The only person he passed on the stairs was the young Swedish guy who lived in the flat below. His blond hair stuck out in clumps, his oversized coat slapped around his legs. He gave Damian a frightened nod, then scurried past.

Damian had caught him in Amy's apartment a couple of

months ago, sprawling on the sofa, drinking coffee as if he owned the place. Afterwards, Damian had paid him a visit and made sure he never came calling again. There was only room for one cockerel in that henhouse.

He set the cookie on a plate and placed it on the end of Clara's bed where she'd be sure to see it. Then he locked up, slipped his spare keys into the cash-filled envelope, addressed it just as the Egyptian had described and hurried across town to make the drop in a derelict bottle bank on the edge of the red-light district.

When Damian finally arrived back at Gift World, he found a group of Japanese tourists waiting, their faces against the windows as they peered in through the glass. He let them in with theatrical bows and profuse apologies and set his mind, for the next few hours, to selling as much of the garish stock as he could, to whichever tourists appeared. He took care to stand in full view of the security cameras at regular intervals. He didn't expect to need an alibi for the afternoon but it certainly wouldn't hurt to provide one.

That night, Amy and Clara both came off shift at ten thirty. Damian, who'd been hogging a corner table at Galileo's since shutting up the shop for the evening, grabbed Amy's hand as she hurried over to him in her coat.

'Can we make it my place tonight?' he said in a low voice. 'I know it's silly but I want you to myself. I want us both to feel uninhibited, you know? Free to make as much noise as we like.'

Amy flushed with pleasure. 'OK. What about the morning, though? Are you planning to kick me out at nine when you go to work?'

'Absolutely not.' He smiled. 'I've booked the morning off. That's part of my evil plan. A lie-in, then a lovely, long breakfast together, and, maybe afterwards, a stroll by the canal. Sound good?'

He looked up. Clara was waiting for them near the door.

He indicated her to Amy with a discreet nod. 'Clara won't mind, will she? If I whisk you away for the night?'

Amy grinned back at him. 'She'll be fine. Let me just tell her.'

55

Damian didn't like Amy in his apartment.

As soon as he woke, he took her for breakfast in an Italian café and let her tuck into pastries while he drank his coffee. It wasn't only the pregnancy that was thickening her waistline.

He was finishing his coffee when a message came through on his phone from an unknown number:

Job done.

He deleted it, drained his cup and got to his feet.

As they headed back to her place, a surge of adrenalin made his heart quicken. He was exhilarated. He'd been impressed by the Egyptian and the way he'd done business. Now, he needed to be certain that his friends had delivered the goods. Or rather disposed of them.

'What're you smiling at?' Amy pulled on his hand, teasing.

'Oh, nothing,' he lied. 'Just thinking about last night.'

She stood on tiptoes and kissed him. Her breath smelled of milky coffee.

They approached the street-level entrance. He made a show of searching his pockets.

'Damn. Can't find my keys. Must've left them somewhere. You got yours?'

'You muppet!' She laughed, drew out her own set and let them in.

Damian felt every stair keenly as they climbed. His breath came in short, sharp bursts of anticipation. As they approached the top, he hung back, feeling the blood pulse through his temples.

Amy twisted round to him and put a warning finger to her lips. 'Clara might still be asleep.'

She turned the corner to take the final flight to the apartment, then stopped and stared. Her jaw slackened stupidly. Her hand reached blindly back to him and grasped his arm.

'Look!' she whispered.

The front door stood open. Together, they headed inside.

Sofa cushions were scattered across the floor. The cheap coffee table was knocked over. A wine glass lay on its side, its spilled contents making a long, thin stain across the rug.

'Stay there.' He pushed past her and made a show of searching the apartment. He checked Amy's room first, peering in the wardrobe and behind the door. Then the narrow kitchen. Then Clara's room.

The pillows had been thrown across the room. A sheet trailed half off the mattress. The bedside lamp lay on the floor near the headboard, surrounded by fragments of smashed bulb. Beside it, half hidden by the edge of the sheet, were the remains of a broken plate and a scattering of cookie crumbs.

He nodded. She'd taken the bait. That concoction of drugs would have left her stupefied by the time they burst in, in fact probably out cold. She'd made their job easy.

He looked again at the bedding. The duvet was gone. They'd done as they'd been told and used it to carry her out. He just hoped they'd had the brains to destroy it after they'd tossed her, as agreed, in a desolate stretch of canal.

Back in the living room, he set the sofa cushions back on the frame, then eased Amy down onto it. She was trembling.

'Don't move.' He removed her shoes, righted the coffee table and gently lifted her feet onto it.

She started to emit a strange bleating. A high-pitched murmur of shock. He ran the tap and handed her a glass of cold water, then stood over her while she drank.

'Close your eyes. Take deep breaths.' He reached down and patted her hand. 'OK?'

'But what the hell happened?' Her eyes were glassy. 'Where's Clara? I mean, is she OK?'

Damian ran his hand through his hair. 'She's not here.'

'What do you mean?' She sat up straighter and tried to crane past him to Clara's room.

Damian sat beside her. 'Listen. You need to stay calm. OK? I'm worried something's happened to Clara. Something terrible.'

Amy stuttered: 'What?'

He shook his head sadly. 'Whoever came here, whoever did this, they were violent. You can see that from the mess they left. God knows what they've done to her.'

The colour drained from Amy's face. 'So what—? Where?'

Damian shrugged. 'I don't know. I'm sorry but I don't think it looks good.'

Amy's face contorted. 'But why? Who'd hurt Clara?'

He paused for dramatic effect. 'This isn't easy to say but—' he squeezed her hand '—remember I told you there was another side to Clara? A dark side. Not one, I think, you ever saw.'

'But surely no-one would—?' Her mouth flapped.

He spoke carefully and slowly as if he knew she'd struggle to understand. 'She did like rough sex. With more than one guy, apparently. I'm wondering, well, maybe she had some men over last night, once she knew the coast was clear, and things got, well, out of hand.'

She stared at him, wide-eyed with disbelief. 'Surely she wouldn't—'

Damian hung his head. 'I saw her phone the other day, on the counter. She did have that dodgy sex app. I didn't want to mention it to you. I mean, you two were already fighting, you know? I didn't want to cause trouble.'

'I just can't believe—' Amy trailed off. She looked stricken.

Damian pressed on. They didn't have much time. 'And then yesterday morning. You remember I went into her room, to ask what she wanted for breakfast? Well, she was on her phone, on that app. She tried to hide it from me but—' He shrugged. 'I didn't know what to say. That's not my thing. You know that. But it's quite a scene here. I've seen guys arranging all kinds of hook-ups. It's all anonymous. I guess the risks are part of the thrill.'

Amy was shivering, as if she had a chill. 'So you think she hooked up with some guys last night, here, and—?'

'And it went very wrong.'

'But where is she now?' Amy reached for her phone. 'We need to call the police.'

Damian reached over, prised the phone from her hands and slipped it into his pocket.

'Amy, listen. Please.' He snaked an arm round her shoulders. 'I've read online about stuff like this. It's serious. Girls can wind up dead.'

Amy seemed to dissolve into the sofa. 'Dead?'

He went on: 'Do you remember that awful murder case in

Italy? An English student was murdered. Her room-mate was an American girl.'

Amy blinked. 'Foxy Knoxy?'

'Exactly. Don't you remember what happened? Amanda Knox and her boyfriend were prime suspects from the start. And here's the thing. If something terrible's happened to Clara – and I really fear it has – we've got to get out of here right now. You hear me? No police. Nothing. We pack up and go. Lie low somewhere, for a while.'

She blinked, slow to understand. 'Lie low?'

Damian gestured round the apartment, trying to tamp down his impatience with her.

'Don't you get it? Whatever sex game she got mixed up in last night – and the more I think about it, the more I'm *convinced* that's what happened – it must have turned nasty. And if it did and we're found here, we'll be finished. Can't you see how it'll look? Kinky sex, a murdered girl. It'll be like the Knox case all over again. We won't stand a chance.'

'But we didn't do anything? We weren't here!'

He found his most soothing tone. 'I know that. But we can't prove it. Our only alibi is each other. They won't believe us.' He sighed. 'You don't know what the police are like. They'll be under so much pressure to convict someone, anyone. They'll pin it on us.'

Amy stuck out her jaw. 'We've got to do something. Call round the hospitals. See if anyone—'

'Stop it!' Damian changed tack. 'Amy, it's not just about us any more, is it? It's about the baby. Don't you see? If Clara's been hurt...' he took a theatrically deep breath '...if she's *dead*, the criminal case could drag on for years. If we're stuck in prison, they'll take the baby away from you the minute it's born.'

'They can't! No!' Amy burst into tears. 'What do we do?'

Damian got to his feet. 'I'm going to clear up. You go and pack. Only take what you can carry.'

While she was busy in her bedroom, he set about restoring Clara's room. He gathered up the pillows and straightened the sheet, then swept up the fragments of broken china and glass and replaced the light bulb in her lamp. Finally, he rummaged through Clara's drawers.

'What are you doing?' Amy had appeared at Clara's bedroom door. She leaned heavily against the frame.

'Everything's still here. See? Her passport. Her phone. I'm right – I know I am. She'd never leave her phone behind. Do you know her password?'

'Her sister's birthday: 2407.'

He keyed it in and flicked through the apps, then, tilting the phone away from Amy, quickly downloaded an adult hook-up app.

'I'm going to delete this, just in case. See?' He shook his head, sadly. 'Silly girl. I guessed she must be using something like it.' He flicked Amy a quick glance of the app, then made a show of deleting it.

He crouched down, dropped the phone into the front pocket of Clara's backpack, then added her passport. He pulled random armfuls of clothes from her drawers and stuffed them in the main section. 'We can sort through these later. I just need to make it look as if she packed before she left.'

'But we can't take her passport!' Amy wailed. 'How's she going to get home?'

'Oh, Amy.' Damian sat back on his heels and forced such sadness into his eyes that even he was moved. 'I really don't think, where she's gone, she's going to need a passport.'

They stared at each other for several moments in silence. Slowly, he thought, the penny is starting to drop. From outside, everyday noises intruded. A boat engine churned down the canal and the tinny strains of pop music drifted across the water towards them.

Amy murmured to herself: 'This can't be happening. It's not true. Tell me it's not true.'

Damian made a show of shaking himself out of his thoughts. 'I've got a plan. But you need to trust me. And do exactly what I say.' He blinked hard. 'I don't care what happens to me. This is about you. You and the baby.'

Amy nodded, dumbly.

Damian shouldered Clara's backpack and grabbed Amy's hastily packed suitcase. He ushered her towards the front door.

Amy let out a shuddering breath. 'What about the rest of my stuff?'

'Forget it. I'll send someone round to clear the place once we've gone.' He planted a distracted kiss on her forehead.

Amy seemed lost. She paused on the threshold and turned to take a final look back at the home she'd never see again. He had to shove her hard in the small of the back to make her move on.

56

Damian pressed in closer to Amy. He drew the duvet around their bodies, protecting them from the dank chill of the cheap bedsit he'd found in Walthamstow. Cash in hand, week by week, no questions asked. It would do for now.

So far, London was proving marginally better than the two nights they'd had in Paris, when they'd first fled. Two nights had been as much as he could stand in that crumbling dive. He planned to head back to Amsterdam soon, anyway, and keep his business interests afloat. While he was there, Amy could fend for herself here in London. It wouldn't be for long.

His stubbled chin rubbed lightly against Amy's bare shoulder and he lifted his face. His lips found the warm hollow of her neck and she twisted a fraction to accommodate him. She'd think he was being affectionate when, in fact, he was positioning himself better to hear Maddy's voice.

It was tantalising to hear the faint ring down the phone line. His body tensed with anticipation. It was seven in the morning in Ann Arbor. He imagined Maddy sleepily waking to the sound of her chirping phone, all alone in bed, with no inkling of the news to come.

There was a short silence, then, all of a sudden, Maddy's voice, tense and uncertain. 'Amy? Is that you?'

'Hey, Mom.'

'How are you?' Maddy seemed to struggle to the surface, senses quickening. 'You OK?'

Amy took a deep breath. Damian prompted her with a nudge. They'd rehearsed all this but, for a moment, she seemed unable to speak.

'I've got news. Just listen a minute, can you? Don't say anything, not yet. Let me explain.'

Damian sensed the silence of a held breath down the line.

Amy blew out her cheeks, struggling for the words. 'I've met someone, Mom. Adrian. And, well, it's got pretty serious.' A pause, before Amy blurted out: 'We're having a baby.'

'A *baby*?' Maddy sounded winded.

'Yeah. Isn't it amazing? I'm having it, Mom. I really want it.' Amy's body was stiff with tension. '*We* really want it. But – I need your help.'

Nothing, for a moment. Damian sensed Maddy's shock, washing towards them in waves. He'd expected that. Of course, Maddy would be stunned. It was a lot to take in. What she didn't realise was how much more there was to come.

Finally, Maddy said: 'Come home. I can send you the fare. We can talk properly, figure out what to do.' Maddy seemed to be groping her way in the dark. 'I can fix a good doctor for you and check everything's OK, you know?'

Amy twisted back to check in with Damian. He nodded, reassuring, and kissed her bare shoulder, urging her to carry on.

'I will come home, Mom, soon. We'll both come. But, right

now, we're in trouble.' Amy's voice faltered. 'Something happened in Amsterdam. Clara, my room-mate...' She tailed off.

Maddy said sharply: 'What, Amy? What happened?'

Damian imagined her pressing the phone to her ear, desperate to hear.

Amy gave a shudder. 'We think someone killed her. In our apartment.' Tears came. 'We didn't do anything. You believe me, don't you? We weren't even there.'

Damian patted her arm. *Good job*, he wanted to say to her, as if she were a child. It wasn't even a performance. Her distress was perfect.

'Oh, Amy.' Maddy's mind seemed to work rapidly, trying to adjust. 'Where are you now?'

'London.' Amy could hardly speak for sobbing. It was all becoming more real to her, now she was telling her mother. 'We left as soon as—'

'Good. Amy, you did the right thing.' Maddy sounded in crisis mode, suddenly taking charge even as her daughter started to fall apart. 'Listen, you need to get home. Soon as you can. Can you do that?'

Damian shook Amy and whispered the next part of the script in her ear.

'I will. I want to. But I can't – not yet.' Amy pulled herself together enough to carry on. 'I really need your help, Mom. You mustn't tell anyone. *No-one*, do you get that? *Please*. I can't go to prison. I can't have my baby taken away.'

'Prison? But why would you – Amy, tell me what happened!'

'It wasn't me, Mom, it wasn't. But the police – they won't believe it. We'll be prime suspects. Unless—'

'Unless what? What are you trying to say?'

Damian plucked a tissue from the box and handed it to Amy to wipe her eyes. This was important. She needed to explain their plan clearly and carefully, just the way they'd practised. They really needed Maddy to buy into this.

Amy took a gulp of air and stuttered on. 'Are you listening? This is what we need you to do.'

She outlined Damian's plan. Maddy would have to contact Clara's mother and lie to her, tell her that Amy was missing and persuade her to join the search. In Amsterdam, Maddy would have to make a false statement to the police about Amy being missing, and, if Clara's body was dredged up, she must falsely identify her as her own daughter.

Maddy could turn this into an open-and-shut case. Just another drowned party girl with drugs in her system. With a positive ID from the distraught mother, the police wouldn't take the extra step of cross-checking with DNA.

At the end, Amy said tremulously into the silence: 'Will you do that, Mom? Please. For me. For the baby. If you don't, they're gonna find out what happened to Clara and I'm gonna be a prime suspect, do you see? I didn't do anything, I swear I didn't. But they'll never believe me. If they arrest me, it could take years, with the legal process and the trial and everything. And, by then, the baby—' She dissolved again into tears.

When Amy had finished setting it all out, Maddy fell silent. Damian could almost hear her brain churning.

Finally, Maddy said: 'I don't understand about Clara's mother. Why does she need to be there? Won't it be less risky if I go without her?'

Damian nodded. Smart question. Maddy hadn't dismissed it out of hand, she was thinking it through. That was a good sign. He whispered a rejoinder in Amy's ear.

'She needs to see what happens with her own eyes,' Amy said obediently. 'She needs to be absolutely convinced that if Clara's body turns up, it's mine. Adrian will be there in

Amsterdam to back you up. He'll lay a false trail for Clara's mom. He'll tell her that Clara's already left the country.' She paused. 'See?'

Damian held his breath. Maddy was no fool. She wouldn't enter lightly into a scheme involving lying to the police and deceiving another mother.

They waited. Finally, Maddy said: 'Amy, I don't think we can do that. Come home. Let me take care of you. We'll hire the best lawyers. Once you're here, in the US—'

'No, Mom! You're not listening!' Amy started to cry again. 'If Clara is dead and they find her, they'll be under so much pressure to arrest someone, to blame someone, don't you see? And I'll be a perfect target. The room-mate. Young American blonde, rich family. My name, my picture, they'll be all over the news. The media won't stop digging. They'll twist and exaggerate everything I've ever done, make me out to be a monster. And Dad. They'll dredge all that up again – you know they will. I'll be guilty before we even go to trial. *Please*, Mom. I need this from you. Then, I'll come home. We'll be together. Everything you wanted, OK?'

Damian waited. It was a risk but a calculated one. Maddy had lost her husband. She'd lost her professional integrity and her high-flying career. Amy was all she had left now, Amy and this new prospect of a grandchild. Her overpowering drive must be to protect them both.

'What about Clara's mother?' Maddy asked in a low voice. 'She'll find out eventually. I mean, she'll have to. Clara won't ever come home.'

Damian whispered into Amy's ear.

'She'll be missing, yes, but there'll be no evidence, no body, nothing to link her back to me,' Amy explained. 'Her mother won't know where to look. Clara's an adult. She could be anywhere.'

'Even so.' Maddy sounded troubled, as if she were imagining the pain Clara's mother would feel, the agony of living forever in uncertainty, never knowing if her daughter was alive or dead.

Damian smiled to himself. Getting rid of Bella had been a triumph, killing Maddy's husband had been a joy, but this final vengeance on both women trumped everything.

Amy said tightly: 'I'm sorry about Clara, Mom. Maybe I'm wrong and she isn't even dead. Maybe she's recovering in some hospital. But we need to assume the worst and figure out what happens if she does turn up dead. That's when I need you.'

'I need to think it through.' Maddy's voice held the slightest tremor. 'How long can I have?'

Damian whispered to Amy: 'Until evening, her time, max. Then she needs to make the call to Clara's mother and set the ball rolling. That body might show up any minute.'

Damian nodded to himself as Amy finished the call. Maddy would do it, he was sure. If she wanted to see her daughter again, to be part of her life from now on, she had no real option.

It had been satisfying to hear Maddy's voice again. In a few days, he'd be back in Amsterdam and, once she arrived, he'd arrange to meet her in some remote bar or poky restaurant.

He couldn't wait to see her face when she walked in, thinking she was meeting a stranger, her daughter's new boyfriend, then realised who he really was.

Hi, I'm Adrian, Amy's boyfriend, the father of your future grandchild.

Yep, that would be quite a moment.

57

'I need to go back there.'

Kate stood by the living room window and looked out into the street. A cat was making its way with stealth along her neighbour's fence. Further down, a car was trying to reverse into a tight parking space. The driver misjudged the angle, came out from the kerb and started again.

Kate's eyes drifted over it all, observing without seeing. The world seemed meaningless to her. She resented its ability to carry on.

Some deep, essential part of her had died in the US. Nothing would be the same again.

At night, she played out scenes in her head. Sometimes, she pushed her way into Maddy's home and attacked her, hands slapping and punching, nails scratching.

She imagined screaming in Maddy's face, half-mad with grief: *How could you do that? I helped you. I cared for you. My heart bled for you. And you were lying to me, all that time. You're a monster. You dispersed my daughter's ashes in front of me – my daughter's remains. You robbed me of the chance to say goodbye.*

Why hadn't she barged into Maddy's house that day? Why hadn't she screamed at Maddy? She couldn't explain it. Maybe someone else would have done. Maddy certainly deserved it. But Kate had never hit anyone in her life. Her instinct had been to crawl back to the hotel, to curl into a ball and weep, to get home as fast as she could.

This wasn't about Maddy, not really. Kate couldn't allow her to be that important. This was about Clara. Losing her had opened up a chasm inside Kate, an all-encompassing darkness. She'd never see her daughter's lovely face again, never kiss her cheek, never hold her.

'What are you hoping to find?' Rosa was sitting, still and calm, on the sofa. She'd fallen into the habit of coming by Kate's house every day, invited or not.

Kate didn't have the will to answer. How could she explain? *Hoping?* She was without hope now. This grief that overwhelmed her was more physical, more feral, than even her grief for Simon, for Bella. Clara was dead and it was the end. Kate had nothing left to live for. She'd had a family once. A happy family with a husband she adored and two beautiful daughters. Now, she had no-one. She was alone.

So much of what had happened made dreadful sense now, even as she'd tried to push it away.

The message she'd received from Clara's phone, telling her about the baby and asking for money, hadn't been written by her daughter. She understood that now. Amy must have taken Clara's phone and her passport too, after her death.

The trail Kate had followed through London and to Detroit, thinking she'd been pursuing Clara, had been a false one. Amy had simply stolen Clara's hat, along with other clothing, and used Clara's passport to collect the cash, to throw Kate off the scent. The two young women had looked enough alike, even walked enough alike, for her to get away with it.

Maddy had played her. She'd falsely identified Clara's body as Amy's. The thought of it made Kate feel physically sick. How could one mother do something so cruel to another? And why?

Kate's thoughts returned again and again to the simple cremation, to the slow, black dispersal of the ashes through the water. They had been *her* daughter's remains. It had been *her* right to carry out that final ritual for Clara. It was a final farewell she could never take back.

'I don't know what I'm hoping to find,' Kate said woodenly. 'I know she's dead. I just want to be there. I just need to say goodbye.'

Rosa didn't answer for a moment, then said: 'Do you want me to come with you?'

Kate turned back from the window. Rosa was gazing steadily at her. She would go with her, Kate knew, if she asked. Whatever upheaval it involved, Rosa would do it in a moment and without complaint.

Kate shook her head. 'I think I need to do this on my own. But thank you.'

58

In Amsterdam, the taxi from the Eurostar terminal swept Kate through the commercial districts, with their glass-fronted shops and brash fast-food outlets. It took her through the heart of the city, past churches with squat towers, picturesque bridges studded with bicycles and, on every side, the tall, narrow, closely packed houses that dominated the central canals.

Kate left her bags in the hotel room and, restless, set out on foot. It hurt to see the city again. Its mood had shifted while she'd been away. The grey skies and rainfall that had dominated her previous visit had given way to the start of spring. The canals glistened with weak sunshine. Hump-backed bridges and windowsills bloomed with vibrant hanging baskets. The flower market, hard by the water, was ablaze with colour. The sense of quickening, of bustle, made a sharp contrast with Kate's own feelings of loss.

She walked for miles. She wanted to wear herself to the core, to make her body so exhausted it might sleep, at least a little, and give her relief from her mind. She made ragged loops through the old city, only going back to her hotel room briefly to eat, then setting out again.

She passed Gift World where she'd first met Adrian, unaware that everything he'd told her had been lies. How could he? She glared through the window, catching the startled eye of a young girl perched on the same stool at the back of the shop.

Kate thought of Adrian, safe in Ann Arbor, playing happy families with Maddy and Amy. Why had he lied to her? He'd said he hardly knew Amy, the woman who was pregnant with his child. He'd described meeting Clara and going with her to the airport as she fled the country. All of it lies.

As evening drew in, the garish lights of the bars and restaurants bloomed into life. Music spilled from souvenir shops and food outlets. The serious business of the day was ending and the revelry set to begin.

Kate turned away from the main routes and lost herself in backstreets. The pavements became deserted. The shadows stretched, no longer broken by artificial light, apart from the occasional circles cast by wrought-iron street lamps. Above, the towering buildings leaned in towards her as if they were watching her pass.

She reached a small, silent section of canal and paused against its low wall.

Her body ached. She felt a profound sense of having lost herself, along with everyone she most loved. She was frayed, rapidly unravelling. Nothing else seemed to matter. Her empty home, the petty details of everyday life. It all seemed so inconsequential, so meaningless. She wasn't sure that she could ever go back and be whole again.

She thought of Rosa's question: *what are you hoping to find?* She didn't know any more. This wasn't the launch of Project

Clara. She wasn't here because she was driven to find clues, to search out answers about exactly what had happened to her younger daughter. That was a lost cause and, besides, she was too shattered, in body and spirit.

But she had longed for something. A sense of her daughter, perhaps, in the places Clara had last seen. A final connection. And there was nothing of that. Only emptiness.

Kate's eyes fixed on the black water below. It slid endlessly past. In places, it glided invisibly in the darkness. In others, it glistened intermittently where the surface was caught by stray fragments of light.

She stood with her hands pressed into the cold, sharp stones along the top of the wall. Now the sun had set, the air had become chill. As it blew down the length of the canal, it carried a musty smell of damp, infused with something sour and rotten.

She peered more closely into the water. She wondered how deep the canal was and how deadly. Whether, if she were to topple forward and plunge into it, she would manage to save herself. Whether she'd want to.

On the far side of the canal, a van bumbled into view. It splattered light in a softly spreading arc as it came nearer, bouncing lightly on cobbles. It drew level with her.

As the light spilled across the surface of the water, Kate saw her own pale face gazing back at her. It was ghostly and insubstantial. She watched it as it elongated and contracted, twisted and rippled as the flowing water moved through her reflection.

For a second, another face, smaller and more diaphanous than her own, swam with hers. Her own features were distorted as the two images blended. Her breath stuck in her chest. Clara. It was her.

She spun round and stared behind her into the darkness.

'Clara?' Her voice was thin and wavering in the quiet. 'Are you there?'

The van on the far side of the canal turned and disappeared, taking its cone of light with it. When she looked back at the water, the surface was again black. Whatever mirage she'd seen had gone.

She stood there for a long time, pressing forward against the low barrier of the wall. She felt drawn to the water and, at the same time, deeply, heavily anchored on the land.

Eventually, aware of the stiffness in her limbs, she turned and made her way, shivering now, back to the hotel.

She crossed the hotel lobby and headed for the bank of lifts. When the lift reached her floor, she stepped out, then stopped abruptly.

She'd sensed something. It hit her hard in the chest. A smell. Slight and subtle. She couldn't even have described it. She just knew it. Her senses quickened.

She didn't move, just stood at the end of the shadowy corridor that led to her room and tried to recover her wits. At first glance, the corridor ahead seemed empty. What had startled her?

She strained to see. Partway down, close to her own room, a failing light bulb flickered dimly in the ceiling. She listened hard, trying to quieten her own breathing.

She couldn't see anything and yet she sensed it. Someone or something was there. Concealed in the shadows. Waiting for her.

She didn't speak, just crept forward, a step at a time. As she approached the door to her room, the shadows shifted. She froze, staring.

There. Something down low, pressed back hard into the

slight recess in the wall, huddled against her door. A pair of wide, frightened eyes stared up at her from the gloom.

Kate threw herself forward, closing the gap in a moment, her heart exploding in her chest.

59

'Clara?'

The crouching figure didn't move.

Kate choked on the words: 'Is it you?' She sank to her haunches, there in the corridor, and brought her eyes close to the pale face, doubting her mind, her own senses. She was hallucinating, surely.

Clara burst into tears.

'How are you—? What are you—?' Kate seized hold of her daughter with all her strength, wrapping her arms around her and pulling her close. If this were real, if this were true, Kate would never let go of her daughter again. She rocked her, clasping her as tightly as she could, as if her life depended on it. Kate started to shake as her eyes filled.

'I thought you were dead. My God, Clara. I thought—' Kate could hardly speak for sobbing. Her face pressed wetly into her daughter's soft hair. The familiar smell of her daughter's skin washed over her.

This was what she'd imagined so often in the small hours of the night when she'd paced around the house, desolate, grief-stricken. This grasping of her daughter in her arms, this squeezing her close. Was it really true?

'I'm sorry. I'm so sorry.' Kate's words tumbled out. 'I love you so much, Clara. So much.'

Kate pulled suddenly back from her daughter, afraid. Was it her? How could it be? She held her daughter's damp, blotchy face between her hands and studied it. 'Is it really you? I never thought I'd ever—' She swallowed hard. Her hands trembled. Clara's skin was warm and wet and real. 'How did you—?' Kate didn't understand anything. Her mind was upside down. It didn't matter. Clara was here. Alive. 'I love you. You know that, don't you? You're everything to me. These past days, when I thought I'd lost you, when I thought I'd never see you again, I didn't know how I could bear it.' She broke off, took a shuddering breath as she forced herself to carry on. 'I don't think I could live without you.'

Clara, staring with desperate eyes into her mother's face, gave a jerky nod.

Kate pulled her close again, squeezing her. 'I'm so sorry. For everything. If I could turn the clock back, if I could do it all again, I'd be so different. I was lost after Bella died. Broken. I wasn't there for you, Clara. I didn't listen to you. I see that now. I'm so sorry.'

Clara started to cry harder. Kate stirred herself at last, opened the door to her room and propelled Clara inside.

Sprawled on the bed, Kate rocked her. Clara was her baby again, her toddler, climbing into Kate's lap to be held, to be comforted. As they rocked back and forth, time seemed to concertina, to compress their shared lives into that one moment.

Kate felt a dam of fear and tension inside her daughter finally burst. She held her as Clara began to sob helplessly, as she let go at last. Kate murmured in her daughter's ear, as she had when Clara was a child: 'It's OK, my love, it's OK. I've got you, now. You're safe. It'll be OK, I promise.'

When Clara's crying finally subsided, she lay, exhausted, eyes closed, in Kate's lap. Her body seemed limp. Kate tried to drink in every detail of her daughter's face. Gently, she stroked the matted hair from Clara's forehead, from her flushed cheeks.

Clara opened her eyes and blinked up at her mother. 'I'm sorry too. I was awful to you. I was just angry and hurting so much. Losing Dad and then Bella and—'

Kate put a finger on her daughter's lips to silence her. 'I know,' she said. 'It's OK.'

Clara's eyes fell closed again and, gradually, as she relaxed, her breathing deepened.

Kate sat very still, watching over her daughter. There was so much she needed to know, so much she didn't understand, but, for now, all she wanted was to hold her, to look at her, to feel that she was here, in Kate's arms, safe and very much alive.

Thank you, God, she thought. *Thank you so much for giving her back to me.*

60

When Clara opened her eyes, Kate saw in them the echo of the little girl she remembered. Her look was lost and frightened, a mute appeal to her mother to put things right.

'Take a deep breath.' Kate reached across to the box of tissues on the bedside table and plucked some out. There were so many questions she needed to ask, jostling and pressing, but she could also see what a state Clara was in. She remembered what Rosa had said: *you can be a bit, you know, full on. Maybe Clara doesn't need that right now.*

Kate took a deep breath and said, as calmly as she could: 'How about getting you something to eat? Good idea? I'll order room service.'

Clara hid in the bathroom while the room service tray was left. When the coast was clear and the room door had been locked again, Clara fell on the burger and fries as if it was the first hot meal she'd had in a long time.

Kate sipped her coffee and struggled to stay quiet until her daughter seemed ready. Her forehead creased with concern as

she scrutinised Clara's face. Her cheekbones were more prominent, her face less full. She'd lost weight.

Afterwards, Kate settled Clara next to her on the bed. She
laced an arm round her daughter's shoulders and forced herself
to sound calm.

'Now,' she said, 'can you tell me what happened?'

Clara pursed her lips. 'It was him. Adrian.'

Kate hesitated. 'Amy's boyfriend?'

Clara nodded. 'He tried to get me killed. It was him, I'm sure
of it. He thinks I'm dead.'

'He tried to get you *killed*?' Kate felt the tension stiffening her
daughter's body. 'But why? Why would anyone—?' Kate struggled to breathe. How dare he. It made no sense. Her lovely
daughter. Clara wouldn't hurt a fly. She wasn't a threat to
anyone. How could—?

Kate took a deep, steadying breath and tried to slow her
racing heart. 'Why don't you start from the beginning, OK? Tell
me everything. Just take your time.'

They sat for a moment in silence.

Finally, Clara shuddered and began to talk.

'I didn't trust him, Mum. There was something about him,
about the things he said, that didn't ring true. I tried to warn
Amy. We had, I don't know, a big argument about it. And then I
realised he'd been there, in the apartment, all the time. He'd
heard every word.' She closed her eyes for a moment and shivered. 'The look he gave me. It was poison. That night, I hardly
slept. I just wanted to pack and move out. But the next morning,
he was a different character. He can be charming, sometimes.'

Kate nodded grimly. She knew. She'd seen that for herself.
'So you changed your mind about leaving?'

'Not really. I just pretended. I knew it might take me a few
days to find another place.' She picked at the sides of her finger-

nails as she remembered. 'That evening, I was on shift at Galileo's until late. Amy was too but she said she was going back to Adrian's place with him. They left and, just after that, Gino, the boss, called me and told me I needed to finish setting up for the next day. By the time I'd finished, it was pretty late. I headed back to the apartment.

'It was cold but it was such a relief to be on my own in the quiet after all the noise of the restaurant. So I didn't hurry back. I went for a bit of a walk instead.'

She paused, scanning her mother's face to make sure she was listening before she carried on.

'It must have been midnight by the time I reached the apartment. I was frozen half to death. I slowed my footsteps. Upstairs, the rooms were dark. But as I looked, I saw a faint light, a weak, bouncing gleam. Like a torch.

'Burglars, that's what I thought. I was scared. Instead of going up, I crept past the entrance to the building and hid. There's an alleyway a bit further on and I crouched there, in the darkness, breathing in the stink of rotting rubbish, and watched.

'After a while, the main entrance door opened and two guys came out. Thick-set types. They were breathing heavily. Their armpits were stained with sweat. They were carrying something bulky between them. It sagged in the middle, hanging between their hands. I thought it was an old carpet. I doubted myself, almost laughed at how scared I'd been. Maybe I'd been mistaken about seeing a light inside. Maybe the flickering I'd seen had just been reflections on the glass from the water flowing in the canal. A trick of the eye.

'Then I looked again at the shape. The proportions, the rounded contours. I started to gag, my hands pressed over my mouth, trying to stop myself from retching.

'There was a white van parked down the street and the men

opened up the back, groaning and grumbling to each other, threw it inside and drove off.

'Once they'd gone, I just collapsed. That shape was a person. I just knew it. Whether they'd been dead or just unconscious, I wasn't sure. But whoever it was, I was terrified for them.

'I stayed there until my legs were so cold, I could barely move. They didn't come back. No-one else came out.

'In the end, I hobbled in through the main entrance. The warm air from the building's central heating washed over me and I crept up the stairs. Ahead, I saw at once that the door to our apartment was open. I inched closer and stood with my back pressed against the wall for some time. I strained to listen for sounds inside. It was silent.

'Gently, I pushed the door further open and headed into the apartment. I was braced for attack, for a sudden explosion of movement, but there was nothing.

'I stood in the living room, breathing hard, and looked around. It was a mess. Amy and I weren't the tidiest people but this was different. Cushions were strewn across the floor. The coffee table had been knocked over.

'On the far side of the living room, my bedroom door was flung wide open. I headed over there, heart pounding. It wasn't the way I'd left it. Not at all. Pillows everywhere. Sheets dragged off the bed. I took a few steps further in and crunched on shards of glass. My bedside light was on the floor, smashed. My duvet was missing. The body – it must have been wrapped inside it.

'I stood, trembling. I didn't know what to do. I couldn't move. I didn't want to touch a thing. I just felt sick. Then I turned and ran.'

Kate softly stroked her daughter's tight back and shoulders. Her mind was working hard. No-one had stumbled, drunk and drugged, into the canal. It hadn't been an accident. It had been a murder. Judging by what Clara had described, a hit job by thugs. Thugs who had apparently made a terrible mistake.

Kate said, as calmly as she could: 'Those guys...' she hesitated '...you think they came to kill you?'

Clara's lips pressed into a hard white line. Her eyes brightened with tears.

'But *why*, Clara?' Kate tried to keep her voice level. 'Why would Adrian – or anyone else, for that matter – want to hurt you?'

Clara's eyes were wide. 'That's what I keep thinking. I don't know.' She seemed barely able to speak. 'He's weird, that's all I can say. Always pushing drugs at everyone, soft and hard.' She seemed to read Kate's expression and added hastily: 'Not me, Mum. I don't do that stuff.'

Clara considered. 'Maybe he's angry that I saw him for what he is – a phoney. That I tried to warn Amy.' Tears squeezed through her lids and splashed down onto clasped hands. 'But that's no reason to *kill* me, is it?'

Kate shook her head. Something about all this didn't add up. 'And Amy's mother. She flew all the way to Amsterdam to identify a dead body as her own daughter – when she knew it wasn't true. But why? Why would she lie like that? Just because she was frightened of Amy getting into trouble? There must be something—' Her thoughts were racing, searching for answers, for connections. 'There's nothing else you can think of?'

Clara, crying again now, shook her head.

'You're still frightened, aren't you?' Kate threaded her arms around her. 'You think, if they find out, if they know you're still alive, they'll come after you again?'

Clara could barely speak. Kate stopped probing, tightened her arms and held her daughter close.

Kate ran a hot bath for Clara and sat outside, her back against the bathroom door, while Clara took it.

She was trying to give Clara as much space as her small hotel room could allow. It was hard. She had a visceral need to hold her daughter, to touch her, not to let her out of her sight.

She hunched there, guarding her, and smelled the pungent hotel bubble bath, listened to the soft splashes as Clara shifted her weight in the water.

Afterwards, Clara wrapped herself up in the fluffy hotel dressing gown and stretched out on the bed. She looked exhausted. Kate lay close alongside her, an arm threaded round her daughter's waist. The tension, the hostility, which had separated them from each other since Bella's death, seemed to have melted to nothing. Kate could still hardly believe it. She had her daughter back, in every way.

Quietly, Kate started to explain everything that had happened to her, as Clara, lying close, listened.

Kate talked her through that first transatlantic phone call from Amy's mother, Maddy, and their search for both girls in

Amsterdam, the way Maddy had identified the body as Amy's and Kate had helped her arrange a hasty cremation and release her ashes into the water. Later, in London, Kate's anguished attempts to reach Clara, imagining she was somewhere in Italy, as Adrian had suggested, then her sightings of Clara in London, wearing a hat so like the one Bella had crocheted. Then, that final journey to Ann Arbor where Kate had seen Amy and Adrian with Maddy and been devastated by the conclusion that, all along, the dead girl had been Clara.

Clara twisted round to look her mother in the face. Her expression was full of pain. 'Oh, Mum. I'm so sorry. I should have found a way of telling you I was OK. I was just so frightened. I thought, if anyone found out, those guys would come after me—'

'Don't. It's OK now.' Kate shook her head. 'I'm just so glad. So grateful it wasn't you.' She took a deep breath. 'But, Clara, if it wasn't you and it wasn't Amy, who was it?'

The two of them looked each other full in the face.

Clara said slowly: 'Did Amy's mum ever talk about another American girl? Amy had a flatmate before me. A girl called Honey. She was a bit—'

'She was into drugs,' Kate cut in at once. She remembered Gino's flare of anger when Maddy had asked him about Honey. *A dopehead*, he'd called her. *Too much into parties*. 'I thought she'd moved out?'

Clara pulled a face. 'Well, she had. Technically. But she never stayed anywhere for long. And Amy never made her give the key back. She was always coming round uninvited and hanging out, making a nuisance of herself. Once or twice, I, well, I came back late from work and she was asleep in my bed.'

Kate understood at once. 'But how – I mean, if it was her, wouldn't someone have raised a stink by now?'

Clara stared, her eyes full of pain. 'I'm not sure. She did sort of disappear at times. We just assumed she was stoned.'

Kate frowned to herself. 'Did she have family?'

Clara looked anguished. 'She had a mum in the States, somewhere. And maybe a brother. She didn't talk about them much. They didn't get on.'

Kate shook her head. She imagined the girl's poor mother, still unaware of the grief to come.

Clara said: 'Amy might know.'

'Oh, Clara.' Kate sat very still, thinking. She thought of this young girl, Honey, rootless and lost, unable to hold down a job, endlessly surfing couches and sleeping in other people's beds. A girl who, even after all this time, hadn't been reported missing because no-one had noticed she'd gone.

'Was she blonde?' she said suddenly.

'Ash blonde.' Clara nodded. 'Even lighter than Amy.'

So that was one thing Maddy hadn't lied about, after all.

'Poor kid,' Kate said simply. It sounded as if Honey had let herself into the apartment at the wrong time on the wrong day and, finding the place empty, climbed into Clara's bed to sleep.

'I keep thinking, if I hadn't gone for that walk—' Clara started to shake. Kate tightened her arms around her. 'Or if Honey hadn't been there, in my bed, maybe they'd have waited for me. Maybe I would have been—'

'Don't.' Kate rocked her. 'You can't know that.'

Kate thought back to the cremation and the dispersal of the ashes. It was all such a mess. Maddy's lie stretched on and on. Kate had unwittingly been part of destroying the evidence. It did seem likely that Honey had been the victim that night but there seemed no way now of proving it.

She held Clara very close, thinking. She had to focus on her own daughter. Her priority was on keeping Clara safe.

Kate said: 'So where've you been living?'

'Axel let me stay with him.'

'Axel?'

'Swedish guy. Lives in the flat below. A student.'

Kate remembered the young Scandinavian man who'd fled on his bicycle when she and Maddy had tried to question him. She'd sensed at the time that he'd known something. She wanted to kick herself. She should have trusted her instincts and followed up.

'He's just a friend,' Clara went on. 'He wouldn't come up to our place. He and Adrian didn't get on. But I used to sneak down to his apartment, now and then, for a coffee and a chat. When I fled down the stairs that night, he had his door open a crack, listening, trying to figure out what was going on. I'm sleeping under his bed.'

'*Under* his bed?'

'He's draped a bedspread over, to hide me. In case they burst in, at night, searching for me.' She pointed at her clothes. 'This is all I've got. That night, I was too scared to take my stuff, even my phone, in case they came back and realised it was missing, that I was still alive.

'The next day, Amy and Adrian came over and cleaned the place up. They took a load of my clothes, including that hat Bella made me. You were right – Amy must have been wearing it in Covent Garden when you spotted her. And my phone. And my passport. I've no way of getting home.' She shivered. 'Then a group of men came in and emptied the place completely. Someone else lives there now.'

Kate took in Clara's pinched face. 'What've you been living on?'

'Whatever Axel could afford.'

Kate imagined her daughter curled in the darkness under a

bed every night, terrified that the murderers would come back for her. 'Why didn't you call me? Or get Axel to send me a message?'

'I was just so frightened. I thought, if I reached out to you, Adrian might find out and he'd kill me.' Clara started to cry again. 'I saw you. When you came to the apartment building that time.'

'With Maddy, Amy's mum?'

Clara's voice was ragged though her tears. 'I heard your voice. I thought I was dreaming. I peered out of Axel's bedroom window and you were there, looking up at me. You were so close.' Her sobs intensified. 'Didn't you see me? I wanted so much to bang on the glass, to shout out, but I was too frightened. What if those guys were watching the building? I couldn't risk it.'

'But you've risked it now.'

'Axel saw you today in the street. He remembered you. He followed you back to your hotel and saw which room you went in. Later, when it was dark, he sneaked me over in the back of a taxi. I just waited there, outside your door, until you came back.'

'I'm sorry I wasn't back sooner. But you did the right thing.' Kate felt a surge of adrenalin. Life had given her a second chance, a chance to save her daughter. She was going to seize it. 'I'll keep you safe, from now on.'

Clara pulled back. Her eyes were full of fear. 'But what if someone saw me? What if they know?'

Kate gave her a long look. 'You're convinced Adrian is the guy behind this?'

Clara nodded emphatically. 'He wants to get rid of me. He's dark. He's the reason I came to Amsterdam, did you know that? He messaged me online and invited me over. Said his girlfriend was looking for a room-mate.'

Kate frowned. The plot was getting weirder by the second. 'Why? Why did he want you here?'

'I don't know.' Clara looked beside herself. 'I thought he was OK. He said he knew Bella.'

'He knew Bella?' Kate tensed.

'He said he was friends with her at uni, but now I don't believe he even went. He lies all the time. Maybe he just read online about how she died. Anyway, he knew I was onto him. And if he finds out I'm still alive, he'll come after me. He wants to shut me up.'

Kate considered, perplexed by Adrian's connection to Bella. 'What about Amy? Where does she stand in all this?'

Clara blew out her cheeks. 'I don't know. Whatever line he's spun her about what happened, she must think I'm dead. She adores him and she'll be terrified. She'll do whatever he tells her, see?'

Suddenly, Kate did see. She could almost hear Amy's panicked phone call to Ann Arbor, begging her mother to save her. Adrian was smart. It was such an audacious idea, to spirit Amy away to London, and then, finally, once the trail was well and truly muddied, to fly to Detroit and hide away there.

Meanwhile, Maddy had pretended to be so worried about her precious daughter that she'd jumped on a plane and flown to Amsterdam to look for her. She'd made sure on arrival to highlight Amy's disappearance to the local police. It had put her in pole position when a body was found in the canal. The desperate mother, ready to identify the young, dead female as her missing daughter. The murderers' mistake had played to their advantage. They'd ended up with a dead blonde who, after days rotting in the water, could indeed pass for Amy.

'Why did she need me?' Kate was thinking aloud. She'd

been played. She saw that. Cleverly played. But what use had she been? 'Why involve me at all?'

Clara looked thoughtful. 'I've wondered about that. I don't know. Maybe it's got something to do with Bella. You know, Project Bella.' She hesitated, her eyes on Kate's face. 'I'm not having a go. I'm just saying. You're all over the internet, talking about Bella's death, saying it's torn the family apart. That you won't rest until you get justice. All that stuff.'

'How does that help them, though?' Kate didn't see where Clara was going with this. 'Surely a relentless, campaigning mother is exactly what they don't need if they're trying to cover up a murder.'

Clara paused, marshalling her thoughts. 'I think it's the mother card. Maybe she reckoned you'd empathise, you know; you'd see her as a kindred spirit, another desperate mum trying to save her missing daughter. Your own emotions about losing a daughter, your grief for Bella, would blind you. So, you'd be more likely to believe her, when she pretended it was Amy's body.'

'Maybe.' Kate thought back to the intense days she and Maddy had shared together in Amsterdam. 'But it still doesn't really explain why she needed me.' Kate had felt so desperately sorry for Maddy and guilty too because she was grateful the body in the canal was Amy's and not Clara's. There was no doubt her emotions had been intense. Still, she had the sense that something else was eluding her. Something important.

'We're missing something,' Kate said. 'Some connection. Something that ties all this together and helps it make sense.'

They sat quietly for a moment, both lost in thought.

After a while, Kate murmured: 'All that nonsense about Amy's jewellery.' She remembered Maddy's grief-stricken expression as she'd handled the pieces of hand-painted wooden jewellery. They were unique pieces, Maddy had said wistfully. She'd told Kate that whole story about buying them in New York and giving them to Amy when she went travelling. She'd been so convincing. Kate shook her head. She knew now that it was all lies. But why?

Some of Maddy's other behaviour made more sense. No wonder Maddy had been so determined to sever contact with Kate, once it was all over and she was ready to leave Amsterdam. Kate had played her part. The last thing Maddy wanted was for her to stay in touch. She didn't want her to find out the truth.

Beside her, Clara was relaxing into sleep. Kate saw her daughter's eyes grow heavy, felt the sudden tremor through her body as she struggled to stay awake.

Kate pulled back the duvet. 'You need to get some rest. You're safe here. I won't leave you.'

She helped Clara under the covers and lay quietly beside her. Clara's eyes closed. A moment later, her breath settled into a deep, steady rhythm.

Kate kept vigil. She thought of all the times she'd watched her daughter sleep.

Those first days when Clara was a new baby with impossibly long eyelashes, cradled in her arms. Kate remembered simply sitting, exhausted but too enraptured to move, and gazing at her daughter's face. Her tiny, perfect miracle. Her beautiful second-born, with her whole life ahead of her. She'd sat like that for hours, sometimes, her arms stiffening, determined not to set her down.

She thought of the times Clara had fallen asleep in her car seat as a toddler, her head gently lolling, her eyes gradually closing, lulled by the engine. The car had become heavy with silence. Kate had driven with exaggerated care, then, sometimes, added extra circuits of the neighbourhood, just to extend the peacefulness. She remembered the sleepy weight when she'd lifted Clara at last into her arms, small head flopping, and carried her, stirring and protesting, into the house.

Now, her daughter was a young woman. Kate thought of the horrors she'd seen and of how frightened she'd become, how exhausted. The very thought made her heart ache.

'Oh, Maddy,' Kate murmured. 'Why did you go along with it?'

Maddy had done a wicked thing. How could anyone lie about something as important as a dead girl's identity? Kate sighed to herself. She guessed Maddy had seen it as the only way of saving her daughter. Perhaps, from the police. Perhaps, even, from prison.

Kate shook her head. She wondered if she would be capable of the same lies, if she found herself in the same situation.

She propped herself up on one elbow and watched silently as Clara slept, relishing each even, rhythmical breath, each flutter of her daughter's eyelids. She felt her own heart rate slow. Clara was alive and Kate knew, as she watched her sleep, that she'd do whatever it took to keep her safe. Maybe, she thought, she and Maddy weren't so very different, after all.

62

The following morning, Kate woke early and spent a productive couple of hours phoning and emailing.

When Clara finally woke, Kate ordered room service breakfast and hid Clara in the bathroom while it was delivered. Then, she tried to encourage Clara to tuck into the eggs, sausages and pastries.

'I've been making some calls,' Kate said. 'One of them was to the British Embassy in The Hague. It sounds a fairly straightforward process, getting you an emergency travel document, but it'll take at least a couple of days. Rosa says she can help. We need to dig out documents from home, like your birth certificate.' Kate hesitated, watching Clara's reaction. 'And it's possible you'll have to go to the embassy for an interview.'

'In The Hague?' Clara looked up from her food, panic in her eyes. 'Mum, I can't go anywhere. What if Adrian finds out?'

Kate reached for her daughter's hand. 'As far as I know, he's still in the US. He took Amy there to be with her mother. But, you're right, he could be back any day. So we need to move fast.'

Kate paused. She could see how distressed Clara was

becoming but there was something else she really needed to raise. 'I've been wondering whether or not we should go to the police. If we report your passport stolen, we could get an official document to submit to the embassy and—'

'No!' Clara set down her knife and fork with a clatter. 'It's all too risky. You don't know Adrian. He's got friends everywhere. And anyway, what's the point in going to the police? The story sounds too far-fetched. They'll never believe me.' She looked close to tears.

'Oh, Clara.' Kate leaned across and held her, briefly. 'We will get through this. There are risks whatever we do. You're right, we don't know who we can trust.' She took a breath. 'The police may not believe you. You can't prove that you saw what you did. And, when it comes to accusing Adrian, we've no real evidence.'

Clara blew out her cheeks. 'Even if they interviewed him, we both know what he's like. He'd fool them.'

Kate nodded, thinking. 'We might be able to prove that Maddy lied. If they took us seriously and made enquiries with the US, they could confirm Amy's back there, alive and well. But it would take time.'

'Mum, please. Forget about the police.' Clara's voice was pleading. 'If Adrian finds out I'm alive, he'll kill me. I'm sure he will.'

'That's what I thought you'd say.' Kate considered. 'But—'

'No, Mum! You promised!' Clara was shaking. 'You promised you'd keep me safe!'

Kate had promised that. She couldn't let her daughter down. 'All right, let's leave it, at least for now.' She reached out and stroked Clara's hair. 'Don't cry. It's OK.'

'It isn't OK, though, is it? It's never going to be OK,' Clara sobbed. 'I'm never going to be safe from him, am I? He's always going to be out there. I'm going to be looking over my shoulder for the rest of my life.'

'Clara, listen.' Kate forced her daughter to look her in the eye. 'Calm down and listen to me.'

Clara looked back at her, her eyes red, her breath ragged as she tried to stop crying.

'Good. You listening?'

Clara gave a shudder, calming herself, and nodded.

'OK. I've been thinking a lot about this,' Kate said softly. 'You're right. I think you will always be in danger, as long as that man's alive.'

The silence between them stretched.

Clara swallowed hard. 'So what do I do?'

Kate looked away for a moment. She looked at Clara's hand in hers. She remembered how tiny it had been once, such minute fingers, a whole hand of them curling round one of her own. She'd promised her daughter then, when she was just a newborn, that she'd love her, that she'd look after her.

'You need to trust me.' She stroked the back of Clara's hand. 'And you might need to be brave. Can you do that?'

* * *

Without a police report, Clara did need a face-to-face interview at the embassy.

Kate travelled with her to The Hague and installed her in a small, inconspicuous guesthouse within walking distance of the embassy building. Clara barely left their room, a shrunken shadow of herself, frightened half to death.

On the second day, Rosa arrived to take Kate's place, Clara's birth certificate in her bag.

'Have you got to go, Mum?' Clara clung to her mother like a small child.

Kate held her close. She thought of all the partings. All those mornings at nursery, when Clara had looked so vulnerable as she was ushered in through the door, without time for a backwards glance. All the drop-offs at primary school when Kate had forced herself to kiss Clara brightly on the cheek at the school gates and watch her head in, plaits flying, school bag bumping on her back.

Now, all over again, Kate felt as if her heart was being ripped from her body. She didn't want to turn around and go. She didn't want to leave her daughter.

'It sounds as if you'll get the emergency travel document approved tomorrow. Then, you and Rosa can head straight back to London. OK?' Kate attempted a smile. 'I'll be home before you know it.'

Kate climbed into the rental car, drove to Schiphol Airport and caught the next flight to Detroit.

63

Ann Arbor had changed in the short time Kate had been away.

Just as it had in Amsterdam, the weather had shifted gear as it moved into spring. Plants, dormant during the cold winter months, were in bud. Cafés and restaurants had set tables out on the street. Mobile coffee shops, operating from brightly coloured vans, had appeared along the edge of main streets.

The mood on campus had lightened. Students strolled in the open air between classes, unhurried, relishing the warmth of the sun on their faces. They lingered with takeaway coffees on benches and walls. They threw frisbees and American footballs on the stretches of grassy lawn.

Kate looked down on it all from her hotel room. Her mind was far away, twisting and contorting. She gripped the edge of the curtain until her knuckles blanched, then realised and let it fall.

She thought about Simon and Bella and the horror of losing first one, then the other. Their absence gnawed at her, always. She remembered the feeling of hopelessness that had consumed her that evening in Amsterdam when she had stood in the shadows on the edge of the canal and believed Clara too was dead. The shine on the surface of the black, fast-flowing water and the dark pull beneath. The lure of obliteration.

She reached out and steadied herself against the wall. It was still and solid in a world that seemed to be spinning out of control. Something was opening up in front of her, something sinister. It frightened her. She thought of Simon and his softness, his kindness, his determination to do the right thing. He would be horrified, she knew, if he sensed what she was planning. He'd beg her to stop, to step away while she still could.

She shook her head. She couldn't afford to let herself think like that. He wasn't here. This was her choice.

She pulled herself straight again and focused on the students idly crossing the campus. She thought of Clara, soon to board a flight to London. Her arms ached to hold her again. She'd made a promise to her daughter, to keep her safe, whatever the price. It was a promise she would keep.

A smart, middle-aged woman appeared from the main road and tripped briskly along the paved path towards the entrance to Kate's hotel. Maddy's pale blue coat was nipped at the waist by a belt. The breeze lifted strands of her blonde hair. She reached the hotel, passed under Kate's window and disappeared from sight.

Kate nodded to herself. She imagined Maddy downstairs, striding through the reception lobby to the lift and heading up towards her room. She waited for the knock on the door. It was what she'd expected, what she'd hoped, but she still hadn't been certain if Maddy would come.

She closed her eyes and took a deep, slow breath.

As soon as Kate opened the door, Maddy darted inside the room. The two women stood, face to face. Maddy's lips and forehead were etched with tension. Her eyes were hard. They seemed to search Kate's face.

Kate said: 'Does anyone know you're here?'

Maddy shook her head. Her eyes didn't leave Kate's.

'How did you find out?' Maddy said. She sounded defeated.

'It doesn't matter. The fact is, I did.'

Kate gestured to the chairs she'd moved to the centre of the bedroom and the women sat, facing each other. Outwardly, Maddy seemed composed, her legs neatly together, her hands clasped in her lap. Kate wasn't fooled. She saw the tension in her jaw.

'I suppose you want money.' Maddy's voice was jagged. 'Is that what this is about?'

Kate said in a measured tone: 'I'm not a blackmailer.'

'Anyway, why should I believe you?' Maddy narrowed her eyes. 'You implied in your email that you know what really happened. How do I know that's true?'

Kate's tone was measured. 'I know why you flew out to Amsterdam, why you lied and claimed that Amy had gone missing and then, when a dead body showed up, pretended it was your daughter. You were protecting her, weren't you? You were worried that, if you didn't cover her tracks and give her the chance to get out of the country, she might get caught up in a murder investigation.'

Maddy flushed and looked away, towards the window.

'You used me.' Kate struggled to keep the anger out of her voice. 'You lied to me and let me comfort you, even though you thought my daughter was the one who'd really died. But that's the bit I still don't understand.'

Maddy couldn't look at her. 'It was his idea. All of it. Amy was terrified. It was too late for your daughter. She was already dead. But Amy – she'd had her whole life ahead of her.'

Kate swallowed hard. She'd already figured out the truth of this bit for herself, but it still hurt to hear it.

'Well, it wasn't my daughter,' she said at last. 'They got the wrong girl.'

'I don't believe you.' Maddy's eyes flicked uncertainly to Kate's face.

Kate shrugged. 'Suit yourself. But I can tell you Clara's very much alive.'

Maddy blinked rapidly. 'So who—?'

'We think it was another American. Honey. A friend of Amy's.'

'Honey?' Maddy let out a tight breath. 'Yeah, Amy talked about her. They were room-mates for a while.'

'Exactly.'

'And she—?' Maddy tailed off. 'My God.'

They fell silent, lost in their own thoughts. Outside, a young man hollered across the campus. A football thumped and bounced on the paving below.

When she felt Maddy was ready to listen, Kate carried on. 'I should hate you for what you did. It was despicable. You thought you'd tricked me into organising my own daughter's cremation, without even knowing what I'd done. How could you be so cruel? And letting me watch while you dispersed her ashes.' She shook her head in disgust. 'There've been nights I've been so consumed with grief, with bitterness, that I've wanted to hurt you, really hurt you. Believe me.' She took a deep breath. 'But Clara's alive. All I want now is to keep her safe. And, suddenly, I think we find ourselves on the same side, you and I. We're both mothers who'll do anything to protect our daughters.'

'Protect them?' Maddy gave a hard laugh. 'It's a bit late for that. You don't know him. You don't know what a monster he is.'

'Then tell me.' Kate sat forward, her eyes sharp. 'I'm missing something. I know I am. Something that ties all this together. You. Me. Our daughters.' She hesitated, watching Maddy's reaction. 'If we do this, if we join forces, there are no half measures. We'd have to trust each other absolutely. And it must be just us. The things we're going to talk about today, the things we might do, no-one else can ever know. Not Clara, not Amy, not anyone. Do you understand?'

Maddy frowned. She opened her mouth, as if she were about to speak, then closed it again.

Kate persisted, speaking slowly and clearly. 'Look, we can carry on working against each other. Or we can work together. You choose.' She hesitated, weighing up the tension in the room. 'Be aware that if you go to the police, I'll deny everything. And if I tell them what I know, if I tell them what really happened in Amsterdam, well, you can imagine what that would mean for Amy. And her baby.'

They sat in silence for a moment, eye to eye, each taking the measure of the other.

Kate lowered her voice. 'I've got a plan but it's still sketchy. I need your help.' She hesitated, then continued. 'Remember, Maddy, I want the same as you. I want to save my daughter from him. And I'm willing to do whatever it takes. The question is: are you?'

Maddy slowly nodded. Kate felt her shoulders slacken as she sensed something shift between them.

'So,' Kate said. 'What else can you tell me about him?'

'He murdered my husband,' Maddy said softly. 'In cold blood.'

For a moment, Kate couldn't speak. Finally, she whispered: 'My God.' Her anger towards this woman morphed in a heartbeat to pity. She thought of Simon and the pain of losing him.

'I'm sorry, so sorry.' She shook her head, struggling to understand. 'But why?'

'Revenge.' Maddy swallowed hard. 'I made a mistake. A dreadful mistake. Involving his mother.'

'His mother?'

Maddy nodded. 'She killed herself.' She hesitated, as if she were choosing her words with care. 'I was her psychiatrist, in New York. I'd prescribed medication. Sertraline, an antidepressant. I should have monitored her, to make sure she didn't have a paradoxical reaction.' She glanced at Kate to see if she understood. 'A reverse effect. That happens sometimes. Instead of alleviating depression, medication can make a patient suicidal.'

Kate frowned. 'And that's what happened to her?'

Maddy inclined her head. 'I doctored the notes. It was stupid. I panicked. I pretended I'd checked up on her when I hadn't. To save my skin.' She looked down at her hands. 'I was on fentanyl at the time. You know what that is? An analgesic. Highly potent. Highly addictive.' She paused. 'I'm clean now.'

'And he found out?'

'He knew about all of it. After he'd murdered Arthur, he came right out and told me. He seemed to take pleasure in it, in knowing there wasn't a thing I could do. He didn't just threaten to expose me. That's the easy part. He threatened to kill Amy if I went to the police.'

'Amy?' Kate stared. 'But they're having a child together.'

Maddy gave a crooked smile. 'Isn't it perfect? So I'll never be free of him. Neither will she. Or my grandchild.'

Kate's mind spun. Stray pieces of information wheeled in front of her. Clearly, Adrian had proved himself capable of murder. Clara's instincts had been right. But why? Why had he tried to kill Clara?

'Tell me about his mother. What was she like?'

'Monica?' Maddy shrugged. 'I'd only seen her for a few sessions. She seemed—'

'Monica?' Kate sat up, her voice sharp. 'Monica what?'

Maddy looked thrown for a moment. 'Bancroft. Monica Bancroft.'

Kate felt the blood drain from her face. Stray pieces, flying haphazardly around her head, suddenly coalesced and started to fall abruptly into place.

Jonathan. She remembered what a strange boy he'd been, how disturbing she'd found him. She remembered Coco, cold and stiff in the water. Clara's doll, Mimi, grotesquely strung up.

Kate's mind whirled. Of course, he wanted to kill Clara. He hated them. He always had. *He's the reason I came to Amsterdam*, Clara had said. *He wants to get rid of me*. It was no accident. He'd lured her there.

'His name isn't Adrian,' she said aloud.

Maddy looked surprised. 'That's right. It's Damian.'

Kate shook her head. 'It's Jonathan.'

'Wait.' Maddy looked shocked. 'You know him?'

Kate was only half listening. Her thoughts raced ahead. What else had Clara said about him? Drugs. *He's always pushing drugs at everyone, soft and hard*. Kate's lungs seemed to explode in her chest. *He knew Bella. At uni*. Her breath came in shallow puffs.

'He killed my daughter.' The knowledge of it burst over her like a tidal wave, sweeping everything in its path. Kate heard her voice, strangely disembodied, say again: '*He* killed her.'

Maddy stared at her. 'But I thought you said—'

'Not Clara.' Kate took a shuddering breath. 'My other daughter. Bella. He didn't only kill your husband. He killed Bella too.'

64

DAMIAN

Damian was beginning to wonder how long he'd stick around, after all.

For the first few days in Ann Arbor, he'd been riding high. He'd taken pleasure in Maddy's pain and her struggle to hide it from her daughter. He'd seen the way she turned away from him when he spoke, as if she were stopping her ears, the way she left the room if he found her alone and, when the three of them were together, how she lavished her attention on Amy, as if he weren't even there.

He saw the difference in her, compared with the woman he'd seen in New York, and enjoyed knowing it was because of him. She was clean now, free of fentanyl. But, despite that, she was a deeply diminished version of herself. Her high-profile career had gone. No more Manhattan power couple. She was a solitary widow who seemed to have cut herself off from the world.

Only Amy seemed to bring her joy. Damian had expected Maddy to be devastated by the news of Amy's pregnancy, not least because it made her husband's murderer a permanent part of her family. But Damian saw the light in Maddy's eyes when her daughter walked into the room, the pride in her face when they sat together and talked in low voices about Amy's plans for the baby, for the future.

Damian was already bored by Amy. He liked the idea of a son but not while it was a mewling infant. He'd find a way of taking the boy over once he was old enough to be interesting. At the age of seven, maybe, or eight.

He wondered about spending another year or two in Amsterdam and then heading back to England. He thought often about Clara's mother, imagining her pain now she was alone, her husband and daughters gone. He wondered how long it would be before she realised Clara was not just missing but dead. Legally, it would take seven years, of course, until the courts could declare Clara dead and then Damian would pursue his inheritance. He could wait.

As for a mother, he didn't know. Maybe some mothers never accepted that missing meant dead. Maybe they never gave up. Maybe they kept searching for that missing child all their lives.

Then, just when Damian was feeling at his most restless, something happened. Maddy came home from the university one evening and he sensed a change in her.

When she brought him a beer before dinner, she paused and lifted her eyes to his, as if she really saw him, for the first time. He hesitated, trying to read her look. Furtive. Thoughtful.

'Everything OK?' he said carefully.

Maddy opened her mouth, then hesitated and closed it. Finally, she just said: 'I guess so.' She glanced towards the window. 'Is Amy outside?'

He nodded. Something was definitely different. 'Yep, soaking up the last of the sun.'

Maddy wandered back to the kitchen and he joined Amy out on the patio. She was resting her feet on the table, crossed at the ankles. Her legs were bloated with pregnancy, her skin dull. She made some inane remark about the squirrels digging up the lawn.

He pulled out a chair and sat beside her. He was barely aware of her. He was intrigued by Maddy and the hint of the old sparkle he'd detected in her eyes.

He gazed out across the stirring trees, sipped his beer and reasoned it all out. Maybe Maddy was finally getting over the shock. He remembered how furious she'd been when he'd met up with her that final night in Amsterdam and she'd seen who he really was. *Adrian, your daughter's boyfriend. Also known as Damian, your husband's killer.*

He smiled to himself. He'd played a blinder, by anyone's reckoning. Maybe she'd finally accepted that they were even now. Their score was settled.

Amy leaned over and put a hand on his arm.

'Hey, anyone home?' She grinned up at him, interrupting his thoughts.

He managed a smile back. 'How're you feeling?'

The miracle of her pregnancy and the changes to her body was a topic close to Amy's heart and, encouraged, she prattled on. He nodded, his features sympathetic, while his mind wandered.

He'd taken some calculated risks but, so far, they'd all paid off. When he'd first seduced Amy in Amsterdam, he'd impressed on her the need to keep him secret from her mother. No photos. Nothing that might give the game away. He'd known the name Adrian would mean nothing to Maddy.

Amy hadn't been hard to convince. He'd simply told her that he wanted to get to know her properly first. *I love you so much and I'm worried your mother mightn't think I'm good enough for you.*

Then, once the trap was sprung, he'd lured Clara out too and—

'Are you even listening?' Amy looked exasperated. 'You're miles away!'

'Am I? Sorry.' He reached over and ran a finger along the curve of her jawbone.

'Do you really have to go back?' Amy's voice descended into a whine.

He tried not to let his irritation show. 'You know I do. It won't be for long. But I've got work to finish off in Amsterdam.' He didn't intend to walk away from the Egyptian just yet. There was money to be made; he could smell it. He softened his voice. 'I want to work hard and provide for you. You know that. You and the baby.'

She nodded, mollified. He sipped his beer. He was ready to head back to Amsterdam for a while. It was all very pleasant here in Ann Arbor, with Maddy waiting on him and picking up the bills, but he needed some space.

Behind them, he heard the rattle of dishes in the kitchen.

'Sounds like your mother's starting on dinner.' He disentangled himself from Amy and scraped back his chair. 'You rest here. I'll see if she needs any help.'

He found Maddy at the counter, her hair swept back behind her ears, her head dipped as she put together a salad. She turned when she heard him and he saw again that quick, conscious look.

'What can I do?'

She set a punnet of tomatoes and a chopping board on the table in front of him. 'You could halve those.'

For a while, they worked in a silence broken only by the swish of cold water as she washed salad leaves and the pulpy suck of the knife through the soft flesh of the tomatoes. He waited.

'I've been thinking.' Maddy's voice was low. 'I need to talk to you. About your mother.'

Damian felt his body tense. 'What about her?'

Maddy glanced past him towards the patio, as if checking that Amy wasn't listening.

'Things she told me. She talked a lot, you know, in her sessions with me. About her feelings for you. For your father.'

Damian stopped cutting. His fingers tightened round the knife. 'Why did you never—'

Maddy put a finger to her lips. She nodded at the window. Amy, her back to the house, was still sipping her soda and gazing out across the garden.

Maddy said quietly: 'Look, it's delicate. I need to keep Amy out of this, OK? If I share what your mother told me, it's, well, for one thing, it's a clear breach of client confidentiality.'

Damian blinked. 'She's dead.'

Maddy shrugged. 'Even so. Still stands.'

Damian narrowed his eyes, considering her. 'So why raise this now?'

Maddy dipped her eyes to her hands. 'I've given it a lot of thought. I mean, it's a pretty unusual situation, right? You're family now. You're here for the long haul. So, I just figured...' she paused as if she were searching for the words '...there are things she said, about your childhood, about her feelings for you, well, I think you have a right to know.'

'OK.' Damian's interest was quickened. His mother had been such a remote figure, all his life. The drinking, the men. It never felt there was much left over for him. Something inside him stirred. Yes, he'd like to know more. He wanted to know what she'd really felt. 'When, then?'

She dumped the salad roughly in a bowl and said at volume: 'You finish the tomatoes, could you? I'll sort the chicken.' She twisted from the counter and headed across the kitchen towards the fridge.

Damian sensed movement outside and turned. Now, he understood. Amy had dropped her feet from the patio table and was heavily getting up, looking in on them through the window as she righted herself. He winked at her and blew her a kiss, wondering how much she'd heard. She merely smiled and turned back to the table to collect her empty glass.

She disappeared from sight. In a moment, she would walk through the doors to join them.

Maddy, glancing across at him, said in a low voice: 'Look, there's a lot to talk about. We can't really do it here. How about we fix some time together, somewhere quiet, before you go back to Amsterdam. I'll sort something out. Deal?'

He considered her for a moment, then nodded. 'Deal.'

65

Damian waved a final goodbye to Amy.

She twisted round in the passenger seat, her eyes brimming with tears, straining for a last glimpse of him as Maddy pulled away from the airport terminal to drive home.

Damian waited until the car had disappeared into the flow of traffic, then wheeled his case into the departures hall and counted to fifty, to be sure they were gone. As far as Amy was concerned, he was catching a flight to Amsterdam that lunchtime. He finished his count, smiled to himself and headed for car rentals.

He'd reserved a low-slung, sporty model for the next few days. He jangled the keys in one hand as he climbed in and checked over the controls. It wasn't bad. Ideally, he'd have liked a top-of-the-range convertible but that hadn't been an option. His mental image of himself speeding through open country-side, the crook of his elbow resting stylishly on the door, his expensive sunglasses dazzling, well, it would just have to wait for another day.

He found a rock station on the radio and lightly tapped the

steering wheel to the beat as he weaved his way through the traffic. The roads around Detroit were always clogged. He was glad when he could finally pick up the interstate and put his foot down, letting the car eat the miles towards Lansing and Grand Rapids. His destination lay far beyond, in the Upper Peninsula itself.

Gradually, the tight suburban sprawl, peppered with retail parks and hypermarkets, gas stations and hardware stores, opened up into a more rural landscape. He drove with growing excitement past fields of dairy cows and horses and freshly planted sugar beets and beans.

Impatient, Damian tried to distract himself by focusing his mind on the next two days. He'd been happy to leave the arrangements to Maddy. She'd heard about an old cabin, she'd said, on the upper shores of Lake Michigan, owned by a friend of a friend. He pictured a cosy wooden lake house, with a log fire and fabulous views.

He checked the time. Maddy should be setting out soon, heading there straight from Ann Arbor. She'd spun Amy some story about attending a two-day conference at Yale. He'd had no idea that she could lie with such conviction. It amused him.

An old classic came on the radio. He knew it from the opening chords and reached over to twist up the volume. He remembered listening to it at boarding school as a lonely teenager, dreaming of the future he'd make for himself. He hammered out the chorus, banging the steering wheel with the palm of one hand. Why the hell not? He grinned to himself. Why shouldn't he be in a great mood? He was smart. He'd worked hard. Finally, things were going right.

He'd taken revenge on his stepmother and bolstered his claim to his father's estate by ridding himself of both his stupid half-sisters. Kate might kick up a fuss about Clara being missing but he'd covered his tracks well. If the police bothered to take up the case, the most they could do was figure out that Clara had never left Amsterdam. Amy had kept hold of Clara's passport – it had helped her collect all that cash at Heathrow – but she'd travelled on her own US passport, no questions asked. Clearly, communications between the Amsterdam police and the airport immigration authorities hadn't been as close as they should have been.

As for him, he'd just stick to his story and play dumb. The trail had gone cold. There was no body.

In the meantime, he planned to carry on making money in Amsterdam. He'd earn enough to hire some big-gun lawyers to press his claim to the family money. And if his stepmother proved obstinate, well, there was always the risk she might have a terrible accident, like her daughters. He smiled to himself as he drove.

It was mid-afternoon by the time he skirted round Grand Rapids and, soon after, he decided to pull off the road to refuel and grab a burger. He'd already been driving for more than two hours and, according to the sat nav, it was still another four to the cabin. He wondered how far Maddy had got.

His mood shifted. The euphoria he'd felt earlier gave way to something more sombre. He wanted to hear what Maddy had to say about his mother. It must be something significant to warrant all this fuss. What beans had his mother spilled, in those counselling sessions? About his childhood, Maddy had said. And his father.

He didn't remember ever seeing his father, when he was very young. When he'd asked his mother about him, she made up crazy stories, different each time. Once, she said his father was a pirate who'd sailed away to find treasure and never come home. Once, when she was in a sour mood, she called him a tramp who smelled and slept under bushes. Another time, when she was very drunk, she'd told him to shut up about his father. *He didn't want you and neither do I.*

He wrapped up the remains of his fries, dropped them in the trash and wiped off his fingers. He headed into a 7-11 for a couple of bottles of Californian wine and a bag of snacks, stowed them on the back seat and drove on.

Gradually, the world around him became increasingly rugged, the domed sky above more open and vast. The towns along the route shrank in size and the fields were replaced by dense woodland, bursting with sap. Every now and then, he saw the flash of a scut as a rabbit darted for cover. A hawk, maybe even an eagle, skimmed the tops of the trees. He noted signs for walking and cycling trails, disappearing into the hinterland. Traffic thinned to a trickle.

Damian sat back, enjoying the drama of the landscape. The sheer scale of the US, with its epic, rolling wilderness, took his breath away. The music on the radio spluttered and spat as he dipped in and out of range.

The light started to fade. He blew out his cheeks, getting tired now. Overhead, clouds congregated, further blocking the dimming sun. Just when he was starting to despair of ever arriving, the sat nav guided him off the highway and onto a smaller, winding road, fringed by beeches and elms.

Now and then, through gaps in the treeline, he glimpsed the dark waters of Lake Michigan to the west. Above the surface of the lake, towering limestone cliffs gleamed in the dying light. The barren, vertical rock was as bleached and ridged as bone.

Rain spattered the windscreen. A storm was blowing in. He shrugged. It didn't matter. They'd be talking, not hiking. There wasn't even a phone signal at the cabin, she'd said. No way Amy or anyone else could interrupt them.

Darkness was descending rapidly. He put his headlights on full beam and slowed, made more cautious by the rain and the failing light. Far from dipping down towards the shore, as he'd expected, the road was climbing steadily, lifting him high above the lake. He found himself driving parallel to a tree-lined ridge, a last defence before a dramatic dead drop to the water below. The cliffs were clearly as sheer on this side of the lake as on the far side. In daylight, he was sure, the views would be spectacular.

If it hadn't been for the sat nav, he would have missed the turning for the cabin completely. The approach was no more than a dirt track, partly concealed by untamed bushes.

He nosed the car down it, bumping on the stones and ruts. His headlights picked out the structure ahead. It had a sharply angled roof and brown, clapperboard walls. A rough stone chimney rose through the centre, like a stalk.

As he drew closer, he saw the peeling paint on the window frames. Weeds were thick around the squat front door and along the sides of the building. It looked almost abandoned.

He parked in a flurry of loose gravel and cut the engine. When he opened the car door, his senses were assailed at once. The buffeting wind threw rain hard in his face. He tasted the heady scent of wet woodland and the sodden remnants of winter mulch. He struggled to the relative shelter of the narrow porch with his case in one hand and the carrier bag of wine and snacks in the other.

The door creaked and stuck in its frame as he shouldered it open. The shadowy interior smelled of stale smoke and rot.

'Hello!' he hollered, just to amuse himself. 'Anyone home?'

No reply. The only sounds were the muted whistle of the wind outside and the rain stippling the windows.

He set down his bags and carried on into the cabin. It was a tiny, ramshackle place, not at all what he'd envisioned. He could only think that Maddy had been misled.

He made his way down a grimy corridor towards the far end of the property. The light switches he found along the way didn't work. He shook his head and switched on his phone torch instead.

The corridor opened out into a cramped living room. He stood in the centre, training his torch on one object and then another, looking around.

A picture window dominated the far end. The darkness turned it into a black mirror, reflecting back to him the tiny circle of light surrounding the phone in his hand and, beyond it, barely visible, the ghostly outline of his own figure. He stood for a moment, regarding himself. His dark jeans and sweater disappeared into the gloom, leaving the pale shine of his skin, hands and face eerily suspended.

He approached the window and put his face to the glass, shielding it with cupped hands. All he could make out was a narrow strip of land with a single tree and, beyond it, the ragged edge of the cliff, giving way to nothingness.

He turned his attention back to the room. The furnishings were shabby. He found a heap of old woollen throws by the fireplace and shook them out, draping them over the threadbare sofa cushions. He discovered matches and a basket of logs in the grate and busied himself with laying and lighting a fire. The wood seemed damp.

It was just after seven o'clock. He opened a bottle of wine and drank off a glass, smoked some of the dope he'd secreted in his case and settled himself by the fire, watching the flames.

He sat back and let his mind drift to memories of his mother. He'd learned, from an early age, to ride her moods. There had been crazy days, now and then, when she danced in the kitchen and, in the park, dared him to climb trees with her, frightening him by going too high. More common were the black days when she didn't get out of bed.

He remembered the first time he'd fed himself from the biscuit tin. He was three or four, not yet in school. His mother hadn't got up that morning and he knew better than to wake her. He'd played quietly downstairs but when it got to afternoon, the hunger had become overwhelming. He hadn't known how to fix himself anything, not even a sandwich, so he'd turned to biscuits. Afterwards, he'd thought he'd be in big trouble for eating so many but his mother, when she finally appeared, didn't seem to care. After that, biscuit meals were a regular fixture.

He refilled his glass and drank it off. The wine and the dope together were melting away the tension in his body and he felt his senses blur. Where the hell was Maddy? She'd warned him that she might be late but, even so, he'd expected her by now. He wanted to hear what she had to say. He'd waited long enough.

He reached for his phone to message her, to tell her to hurry, then realised there was no signal. Of course. He'd just have to wait.

By eight thirty, he'd finished the first bottle of wine and opened the second. The room was fuggy with the acrid scent of dope. He felt his head loll as he started to doze and shook himself awake again. He stirred the fire into life and added more logs, sending up a shower of sparks. He stretched out the cramp in his legs and lit a fresh joint.

He jumped. A sound, outside. He listened hard, trying to make it out through the wind. Were those footsteps, close at hand, crunching across the loose stones? He hadn't heard her car. He drank off his glass and hurried back through the house to the front door.

The darkness was broken only by a faint wash of moonlight. He held up his phone torch but it was useless, dispersing at once into the night. He stood, blinking, on the threshold, as his eyes adjusted to the gloom. He made out the low shape of his own rental car, parked there by the side of the house. There was no sign of Maddy's. Where had she left it?

A strange sound came to him in the wind. A girlish laugh, drifting in from the far side of the house.

'Maddy?' His voice dispersed and disappeared at once. 'Are you there?' The night breeze chilled his skin and he shivered. What was she playing at?

The laughter sounded again. It sounded odd, disembodied, unravelled by the air.

He shook his head, irritated by her, and followed the sound, wading through unkempt, damp grass, close to the side of the cabin. When he reached the far end of the building, the full force of the gusts blowing up from the lake almost knocked him off his feet. He staggered and steadied himself against the rough wooden wall.

The moonlight shone more brightly here, silvery in the darkness. It shimmered in waves on the surface of the water, far below. He narrowed his eyes and looked around. Where was she?

He wondered if she'd sneaked past him and was already inside in the warm, laughing at him. He spun to face the picture window, twisted, cupped his hands against the cold glass and peered through. All he could make out was the yellow and orange glow of the fire, the darting shadows on the wall.

A pebble hit the glass beside him. A second struck him lightly on his back. He spun round. *For heaven's sake.*

'Maddy! What the hell are you playing at?'

He stared into the flurry of wind. Rain stung his cheek. He

felt himself sway, his senses befuddled by the alcohol, the drugs. He didn't have time for this. Impatience bubbled up in him. This was the sort of silly prank Amy might play, not her mother.

'Stop it.' His tone was sharp now. 'That's enough.'

She couldn't be far if she'd lobbed a pebble. He took a step away from the back of the cabin towards the solitary tree. His head craned forward. His eyes scanned the shadows in the half-light.

There weren't many places to hide. The narrow strip of land between the back of the house and the edge of the cliff was uncultivated scrubland, carpeted with sharp-bladed, wild grass and dotted with shrubs.

'Come out, Maddy. I know you're there.' His eyes ached from the dry chill of the wind.

A shape stepped out from a copse of trees further along the cliff. The figure of a woman.

'Maddy?' His mind struggled to be certain in the half-light.

Maddy's blonde hair was tousled and wild.

She spoke but she was too far away. He couldn't make out the words.

Maddy took a few steps closer and beckoned to him. 'Come over here, I've got something to show you. It's to do with your mother.'

The words reached him in fragments in the squall. He bit down on his lip. His mind was dulled by alcohol and dope. 'What're you doing out here?' He tried not to shout, to tamp down irritation. 'Come inside.'

'In a minute.' She frowned. 'Come on.' He shivered. He took a few tentative steps towards her, conscious of the strength of the driving wind and the sudden limestone drop of the cliff to his left.

What was she playing at, dragging him out here? It had

better be good, whatever it was she had to show him. He tutted to himself, then pushed forward against the blast, his body leaning in, battling the storm.

A sudden squall knocked him off balance and he staggered. He crouched for a moment, centring himself. He was close enough now to the edge to feel the pull of the black water in the lake below. It was a dizzying drop. He moved away.

Maddy glared at him. 'Get a move on. I'm freezing my butt off.' He found his balance again and took a few tentative steps towards her.

All at once. From nowhere. Something crashed into him. Hurtled from the shadowed side of the house, knocking him towards the edge of the cliff. He grasped at it, grabbing a handful of hair, the waxed material of a jacket. A woman. That was a woman's hair.

She butted him hard in the stomach, winding him, then kicked him in the groin, making him double up in pain.

He pummelled weakly at his assailant as her blows rained down. He tottered sideways, struggling in vain to right himself again, to find purchase in the slippery grass.

To the left, he sensed the soil start to crumble and give way. His foot scrambled on the disintegrating earth, desperate for solid ground. Clods flew down into nothingness, dropping endlessly.

Maddy came running towards them, her skirts billowing. Thank God.

His attacker, sensing his distraction, seized his wrists and twisted them out of her hair. She shoved him hard and he faltered, his feet paddling frantically. He pitched backwards, hands grappling, feeling the emptiness reach for him. His desperate fingers scratched at the rock as he fell, scraping his wrists and breaking his nails.

Wind rushed past him. His body jerked to a halt. His shoulder jolted in its socket. His flailing hand had caught something solid. A gnarled knot of root, protruding from the stone. He grasped it, hung there, dangling, clinging to life.

'Help!' His voice dispersed. 'Please.'

His feet scrambled uselessly at the slippery surface of the cliff. Fragments of stone and grit broke free as he kicked and bounced down the rock face into the darkness.

Terrified, he pulled his eyes away and stared upwards. The edge of the cliff drew a dark line against the sky.

As he looked, a woman's face loomed, moon-like, and hung there, close to the ground. She must be flat on her stomach. Only her head and shoulders protruded.

He stared. He was hallucinating. Her eyes fixed on his. Kate. His stepmother. His stomach chilled. What the hell was she doing here?

Time seemed to fold as a memory stirred. She'd looked at him that same way once, with those cold, hard eyes, when he was a boy, when he'd been sent to visit.

How was it possible? His mouth hung open. Through his body he felt the rush of a hollow, terrible knowledge.

The truth burst on him. Maddy had tricked him, with her promise of the chance to hear his mother's voice from beyond the grave.

He remembered in a flash how brilliantly she'd played the grieving mother in Amsterdam, how she'd fooled both the authorities and his stepmother into thinking Amy was dead. Was it possible that—? He could scarcely believe it. Had she fooled him too? Had these women, Maddy and his stepmother, conspired against him?

Already, his fingers, cut by the rough surface of the root, were becoming numb. He strained to yank himself higher, to reach up his lower, dangling arm and grasp with that hand too. He bulged with effort but couldn't reach.

'Help me!' he screamed at his stepmother. 'Please.'

She'd heard him, he knew. But she didn't move to save him.

Instead, her voice cut through the wind. 'You took Bella from me. I know it was you. I hope you rot in hell.'

Maddy's face appeared at her side. 'You killed my husband,' she screamed. 'And seduced my daughter, just to hurt me. You don't love her. You don't know what that means.'

His eyes bulged in his skull. He was losing feeling in his fingers. He couldn't hang on much longer.

His stepmother's mouth twisted. 'It wasn't Clara who died. It was Honey.' Her eyes gleamed. 'Clara's alive. And you'll never take her from me.'

He locked eyes with Maddy, pleading silently for help. He didn't have the power to cry out again.

'You want to know what your mother called you?' Maddy spat out the words.

His frozen hand was slipping. He was gripping the root by little more than stiffening fingertips.

'A freak,' she shouted. 'A psycho. She cursed the day you were born.'

His muscles shuddered. His eyes fastened on his own fingers as if they were those of a stranger. He watched his dragging, hanging weight prise them, one by one, away from the root.

Helpless, he fell. The wind dried his open mouth, stopping his cry. He paddled the air, striking jagged outcrops as he plummeted past the rock face.

He was in New York, sleeping in his dead mother's shabby apartment, plotting to avenge her.

He was a young man in London, dealing and hustling,

obsessed with punishing the stepmother who'd rejected him, who'd inherited his father's money.

He was ten years old and stepping out of his father's car onto a gravel drive, looking in awe and bitterness at the grand, rambling family house that would never be his home.

He burst at last on the sharp-toothed rocks far below.

66

KATE

Kate's body shook.

Damp seemed to reach up from the earth and seep into her bones. It was a deep chill, one she might never again escape. She sensed Maddy, lying still and silent beside her, a narrow strip of human warmth.

Kate's eyes fixed on the distant foot of the cliff, on the water stirring against the rocks. Her eyes spangled with strain. All she could see was blackness, dappled with fragments of low moonlight shimmering across the surface of the water. No sign of him. No sign of life. The wind swirled and whipped around them, heavy with rain. He was dead. He had to be. No-one could survive that.

Kate shrank away from the edge, forced herself onto her hands and knees and crawled backwards, away from the drop. She stretched out a hand for Maddy and drew her up. Their palms were clammy with fear, slippery with rain. When they left, the coarse grass seemed to spring back into place behind them, as if they had never been.

By the time they reached Maddy's car, hidden some distance

away in the trees, they were both shivering hard. Maddy pulled off the thin, white dress, stuffed it in her case, and dressed in jeans and a thick sweater. It took her three fumbling attempts to slot the key into the ignition.

Kate, in the passenger seat, reached over and placed her hand on Maddy's. She felt the jerks and tremors in her body and tried to ground her.

'You OK?'

Maddy nodded. She didn't look OK. She looked wrecked. Her cheeks were bloodless, her breathing fast and shallow. *She'll carry this for the rest of her life*, Kate thought. *We both will.*

Maddy said: 'Amy? How do I—?'

They'd already been through this. 'You don't do or say anything.' Kate squeezed Maddy's fingers in hers. 'She'll find out, eventually. Someone will find him. The police will go through his stuff in the cabin. After that...' She shrugged. After that, the lies would come tumbling out, one after another. Amy's life would be shattered, at least for a while. But she'd rebuild it. Maddy would be there for her.

'Now.' Kate nodded at the steering wheel. 'We need to get out of here. You OK to drive?'

The long drive to Grand Rapids was one Kate never forgot. It took on the quality of an endless dream. The headlights forever skimming across the moving surface of the black road. The heavy darkness of the trees leaning in overhead. The silence in the car.

They would soon separate. After that, they'd never see nor speak to each other again.

Once Maddy dropped her in Grand Rapids, Kate would check into an airport hotel to shower and lie, rigid, on a bed, eyes glassy, unable to sleep. The next day, she'd fly to Chicago and onwards, back to London, back to Clara.

Maddy would drive on alone to Detroit, ready to pick up her own flight to Connecticut and the conference waiting there.

Finally, Maddy pulled into the kerb in the shadows, a short walk from Kate's hotel.

Kate made to get out, then hesitated and turned back. 'Well, good luck.' She extended her hand and they awkwardly clasped fingers. It all felt unreal.

Maddy said: 'What if someone saw us?'

'No-one saw us.'

A moment's silence. Maddy started again: 'What if—?'

'Stop it.'

Maddy blinked. For a moment, she seemed lost. She whispered: 'What have we done?'

'What we had to do.' Kate fixed her eyes on Maddy. 'Never forget that. We did it for them. For our daughters.'

They squeezed each other's hand one last time before their grasp loosened.

67

KATE

Six Months Later, London

Kate sat quietly in the window of the café, distracted by the weave and bustle of Oxford Street.

Shoppers streamed past in clusters of two or three, laden with bags. A tight-faced middle-aged man shoved through the throng. A gaggle of young women shrieked and clutched at each other as they ran into the road. Handbags swung in the crooks of their arms. They threaded their way between the cars, narrowly avoiding a speeding motorbike.

It was early afternoon. The late September sun was already losing its potency.

Suddenly, there was Clara, bursting into the café, waving a hand, bristling with shopping. She picked her way between the crowded tables. Kate scraped back her chair and got to her feet to greet her. Clara's cheek was warm and smooth against her lips.

'Did you find what you wanted?'

'Pretty much.' Clara heaped her packages and bags on the

spare chair and slid in beside her mother. 'I'll show you but, first, I'm starving. Did you order?'

'Only a coffee, so far. I was waiting for you. Here, have a look at the menu.'

While Clara studied it, Kate took the opportunity to gaze at her. Blonde hair fell forward across her face and, with an automatic hand, Clara caught it up and tucked it back behind her ear.

Her face was no longer gaunt. She'd gradually gained back the weight she'd lost during those traumatic days hiding in Amsterdam. The purple smudges under her eyes had faded. She was animated, flushed with excitement about her next great adventure, heading off to Leeds in a week's time to start university.

Kate imagined Clara's bedroom falling empty again. She knew she'd find herself in there on her way to bed, dutifully closing the curtains for no reason, only to open them again the next morning. It would be a fresh loss but a welcome one, oh so welcome, compared with losing her daughter forever.

'Ham and cheese toastie, please.' Clara looked up. 'And share some fries?'

'Sure. Anything to drink?'

When Kate came back from placing their order at the counter, Clara held out her phone.

'Hey, Mum. Look!'

Kate took in the photo that Amy had posted on social media.

'She's *Freya Olivia*, apparently. Cute.'

Amy's baby girl looked three or four months old. She was propped up in Amy's lap, her cheeks chubby, her mouth open, laughing.

Clara pulled back her phone and flicked to another page.

She and Amy hadn't been in touch since Amsterdam. Kate was surprised she'd come across the post.

Clara, lost to her screen, had already moved on. Kate hadn't. It wasn't the sight of the baby that had struck her so forcefully. It was the look on Amy's face as she gazed down at her daughter, her eyes radiant with love. She looked utterly besotted, as if she were already a mother who'd do anything to protect her daughter. Whatever it took.

Bella. Memories hit Kate with sudden force. Such a beautiful baby. She remembered how weightless Bella had felt, the first time she'd held her. The bones of a bird. Kate had laughed and wept at the same time, crazy with exhaustion, floored by a rush of love so overwhelming it astounded her.

Now, she nodded to the shopping bags and asked Clara brightly: 'So, show me! What did you get?'

'Well...' Clara set down her phone and reached over to the spare chair. 'I hope you're going to like them. I wasn't totally sure about this one, at first, but it looks great on.'

Clara chatted about the clothes she'd bought, pulling out one piece after another. Kate pored over each garment with care, murmuring approval as Clara talked her through the prices and why she needed this one for every day, for lectures, this one for hanging out at the weekend, that one for going out in the evening.

Even as Kate listened, an encouraging smile on her face, part of her was still with Amy. She wondered what Amy would tell her daughter about the father she'd never meet.

According to news online, officials had ruled Damian's death a tragic accident. By the time his body was found, spotted by a local amateur fisherman, it was badly decomposed. Forensic reports showed high levels of alcohol and marijuana in his blood. It explained perfectly how he'd come to stumble so tragically from cliffs known for their strong winds and treacherous drop.

The waitress interrupted, banging their tray of food down on the table and turning away.

Kate set the toastie in front of Clara, along with her coffee and fries. She made a show of eating one or two but they were for Clara, really. She watched her daughter push the clothes back into their bags and start enthusiastically on her food.

Clara too thought Damian's death had been accidental. *You don't ever have to worry about him again*, Kate had told her, showing her the news reports. *It's over.*

It was the most she would ever say.

Clara finished and they scraped back their chairs and gathered their bags, ready to head back out into the world.

'How about a movie, later?' Clara said. 'I feel like a girls' night in.'

'Sounds good to me. Pizza?'

'Deal.'

Kate felt her body ease its hold on the day. This was what mattered. Clara was alive. She was happy. Normal life was reaching for her again, a warm, strong tide, gently stirring, ready to lift her and draw her back into its flow.

They were standing at the bus stop when Kate was jolted by the feel of her phone, vibrating in her pocket as it rang. She dug it out. It was a US number. Not one she knew.

A woman's voice, with the lilt of a Midwest accent. 'Hello? Is this Kate Grosvenor?'

She mispronounced Kate's surname, as if she'd only seen it written down.

Kate spoke loudly, battling the noise of the traffic. 'Hi. This is Kate. Who's speaking?'

There was a heavy breath down the line, as if the woman

were steeling herself for what was to come. Kate pressed her phone against her ear to listen.

'I don't know if you can help me? I got your number from a guy in Amsterdam. Gino Mariani? He thought you might be able to help.'

Kate couldn't speak. Her stomach chilled. Somehow, she sensed exactly what this woman, this fellow mother, was about to say.

Suddenly dizzy, she bent forward. It was the call she'd been dreading, the call she'd hoped would never come, the call that threatened to undo them all.

'It's about my daughter, Honey,' the woman said. 'She's kinda gone missing.'

ACKNOWLEDGEMENTS

A big thank you to my brilliant editor, Emma Beswetherick, for championing this book from the start. I'm so grateful for the vision, creativity and enthusiasm you've brought to it. It's such a pleasure to work with you. Thank you too to the rest of the dynamic, talented team at Boldwood. I'm thrilled to be on board.

Thank you to my sister, Janet Shepherd, for professional expertise and great suggestions around psychiatry, addiction and paradoxical reactions to medication.

Thank you, as always, to my wonderful agent, Judith Murdoch, the best in the business.

And thank you to all my family for your support and love. Ann, this one's for you.

ABOUT THE AUTHOR

Building on a lengthy career as an award-winning BBC foreign correspondent, editor and presenter, **Jill Childs** is the author of several bestselling novels, selling over a half a million copies. She lives in South-West London with her husband and twin daughters.

Sign up to Jill Childs's mailing list for news, competitions and updates on future books.

Follow Jill on social media here:

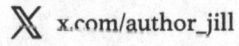 x.com/author_jill

THE *Murder* LIST

**THE MURDER LIST IS A NEWSLETTER
DEDICATED TO SPINE-CHILLING
FICTION AND GRIPPING
PAGE-TURNERS!**

**SIGN UP TO MAKE SURE YOU'RE ON
OUR HIT LIST FOR EXCLUSIVE DEALS,
AUTHOR CONTENT, AND
COMPETITIONS.**

**SIGN UP TO OUR
NEWSLETTER**

BIT.LY/THEMURDERLISTNEWS

Boldwood

Boldwood Books is an award-winning fiction publishing company seeking out the best stories from around the world.

Find out more at www.boldwoodbooks.com

Join our reader community for brilliant books, competitions and offers!

Follow us
@BoldwoodBooks
@TheBoldBookClub

Sign up to our weekly deals newsletter

https://bit.ly/BoldwoodBNewsletter

www.ingramcontent.com/pod-product-compliance
Lightning Source LLC
Chambersburg PA
CBHW011640010726
47495CB00011B/2837